Tyrranis very deliberately removed his sword belt, the breastplate, and his military cloak and laid them carefully aside. Then he brought out a pair of leather gloves and slowly began to pull them on, one finger at a time. "Now," he said with cold malice, "let us discuss magic."

Valorian's mouth went dry. "What do you mean?" he managed to ask.

The general picked up a short, heavy club and came to stand in front of his prisoner. His muscles were tense, as if his body were tightly coiled beneath his knee-length tunic. "Magic," he hissed. "The power of the immortals." Without warning, he brought the heavy club smashing down on Valorian's upper right arm.

The clansman stiffened in pain; his jaw clamped shut. The blunt instrument hadn't broken his arm, but it felt as if it had. Valorian strained vainly against his chains, but the soldiers had pulled them tight, leaving him stretched flat against the wall with no room to escape Tyrannis's attentions. Queasy with fear, he stared as the general raised the club again.

"We have all night, clansman," Tyrannis informed him. "You will tell me the secret of your magic, or it will be a long night indeed. . . ."

Other TSR® Books

Valorian

Mary H. Herbert

VALORIAN

First Printing: February 1993
Printed in the United States of America.
Library of Congress Catalog Card Number: 92-61079

9 8 7 6 5 4 3 2 1

ISBN: 1-56076-566-6

TSR, Inc.
P.O. Box 756
Lake Geneva, WI 53147
U.S.A.

TSR Ltd.
120 Church End, Cherry Hinton
Cambridge CB1 3LB
United Kingdom

For my parents, Bond and Mary Houser,
with all my love.
(and thanks, Mom and Dad, for not getting
mad at me when I spent that entire family
vacation reading *The Lord of the Rings*)

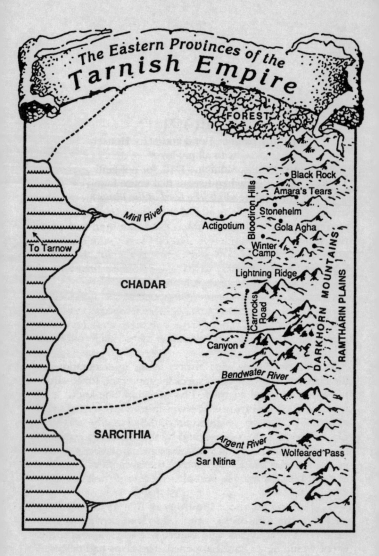

The Eastern Provinces of the Tarnish Empire

FOREST

Black Rock
Amara's Tears
Bloodiron Hills
Stonehelm
Gola Agha
Actigotium
Winter Camp
Lightning Ridge
To Tarnow
Miril River
CHADAR
Carrocks Road
Canyon
Bendwater River
SARCITHIA
Argent River
Sar Nitina
Wolfeared Pass
DARKHORN MOUNTAINS
RAMTHARIN PLAINS

Prologue

ady Gabria rose with the rest of the crowded clanspeople and watched with shining pride as six young warriors entered in single file through the huge double doors of the chieftain's hall. In the ancient tradition of the Khulinin Clan, the men had completed their rites of initiation into the werod, the clan warriors, and now they followed the priest of Surgart, the god of battle and warriors, into the hall to make their final vow of fealty to their chieftain, Lord Athlone.

Gabria clasped her fingers tightly together, as if to lock in the joy that threatened to burst out. This was supposed to be a solemn moment for these six young men, and she wasn't going to embarrass them by shouting her pleasure out loud. But it was a difficult effort.

The Warriors' Rites were always a time of celebration for the clan, but this year was especially important, for Savaron, her eldest son, had completed his initiation. She knew, if all went well, Savaron would be wer-tain in a few years and eventually take over as chieftain of the clan. She was very pleased with the succession and by the clan's ready acceptance of her son. Savaron was a capable, courageous, intelligent man, who had already shown the strength of character of both his parents. He had also inherited their talent to wield magic.

Gabria thought about the irony of that as the warriors strode to the foot of the chief's dais and bowed to Lord Athlone. Twenty years ago, before her son was born, this event would never have happened. The clans had despised magic for over two hundred years and put to death anyone who tried to use the natural power. It wasn't until Lord Medb of Clan Wylfling found an ancient book of sorcery and tried to conquer the twelve clans of Valorian that the clanspeople began to realize that they had been mistaken to turn their backs on magic. Only she, Gabria, had dared oppose Lord Medb's evil sorcery with magic of her own. She had defeated him and set in motion within the clans a difficult but gradual reacceptance of the use of sorcery.

With the help of her husband Athlone, the chieftain of the most powerful clan on the Ramtharin Plains and a magic-wielder in his own right, she had struggled for twenty years to return sorcery to its respected place within the clans. It hadn't been an easy task. The laws of the clans had been gradually changed to accommodate the magic-wielders and protect those people who didn't have the inborn talent. But generations of clanspeople had grown up being taught that magic was heretical, evil, corrupting. Even after twenty years, the old prejudices still ran deep in the clans.

Thankfully the Khulinin had grown quite tolerant of magic. After the initial shock of learning their chieftain was a sorcerer, they had come to accept magic much as he did: as a gift and as a blessing of the gods. Now, twenty years after the return of sorcery, the Khulinin were watching as another sorcerer prepared to take his vow of fealty and follow in the footsteps of his father.

The young men knelt before their lord on the dais, their strong, tanned faces bowed before him. A hush fell over the watching crowd as the priest of Surgart withdrew a mask from the folds of his robes and raised it high above his head so that the eyeholes seemed to look down on the kneeling warriors. The mask was solid gold, brilliantly polished, and lovingly tended. It was the most treasured possession of the Khulinin Clan, for it was the death mask of the hero-warrior, Valorian.

A warm, throbbing sense of wonder filled Gabria at the sight of the gleaming mask. Its face was as familiar to her as her husband's and almost as beloved. She had found the old mask many years before in the ruins of the sorcerers' city, Moy Tura, and had brought it home proudly to Khulinin Treld. The man whose face had formed the mold had died over four hundred years earlier, but his legacy still influenced the clans of the Ramtharin Plains. The Khulinin often used the mask to evoke Valorian's presence at special ceremonies, and Gabria knew he would have been pleased by today's ceremony and by her son, who would help pass on the gifts Valorian had given to his people.

Before the eyes of the clan and the enigmatic face of the death mask, the six warriors repeated the ancient vows of loyalty one by one and received their first warriors' gifts from their lord: the traditional bag of salt and a dagger. When the last one finished his vows, the six men stood together, raised their swords to the raftered ceiling, and shouted the Khulinin war cry.

Their shout had barely begun to fade when Savaron turned quickly to his father and cried, "A boon, my lord! I ask my first boon."

Lord Athlone looked slightly startled by his son's request, but he nodded, wondering what the young man was up to.

"It is early yet," Savaron said with a grin. "There is time for a tale before the feasting."

The Khulinin called out their agreement. They were always ready to hear one of the wondrous tales told by their bards. But Savaron raised his hand, and the crowd fell silent. He went to the priest of Surgart and, looking inquiringly at the man's face, reached out to take the death mask into his own hands. The priest nodded once before he passed the precious burden to the warrior.

To everyone's surprise, Savaron winked at the clan bard nearby, then strode through the crowd to his mother, Gabria. "I wish to hear the tale of Valorian," he said loudly and placed the golden mask in her arms.

For a moment, Gabria hugged the heavy mask to her chest, too startled to say a word. Savaron knew of her deep, abiding respect for Valorian, and he knew of her efforts over the years to compile the ancient stories of the hero-warrior's deeds into a single great tale. But why did he want to hear her tale now? Had his own wonder filled him when the mask was brought out, or did he simply feel the appropriateness of the story at this time?

She glanced around at the clanspeople and saw the curiosity on their faces. She had never told this tale before, because it had taken nearly twenty years to peel away the myths and fables surrounding Valorian and gather the scattered stories, fragments of histories, and forgotten songs into one cohesive tale. Even now she wasn't certain she wanted to share her tale . . . except for her son.

Taking her silence as acquiescence, Savaron led her to the dais, where Lord Athlone willingly gave up his chair for his wife to sit. The two men found stools and sat by her feet while the other clan members gathered closer.

Gabria hesitated for a long moment, gazing down into the face of the mask on her lap. The eyeholes stared back at her, dark, empty, and bereft of life. She remembered a fleeting minute long ago when those eyes had stared back at her, as blue as an autumn sky, and she held that memory firmly in her mind while she gathered her thoughts.

"May my words please you, my lord Valorian," she whispered, then, raising her voice so all could hear, Gabria said, "The journey began with a dead deer. . . ."

alorian crouched, poised immobile behind a clump of boulders, his ears trained to the voices in the valley below. He listened intently for a few breathless moments before he slowly lifted his eyes over the edge of the rock and peered down into the narrow, wooded valley. They were directly below him, making camp as best they could under the dark, wet trees. Several thin horses were tethered nearby, picking at a sparse pile of fodder.

A heavy drizzle obscured the details of the men's faces and dress, but Valorian saw enough to recognize the occupation of the five men. They all wore the black eagle emblem of the XIIth Legion of the Tarnish emperor. Strangely, though, the legion was supposed to be on the other side of the Darkhorn Mountains. What was this small group doing so far from home?

Valorian studied the soldiers for a few more minutes, then slipped down behind the rocks again. He leaned back on his haunches and scratched the four-day stubble on his jaw thoughtfully. The men below posed a real problem to the hunter. Normally he would avoid Tarnish soldiers like lepers. In the many years since the Tarnish armies had invaded his homeland of Chadar, Valorian had never known the soldiers to be anything more than merciless, greedy curs who helped their emperor maintain his conquests with ruthless efficiency. Valorian knew that if he went down among them alone, they were as likely to kill him as to talk to him.

The hunter risked another glance over the boulder. The

men were still grouped together, trying vainly to light a fire. Valorian curled his lip. The fools were going about it all wrong, and from the appearance of their haggard faces and dirty tunics, things had been going wrong for them for a long while.

Valorian loosed a sigh and looked back up the hill to where his stallion stood out of sight in a copse of trees. On the horse's back was Valorian's prize, the result of four days of difficult tracking and nearly fruitless hunting: one thin, field-dressed deer. The deer would mean fresh meat for his family for the first time in many days.

And yet perhaps those men in the valley had a greater prize, a prize worth the danger of facing the soldiers alone and unarmed. Information.

Valorian believed the XIIth Legion was garrisoned at the Tarnish stonghold of Ab-Chakan, to the east, on the other side of the Darkhorn Mountains, in a tantalizing land Valorian knew only by the tales he had heard. The land was named the Ramtharin Plains and was described as a vast, empty realm of grass and endlessly rolling hills—a land perfectly suited for his nomadic people and their horses. Unfortunately the Tarnish Empire had extended its hold over the plains as far as the Sea of Tannis nearly seventy years ago and still held it in the name of the emperor.

Now, however, the empire was beginning to lose its grip on its far-flung provinces. Enemies were plaguing its borders, several tribes far to the west were rebelling, forcing the emperor to send thinly stretched legions to quell the uprisings, and three years of bad weather had played havoc with the crops that fed the great capital city of Tarnow. The Tarns themselves were growing unmanageable. To make matters worse, the old emperor, who had doubled the size of his empire and struck terror in the ranks of his enemies, had died, leaving his throne in the hands of his weaker, less capable son. In just eighteen short years, the empire had lost a fourth of its outlying provinces and had been forced to abandon many of its fortresses. Ab-Chakan was the last

Tarnish garrison on the eastern side of the Darkhorn Mountains and the only one left on the Ramtharin Plains.

Perhaps those soldiers down in the chilly, wet clearing knew some news that would be useful. There had to be an important reason for them to be so far from their garrison, and there was nothing like a hot meal and a warm fire to loosen a man's reluctance to talk.

All of these thoughts passed through Valorian's mind while he debated his decision. Then, with a curse of resignation, he slipped out of his hiding place and made his way quickly uphill toward his horse. The meat would help his family temporarily, but the information he might gain could help his entire Clan for a long time to come.

The stallion, Hunnul, standing quietly in the gathering shadows of night, nickered softly to the man when he entered the copse. Valorian paused to run his hands down the horse's powerful black shoulder. The clansman smiled a rueful grimace.

"After all that work, Hunnul, we're going to give our prize away to some Tarnish soldiers."

The big stallion snorted. His dark, liquid eyes watched his master with unusual intelligence and affection.

"Perhaps I'm crazy," Valorian muttered, "but they're from the Ramtharin Plains! I've been trying to learn more about that land for a long time." With brusque movements, the hunter packed his bow and short sword out of sight in his gear, keeping only his hunting knife in his belt. Then he mounted Hunnul's saddle in front of the wrapped body of the deer and drew a deep breath to help still the faint trembling of his cold hands. "Let's go," he said to the horse. "We have Tarns to feed."

Obediently the stallion walked out of the trees and began to pick his way down the rock-strewn hillside. Twilight was settling heavily into the valley under a gloomy shroud of drizzle and mist, enabling Valorian to ride almost to the edge of the soldiers' camp before one man saw him and shouted a warning.

The others whirled in surprise. Dirty and disheveled they might be, but Valorian immediately saw the soldiers still maintained the strict training of the crack XIIth Legion. In a blink, the five men had drawn their swords and stood back-to-back in a tight circle, their faces grim and their weapons ready.

"Well met!" Valorian called as cheerfully as he could muster. He slouched his tall frame to look as innocuous as possible and pushed back the hood of his cloak. Hunnul stopped at the edge of the clearing.

The five soldiers didn't move, staring balefully at him.

"Identify yourself," one man ordered.

In answer, Valorian untied the deer from the back of his saddle and dumped it on the ground in front of Hunnul. He allowed the hungry men a moment to eye the meat before he slowly dismounted. The soldiers didn't budge from their defensive positions.

"I am called Valorian," the hunter told them, opening his cloak so they could see he wasn't armed.

The men in front of him studied his iron-bound leather helmet, his long wool cloak, his sheepskin vest, and his tattered tunic and leggings. They didn't bother to look past the grime and the patches to the long, lean man with the face hollowed by days of hunger and the quick flash of intelligence in his deep-set eyes. "A clansman," one soldier snorted derisively. The five Tarns visibly relaxed.

Valorian stifled a surge of anger at their disdain and tried to smile. The effort was thin at best. He knew the Tarnish Empire and the Chadarians held his people in low esteem. The clanspeople of Fearral were regarded as slovenly, weak, cowardly, and of little account. The only useful thing they could do, and the only thing that kept them out of slavery in the emperor's galleys or salt mines, was breed and train horses. Valorian had anticipated the soldiers' reaction to his origins, but that didn't mean he had to like their attitude. What really galled him was there was too much truth behind their scorn.

The Tarn who had spoken stepped out of the circle and thrust his sword point toward Valorian's chest.

The hunter didn't flinch, but stood still as the point came to a stop a hairbreadth away from his ribs. He forced his eyes to widen in fear and his mouth to hang open.

The soldier eyed the clansman suspiciously from helm to boot. He was a big man, as tall as Valorian himself, with a strength and brutality forged from many battles. His hard, craggy face was clean-shaven, and his uniform and weapons were well cared for despite the obvious wear of long travel.

Valorian recognized the insignia on the man's shoulder as the rank of a sarturian, a leader of usually eight to ten men within a legion. Gritting his teeth, Valorian swallowed his humiliation and bowed his head to the soldier. "I have a deer I thought to share, General."

"I'm no general, you stupid dog!" the man snarled. The tip of his sword slowly dropped away from Valorian's chest.

"Share, hah!" a short, bandy-legged soldier snapped. "Just kill him. That'll leave more for the rest of us."

The sarturian cast a speculative glance at the clansman to see his reaction.

Valorian shrugged, his eyes still downcast. "You could kill me, but then who would you have to light the fire and roast the meat?"

"Good point," a dark-haired Tarn said. "We're not having much luck with the fire."

The circle of soldiers began to break apart as they edged around to stare hungrily at the deer.

"Let him cook it, Sarturian. Then we can kill him," the short Tarn urged.

Their leader made an irritated sound and slammed his sword back in the scabbard. "Enough! The Twelfth Legion doesn't deal in treachery. You and your deer may join us, clansman."

For just a moment, Valorian lifted his gaze and came eye to eye with the Tarnish sarturian. He despised Tarns with a hatred born of thirty-five years of bitter experience. His common sense told him to look away and maintain his harmless, weak facade, but his pride overrode his sense for just a heartbeat. He let his silent hatred bore into the man's dark stare. When he saw the Tarn's eyes begin to narrow, he thought better of his intentions, swallowed his pride, and let his eyes slide away. His jaw clenched, he turned before he could damage his credibility as a harmless clansman any further and went to his horse to unpack his saddlebags.

The sarturian stood for a minute as if deep in thought, a scowl on his face. Finally he gestured to his men. "If you want to eat tonight, help him."

The four other men obeyed, spurred on by the hunger that gnawed in their bellies. Two hauled the deer carcass to the edge of the clearing while the other two came to help Valorian as he undid the girth of his saddle.

"Fine horse," remarked the short legionnaire. He reached for Hunnul's head and cursed as the stallion whipped his nose away from the strange grasp. The horse wore no bridle or halter, so the soldier could not get a good grip on the muzzle.

Valorian was slow to reply. Hunnul *was* a fine horse, probably the finest in Chadar. Tall at the withers, long-legged, and beautifully proportioned, the stallion was a magnificent animal—and Valorian's pride and joy. The horse had been carefully bred, hand raised, and trained to the clansman's utmost skill. Oddly enough, he was totally black, without a single white or brown hair. Such a horse would be valued highly by the soldiers of the Black Eagle Legion.

Valorian shrugged nonchalantly at the soldier, thrust several bundles in the man's arms, and said, "He's not bad. Rather vicious, though." Before the soldier could react, the clansman slipped off the saddle and spoke a command.

The big stallion tossed his long mane. With a neigh, he turned on his heels and plunged into the darkness.

The five soldiers looked after the horse in amazement.

"Planning on walking home?" the sarturian asked.

Valorian ignored the remark and picked up his gear. "He'll

be nearby if I need him."

The men exchanged glances of mingled surprise and doubt, but Valorian gave them no more time to speculate on the magnificent stallion. He set them to work immediately, butchering the deer and gathering more firewood. From his saddlebags, he removed a small pack of dried tinder, his fire starter, and a small hatchet. With the skill gained from over thirty years of practice, Valorian swiftly cleared out a space on the ground for his fire, built a lean-to of woven vines and branches to protect the flames from the rain, and gathered the necessary materials for the blaze.

The soldiers watched as he quickly piled his tinder—a handful of dried fluff, grasses, and tiny twigs—on the cleared ground. Using his knife, he feathered the ends of several larger twigs and added them to his pile, then he brought out his most precious traveling tool: a small, glowing coal, carefully nurtured inside a hollow gourd. In a moment, the hunter had the fire blazing merrily in the dark, wet clearing.

The Tarnish soldiers grinned in a sudden release of tension and frustration.

"As good as magic," one man said, slapping Valorian on the shoulder.

"Magic," the sarturian grunted. "You ought to know better than to waste your time with that nonsense! Magic is for self-deluded priests and fools."

The clansman sat back on his heels. "What do you know about magic, Sarturian?" he asked out of interest. Unlike many of the Tarns, the clanspeople didn't believe in a power of magic, only in the powers of their four deities.

The leader gestured to the fire with a broken length of deadwood. "Magic doesn't exist, Clansman. Only skill."

"Don't tell General Tyrranis that," the dark-haired soldier said with a smirk. "I've heard he's trying to find the secret of magic."

"Shut up!" snapped the sarturian.

The mention of General Tyrranis made Valorian grit his

teeth. The general was the imperial governor of the huge province that encompassed Chadar and the foothills where Valorian's clanspeople were forced to live. To say he was hated was putting it mildly. Tyrranis was an ambitious, ruthless combination of astute politician and merciless military man who crushed anyone who tried to thwart him. He ruled his province with enough violence and fear to keep the people firmly under his heel without any thought of rebellion. Valorian had heard rumors that the general's ambitions reached as high as the imperial throne, so the mention of Tyrranis's search for magic didn't surprise him.

Perhaps with luck, Valorian thought to himself, Tyrranis would kill himself in some foolhardy experiment looking for something that didn't exist.

Seeing the sarturian watching him, Valorian quickly removed any expression from his face and set to work. He didn't want to stay with these men any longer than necessary. He wanted to feed them and get their tongues talking about more useful information—such as why they were in Chadar, what was the Ab-Chakan garrison doing, and where was a good trail to the Ramtharin Plains.

As rapidly as he could, Valorian built his fire hotter and roasted strips of deer meat over the glowing coals. The soldiers plunged into his cooked offering with the voraciousness of hungry wolves.

By the time they stopped eating, the deer carcass was virtually stripped, and the rain had died to a heavy mist. The soldiers leaned back, laughing and talking and drinking from their last flask of wine. No one offered wine to Valorian or paid him any heed as he sat in the shadows under a tree and gnawed on the last of the venison.

The clansman felt a brief pang of guilt for filling his stomach with meat while his family was probably eating watery soup and the last crusts of old bread. The winter had been hard, and there were very few stock animals left in their herds. The family was counting on him and the other men to bring in meat for the cooking pots. Perhaps, he hoped, one of the other hunters had had some success. He drove the feeling away and concentrated instead on the talking soldiers.

The meat and wine had indeed soothed their tensions, setting their tongues free to air their gripes and worries. Their disregard for the clansman was so complete, they seemed to forget he was there.

For a while, the five men simply conversed about the everyday complaints of soldiers: bad food, hard work, loneliness. Warm in his cloak and weary from the days of hunting, Valorian listened to their conversation with growing drowsiness. His eyelids drooped. He was beginning to wonder how he could turn their talk toward the Ramtharin Plains when the short legionnaire said something that jolted the clansman wide awake.

"I don't know about the rest of you, but I'm glad to be leaving that forsaken pile of rocks." The man took a long swig from the wine flask and passed it on. "Good riddance to Ab-Chakan!"

"How can you say that?" another soldier said, his voice thick with sarcasm. "I'm going to miss the place—the cold, the wind, the heat and the fleas in the summer, no town in sight for league after league after league. Why would we want to trade that for a comfortable billet in Tarnow?"

One man slapped the eagle emblem on his chest, grinned, and said, "By the sacred bull, I'll be glad to see Tarnow again. I haven't been home in ten years." The speaker, a dark-haired soldier, slid off his seat to stretch out full length on his back. "Say, Sarturian, has General Sarjas said when we're being withdrawn?"

A grunt escaped the sarturian's lips as he retrieved the flask of wine. "You think the commanding general of the Twelfth Legion discusses his plans with mere sarturians?"

"No, but you must have an opinion. You've been around long enough to figure out officers."

The sarturian shifted his position and snorted. "No one understands officers . . . still, I'd say we'll pull the garrison out by late summer. The legion's supply wagons have to get over Wolfeared Pass before snow blocks the trail."

Three of the legionnaires grinned at each other. It wasn't often they could get information out of their closemouthed sarturian, and this was a chance too good to let pass.

Under the tree, Valorian leaned back, his heart pounding. He could hardly believe what he was hearing. Breathlessly he remained still, closed his eyes, and willed the soldiers to continue talking.

"So which way do you think we'll go home?" the short Tarn probed his leader. "North through Chadar to Actigorium or south through Sarcithia to Sar Nitina?"

There was a long silence that dragged out until the soldiers began to think the sarturian wasn't going to reply. Finally he shrugged and said, "I'd lay my money on the southern route. It's longer than going through Chadar, but it's easier than risking General Tyrranis's political traps. He'd sell his wives to have a full legion under his jurisdiction. If we want to get back to Tarnow without delays, we'd better go by way of Sar Nitina." He took a long swallow of wine as if to end the conversation and passed the flask on to the next man.

"Then why are we going to Actigorium to see General High-and-Mighty Tyrranis?" asked a soldier.

The dark-haired Tarn snickered. "General Sarjas doesn't see things as clearly as our sarturian, so he's probably sending us for the general's written permission to cross Chadar just in case he decides to go that way. Isn't that right?" he demanded.

The sarturian cocked an eyebrow at him. "You have a big mouth, Callas."

Callas pulled his lips into a triumphant grin. "I am right! Well, I don't care which way we march as long as we get out of those plains. Gods, I miss cities." Suddenly he noticed the fourth soldier sitting quietly across the fire, looking glum. "What about you, Marcus?" he jibed. "You haven't said a word. Aren't you glad to be going home?"

"Not this way!" the older man said bitterly. "The Twelfth

Legion has never retreated, and yet here we are about to abandon a perfectly good fortress and withdraw because our all-powerful emperor can't even hang on to what his father left him!"

"Keep such thoughts to yourself, Marcus," the sarturian growled. "Talk like that can separate your head from your shoulders."

The old soldier gestured angrily. "It's the truth and you know it! Ab-Chakan is the last occupied fortress on the plains. When it's abandoned, Tarn will lose the entire Ramtharin Plains."

The short Tarn shook his head. "The plains have given us nothing more than grass, copper, hides, and a few miserable slaves. We can find those anywhere. Better to lose a distant, unprofitable province than our own homeland."

"The loss of the province isn't so bad," Marcus agreed. "It's the cost that angers me—the loss of pride and honor for the legion, the loss of confidence and respect in the empire. The man who sits on the throne of Tarn is throwing away a mighty realm out of weakness, stupidity, and—"

"That's enough!" commanded the sarturian sharply. "You don't need to shout your views across all of Chadar."

The soldiers fell quiet. Although Valorian kept his eyes shut, he could sense their attention had abruptly turned toward him.

"What about the clansman?" he heard one soldier ask softly. "Do we kill him or let him go?"

"Let him go. The meat was worth his life," answered the sarturian.

"What if he's heard everything we've said?"

Their leader laughed a sharp sound of derision. "He's a clansman. He can't do anything about it, and the rest of the empire will know soon enough."

Even the sarturian's scorn couldn't stifle the thin smile that twitched across Valorian's lips. Fully alert now, the hunter continued to feign sleep while the Tarnish soldiers bedded down under their blankets and the fire died to embers.

When the men were snoring and the clearing was dense with mist and darkness, the clansman rose from his place under the tree. He retrieved his saddle and slipped away silently into the night.

At dawn, Valorian found Hunnul in a meadow down the valley, not far from the clearing where the Tarnish soldiers were beginning to stir. The hunter whistled to the stallion, and he watched with satisfaction as the big horse came cantering toward him, his mane and tail flowing like black smoke. Quickly he saddled Hunnul, then turned his mount south, away from his home camp.

Valorian had some time to think about what he had heard that night as he tried to sleep in the meager shelter of a thicket. He mulled over the soldiers' words with growing excitement until he had decided to extend his hunt. His family's winter camp lay to the north, and he had already been gone longer than he had intended; his wife, Kierla, would be worrying. But he still had no meat, and somewhere—to the south, he believed—was a pass—the only pass he had ever heard of that was low and wide enough to allow wagons to travel over the towering Darkhorn Mountains. He would hunt to the south. Perhaps if the gods were watching over him, he would find both meat and the pass.

For two more days, the hunter rode south toward the borders between Chadar and Sarcithia, deep into country where he had never traveled before. He studied the unfamiliar peaks with the practiced eye of a man born in the shadows of the mountains and saw nothing that resembled a usable pass. He searched for game, any game that would feed his people, but he didn't even see a hoofprint. The rain continued to fall from a low, dismal roof of clouds, washing the streams out of their banks, turning the earth to glutinous mud, and washing out all signs of game. Valorian's clothes and gear grew sodden, and even his skill as a woodsman couldn't coax the soaking wood to flame.

On the third day, he turned Hunnul deeper into the foothills. Throughout the morning, they rode higher and higher into the skirts of the towering Darkhorns toward a tall, bare ridge that afforded an unobstructed view of the long range of peaks.

"If we don't find something soon, Hunnul, we'll have to go back home empty-handed," Valorian remarked as the horse struggled up the steep slope of the ridge.

Hunnul scrambled up to the top of the crest before he paused to snort as if in reply. His sides heaved with his exertion, and his nostrils flared red.

Valorian patted the stallion's damp neck. He saw nothing strange in talking to his horse as if to a good friend. Hunnul was an intelligent animal and seemed to understand much of what his master said to him. The hunter only regretted that the stallion couldn't respond in kind. He spent so much time on horseback, it would be pleasant to have someone to talk to once in a while.

The clansman let his horse rest for a time while he gazed at the land around him in disgust. There wasn't much to see. Rain was everywhere. It hid the mountains in an impenetrable cloud, effectively blocking any hope Valorian had of spotting the pass or any game.

He slammed his fist against the pommel of his saddle. "By the gods," he exclaimed. "It's rained for fourteen days! When is it going to stop?"

A sudden crack of thunder made him flinch. He stared up at the iron-gray sky in surprise. This was early spring, rather soon for thunderstorms. But all clanspeople knew the thunder was really the sound of the steeds of Nebiros, the messenger of the god of the dead. Perhaps Nebiros himself had been sent to fetch a soul.

Another bolt of lightning seared across the sky, followed by a tremendous crack of thunder. The wind suddenly gusted over the ridge, snapping at Valorian's cloak. Hunnul flattened his ears and pranced sideways.

Valorian felt his muscles tighten with nervousness. He had never liked lightning. "Come on, boy. Let's get off this ridge and find some shelter."

The horse was quick to obey. They found an outcropping on a hillside nearby that offered some relief from the wind and the torrent of rain that poured from the sky. The lightning and thunder continued unabated for a long time until the hills reverberated with the sound and fury.

Irritably Valorian stood by Hunnul's steaming side and ate the last of his trail bread while his thoughts slogged morosely through his mind. When the afternoon was late and the rain was still falling, Valorian reluctantly decided that, meat or no meat, it was time to go home. He would have to try again some other time to find the pass.

At last the rain eased to an intermittent drizzle, and the wind died to mere gusts. The lightning and thunder seemed to move farther to the south.

Depressed and weary, the clansman rode his horse to the top of the ridge again for one final look at the mountains. The clouds had lifted a little with the passing of the thunderstorm, revealing a glimpse of the imposing ramparts of the Darkhorns.

Valorian's mouth tightened. He hated those mountains. As long as those great peaks blocked his people to the east and the Tarnish Empire forced them out of the west, they had no hope of survival. If the Clan was to continue, they had to escape. They had to find a way over the mountains and out of the grasp of the Tarns.

"We have to locate that pass, Hunnul," Valorian said forcefully. The stallion's ears cocked back to listen. "If we could just find it, I could give Lord Fearral positive proof that a path over the mountains really exists. Then he'd have no excuse not to bring the Clan together and seek the Ramtharin Plains!"

There was a pause, then the man threw his hands wide. "Imagine it, Hunnul! A realm of sky and grass, there for the taking. No Tarns, no tribute or taxes, no General Tyrranis. Freedom to raise our horses and our families. Freedom to be as we once were! If I could only convince Lord Fearral . . ."

Valorian lapsed into silence and stared morosely at the

curtains of clouds and rain to the south. If the clanspeople deserved the ridicule and scorn of the Tarnish Empire, Lord Fearral was one reason why.

In the time of Valorian's grandfather, the Clans had been a proud people who had roamed the fertile lands of Chadar in large, loosely knit nomadic bands, each ruled by a lord chieftain. They had been fierce warriors, excellent stockmen, and good neighbors to the sedentary tribes of Chadarians who populated the riverbanks and valleys of the country.

Clan life had followed a smooth and natural course, until the armies of the Tarn had invaded Chadar. The clansmen had tried ferociously to defend their land, but the Chadarians surrendered to the armies and refused to help. The large, heavily armed infantry legions decimated the mounted Clan warriors, massacred entire camps of women and children, and drove the survivors into the bleak and barren Bloodiron Hills in the northern Darkhorns. The people had remained there ever since, penned in, isolated, and rejected.

Since that time, nearly eighty years ago, the Clans had lost many of their traditions and much of their pride. They had dwindled to a single Clan composed of a few ragged family bands who paid homage to one old lord chieftain. Their rich pastures, large herds, and the accumulated wealth of generations were gone. They managed to eke out a bare subsistence through hunting, foraging, and petty thievery. Everything else they had went as tribute to General Tyrranis.

Valorian recognized the futility of fighting the Tarnish Empire to regain what was lost, but he couldn't give up hope for his people. If they couldn't survive where they were, then he firmly believed they had to seek a new home.

The problem was convincing his wife's uncle, Lord Fearral. The timorous old chieftain was as hidebound as an old cow. Valorian had tried several times to plead with the chieftain to bring the scattered families together and lead them somewhere to new lands. Fearral had refused. Without more definite hope and specific information about their destination, the aged lord wouldn't even attempt a move. The

Darkhorns were too dangerous, he told Valorian repeatedly, to warrant such a foolhardy journey. Besides, General Tyrranis would never allow the Clan to leave their place in the hills. The chieftain was adamant.

Now, though, Valorian hoped that if he could bring news of a pass over the mountains and a land free of Tarn's grip, it would sway Fearral to at least send out scouts and begin making plans.

If only he could find the pass so he could be certain. A sudden impulse born of deep emotion brought his hand to his sword. With the ancient war cry of his people, Valorian drew his weapon and flourished it at the sky.

"Hear me, O gods!" he shouted. "Our people are dying! Show me a way to save them. Help me find Wolfeared Pass!"

At that instant, in the heart of the thunderstorm south of the high ridge, an incredible power burst into incandescent existence. Brilliantly hot and deadly, it knifed through the cold air like a divine bolt and exploded out of the confines of the storm. In the space of a heartbeat, the lightning arced to earth and found a conductor of metal as its target.

With unearthly force, it struck the helmet and sword of the clansman. Its power seared down his arm, through his head, into his body, and continued down through his horse.

Valorian arched over backward, connected for an eternal second to the power of the gods, and then his world exploded in fire and light. The thunder boomed around him, but he didn't hear it. Both horse and rider were dead before their bodies crashed to earth.

2

he first thing Valorian grew aware of was a vast, unutterable silence. It pressed against his senses with a strange heaviness as empty and still as death. Gone were the sounds of the wind and rain, of wet leather creaking, and the clop of Hunnul's hooves on stone. There was simply nothing.

Ever so slowly Valorian raised his head and opened his eyes. The world he had known was still there, but it seemed to be fading into a pale, slightly luminous light, like a dream that ends before waking. Valorian was shocked to realize that he was standing upright, yet he couldn't feel anything. He had no weight on his legs, or soggy clothing on his cold skin, or even a headache from his fall.

All at once the revelation hit him as hard as the lightning. With a cry, he whirled around and saw his body lying twisted and motionless beside the still form of his horse. A wisp of smoke rose from his broken helmet.

There was a feeling in Valorian's mind like the shattering of glass that shook him to the depths of his soul. Fury filled him, and he bellowed with all his might, "*No!* This cannot be!" His voice sounded strange in the unearthly stillness, yet it was a relief to hear any noise. He shouted again just to break up the frightening silence.

Something moved close by, causing him to turn again, and he came face-to-face with Hunnul. The black stallion, apparently unmarked by the drastic change that had befallen them, nickered nervously and crowded close to his master. The saddle, or the image of the saddle, with all of his gear, was still cinched to Hunnul's back.

Valorian's anger receded a little in the comfort of the stallion's presence. He reached out to touch Hunnul, and his fingers felt the warm, black hide—until he pushed a little harder and his hand went right through the horse.

Frightened and furious again, Valorian shook his fist at the sky and shouted. "We're dead! All you holy gods, is this how you answer a prayer? Why now? Why *us?*"

The clansman abruptly paused. A faint sound intruded into the silence, a sound like distant thunder. Gradually it grew louder, drawing closer from a distance that had no direction.

Valorian drew a harsh breath. "The Harbingers." He should have remembered they would come. They were the riders of Nebiros's steeds and the messengers of Sorh, the god of the dead, who came to escort every soul that passed beyond the mortal world. They took the newly deceased to the realm of the dead to face the judgment of Lord Sorh.

"Not this time," Valorian cried. "I won't go. I can't, Hunnul. I won't leave my wife and family to the Tarns and starvation. Not while I can bring the hope of escape." Even as he spoke, the thundering noise became audible as hoofbeats.

From out of the glimmering light where the mountain range had vanished came four white riders on pale steeds galloping toward him with the speed of diving eagles.

The hunter looked around angrily for a weapon or some means of holding off the Harbingers. He spotted his sword lying several paces away from his dead body, and in more hope than knowledge, he lunged for it. His hand closed around the hilt and hefted it. It felt real enough to him.

Forged of braided iron and decorated with silver, the weapon had been burned black and its tip warped by the power of the lightning. At that moment, Valorian didn't care. The hilt still fit comfortably into his grip, and the weapon sang through the air as he swung it in a wide arc.

The clansman shouted with relief, sprang to his horse,

and brandished his weapon at the oncoming steeds. "Sorh honors me by sending four," he shouted to Hunnul, "but they will have to return without me."

Hunnul pranced sideways, infected by his master's agitation. Together they watched the four immortal escorts come galloping out of the sky to take them to the realm of Sorh. As the Harbingers drew closer, Valorian could see they were male in appearance, dressed in battle gear that shone with an icy light, and apparently unarmed. He studied them curiously. No living person knew what the Harbingers looked like, for very, very few souls died and returned to life. Valorian had never personally known a man or woman who had come back from death. Nevertheless, it was said that others had done it, and their success gave him hope. If he could just hold off the shining riders, they might let him go.

The four riders were almost upon him when he kicked Hunnul and shouted the Clan war cry. The stallion lunged forward into the midst of the white horses, squealing and snapping like a maddened creature. Valorian, his expression carved in adamant fury, swung his sword left and right at the riders. His weapon passed through two Harbingers and met nothing but air. Yet his attack seemed to surprise them.

They broke away from him and gathered at a distance to watch him. Their faces—if they had any—were invisible behind the visors of their helmets. Their postures were alert yet relaxed. They didn't seem to be particularly angered by Valorian's attack, only cautious. Most souls did not object so vigorously.

In a flash of worry and irritation, Valorian realized that they didn't have to fight or subdue him. They could simply outwait him. The Harbingers had all eternity.

Valorian noticed something else, too. The land around him was almost gone. The mountains and the ridge had faded out of sight, leaving only the small patch of stone and earth where their two bodies lay. Around him was only the gentle light. Alarmed, Valorian kneed Hunnul back to stand by the bodies. He knew instinctively that if they left their mortal shells, they would lose their only chance of returning to the living world.

"Valorian!"

The clansman started violently at the sound of his name.

"Sorh has called for you."

It was one of the Harbingers. His voice was low, masculine, compelling. Valorian felt a strong desire to obey his command. He forced it down with all his might.

"Not this time!" he shouted. "There is too much left for me to do."

"What you have left undone shall have to be done by others. Your time is over."

"No!"

"You must come, Valorian." The Harbingers' steeds took a step toward him.

All at once and without any warning, a great wind blew up around Valorian and the death riders. Like a living creature, it howled and roared and pushed between the startled clansman and his escorts.

Out of the raging wind, Valorian thought he heard a voice say, "Tell Sorh he will have to wait."

Suddenly the wind swooped up Hunnul and Valorian and carried them with giant, unseen hands up and away from the small patch of mortal earth. The man was too stunned to protest. The powerful wind had no adverse physical effect on his soul, but it left him mentally breathless as it bore him with incredible speed into the glowing, unfamiliar boundaries of the realm of the dead. The world of mortality and the Harbingers were left behind.

Beneath him, the stallion tried to neigh. Hunnul was terrified, but he couldn't move a muscle in the grip of the roaring, rushing wind.

Gradually the wind began to ease. Its force gently dissipated; its grand roar quieted until the strength of its passing was nothing more than a breeze. Ever so carefully the unseen hands of the wind set Valorian and Hunnul down, unharmed, and whisked off in a gust that sounded like laughter.

Both man and horse let out their breath in a great gust of relief. Hunnul stamped his hoof and snorted, as if to say, "Well!"

"Great gods of all," the clansman exclaimed, staring around. "What was that all about?"

There was no immediate answer. He and Hunnul were standing on what looked like a vast, featureless plain of gray stone—granite from the look of it, the substance of mountains unborn. The sky above them, if that's what it was, was a pale shade of gray and equally as empty. There was nothing else as far as they could see.

Valorian noticed he was still holding his sword. He hefted it once, then slowly slid it back into the sheepskin scabbard at his side. He had a feeling that no weapon would avail him here on this strange plain of stone. Something or someone of great power had brought him here with deliberate intent. He could only wait to see what would happen now. Swinging his leg over Hunnul's mane, the clansman slid off the horse and came to stand by the animal's head.

Together they looked at the stone around them.

"Now what?" Valorian murmured, nonplussed.

Hunnul nickered. The big stallion dipped his nose toward something on the ground in front of his hooves.

Valorian looked once and bent over for a second look. A tiny green plant had somehow taken tenuous root in the stone. As the man watched, the plant grew larger, spreading its tiny roots wider and deeper into the rock. The granite began to crack beneath the force of the roots. Tiny leaves popped out of the stem, opened, and spread wider. Tendrils curled toward the sky. Still deeper went the roots into the hard rock, but now Valorian could see the masses of fragile, hairlike roots were crumbling the granite into sand. He gasped in surprise and stepped back. Excitement, wonder, and dread crowded into him until he was shaking with emotion.

Swiftly the plant grew taller, without water, earth, or real sunlight. It stretched its stems and leaves up toward the sky in joyous, quivering life and suddenly burst into brilliant bloom. The flowers were of every hue imaginable, glistening bright with morning dew and filled with a delicate unearthly fragrance that was sweet and alluring.

Valorian's mouth dropped open and he fell to his knees. "The flower that shatters the stone," he breathed. The power of life. The power of the goddess Amara.

As the truth clarified in his mind, the plant began to shimmer with a pearlescent glow. Its stem, leaves, and flowers wavered and shifted before the man's eyes into the shape of a woman.

She was a glorious woman to Valorian's mind: tall and fair, with strong limbs, wide hips, and a noble figure. Her long, heavy mane of hair hung to her waist like a swirling cloak of pale spring green. Her eyes were as brown and deep as the earth. She wore a gown that belied description of its color, for it shifted in rainbow hues with every move of its wearer and clung to her body from her neck to her feet like gossamer webs of silk.

Valorian bowed low before her.

Amara, the goddess of life and birth, of the rejuvenation of spring and the grace of fertility, the beloved mother of all to the clanspeople, stepped forward and raised the hunter to his feet.

He looked into her face with awe and felt her love for him surround him with comfort and warmth. His anger and fear fell away in the joy of her presence.

"Amara," he whispered.

A smile lit her face, and Valorian wondered at how ageless she was. Her eyes were as ancient as the bones of the mountains, but her cheeks and her smile glowed with the youth of dawn.

"Please, my son, walk with me awhile," the goddess said to Valorian. Then she turned to the horse. "Hunnul, you must come, too, for this concerns both of you." With one hand on Valorian's arm and the other on the stallion's shoulder, the goddess walked slowly across the empty plain of stone.

She said nothing at first to her two companions, only strode majestically by their sides. Valorian respected her silence, even though a thousand questions burned in his mind.

They walked a little farther, to nowhere in particular, before Amara turned to face the man and horse. She seemed to study them both from head to foot and from the inside out before she nodded in satisfaction.

"Valorian," the goddess spoke sincerely, "a great misfortune has befallen me. To my distress, I have lost a possession that is very dear to me and very important to your world."

Valorian said nothing, only lifted an eyebrow to punctuate his interest. It was obvious to him that Amara had snatched him away from the Harbingers for her own purpose, but he couldn't imagine why. What would a goddess as powerful as Amara need with a simple mortal clansman? He tilted his head slightly to watch her face and listened as she continued.

"By the reckoning of your world, it happened fourteen days ago. My brother, Sorh, opened the mountain fastness of Ealgoden to imprison the soul of a particularly loathsome slave collector, when he made the mistake of allowing several gorthlings to escape."

Valorian drew a sharp breath.

"Exactly," the goddess said flatly. A grimace of disgust marred her exquisite face. "The little brutes were quickly retrieved, but not before they wreaked havoc on the mountaintop where we reside. One of the gorthlings stole my crown and took it back with him into the mountain."

The clansman's hand tightened around his sword hilt. He wasn't certain whether to be furious with indignation at the crime perpetrated on the Mother of All or horrified by the thought that was beginning to form in his mind. "Have you asked Lord Sorh to return your crown?" he asked quietly.

"Naturally. However, my brother is in perpetual competition with me. What I bring to life, he brings to death. We battle constantly. He feels this is just another game and that I must fetch the crown myself."

"Which you cannot do," Valorian stated. He thought he knew now what she wanted . . . and it terrified him.

The goddess turned her ancient eyes on the man. "As you have wisely deduced, Valorian, I cannot. I have very little influence over Sorh's minions, so I dare not go myself." She gestured angrily at the sky, setting her dress shimmering with her agitation. "The crown stolen by the gorthlings is one of three divine emblems that I bear. My scepter controls the wind and my orb governs the clouds, but it is my crown that carries the power to rule your sun. Without my three regalia working in harmony together, I cannot properly control the natural forces of the weather."

"That is why there has been so much rain?"

Amara swept her arm down. "Yes! Without the power of the sun to balance the wind and clouds, your world will eventually drown in rain."

Valorian made no reply, but a host of unpleasant thoughts trooped through his mind. He was horrified by the idea of entering the sacred mountain of Ealgoden. The mountain in the realm of the dead was both the home of the gods on its peak and the prison of the souls of the damned. Within its dark heart, named Gormoth, the fearsome gorthlings of Sorh kept the souls of those unworthy for peace trapped in eternal torment. No one went willingly to seek the gorthlings inside Ealgoden. Valorian knew if he failed to escape, he would be trapped inside forever.

Still, he believed he had to try, not only for the sake of his Clan's beloved goddess, but for his people as well. If he had to be dead, he could never be at peace knowing he had failed to try to save them from a world doomed to die.

A sudden glint lit his blue eyes at another thought. If he were successful, the goddess might want to reward him, and he could think of several things the goddess of life could do for his Clan.

But the gorthlings of Sorh! By Surgart's sword! He just

hoped the goddess's trust in him was not misplaced. He took a deep breath to steady his voice.

"I will find your crown," he told her.

Amara smiled a long, knowing smile. "Thank you, clansman." She turned to Hunnul and laid her fingertips on his soft muzzle. The stallion didn't budge. "What of you, my worthy child of the wind? Will you go also?"

Valorian wouldn't have thought his horse had understood what was being said, but Hunnul bobbed his head and neighed in reply.

The goddess stepped back, satisfied. "He is a good horse. He will follow you where you need to go." Her soft tone hardened to a command. "Now, mount, my son. I have something to give you before you go."

Valorian quickly obeyed. Now that his decision was made, he didn't want to risk having any second thoughts. He sprang into the saddle and faced the goddess, his expression set.

"Lord Sorh will give you no trouble. I will see to that," Amara said. "However, the gorthlings will be more than trouble. Your sword will not avail you in the tunnels of Gormoth. Therefore I give you a greater weapon." Raising her arms high, the goddess cried, "By the power of the lightning that brought you here, I name you magic-wielder." She abruptly flung her hands out toward the man, and Valorian gasped as another bolt of lightning hurled toward him. He had no chance to flinch before it struck him full on the chest.

Yet this strike did not hurt. It pierced through his chest and sizzled to the ends of his soul, warming him to the core of his existence, strengthening him, empowering him with a strange new energy.

Surprised, he stretched out his hands and saw a pale blue aura covering his body like a second skin. "What—what is it?" he managed to ask.

"You now have the power to wield magic, clansman."

"Magic!" he said, dumbfounded. "There is no such thing."

Amara's hands gestured again in a wide embrace of the plain, and her hair waved like summer grass. "Of course there is! When the world was created, a vestige of the power that fueled that creation remained behind in every natural thing. It permeates your world, Valorian, and our immortal world as well. You have seen its effects. Magic forms rainbows and unexpected things you call miracles. It is responsible for creatures that you have never seen and know only in legends. It has always been and always will be."

"Then why haven't men known of this power and learned to control it?" he demanded.

"Some people do know of the existence of magic. None have been able to control it. Until now."

Valorian stared dubiously at his hands. The blue aura was fading; in a moment, it was gone. "How do I use this power?" he asked, his doubt still clear in his voice.

"Use your strength of will," the goddess instructed him patiently. "Decide what it is that you want to do, clarify that intent in your mind, and bend the magic to your will. Forming a spell of words that states your intention will help. You can create destructive bolts and protective shields, alter the appearance of things, move large objects—just use your imagination. You are limited only by your own strength and your own weaknesses."

"Imagination," Valorian muttered. He was finding this whole conversation very difficult to accept. Still, he couldn't very well argue with the goddess without giving the magic a try. He closed his eyes, concentrating on an image of a small lightning bolt. He didn't feel anything or notice anything different about himself, and nothing happened. This obviously wasn't working.

"The magic is here, clansman! Concentrate!" he heard Amara say sharply.

Startled, he quickly erased his mind of all thought but the one of a bolt of power, a brilliant, sizzling bolt that would terrify gorthlings and bring him safely out of Gormoth.

Something stirred within him. Valorian felt an odd sensation of power that he had never experienced before suddenly fill his mind and flow through his body. Slowly he raised his right arm and threw his hand forward. To his surprise, the strange power surged. He opened his eyes in time to see a blue bolt pop out of his fingers and shoot across the plain of stone. It wasn't large or dazzling, but it was his, and he watched it with his mouth ajar until it dissipated in the distance.

Amara tilted her head up, looking pleased. "Well done, Valorian. You will learn."

The clansman bowed to her, his face full of shock, excitement, and success. "Lady Amara, just one question." She nodded once. "Why did you choose me?" he wanted to know. "Surely there are others who are better warriors or who have greater courage than I."

She laughed, a rich, warm sound of affection. "Perhaps there are others, Valorian. But my champion must have every bit as much intelligence as courage. It would not be wise to rush blindly into the gorthlings' lair."

Without warning, the goddess suddenly coalesced into a glowing cloud of brilliant light and scintillating color that rose high over the clansman's head. She glittered in the gray air like a radiant star.

"Wait!" he shouted. "Where do I go? How will I find you again?"

"The Harbingers will take you," Amara's voice called, "and I will find you when the time comes."

Hunnul neighed a ringing farewell.

Valorian watched the glowing cloud soar high in the dull sky, then streak away with the speed of a comet. A mixture of emotions rose in his heart at her leaving, not the least of which was fear. Now that the goddess and her loving comfort were gone, Valorian felt a rush of cold apprehension at what he had agreed to do. No man in his right mind would deliberately volunteer to enter the foul caverns of Ealgoden and hope to escape unscathed. It was impossible. Nevertheless, he had offered to go, and one way or another—even with this strange power of magic—he was going to try to succeed.

He heard again the thundering hooves of the Harbingers' steeds. Like huge white phantoms they rode out of the sky, swift and shining, to come to a neighing, prancing stop in front of the clansman.

This time Valorian reluctantly bowed his head to their summons. Hunnul stepped forward into the midst of the white steeds, and the clansman and his escort rode forward across the plain of stone.

3

wifter than storm clouds the Harbingers galloped forth, carrying the black stallion along by the force of their impetus. Almost immediately a wall of dark mist rose up before them; they passed through without pause. Valorian glanced over his shoulder and saw that the plain of stone, whatever and wherever it had been, was gone. He and his escort were plunging through a wall of cloud that was unfathomable and totally lightless. There was no sound other than the faint vibration of the horses' hooves on air and no light except for a pale, phosphorescent glow emanating from the four Harbingers. Valorian could just barely make out Hunnul's head in the gloom. The numbing lack of any real sensation began to disorient him, and he locked his eyes on the stallion's flattened ears as a center of focus.

Then, before his mind and eyes had time to adjust, the horses galloped out of the mist into the realm of the dead. The clansman gasped; his eyes screwed shut in the sudden clear light that assailed him. Hunnul, too, faltered and would have stumbled if Valorian hadn't automatically shifted his weight to help steady the startled horse. The stallion jerked to a stop and bobbed his head in confusion.

Valorian had to squint before he very slowly opened his eyes and looked about with wonder. The four Harbingers were still with him, waiting patiently for him to follow them. The dark wall of mist was gone, replaced by what looked like a vast meadow of grass. Far in the distance, he could see a single mountain rising out of the plain like a gigantic sentinel. The light that illuminated the scene shone from the mountain's peak as bright and splendid as the sun of the mortal world. The clansman knew without asking that the mountain was the sacred peak of Ealgoden, where the gods lived in immortal splendor, keeping watch over their people.

Awed, Valorian urged Hunnul forward, and the four Harbingers took their places, two to the front and two behind the clansman. They rode slowly across the vast meadow while Valorian examined and marveled over the unearthly beauty of the place. Never had he seen such a huge, perfectly created plain of grass. It was gently rolling, treeless, and thickly covered with a verdant coat of grass and delicately colored flowers that barely reached Hunnul's hocks. The sky overhead was a vivid azure, and the light from the peak shone warm and mellow.

The only things missing, Valorian realized, were the wind, insects, animal life, and people. The lack of these things seemed very odd to him, since he was used to the lively meadows of the mortal world. After a while, the quiet and the emptiness began to bother him. He was about to try asking the silent Harbingers a few questions when a movement caught his eye.

Several people were coming over the crest of a hill off to Valorian's right. They saw him and waved joyfully, their excitement evident even over the distance. One person broke away from the small group to come running toward him. Valorian realized there was something very familiar about the long-legged stride of the runner. He stared as the person came nearer. Other people were coming toward him now from all directions, men, women, and children, some on foot, a few on horseback, and all waving and calling cheerfully to him. He glanced around at them in growing surprise before looking back again at the person running toward him.

All at once the runner's dark hair came unbound in long waves, and Valorian recognized who it was—his youngest sister, who had died when she was fourteen. Behind her were their parents, another brother, and their grandparents. All had been dead for years, but Valorian hadn't realized until that moment how much he had missed them.

He cantered Hunnul forward to meet them. "Adala!" he cried happily. He was about to jump down to greet her when a small, urgent warning spoke in his ear. Startled, he looked around at the Harbingers, at the air above him, and at the fields nearby. There was no one close enough to have spoken, but the warning remained clear and persistent in his mind. It must be Amara urging him on, he decided, for he knew now that if he dismounted, if he left his horse and his escort to join the throng coming to greet him, he could become enthralled by the lovely meadow and the happiness of his kinsmen. He could lose his sense of purpose and any chance of helping the goddess, thus unwittingly condemning his world to destruction. Reluctantly but firmly he shifted back into his saddle and let Hunnul continue walking.

"Valorian, you old dog! You've come!" Adala shouted gleefully. Her young, lovely face beamed up at him as she came to jog beside Hunnul. "You have a horse with you, you lucky slug. They must have buried you with honors. And four escorts! Sorh does you great honor. Though I don't know why."

Valorian grinned at her. Adala had always loved to talk. She had always loved to do everything with an exuberant gaiety that lit her every move and expression with fire. She had even loved the vicious little mare that one day slammed her headlong into a tree.

By this time, his father, mother, and baby brother had caught up with him, and other people were crowding around. The whole chattering entourage walked along with the horses, calling to him and asking questions.

Valorian looked down at them all and was startled by how many faces he recognized. There were friends, acquaintances, and even a few enemies here, and relatives he knew only by family history. He waved and smiled, but he didn't dismount or stop to meet them.

"Valorian!" a voice boomed over the others. "How are you, lad?"

The clansman nodded with pleasure and saluted the man striding beside Adala. "I am here, Father. That should say something."

The old man, still looking as robust and hale as the day he tangled fatally with three Tarnish soldiers, laughed and slapped his son on the leg. Valorian felt only a slight sensation. Death had certainly limited his sense of touch.

"Father, do you see this horse?" Adala exclaimed. "Isn't he a beauty? What did you do, Valorian, steal him?"

"Hush, Adala!" her mother shushed the girl. "There will be time later to talk when he returns from Lord Sorh."

Valorian winced. He had just found this part of his family. He hated to tell them of his true mission.

Before he could say anything, his father demanded, "Tell me first, Valorian. Two things: How is your brother, and did you fulfill your duty to the Clan before you left?"

Valorian wanted to groan. Leave it to his father to bring up the sore point of his life now. At least he could report the good news first. Maybe he could be gone before his father demanded the rest.

"Aiden was well and happy the last time I saw him. He is about to be married."

"Aiden? He survived unharmed to manhood? Praise Surgart!" his father declared.

Adala snorted indelicately. "That wildcat in a sheep's coat? Married? Poor girl."

Valorian couldn't help but smile. He, too, had often despaired that Adala's twin brother would ever grow up. Aiden had been as wild and reckless as his sister.

"He missed you horribly when you died," Valorian told Adala. "I think some of his deeds came out of his grief."

She quieted for a moment, her shining smile lost in sadness, then she brightened and skipped ahead to Hunnul's head. "At least you're here with us now. May I ride your horse?"

"Perhaps sometime," Valorian replied vaguely. He waved a hand toward the seemingly endless fields of grass. "Is this all there is?"

"My goodness, no," she said. "This is only a small part. The realm of the dead has many places and many more people. You can make of your eternal life what you will."

"Enough chatter, girl," their father said in exasperation. "Valorian, you will not change the subject. Did you and Kierla produce a son?"

"No." Valorian replied flatly and clamped his jaw shut. He didn't want to continue that discussion. His father had chosen Kierla as a wife for him when he was barely a man. She had the looks of a good brood mare, the old man had said—long frame, wide hips, ample breasts. She would bring many children to Valorian's tent. Valorian had had his heart set on another, but he took Kierla reluctantly to please his father. To his surprise, marrying her had been the best decision of his life.

The only problem was that she hadn't borne any children. In the fifteen summers since they had been joined, she had never once been pregnant. Several people had suggested to Valorian that he could turn her out and get a new wife, but he refused. He and Kierla had grown to love one another in a way that transcended the absence of children. Although he knew the lack of babies in her arms was a bitter disappointment to her and that she would leave if he asked, he had never even considered it. Kierla had strengths that sustained them both and a spirit that delighted his heart. It was a shame his father would never understand.

"What?" the old man bellowed. "Why that useless—"

He was interrupted by his wife who put her hand on his arm. "It hardly matters now, my husband. Let our son pay his homage to Lord Sorh."

As soon as she spoke, Valorian reached out and gently touched her hair. His mother's hair was still as gray as on the day she died, but the face she turned to him was radiant with peace and contentment.

"Mother," he said quietly, "it is possible I will not come back."

"Whyever not?" cried Adala.

His parents looked up with questions in their eyes.

"I go to Gormoth in Ealgoden as Amara's champion to face the gorthlings," he replied.

The entire entourage abruptly fell quiet.

"No, you can't!" breathed Adala finally. Their mother's radiant peace faded to a sickly fear.

"Valorian, don't be a fool!" an uncle shouted. "No mortal can best a gorthling."

His grandfather gestured furiously toward the mountain. "Those creatures are evil, don't you know that? They'll destroy you."

Only his father stared keenly into his face with the piercing gaze of an old, wise eagle. "If Amara chose you," he stated with intensity, "then you must go."

The clansman nodded, his cool blue gaze matching his father's. "The goddess gave me a weapon," he said to reassure his parents. "I am not totally defenseless."

The old man clenched his fist. "Then use it wisely, and we will see you when you return."

"Thank you, Father," Valorian said. It was time to move on. He was afraid that even with Amara's warning ringing in his mind, he would lose himself in the reunion with his family. He waved farewell to his relatives and friends and kicked Hunnul into a canter. The four silent Harbingers moved with him.

"Surgart go with you, Brother," Adala cried, waving frantically.

"And Amara, too," bellowed his father.

All too quickly the crowd of well-wishers was left behind on the green fields, and Valorian rode on alone with his escort. Ahead of him, the meadow stretched on in gentle, unbroken waves to lap against the feet of the sacred mountain that rose in solitary splendor to meet the sky.

Even from a distance, Valorian could see that the peak

was bigger by far than any puny mountain in the mortal world. Its gigantic gray-black ramparts dominated the realm around it; its massive, jagged crags thrust high into the rarefied air. A veil of cloud and mist hid the upper reaches of the peak where the gods and goddesses resided, but the eternal light at the summit burned clear and bright.

As Valorian and Hunnul drew closer to the mountain, the clansman noticed that they were following a faint path in the grass. The trail ran straight and true to the mountain's slope and shimmered with its own pale luminescence in the sacred light. He knew they were riding one of the many paths of the dead that led to the throne of Sorh. He studied the path worriedly and wondered how he was going to get away to begin his search for an entrance into Gormoth. The Harbingers weren't going to let him simply wander off, nor did he think he could escape from them. On the other hand, Valorian didn't relish going to the court of Lord Sorh.

By immortal law, he, as a newly arrived soul, was required to face the god of the dead before he could take his place in the realm of the dead, and normally he would have done so. However, this situation could hardly be called normal! Valorian was afraid that if he went to face the god of the dead before he tried to rescue Amara's crown, Lord Sorh could delay him, hinder him, or simply refuse to let him go. The last thing Valorian wanted to do was spend eternity arguing with gods while his world drowned in the fury of unleashed storms.

He sighed between his teeth and settled into his saddle to wait. As long as he had four Harbingers for escorts, there was little he could do except follow them and hope for a chance to slip away.

A short while later Valorian realized there were other people on the trail. Not far ahead was a single Harbinger escorting several men on foot—Tarns, from the look of their clothes and their swarthy skins. Before them, another group of men, women, and a child walked with their escort. Valorian glanced over his shoulder and saw, far behind him, a fair woman of Chadarian blood riding a dun-colored mare and carrying a baby. They, like he, were all moving toward Ealgoden to face the god of the dead—whatever name they might call him.

The trail gradually began to rise. The verdant meadow was left behind and replaced by piles of tumbled boulders, stony slopes, and granite outcroppings. Soon other trails appeared to the right and left and merged with Valorian's path. The clansman saw more people: a few clanspeople, some Chadarians, a Sarcithian, and some from races he did not know, all coming with their escorts. The Harbingers were rather busy that day, he mused.

It was then that he suddenly noticed his own Harbingers were gone. They had vanished without a word or a reason and left him alone on the path. Surprised, he brought the black stallion to a halt and glanced around at the tumbled mountainside. There was no sign of his escorts.

Perhaps Amara had recognized Valorian's difficulty and drawn away the Harbingers. Without them in his way, he should be able to slip off and begin his search for an entrance into the gorthlings' domain. He wished she had told him where to find a door. One could be hidden anywhere on this vast mountain.

Hunnul nickered, startling Valorian from his thoughts. The young woman and her baby were passing by. She nodded to him politely and the baby cooed, but their escorting Harbinger totally ignored him. They rode on, disappearing out of sight beyond a clump of boulders.

The clansman waited only until the way was momentarily clear before he dismounted and cautiously stepped off the glowing path. Nothing happened. The path remained empty, no alarms were sounded, and his escorts did not return. Relieved, he led Hunnul off the trail and into the rugged flanks of the mountain to begin his search.

* * * * *

He has come, Lord Sorh.

The dark, emotionless visage of the god of the dead turned toward the kneeling Harbinger and nodded once. *So, Amara has found her champion. Who is it?*

A clansman named Valorian, replied the escort.

Ah, yes. The son of Daltor. He will need his father's courage and his mother's restraint for this task. It should prove interesting. The god leaned back in his massive throne and steepled his fingers. *Allow the man some time to search, then reveal the entrance. I will give him a chance to show his mettle.*

The Harbinger bowed and backed out of the god's presence.

The goddess Amara stepped out of the shadows of Sorh's hall and came forward to face her brother. Bright and passionate against Sorh's impartial gravity, she shone like a sun in a gloomy, cold cavern. *You will not interfere in this matter?* she asked.

I will not if you will not.

Agreed.

Sorh summoned the other deities. *Surgart and Krath, bear witness!*

The god of war and the goddess of destinies arrived together and stood beside Amara.

We have heard, Surgart told them.

Krath agreed. *The man goes alone.*

Then so be it.

* * * * *

Valorian had no idea how much time had passed since he left the path of the dead. What was time, anyway, compared to immortality? There was no night with its stars or day with its sun to guide his efforts. Instead, there was only the ceaseless golden light and the looming mountain with its impenetrable walls.

The clansman knew that he and Hunnul had circled up

the gigantic peak three times, climbing, scrambling, and fighting their way around the tumbled boulders and steep inclines. So far they had found nothing. The only paths led up to Sorh's throne. There were no footprints, worn places, cracks, or any sort of sign that would lead him to an entrance into Gormoth. The mountain was as impassive and impervious as Sorh himself.

When they had completed their fourth loop around the mountain, Valorian wearily drew Hunnul to a halt and stood staring out over the mountainside. He shook his head. This was the strangest mountain he had ever known. There was no wind, no animal life, no heat or cold, no ice; there was only rock.

Climbing the peak should have been easy, but Valorian hadn't been dead long enough to grow accustomed to the strangeness of his immortal existence. He had no real feeling in his body, and physical exertion did not tire him, yet even the realm of the dead seemed bound by some of the laws of nature. He couldn't simply float around the mountain; he and Hunnul had to traverse it the hard way. After four long circles, he was thoroughly tired of the fruitless struggling.

Valorian hoped they didn't have to go much higher in their search. The way was growing too steep and difficult for the stallion, and they were only halfway up the mountain slope. He didn't want to leave his mount behind if he could help it. At least he didn't have to worry about the two of them falling to their deaths. If they fell, he supposed they would just climb back up again.

The clansman led the black horse along a slippery escarpment to a wide, flat ledge. Close by was the path of the dead they had left some time ago. He stared up the mountain to the curtain of mist that obscured the realm of the gods. Had Sorh noticed he was missing from the ranks of the newly dead who stood before the throne of judgment? Had any of the deities noticed him crawling like a fly on the walls of their home? He leaned against Hunnul's side and wished he were someplace else.

Hunnul's soft muzzle suddenly nudged his arm. Startled, the clansman looked up to see a Harbinger riding down the nearby path leading another man, a Sarcithian marauder, on foot. Valorian pressed Hunnul back into the shadow of a big boulder, out of sight of the Harbinger, then carefully peered around the rock edge. Harbingers usually escorted souls up *to* Sorh, not away from him—unless . . . Valorian worked his way closer to the trail in time to see the shining white rider turn off the main path onto a way only he could see. The dead man followed.

Valorian drew a sharp breath. The Harbinger must be escorting a soul to the entrance into Gormoth, the gorth-lings' lair. If he could just follow them, they would lead him to the door. Quickly Valorian led Hunnul onto the mountain path and down to the place where the Harbinger had left the trail. There on the rocks Valorian saw the faintest track worn into the rock by the countless condemned souls who had traveled that way. The trail angled sharply uphill, tra-versed a steep, boulder-strewn slope, and came to an abrupt end in a tremendous cliff wall.

Valorian watched from behind an outcropping as the Har-binger and the helpless soul came to a halt before the blank stone wall. In a loud voice, the escort called a single word. There was a deep, sonorous noise in the cliffs, and Valorian stared openmouthed at the large door-shaped crack that appeared in the rock wall. He had passed by this cliff before and never noticed the entrance. The noise changed to a grinding groan as the door swung outward, revealing an opening large enough for several horses abreast to pass through. Behind the door was a tunnel, a hole of stygian darkness.

The opening door suddenly galvanized the Sarcithian who stood with the Harbinger. His shriek of utter despair shat-tered the mountain quiet as he whirled frantically to flee.

But the white rider was faster. A bolt of shining energy flew from his upraised hand and caught the man before he had taken two steps. The power wrapped around his chest like a rope and pinioned his arms to his sides. The doomed man screeched and struggled, his face wracked in terror. The Harbinger paid no heed.

Inexorably the power began to draw the Sarcithian toward the open doorway. The condemned man fought his bonds like a madman, but the magic held firm to the threshold of the door. There the man was halted, the white energy vanished, and he was left standing just inside the ominous black tunnel into Gormoth. A high-pitched cackle of glee echoed out of the darkness. The soul froze in horror.

The Harbinger lowered his hand and spoke. "For your crimes, you are condemned to Gormoth for eternity. There is no hope beyond those portals."

Before the Sarcithian had time to react, the heavy stone door slammed shut with a thundering boom, sealing him forever with his doom. The echoes died away; the mountain was left once more in silence. The Harbinger rode back the way he had come, paying no attention to the clansman hidden in the rocks.

Valorian sank back against the stone, appalled by the horror he had seen. Second and third thoughts battered against his resolve to enter that forbidding doorway until he felt as weak and despairing as a condemned man. "Amara," he silently cried, "why did you want *me* to do this?"

Forcing himself to mount Hunnul, the clansman rode to the base of the cliff wall. He stared numbly up at the gray stone, struggling to control his fear. Because he had given his word to his goddess, he wouldn't back down now, but he had never done anything in his life as difficult as voicing the Harbinger's command to open the door. Only the knowledge that the decision to go to Gormoth had been ultimately his gave him the strength to continue.

With every bit of courage he could summon, Valorian forced his mind clear and spoke the Harbinger's strange command, hoping it would work for him. He waited for several moments, yet the door didn't budge. He shouted the command again in an effort to mimic the Harbinger's exact tone and inflection, and still the portal remained solidly closed. His hopes sank into frustration. What could he hope to accomplish if he couldn't even get inside?

He was about to dismount and try beating on the door when a new thought came to him. The Harbinger had used a strange power against the dead man's soul, a power that was quite possibly magic. Therefore, Valorian surmised, it seemed reasonable to assume that the escort had used magic to open the door as well.

Valorian lifted his head. It was certainly worth a try. Amara had given him the ability to wield magic, and it was time he started learning to use it. "Clarify the intent in your mind," she had said. He closed his eyes, concentrated a single thought on the door, and clearly voiced the Harbinger's command.

An unfamiliar energy seemed to crackle through him and surge from his being. There was a long, hesitant silence, then, ever so slowly, the big stone portal cracked open and swung wide. The darkness yawned before him. Looking down the black maw of the tunnel, Valorian wasn't certain whether to be pleased by his success or horrified. But at least the spell had worked.

Valorian reluctantly drew his sword and said, "Let's go, Hunnul."

For once, the big stallion refused. His ears went flat against his head, and he tucked his chin in and backed away several steps.

The clansman could hardly blame the horse. A cold, fetid draft blew from the entrance, heavy with the smell of sulphur and corruption. The darkness within was absolute.

Valorian stared at the tunnel, then gazed up at the light shining from the mountaintop. A wisp of a smile lifted the corners of his mouth. Encouraged by his success with the door, he closed his eyes and concentrated on a desire for light: a small, bright, movable light that would guide his way through the tunnels, calm Hunnul's fear, and perhaps surprise the gorthlings.

He felt again the strange surge of power and cautiously opened his eyes. A light was there, but it wasn't quite what he had in mind. It was too small and feeble. He tried again to focus on exactly what he wanted, channeling the unfamiliar power into his first real spell. To his pleasure, he watched the guttering light transform into a brightly glowing sphere that hung suspended in the air near his head.

Hunnul snorted suspiciously. However, when Valorian sent the light ahead into the passageway, the big horse unwillingly moved forward. Step by step, on legs as stiff as glass, Hunnul approached the entrance. They passed over the threshold into Gormoth, and on its own accord, the door boomed shut behind them.

4

ike a summons, the thundering boom echoed down the tunnel, deep and resonant, shaking the walls and causing the floor to tremble. Hunnul came to a dead stop in frightened surprise. Valorian tried to stifle his own apprehension as he calmed the nervous stallion. He stared around warily at the smooth floor, the rough-hewn walls, and the ceiling that loomed overhead. There was nothing to be seen in the glow thrown by his light. Just ahead, the blackness of the tunnel led downward into the depths of the mountain. There was no noise, no movement, no indication whatsoever of life; even the man who had entered a short time before was gone. Yet Valorian sensed the presence of something close by. There was a coldness in the air that chilled him to the bone and raised the hairs on his neck. Warily he clutched his sword and, mentally pushing his sphere of light ahead of them to show the way, kneed Hunnul forward down into the implacable darkness.

They walked slowly downward for what seemed a very long time. The tunnel ran straight for a few paces, then turned to the right and immediately curved left again. It continued its erratic course, zigzagging through the mountain until Valorian had no idea what direction they were going except down. There were no side openings or forks in the trail; it seemed to be the only way in, leading irrevocably down to some destination known only to the gods and the gorthlings.

The tunnel remained empty and silent. The only noise

Valorian could hear was the soft *clip-clop* of Hunnul's hooves on the floor, yet the clansman knew they were not alone. The feeling of a presence close by grew stronger by the moment. Something was watching them, he knew it. The back of his neck prickled and his body was rigid with tension while he strained every sense into the darkness surrounding them. Every now and again he half saw a whisk of movement at the farthest reaches of his light, as if something was getting out of the way of the strange magical illumination. He imagined the gorthlings, if that's what were out there, were rather surprised by a soul entering their domain with a horse, a sword, and a sphere of magical light. He just hoped their amazement would keep them at bay for a while longer.

The cold, fetid draft was stronger now, and the mountain seemed to weigh heavily over their heads. Hunnul walked on, ever downward, his ears swiveling like a deer's and his nostrils flaring to red cups. The stallion was so tense he was practically stepping on the tips of his hooves.

Valorian lost all track of time. He didn't know how long they walked in the stinking, cold darkness or how far they had gone. His sense of reality shrank to a small circle of light surrounded by unseen evil and imagined horrors.

After a while, he became aware of harsh whispers in the blackness behind him. A pattering sound, like many small feet, echoed down the tunnel, and now and again there was a crashing noise as if a rock had been dislodged. Once Valorian thought he heard an agonized shriek from somewhere in the darkness, but it was impossible to tell from which direction it came, and the hideous sound was cut off almost as quickly as it began. Valorian swallowed hard and wondered where the soul of the dead man had gone—and where were the gorthlings?

Hunnul pushed on until he was almost jogging along the passage. The sound of his hooves rang around them, yet the noise didn't hide the skittering and whispering sounds in the shaft behind them. All at once something small scooted out of the blackness and gave Hunnul's tail a vicious yank. The stallion squealed in fury and lashed back with a foot just a moment too late. The creature was already gone into the darkness before either man or horse could see it.

Valorian cursed under his breath. This journey was growing intolerable. He could hardly bear to continue simply riding into a blind trap while an unseen menace lurked at his heels. He wanted to stand and fight, to see his enemies and drive them away. But the evil things in the darkness stayed out of sight, and all he could do was keep going.

Warily he and Hunnul continued on, winding their way downward into the mountain fastness. It wasn't long before the creatures behind them grew bolder. Their whispers changed to malicious laughter that grated on Valorian's already stretched self-control. Rocks flew out of the dark to land with a crash near Hunnul's feet or strike with stinging pain on Valorian's back. Shadows small and swift dashed maddeningly in and out of the rim of Valorian's light.

"Come forth and fight me, you worms!" he shouted, brandishing his sword at the taunting shadows. They merely laughed at him again with harsh, maniacal voices.

Valorian had ridden what seemed a very long distance when suddenly Hunnul snorted a fierce warning. Before the man could move, three small creatures dropped from the ceiling onto his head and shoulders. They wrenched off his helmet, threw it aside, and clutched at his head. His soul quailed at their foul touch. They reeked of evil, and their tiny, powerful fingers dug into his skin and hair like burning poison. They couldn't draw blood or seriously injure the soul, but they could inflict agonizing pain.

With an oath, Valorian dropped his sword across his legs and tried to wrench the creatures off with his hands. They clung, screeching and yowling in his ears until he was finally able to peel two of them off and fling them against the rock walls. They bounced off the stone unharmed and ran gibbering into the darkness. The third still clung to his shoulder.

The clansman looked around, and for just a moment, he

stared into the wizened, depraved face of a gorthling. Its head looked like a mummified child's; its eyes were large and depthless, like a chasm of horror and despair. With a shudder, Valorian stabbed his sword at the wicked, grinning face. The blade sliced deep into the creature's head, knocking it off his shoulders to the ground, but the creature clambered to its feet and vanished as quick as a rat.

"Gorthlings!" Valorian spat with loathing. Somewhere in the tunnel, a harsh, evil laugh sounded out of the unseen depths.

The man and horse didn't wait for another attack. They hurried on, breathless and frightened, while dry, guttural voices snarled and mocked them.

"Foolish mortal," the voices hissed. "You play your games, but you are ours."

"They're testing us, Hunnul," Valorian said harshly. "They're not yet sure what we can do." All at once he noticed his sphere of light had dimmed during their fight with the gorthlings. He quickly concentrated on it, channeling the unfamiliar magic through his mind and into the light. To his vast relief, it flared, bright and reassuring, once more.

At that moment, he caught a glimpse of something at the edge of the renewed light. A mass of small, gibbering forms was crowding into the tunnel behind them, gathering to attack. If that many creatures caught them, he and Hunnul would never be able to fend them off.

An image of Amara's lightning bolt flashed into his mind, and quickly Valorian raised his hand and sent a small blue bolt of his own burning into the midst of the creatures. The mass fell apart, screaming in furious surprise.

"Run!" he shouted to Hunnul.

The stallion raced forward down the tunnel, his eyes rolling white with fear. Valorian ducked his head and clung desperately to the galloping horse. He could only pray there were no sudden drop-offs or blind walls ahead. His light kept pace with them through the dark tunnel like a guiding star, and Valorian thanked his goddess at every step for the power she had given him.

Behind them, he could hear the gorthlings yowling and screeching as they chased the horse down the underground path. The man knew the creatures wouldn't be too worried about his momentary escape, for he and Hunnul were trapped in Gormoth. The gorthlings had all of eternity to catch and subdue them.

Valorian stifled a shiver and shoved that thought out of his mind. Let the gorthlings think he and Hunnul would never escape. Perhaps then he could catch them off guard. All he and the black stallion had to do was stay out of their clutches long enough to find the crown and a way out.

Unfortunately, that didn't look as if it were going to be easy. The tunnel's quick turns and sharp curves made it difficult for a running horse to maintain a fast pace. Hunnul had to slow down to keep from crashing headlong into the stone walls or losing his balance. The gorthlings behind were gaining at every turn. The creatures were small, but they were fast and very familiar with the black tunnel.

Then, without warning, a hail of stones crashed down on the man and the running horse. Hunnul stumbled, and his sudden movement pitched Valorian over his head. The clansman crashed into the rock floor and lay dazed while stones fell all around them. Gorthlings laughed from the ceiling above.

One particularly large chunk just missed Valorian's head, and the loud crack of stone on stone brought him to his senses. Desperately he scrambled back into his saddle. He was about to urge Hunnul on when several of the swiftest gorthlings caught up with them. The creatures swarmed up the horse's back legs and attacked Valorian like vicious wildcats.

Once again he had to sheath his sword and fend them off with his hands. Three gorthlings clung to his back, so Valorian quickly yanked off his cloak, wrapped it around them, and hurled it as far as he could. Hunnul, meanwhile, had recovered his footing and cantered forward. Another gorthling was still hanging to Valorian's arm, trying to snatch the sword. It scrabbled up his forearm, hissing as he reached for it.

Valorian was about to grab its leg when, to his surprise, the gorthling shrieked in pain and flinched away from him. Without further attack, it dropped off and ran crying into the tunnel.

Valorian stared in amazement at his arm. What in the name of Sorh had hurt that gorthling? Nothing he or Hunnul had done had harmed it. Why did this one flee? He studied his arm as best he could with the erratic movements of his horse, but he could see nothing unusual.

Except maybe one thing. In the folds of his heavy winter tunic glittered the gold armband his wife had given him on their betrothal. It was his most precious personal possession and one he wore on his upper arm at all times. When he had pulled his cloak off, the armband had been exposed, and the gorthling had touched it. Could it be that the gorthlings were afraid of gold?

If this were true, Valorian wished he had a whole chest of gold. One small armband wasn't going to help much against a swarm of gorthlings. Still, it was a fact worth remembering.

While the man was thinking of gold, the horse continued to canter down the tunnel. The path seemed straighter now, but steeper, forcing the black to slow down again. They both could hear the gorthlings following them, for the harsh voices reverberated through the hollow darkness.

Moments later, Valorian noticed the passageway ahead was growing lighter. The brightness didn't come from his sphere, nor was it the clear light of day. The light was yellowish and uneven—more like firelight. The air had changed, too, becoming warmer and more heavy with the smell of superheated rock.

The clansman had only a moment to wonder about it before Hunnul galloped through an archway and into a large grotto. The light immediately intensified; the stench of molten rock struck their nostrils like a blow. Valorian took one horrified look and brought Hunnul to a sliding stop.

Before them, the path continued on through a giant cavern, except now it was no more than a narrow ledge that wound along the wall on the left side of the cavern. About twenty feet directly below the trail was a wide, slow-flowing river of lava that was moving downward toward the center of the mountain. Valorian had never seen molten rock before, and its heat and ponderous, deadly current staggered him. He didn't need an explanation to know that it would be agony to fall into that river of liquid stone.

On the other hand, he and Hunnul couldn't stand around and wait for the gorthlings to catch them. They had to keep going. Swiftly Valorian dismounted and, after a few reassuring words to his horse, led Hunnul onto the thin, crumbling ledge.

The trail was barely wide enough for the big horse. Hunnul had to pick his way very carefully along the cracked and cluttered ledge with his barrel rubbing along the stone wall and his hooves bare inches from the drop-off. He nickered nervously, and Valorian reached back to rub his nose.

It was that movement that saved the clansman from the torment of the lava, for just as Valorian turned to comfort his horse, a blob of molten rock splattered against the wall by his head.

Valorian instinctively spun to face the danger. There, running along the surface of the lava river, were five gorthlings. They didn't seem to be bothered by the heat or the fluidity of the lava but ran over the surface as if it were solid ground. One scooped up a handful of the stuff and lobbed it toward the path above.

At that moment, the pursuing group of about fifteen or twenty gorthlings emerged from the tunnel. They whooped with glee when they saw the man and the horse on the ledge and the gorthling reinforcements on the river. With incredible agility, they scampered like wizened monkeys along the trail after their quarry.

"You can run, nag-rider," the gorthlings on the river called rudely, "but you haven't got much farther you can go!"

"Let's see you jump, you useless heap of guts," one of the gorthlings on the ledge taunted. It flung a rock at Valorian to punctuate his point. The rest of the creatures followed suit, hurling a tormenting rain of stones, lava blobs, and insults.

Valorian and Hunnul frantically forced their way along the trail in an effort to escape the merciless barrage. They had only taken a few steps when two rocks struck Hunnul on the rump, and at the same time a handful of lava splattered around Valorian's legs. The clansman cried out and tried to shake the burning blobs from his leggings. The molten rock didn't actually burn his skin, but the pain was there as real and terrible as in life. The stallion squealed, leaped forward, and nearly plowed the man off the ledge.

Valorian, clenching his teeth to ward off the pain, held on to Hunnul's mane with every ounce of his strength. Panic rose like bile in his throat. He tried to think through the jumble of pain and fear in his mind. He had to do something fast before one or both of them fell off the ledge into the lava or were overwhelmed by the gorthlings. What he needed was a shield, or better yet, a shelter. Then, like a little spark, a coherent thought clicked in his mind, and Amara's words sprang out of his memory. He could use his power as a weapon *or* as a shield.

Immediately he closed his eyes and tried to imagine a shelter around himself and Hunnul, a tent perhaps, clear, so he could see through it, permeable so they could breathe, and impervious to any kind of weapon. He concentrated, ignoring the pain, the falling stones, the frightened horse, and the gorthlings. He felt the power of magic flow through him, a little unsteadily at first, then warm and increasingly more comfortable. Slowly he raised his hands, lifting them over his head and down in the shape of a domed tent. Something seemed to be happening around him, for the stones were no longer hitting him, and the gorthlings seemed to be howling in rage.

Valorian felt Hunnul stop his terrified prancing. Slowly he opened his eyes. He and Hunnul were completely surrounded by a pale red tent of glowing energy, while just outside, the gorthlings leaped and yelled in frustration as their missiles bounced harmlessly off the magical walls.

Valorian took a deep breath. He brushed off the last of the cooling splattered lava from his legs and took a moment to examine Hunnul. The stallion seemed to be well enough. He had calmed down and was standing on the ledge, his eyes warily watching the gorthlings outside.

"Come on, boy," Valorian said softly. "Let's try this again." Step by step they walked forward along the path, the shelter moving with them like a faintly glowing shield. The gorthlings surrounded them on both sides of the trail and followed their every step. The creatures attacked the shelter in a frenzy of rage, but their attempts to break it with their fists and hurled stones were useless.

The man studied his attackers as he led Hunnul along the trail. The gorthlings were small, vicious, evil, and had dominion over the souls that entered Gormoth. But unlike the Harbingers, they hadn't yet shown any power of their own to wield magic. Valorian thanked the gods for that blessing. Despite his luck with his spells thus far, he realized he was barely tapping the surface of the vast reservoirs of magic. He would be in serious trouble if he had to face an opponent who was skilled in using the power.

He was also beginning to notice that wielding magic could be tiring. He and Hunnul were only halfway along the treacherous trail through the cavern, and already he was feeling the effort of maintaining the shelter. It took more concentration and mental willpower than he expected.

To help conserve his strength, he banished the sphere of light and struggled along the trail, leading Hunnul by the flickering glow of the lava river. Ahead, at the opposite end of the cavern, he could see where the trail entered the rock wall once more. Valorian focused on that black hole while he struggled to hold his shelter intact. As his strength slowly drained away, the tent of energy started to fade.

Twenty paces from the tunnel entrance, the trail began to

widen. Valorian hauled himself onto Hunnul's back. He was so weary he knew he would have to stop using his shield. The gorthlings realized it, too, and increased their efforts to break through.

At ten paces from the tunnel, Valorian made his move. In one motion, he clamped his legs against Hunnul's sides, dissolved the magic shield, and bent low over the stallion's neck. Hunnul responded as he had been trained to do. In a violent lunge forward, he burst through the crowd of gorthlings on the trail and plunged into the darkness of the tunnel entrance at a full gallop, leaving the angry creatures behind.

Valorian immediately renewed his sphere of light—it didn't use as much strength or concentration to maintain—and urged on his horse. He wanted to put as much distance as possible between themselves and the gorthlings. He knew with a sinking certainty that he didn't have the strength at that moment to put up another shield or fend off another attack.

The tunnel was straighter now and still sloping downhill. Valorian wondered how far they had traveled into the mountain and how long they had been there. Surely this trail came to an end somewhere. So far he had seen no other paths, other souls, or any sign of Amara's crown. There seemed to be only the gorthlings and the featureless tunnel winding endlessly through the mountain.

After a short while, the clansman felt his stallion's pace begin to slow. He eased Hunnul to a halt, and together they listened in the darkness. The tunnel was silent.

Nevertheless, Hunnul pricked his ears and shifted his feet nervously. Ever alert to his horse's cues, Valorian sharpened his own senses until he, too, was aware of a strange stirring in the tunnel. The cold, fetid draft that had blown into his face most of the way was gone; the air was almost still. Only a faint stir in the heavy, damp atmosphere signaled that something was changing. Valorian reached out curiously and touched the rock wall. To his surprise, he could feel a slight vibration in the stone.

Then he felt another movement. A tiny arm was reaching out of a crevice in the wall for the hilt of his dagger in his belt. As quick as a snake, Valorian grabbed the arm and yanked hard. A struggling gorthling emerged from the crack. At first it fought to get away, but then it changed tactics and clung to his left wrist and hand like a burr. It hissed at him, its sharp, pointed ears flattened against its skull. Hunnul pranced forward nervously.

Valorian tried to flip the gorthling off, but it held on with a painful grip. He was about to smash it against the wall when he saw more gorthlings behind them. The pursuers had caught up with them faster than he had expected.

Still holding the gorthling in his left hand, Valorian raised his right hand and fired a bolt of energy at the pack to slow them down. He felt the magic suddenly erupt through him, and to his complete amazement, a fiery burst of brilliant blue, hotter and stronger than anything he had formed before, sizzled through the tunnel air and exploded in the crowded mob of gorthlings. They fled, screaming, into the blackness.

Valorian didn't waste time wondering how he had found such strength or trying to pry off the gorthling. He clamped his fingers around its neck and sent Hunnul into a canter before the other creatures could regroup. While the stallion moved forward at a fast pace, Valorian used his free hand to slide his gold armband down to his wrist.

The gorthling saw the gold coming and shrieked. It struggled to escape as the clansman's fingers held it in a merciless grip and forced the golden ring over its small head.

Valorian had suspected that gold had some power over the gorthlings, and he was right. As soon as the armband settled down around the creature's neck like a collar, the gorthling stilled and hung limply in the man's hand.

Valorian gave it a gentle shake. "Can you talk?" he demanded.

"Yesss," it hissed sullenly.

"Where is Amara's crown?"

The gorthling laughed a sharp, wicked sound. "So! She sent you! What a choice. You worm-spined, offal-tongued son of a cave rat!" Its ugly face twisted into a sneer. "Follow this path and you will find it."

The clansman tried another question. "Are there other tunnels into Gormoth?"

Again the gorthling laughed and spat at him. "Of course, stupid mortal. There are lots of ways to get in, but you'll never get out!"

Valorian's mouth tightened. The little brute was only telling him things he had already guessed. However, during their talk, he had noticed that his sphere was burning much brighter and his strength had returned in full measure. As an experiment, he set the gorthling on the pommel of his saddle.

"Stay there," he ordered and let go of its neck. Two interesting things happened. First, the gorthling obeyed him, and second, the light dimmed to its previous intensity. Once again Valorian picked up the creature; the sphere brightened.

"Gorthlings have no power of their own to wield magic, do they?" he stated in dawning comprehension.

"Ooooh! The bonehead catches on quick!"

Valorian ignored the gorthling's insulting words. He was too busy trying to understand the puzzles and possibilities of his captive. "Why not?" he demanded. "The Harbingers can wield magic."

The gorthling hissed at the mention of the Harbingers. "Those goodie-boys," it said with a sneer. "Oh, yes! Lord Sorh favors them. He gives them magic; he gives them nags; he lets them go anywhere. But us? His guardians of lost souls? His faithful servants? He says we have no need of magic power. All we get is this prison hole with its fire and winds!"

The clansman pursed his lips, worried. He had seen the fire in the lava river, but where was the wind? "What wind?" he wanted to know.

Abruptly the gorthling burst into laughter that sounded like the howls of a demented child to Valorian. It made the man's skin crawl. "You'll see. It's where all mortals go when they enter Gormoth. Listen and you can hear it now!"

The clansman slowed the stallion to a jog and listened to the darkness. The creature was right. The changes they had noticed earlier had become more apparent. The draft at their backs was growing into a full breeze, the vibration was increasing to a trembling that shook the walls and floor, and both Hunnul and Valorian could hear a distant steady roaring that seemed to originate from somewhere ahead. The gorthling twisted his expression into a rude smile.

Valorian's apprehension rose in a cold wave, and he asked harshly, "What is that?"

"The wind," the creature cackled.

Valorian wanted to squeeze the gorthling to pulp, but he didn't think that would help much. Instead, he asked, "All right, then tell me this—what power does my gold band have over you?"

The gorthling snarled and hissed before it finally answered, "As long as you force me to wear this nasty stuff, I must obey you."

"Why?"

"Gold is the metal of the gods," the creature replied fiercely. "Gorthlings must always bow to the sacred gold of the deities. Mortals aren't supposed to bring it into Gormoth or wield magic. That's not fair!" it said sulkily.

"Why do you increase my power when you are in contact with me?" the clansman prodded.

"I'm immortal, idiot. Immortals have that effect on mortal filth like you. Not that it will do you much good," the gorthling chuckled with malice. "There is no escape, and you can't control us all. We'll have your soul dumped in the pit before you can spit."

The clansman made no further comment. Instead, he wrapped his fingers around the gorthling's neck and stared thoughtfully ahead into the black tunnel while Hunnul

jogged down the slope, deeper and deeper into the roots of
the vast mountain. Gradually the roaring noise increased, the
wind blew harder until it pulled at Hunnul's mane and tail,
and the walls began to shake from the force of some monstrous, unknown power.

The closer they drew to the unknown source of the noise,
the more sounds they could discern in the thundering roar.
There was gorthling laughter and human sounds, too—
shrieks and cries and a wailing that never seemed to stop.
Valorian felt his soul grow cold. There were no tales in the
mortal world that accurately described the innermost secrets
of Gormoth. What happened within its dark heart was
known only to its tormented prisoners, the gorthlings, and
the gods.

Sooner than he wanted, Valorian saw the end of the tunnel. A strange, hot, wavering light gleamed through an
arched doorway not far ahead. The deep-throated roaring
was now painfully loud. The gorthling snickered.

Hunnul slowed to a hesitating walk, stepped cautiously
through the archway, and stopped dead in his tracks. They
had entered a tremendous circular cave as large as any
mountain in the mortal world. Appalled, Valorian rose in his
stirrups and looked down where the trail stopped in a sheer
drop-off into a chasm whose bottom was lost in the unfathomable depths of Ealgoden. But it wasn't the frightening
bottomless chasm, the immense size of the cavern, or the
disappearance of the trail that transfixed the man; it was
what roared in the center of that vast space.

Valorian stared in awe. He had never imagined anything
so horrendous. Down below him, in the middle of the great
cavern, hung a monstrous, thundering tornado of wind and
fire. In the lurid light of its massive form, he could see
where the molten rock of the lava river flowed out of an
opening in the rock wall below and was sucked and swirled
into the tremendous vortex, forming a maelstrom of searing
heat and flailing winds that remained fixed in place over a
pit of darkness beyond imagination.

Worst of all were the souls Valorian could see trapped in the spinning maw of the giant funnel. There were countless numbers of them, indistinguishable in the fire and violent winds, and they all cried in hopelessness and agony from their prison in a ceaseless, eternal lament that tore at Valorian's heart.

"There's the wind, bonehead. Welcome home!" sneered the gorthling. When the man did not reply, it bobbed its head and went on with glee. "Lord Sorh put that there for our prisoners. Once you're in it, we will never let you go."

The man ignored it with an effort. Gritting his teeth, he forced his eyes away from the whirlwind. Instead, he looked up toward the ceiling of the cavern, which was lit by a pale golden glow, and saw something else that made him lean forward with relief. There was the object of his quest at last.

The roof of the vast space was festooned with stalactites of every length and diameter in a startling variety of colors. In the exact center of the ceiling was the largest stalactite: a huge, long spear of stone that hung over the whirlwind like a weapon ready to drop, and there, jammed tightly onto the tip, was a circular object that glowed with a radiance all its own. The clansman didn't need to ask the gorthling if that object was Amara's crown—he knew it was. In the hellish winds and burning fires, the crown shimmered with a pure beauty that did not belong in this evil place.

Now all he had to do was think of a way to reach it. There was certainly no immediate solution. There were no trails in the cave, no ledges or handholds on the smooth, sheer walls, and no bridges. There were what looked like three other tunnel entrances exactly like the one he and Hunnul were standing by, but they were spaced out along the walls of the cavern at equal distances and may as well have been in another world. Valorian shook his head, his hopes almost dead. There was no way to go . . . and almost no more time.

Gorthlings were gathering in the tunnel behind them again, and Valorian could see other gorthlings creeping along the walls of the cavern toward his position.

The creature in his hand cackled. "Save us some effort, nag rider. Jump! We'll go easier on you."

Valorian glanced down at his prisoner, then back to the stalactite and the whirlwind. He studied the black hole far away on the opposite wall for a moment, and a vague plan began to form in his mind. "Quickly," he snapped, giving the gorthling a shake. "What are those other openings?"

"Other tunnels, dung-breath. I told you there were lots of ways to get into Gormoth. You just can't get out!" The gorthling howled in glee.

Four entrances? So there were other ways to get out—if he could reach one. Valorian's hopes rose a little as he silently worked out his plan. It would be tricky at best. He would need every shred of power the gorthling could give him, a huge share of luck, and the help of one black stallion. If he failed, he and Hunnul would fall into the whirlwind, and there would be no escape from that.

He shifted his weight in the saddle, silently signaling Hunnul with his toes. The stallion automatically backed up several steps until they were within the tunnel again. The gorthlings behind them hooted with laughter.

"You've seen your fate, mortal," one shouted. "What's the matter? Are you scared?"

Their crude, harsh laughter made Hunnul flatten his ears. Valorian disregarded their noise, thankful that the creatures were hanging back for the moment. They were probably waiting to see what the clansman with the magic powers was going to do. In the cavern, the other gorthlings were almost to the tunnel entrance.

Valorian leaned forward and said quietly, "Hunnul, you have seen the power Lady Amara gave me. I intend to use it now, but I also need your help." He scratched the stallion's mane in his favorite place until Hunnul arched his neck and his ears came up. "You'll have to trust me."

"Trust me!" the gorthling mimicked snidely. "Don't bother, dog food. This man will only dump you in the stew."

The stallion tossed his head angrily.

Valorian was thoroughly sick of his little prisoner, but he needed it for just a while longer. He shot a look back at the gorthlings behind them, then at the gnarled faces peering around the edges of the tunnel entrance. It was time to move while the creatures were still hesitating. Swiftly he clamped the gorthling between his knee and the saddle leather to free his hands. Then he pictured in his mind what he wanted to do and dug his heels into the stallion's ribs.

Hunnul obeyed without hesitation. He took four running steps forward and with a mighty heave of his powerful haunches, he leaped off the edge into space . . . and abruptly dropped. Instantly the sucking winds of the tornado caught at the horse and man and pulled them with sickening speed toward its burning funnel.

Valorian's mind went blank with terror. The magic hadn't worked even with the gorthling, and now they were plummeting uncontrollably into the whirlwind. Already he could feel the heat scorching his skin and the winds tearing at his body. Hunnul struggled frantically beneath him, but all Valorian could see was the whirlwind filling his sight with its horror.

Under his knee, the gorthling squirmed to get out. "You failed, mortal!" it cried over the thunder of the winds. "There's a thought for eternity!"

Failed! The word struck Valorian like a whiplash. He had never liked to fail, and he was about to spend forever in agony, having failed his family, himself, and his goddess. The realization jerked his head up and his eyes away from the whirlwind. "Think!" he cried to himself. He couldn't have more than a few moments left.

The magic hadn't failed, he suddenly realized. *He* had. It wasn't enough to simply imagine that his horse could jump a mighty chasm, he had to be more exact. He had to decide *how* Hunnul was going to jump that distance, then channel his magic into making that happen.

Valorian didn't waste another second. With the whirlwind

roaring in his ears and the swirling fires burning his skin, he
remembered the great wind like an unseen hand that had
carried him and Hunnul to the plain of stone. Desperately
he held that memory in his mind, concentrated on exactly
what he wanted, and formed his spell.

The spell was faltering and clumsy, but the magic,
enhanced by the gorthling's touch, surged through Valorian,
and this time it worked. Wind from the tornado itself formed
an invisible platform beneath the stallion's body. Their
descent began to slow against the relentless pull of the funnel, and just as Hunnul's hooves skimmed the uppermost
ring of fire, the horse and his rider began to rise. The stallion's legs instinctively moved into a galloping motion, his
hooves plunging through the hot air. Valorian, his jaw
clenched with his effort to force the magic power to his bidding, slowly raised his palms toward the ceiling and lifted
the horse higher and higher above the ferocious winds.

The gorthlings flew into shrieking fits of rage. Some
hurled stones from the tunnel's mouth, while others scampered upside down along the ceiling and threw broken stalactites at him, but their efforts were useless. Swifter than an
eagle, the black stallion soared through the hot air toward
the center stalactite.

Valorian braced himself in the saddle. He could feel the
gorthling squirm under his knee, and he prayed its touch
would enhance his powers enough to do one more thing.

He raised his hand. More magic gathered at his command
until it surged through every fiber of his being. They were
nearing the stalactite when he fired a blazing bolt of energy
that seared through the air to the base of the stone and
exploded in a shower of blue sparks. A crack as loud as
thunder shot over the roar of the funnel. The stalactite shattered in an explosion of fragments, and its precious burden
started to plummet toward the bottomless chasm in the heart
of the whirling winds and fires.

Hunnul stretched out his neck and his legs; his nostrils
flared, and his tail flew like a storm-whipped banner. Valorian

reached out frantically. He caught the crown of Amara with one hand just as it dropped by Hunnul's head. His breath went out in one great gasp. His relief was so strong, his concentration faltered, almost tumbling Hunnul sideways. But with the glowing golden crown held tightly to his chest, Valorian strengthened the supporting wind beneath Hunnul's feet and pressed his heels into the horse's sides.

The black steed responded with all his heart. His hooves dug into the invisible wind and went racing over the bottomless chasm toward the distant wall. The gorthlings yelled in fury and chased him along the cavern roof, but it was too late. With the wind at his heels, the stallion galloped the long distance to the far wall and reached it unscathed.

Carefully Valorian ended his spell just as Hunnul's feet touched down on solid stone at the mouth of the second opening. The horse bounded forward into the passage onto a trail sloping upward and quickly left the noise and light of the cavern behind.

The tunnel was totally black, yet Valorian didn't waste his strength on a light. Instead, he held the crown above his head and let its radiance light their way. It was no great surprise to see that this path was much like the other—lightless, twisting, and steeply sloped. There could be gorthlings watching the passage, too. That thought made Valorian queasy. He'd had enough of gorthlings and had no wish to be caught now. He and Hunnul had come too far to lose their prize.

The gorthling under his thigh finally wiggled its head free. "You'll suffer for this," it howled at him. "We'll flay you alive for a thousand years and make you wish every second of eternity that you had never heard Amara's name!"

Valorian refused to reply. He tuned his senses ahead and behind to listen for any sign of pursuit. He knew the vicious little gorthlings wouldn't let him go without a fight. For the moment, though, he could hear nothing.

Hunnul was cantering now as fast as he could go in the zigzagging tunnel on the rising slope. Because he knew roughly what to expect in the passages, he was able to move faster through the twists and turns and dark halls.

But even Hunnul's agile speed wasn't enough. All too soon Valorian heard what he feared—a screeching, yowling pack of gorthlings coming up the tunnel behind them. He bent low over Hunnul's mane, held tightly to the crown, and prayed that the stallion wouldn't fall, that there were no lava rivers with narrow ledges, and that there were no gorthlings on the trail ahead. The cries of the creatures behind him grew louder.

Hunnul continued to run, his legs thrusting forward, his hooves pounding on the stone path, his head rising and falling with the rhythm of his flight. Black against the deep shadows, he careered through the tunnel ahead of the gorthlings, trusting his master to guide him.

Then, before man or horse realized what had happened, the trail abruptly leveled out and came to a sudden dead end before a black wall of stone. Hunnul skidded to a wild-eyed stop.

"What's this?" Valorian cried frantically to his captive. "Where's the tunnel?"

The gorthling chortled. "It's the entrance, you moron, and it's locked. This tunnel is shorter than the others."

The noise of the pursuers was almost upon them when the clansman raised his hand. He didn't have time to question the gorthling any further or stop to look for some means to open the door. He and Hunnul had to get out now! His power, strengthened by the gorthling's contact, burst from his hand and exploded on the wall before him. The rock exploded outward, opening the entrance in a cascade of blue sparks and flying rock.

Hunnul stumbled out through the shattered door into the bright light. Blinded by the sudden glare, Valorian fumbled for the creature he held under his knee. He could hear the other gorthlings running up the passage and shrieking, and he knew he couldn't let them loose in the realm of the dead. Desperately he yanked the gold armband off the gorthling's neck, turned, and hurled the creature as hard as he could toward the opening. Almost in the same movement, he fired a second bolt of magic into the rock above the door just as the gorthling pack appeared at the entrance. The burst was weaker than before, but it was enough to bring down a massive chunk of rock that sealed the opening shut with stone, gravel, and dirt. The enraged gorthlings vanished behind the tumbling rock.

Bit by bit the stone settled into place, and the mountain returned to silence. Valorian's eyesight adjusted enough to see the ground, so he dismounted and leaned for a moment against Hunnul's heaving sides. The stallion blew out his breath with a loud snort.

Valorian tried to laugh in a wave of overwhelming relief, but he could barely chuckle. Without the gorthling to sustain his strength, the heavy, unaccustomed use of magic had left him completely exhausted. Too tired to even stand, he sagged slowly to the ground and sat by the stallion's front feet. The golden crown hung heavy in his hands.

He stared at the crown as if seeing it for the first time. In the pure light of the sacred peak, the diadem's own radiance was as clear and golden as the dawn and as warm as the summer sun. It had four pointed rays on its front, each set with a large gem of a different shade to represent the four seasons, and its heavy rim was ornately decorated with intertwined rays of silver and vines of gold. It was a crown worthy of Amara.

Valorian was leaning forward, staring at the crown, when another glorious light illuminated the mountainside. He looked up to see four shining figures standing before him: the Clan deities Surgart, Sorh, Krath, and Amara. He knew in his heart who they were without a word being spoken, and he fell prostrate in awe.

The four deities gazed down on him, their faces benign. "You have chosen well, Sister," he heard Sorh say to Amara.

"Do we go ahead with our plan?" she asked.

Valorian jerked slightly in surprise. Plan? What were they

talking about?

Surgart nodded. "Yes . . . it is time."

"Very well." The mother goddess leaned over and picked up her shining crown. "Thank you, Valorian, for your courage. Your deed has won my eternal gratitude. I wish to reward you for your unselfishness and determination. Is there any boon you desire?"

The clansman slowly climbed to his feet. "I would wish something for my people." He lifted his eyes to the goddess. "Help them find a new home somewhere where they can flourish."

A deep smile of satisfaction spread over Amara's lovely face. She nodded once.

A deafening, shattering clap of thunder split Valorian's world. The realm of the dead, the gods and goddesses, the peak of Ealgoden all vanished, and the man tumbled down into darkness. He cried out once and knew no more.

5

omewhere nearby a bird was warbling a song. Its lilting notes lifted on the wings of the wind and mingled with the subtler rhythms of falling water in a distant stream and the sway of evergreen trees. The gentle sounds were familiar and comforting to the clansman as he lay motionless, still swathed in the darkness of his mind. He listened to the natural music for a long time while his consciousness gradually awakened and his other senses returned.

After a while, he became aware of other feelings he hadn't noticed before: the cold of the stone beneath his stomach, the heavy, damp weight of his clothes, the unexpected warmth of sunshine on the side of his face. Very carefully he opened his eyes. Dark storm clouds filled the sky to the south, the direction he was facing, but to the west, the sky was clearing and the blessed sun was shining. The days of rain were finally over. And, praise the gods, there was Hunnul grazing on a patch of grass nearby.

Valorian managed a weak smile before he tried to sit up. Then his smile turned to a groan and he sagged back onto the wet ground, almost blinded by a severe pain that rocked his head. Nausea settled like a cold, squirming thing in his stomach. The rest of his body felt stiff, as weak as a newborn, and achy in every joint. Strangest of all, he felt very warm inside. Not feverish, just hot.

What's happened to me? he wondered. He lay still again to let the pain subside while he tried to revive his memory. He remembered searching for the mountain pass, and he remembered coming up the ridge to see the range of peaks. Everything after that was extremely hazy. There had been rain and thunder, and then something had happened. He clenched his fists in an effort to remember, but he couldn't recall what had occurred or why he should be lying there feeling as if he had just fallen down the mountainside.

The oddest visions passed through his head . . . Harbingers and goddesses . . . the realm of the dead . . . Ealgoden . . . gorthlings . . . and clearest of all, a golden crown that gleamed with the light of the sun. Yet the images were unfocused and jumbled together. None of them made sense. If he had truly died, then what was he doing still lying on the top of the ridge? The visions had to be a dream, and a bad one at that.

The ache in his head had eased somewhat, so Valorian tried to sit up once more. This time he managed to make it to an upright position. He propped his head in his hands. It was then that he realized his helmet and his cloak were missing.

That's odd, he thought, staring around slowly. His sword and his armband were still in place, his other possessions seemed to be intact, and Hunnul was still saddled, so it wasn't the work of thieves. How could he have lost the helmet and cloak while lying on the ground?

The puzzle was too much for him at the moment. His head was still pounding as if thunder was rumbling through his skull, his right arm was numb, and he suddenly realized he was unbearably thirsty. Remembering his water bag tied to Hunnul's saddle, he whistled to call the stallion. Hunnul perked his ears and moved to obey, but Valorian was horrified to see the big black horse was limping off his right foreleg.

All thoughts of his own pain vanished. The clansman climbed stiffly to his feet and staggered to meet the horse. As soon as he reached Hunnul's side, the cause of the stallion's discomfort was immediately apparent. A long, jagged wound ran down the length of Hunnul's right shoulder.

Valorian exclaimed in amazement while he carefully probed the shoulder. The wound wasn't bleeding; in fact, it looked much like a brand burned into the black hide. Whatever had caused the injury had cauterized the broken blood vessels, sealing the edges of the torn skin. Stitching the wound was impossible; it looked as if Hunnul would be scarred for life. What in the name of Surgart had happened to them? How could Hunnul have been burned like that while his rider had only bumps, bruises, and a headache?

Valorian rubbed the stallion's neck for a moment before he dug out the pot of healing salve Kierla always packed for him and rubbed some liberally over Hunnul's burn. Only then did he untie the waterskin and drain it to the last drop.

The water helped clear his head enough for some common sense to take over. He saw that the day was quickly waning and knew he and Hunnul needed more water, rest, and shelter for the night. After a last look around for his missing cloak and helmet, Valorian slowly and with great care led his horse off the ridge to find shelter. They made it as far as a small stream rippling down a nearby valley when Valorian's muscles started shaking from the exertion and his headache returned with a vengeance. He had just enough strength left to uncinch the saddle from Hunnul's back and take a long drink of water before he dropped into the grass and bracken and fell sound asleep.

* * * * *

It was early afternoon of the next day when Valorian awoke. He came out of his sleep suddenly and bolted to his feet in alarm, his hand fumbling for his sword. The visions of his dream played in his mind for a moment longer, then dimmed to a half-remembered, faded feeling of danger. He shook his head, as if to shake the visions back into view. For just a moment, everything had seemed so clear. He had been riding Hunnul in a tunnel of darkness guided by a ball of light that he himself had created. To his great frustration, he couldn't remember anything else, only an intense feeling of danger.

Valorian sighed and straightened to his full height. Such an odd, disturbing dream. At least the sleep had done some good. His head pain had dwindled to a dull ache, and his body wasn't as stiff—despite sleeping on the cold, wet ground without his cloak. In fact, Valorian still felt warm even in the cool breeze blowing off the mountains. He was also still very thirsty.

He walked to the creek, and after a deep, satisfying drink, he sat back on his heels and looked at his reflection ruefully. He looked terrible. A large bruise, probably from his fall off Hunnul, discolored his temple. His dark, curly hair, which he usually kept tied behind his head, was matted and dirty, and his normally clean-shaven face was hidden under an ugly black stubble.

Valorian was not a fastidious man, but he liked to be reasonably clean, and he hated his beard. It always itched and drew bugs and was too uneven to be worth the trouble of letting it grow. He scratched the stubble absently. It would be so pleasant to have Kierla bring warm water and her knife to shave him.

Kierla! Valorian rushed to his feet. By the gods, how long had he been gone? He had told her he would only hunt for two or three days, yet he had been out perhaps seven or eight days. And he still had to get back. Kierla would be frantic. He had to go home!

He whistled for Hunnul, hoping the stallion wasn't far away. The black horse came trotting over the hill where he had been grazing and nickered to his master. Valorian was relieved to see that the rest and the salve had helped the stallion. Hunnul was moving easier, with only a slight limp in his right leg.

A short time later, the stallion was saddled and they were heading north back toward the Bloodiron Hills, where the clanspeople made their home.

* * * * *

Although they tried to travel fast, Valorian quickly realized that neither he nor Hunnul had the endurance to stand their usual pace. Both of them were weak from their injuries and the lack of food, and too sore to move any faster than a colt's pace through the high, rough foothills. They traveled as best they could, stopping often to rest. Valorian walked much of the time to ease Hunnul's shoulder wound. Fortunately the exercise helped strengthen Valorian's weakened muscles and brought some feeling back to his numb arm. After a while, only the odd warmth within his body and the intense thirst remained.

And the visions. No matter how hard he tried, he couldn't shake the tenacious images of his dream. The vivid memory of those strange visions stuck with him day and night, haunting his sleep with terrors of gorthlings and coloring his days with the light of a goddess's smile. He thought about the dream for hours as he and Hunnul walked home, but the pictures remained mixed up in his consciousness like the pieces of a broken mosaic. He could discern no logic to the patterns or any real truth.

There were all the ingredients of an exciting tale to tell the Clan around the fire at night, Valorian thought with a chuckle. If only he could organize the dream into a coherent tale, everyone would love it.

He shook his head and walked faster. His family had probably given him up for dead by now—except Kierla. She would never accept his death, and he didn't want to cause her any more anguish.

To his relief, the weather remained dry and warm during the journey home. Valorian and Hunnul had no difficulty finding water and shelter; only food was scarce. They saw a few other people far in the distance, some Chadarian shepherds and a small merchant caravan on the road for Sarcithia. But despite his hunger, Valorian instinctively avoided contact with strangers. Very few would bother to help a clansman, and many more would likely steal his horse.

Shortly after noon on the sixth day after his accident, Valorian saw the reddish bluffs that marked the valley where his family made its winter camp. Relief, pleasure, and anticipation welled up within him, bolstering the last of his strength. He mounted Hunnul and urged the stallion forward in a trot along a hillside toward the bluffs.

They had nearly reached the first bluff when a shout caught Valorian's attention. On a rise to the west, where an ancient trail led out of the foothills to the flatland below, a rider on a bay horse was whooping to draw Valorian's notice. The rider waved frantically and spurred his horse into a gallop down the broad slope.

A grin spread over Valorian's weary face, for the rider was his younger brother Aiden, Adala's twin.

"Valorian!" The shout echoed off the bluffs with all its joy and relief.

The clansman rolled his eyes skyward as the young rider thoughtlessly jerked his horse's bit to bring the animal to a stop in front of Hunnul. Aiden didn't have rapport with animals, not even horses. His strength, Valorian knew, lay in his enthusiasm, his charm, and his ability to immediately discern people's characters. He was smaller than Valorian, with a thick mane of dark brown hair, gray-blue eyes, and an unquenchable smile.

Valorian dismounted to meet his brother and was nearly knocked off his feet by Aiden's fierce hug.

"By all the gods, Brother!" Aiden cried joyfully. "We thought you were in the realm of the dead!"

A strange spasm passed over Valorian's face and was gone, but not before Aiden's quick eyes noticed it. He held his older brother at arm's length, studying the man's pale skin, the huge bruise, and his filthy, travel-stained clothes. "You look horrible. What happened to you, Valorian?" Aiden asked, the worry strong in his voice. "We searched the hills for days. Some of the men are still out looking for you. Where were you?"

Valorian smiled ruefully. He pulled his brother close again, as if to draw on Aiden's vibrant energy. It felt good to hug another human being at that moment. "I . . . I don't know where I've been." He gripped Aiden's arm to silence the flood of questions. "I'll tell you everything I can when we reach camp so I won't have to repeat myself."

Aiden jerked his head in agreement. "At least you're back." His voice suddenly choked in his throat, and he turned away to mount his horse.

Together the men rode side by side along the grassy hills toward the wide mouth of the valley.

"Is Kierla all right?" Valorian asked after a moment of silence.

"As well as can be expected. She's hardly eaten or slept for eight days," Aiden replied. "That's some woman you have, Valorian. She wouldn't let any of us give up on you. She sent all of us out in search parties and went out herself for several days. No one could even breathe the possibility of your death in her presence."

Valorian felt his heart begin a slow pound. He could hardly wait to see his wife. He wanted to feel her warmth, to see her eyes sparkling at him, and to rely on her wisdom when he told her of his journey. Perhaps she could help him understand the accident that had befallen him and the strange dream that had taken root in his memory. He straightened a little more in his saddle, and Hunnul, feeling his master's cue, walked faster.

They rode down to the shallow stream that flowed out between the bluffs and turned onto a narrow, barely visible path that followed the creek into the valley.

As Aiden rode in front to lead the way, Valorian became aware for the first time that his brother was wearing the split-leg robes, soft leather shoes, and vest of a Chadarian. He also had two baby goats tied in burlap bags behind his saddle, their heads peeking out of the rough fabric.

"Aiden, what have you been doing?" Valorian demanded. "Stealing again?"

Trying to look insulted, Aiden turned in the saddle. "I have not! Not this time. I went as a legitimate trader to sell some of Linna's rugs and hear the latest news."

"In Chadarian clothes?"

Aiden snorted irritably. "You know those Chadarian merchants won't give a clansman a fair deal."

Valorian stifled a grunt of annoyance. It did no good to talk to Aiden about his actions, because he never listened. He was stubborn, willful, and too intelligent for his own good.

One of his greatest pleasures was going to the Chadarian capital, Actigorium, in disguise to gather news and to barter, trade, or steal anything he could get from the Chadarians or the Tarns. It was dangerous work, for if the Tarnish soldiers ever caught him in any suspicious activity, they would whip him to death and hang his body on the main wall of the city. The problem was that Aiden was very good at his work. He spoke fluent Chadarian, could dissemble with the best, and was skilled at disguises. He was also very successful. He had saved the family several times from surprise visits from Tyrannis's tax collectors and had brought back many items from the city market that the clanspeople couldn't make themselves.

Valorian couldn't understand Aiden's attraction to the city. He himself hated the crowds of people, the narrow streets, and the constant noise, yet he couldn't help but respect his brother's daring.

"What are the goats for?" Valorian asked, deciding to change the subject.

"Linna wants them. They're supposed to have very soft, long wool when they grow up. She wants to try the wool in her weaving."

Even through the disgust in his voice at having to haul goats, Valorian could hear the pride in Aiden's voice. Linna, his betrothed, was the finest weaver in the Clan.

Aiden half-turned in his saddle and said, "I also heard that Sergius may pay us a visit in a few days. It seems we're behind on our tribute to General Tyrranis."

Valorian stifled a groan. The last thing he wanted to do now was argue with Sergius Valentius over taxes the family couldn't pay.

They rode on quietly for a while, deeper and deeper into the hills. Gradually the valley narrowed as the surrounding hills rose high above them. Relieved to be almost home, Valorian savored the familiar landscape as never before. Usually he merely tolerated the rocky confines of the valley. It was cold and damp in the winter, it had too many trees and not enough meadows for the horses, the ground was mostly stone, and the high hills made him uncomfortable. On the other hand, it afforded an excellent shelter from the winter winds, and so far it had protected them well from the Tarns.

It wouldn't be long, though, before the family moved on. After the last of the spring crop of stock animals was born, the family would celebrate the Birthright, the festival of thanksgiving to Amara, then they would pack their tents, gather the herds, and move higher into the mountains to the summer pastures.

Their move could be sooner than he imagined, Valorian surmised, for spring had advanced far into the hills while he was gone. The snow had vanished from the valley during the long days of rain, and the warm sun had brought out a thick carpet of green grasses, herbs, and vines. Wildflowers in delicate colors of white, blue, and pink popped out in every sunny patch of earth.

Not far ahead, Valorian could see where the creek took a sharp turn to the right around a rocky promontory. Behind it, the valley widened into an oval-shaped meadow that was fairly flat and grassy. There, Valorian knew, were the tents of the extended family group that called him their nominal leader.

He was so pleased by the prospect of being almost home, he missed Aiden's look of suspicion at the promontory as they passed.

"Ranulf is supposed to be on guard duty," Aiden snapped,

startling Valorian out of his reverie. "If he's asleep again, I'll slit his gut."

Valorian shot a look at the place on the high point where a guard usually stayed, but there was no sign of one. He frowned. Every Clan camp stationed guards to protect itself from unwelcome visitors or surprise attacks. One unwary guard could mean disaster.

The two riders hurried on along the trail past the promontory and through a copse of tall pines. The path rose up a low slope, then dipped down again to the valley floor and the wide, grassy meadow. Valorian and Aiden went as far as the top of the slope before they stopped and looked down on the camp.

At first glance, the valley looked normal. A few horses grazed peacefully at the far eastern end where the grass was the thickest. Some goats and sheep were being herded by several small boys to the stream that tumbled beside the sheer slopes of the northern wall. The camp itself lay quietly in the sunshine, just below the riders' positions.

Valorian's hand edged to his sword and silently drew it. Something was wrong. He could sense it. The camp was too quiet. There was no sign of anyone among the tents or by the central fire, and the surrounding area was strangely empty.

"Where is everyone?" he murmured.

Aiden didn't hear him. "What did that?" he asked incredulously and pointed to Valorian's sword.

The clansman glanced at his blade, then stared at it in amazement. He had had no reason to draw it on the journey home and hadn't looked at it since that rainy afternoon on the ridge. Something incredible had happened to it. The blade had been burned black by some powerful heat that not only scorched the blade down to the hilt, but also melted the edges in ripples at the point. Instead of a straight, hammered blade, the sword looked much like a long flame. In disgust, Valorian slammed the weapon back in its sheath. The sword had been his father's and grandfather's before him. Now it was probably useless, and short of stealing a Tarnish blade, he had no means of getting another.

"I don't know what did that," he snapped. "Now, where is everyone?"

Aiden gazed at the man for a long moment. He loved his brother too much to doubt him, but this mystery of Valorian's reappearance was beginning to bother him. He gestured toward the camp. "Most of the men and boys are either out hunting or looking for you, and Mother Willa said something about taking the women out to gather herbs and greens. I don't know about everyone else."

The sharp tone in Aiden's voice brought Valorian's irritation up short. He didn't need to take his frustrations out on his brother. He was about to apologize when he heard a sound that turned his blood cold.

Voices had suddenly raised in anger from the corrals where the camp's best horses and breeding stock were kept. The pens were near the stream and out of his sight behind some trees, yet he still recognized the shouting voices. One was Kierla, yelling at another voice that belonged to Sergius Valentius, General Tyrranis's tax collector.

"Oh, gods," groaned Aiden. "He came early! That weasel came two days early!"

All at once, Kierla's shout changed to a cry of fury and fear, and Valorian's heart fell to his knees. He reacted instantly by clamping his legs to Hunnul's sides and grabbing the black mane. The stallion rocketed forward from a standstill to a full gallop down the trail through the trees, with Aiden right behind.

Like a thunderbolt, the black charged through the edge of camp, past the refuse pile, and out of the trees into the wide clearing where the corrals stood. At his master's command, he came sliding to a stop almost on his haunches and neighed in excitement. His sudden appearance brought everyone in the corrals to a shocked standstill.

Valorian's face tightened with rage when he took in the scene in the nearest large corral. One Tarnish soldier was leading four pregnant mares out through the gate with the obvious intention of taking them, and two more soldiers held a small group of clanspeople at bay with swords. The mares were the family's last brood mares of pure Harachan blood, the ancient strain of Clan-bred horse, and the finest of Valorian's breeding stock.

Kierla had apparently tried to stop the Tarns with little success. She lay struggling on her back in the dust of the corral where Sergius had knocked her. The Tarnish tax collector was tying her wrists together.

He looked up when Hunnul burst into the clearing, and an arrogant smirk crossed his swarthy, pinched features. "You're late with your tribute, Valorian," he shouted. "I've had to come collect it myself, and that will cost you."

Kierla started violently, nearly pulling her wrists free. Her fact twisted toward her husband with a crazy combination of hope, joy, anger, and outrage as she fought to escape the Tarn's grip.

Sergius merely chuckled with appreciation before he hauled her to her feet and shoved her toward his saddled horse.

Deep within Valorian's mind, an unconscious power flickered to existence. It surged hotter in his anger, coursing through his veins and energizing his tired body. Fiercer and stronger it grew until his skin tingled with its energy. But Valorian didn't recognize the magic. He saw only his beloved wife being pushed toward the Tarn's horse. There had been other women forcibly taken from the Clan to satisfy Tyranis's lust, and they had never returned. He kicked Hunnul forward.

Sergius saw the movement and drew his knife on Kierla. "One more move, clansman, and this woman will feed the buzzards." He curled his lip at the expression on Valorian's face, then deliberately shoved Kierla up against his horse and ripped the bodice of her dress.

Valorian gave no thought to what he did next; he simply reacted. A fragment of his dream suddenly came into sharp clarity, revealing in his mind the picture of a deadly blue bolt of energy. He raised his hand and threw it forward.

Out of his body, formed by the goddess's gift, came a sizzling blast of magic that seared through the afternoon air, struck Sergius full on the chest, and slammed him to the ground. Kierla was knocked off her feet, and the Tarn's horse reared in terror, snapped its rein, and galloped away.

For a long, silent breath, the tableau froze in time. No one moved, no one spoke. They could only gape at Valorian. The clansman was staring at his hand. In one stunning instant the remaining pieces of his dream fell into place, and he knew with utter certainty that what had happened in his memory was true. He had been struck by lightning and died; he had rescued the crown of Amara from the gorthlings, and she in gratitude had returned him to life with his power to wield magic intact. The enormity of his ability suddenly struck him like a blow, and he lifted his eyes to Sergius's smoking body, appalled by what he had done.

The small movement shattered the shocked silence. The three Tarnish soldiers bolted as one for their horses, but Aiden moved faster. He yanked out his bow and shouted, "Stop them!"

The soldier nearest Valorian staggered and fell with two of Aiden's arrows in his back. The second was killed with a dagger thrown by one of the elderly men in the group. The third nearly made it to his horse before he was brought down by a well-aimed rock from a sling.

Valorian didn't move during the killing. He was too overwhelmed by his own thoughts. It wasn't until Kierla walked over to stand in front of Hunnul that he forced himself to look down at her.

Her green eyes were snapping with suspicion, and her expression was cold. Kierla wasn't a beauty at any time in her life, least of all when she was angry. Her look of outrage set over her straight nose, large teeth, and longish face gave her a faint resemblance to a horse ready to snap. The freckles on her fair skin were lost in a red flush, and her dark eyebrows glowered over her eyes. The long, dark hair that hung in a single plait over her shoulder was tangled and dusty. She paid no attention to her torn bodice, letting the shreds hang open.

Valorian thought he had never seen her look so lovely.

"Who are you?" she hissed fiercely. "You look like Valorian, but he cannot do what you have done. Who are you?"

The clansman dismounted like a weary old man and stood by Hunnul's head. The other clanspeople—his two aunts, some cousins, Kierla's uncle, and several children—gathered around him. Their faces were wary and fearful. The look of relief and welcome had even faded from Aiden's expression.

Valorian could hardly blame them. He had appeared out of nowhere with a power only the gods had heretofore wielded.

"Perhaps it's a gorthling," he heard a young cousin say softly.

"Too big," Kierla's uncle stated. "Could be a ghost."

"Maybe he's a Harbinger," an aunt murmured. The people sucked in their breath at that possibility and took a step backward.

Only Kierla didn't back away. She faced the man before her, scrutinizing every detail of his face. She looked past the dirt and the bruise on his temple and the scruffy beard to the unchanging characteristics of the man's face. If this wasn't Valorian, it was an exact copy of him down to the cleft in his chin, the straight line of his nose, and the scar on his forehead. The eyes were the same brilliant blue, too, but there was a cast about them that was subtly different. They were harder, more piercing, as if forged in fire and set with the farseeing vision of an eagle. Her anger began to fade to confusion. She moved closer, and, trembling, she reached out to touch his cheek.

"I *am* Valorian," he said directly to her, and she knew then it was true. Whatever doubt or fear she had, she cast it aside and fell into Valorian's arms.

Later that night the entire family, fifty-two people in all, gathered around the central fire after the evening meal to hear Valorian's tale. He told them everything, from the moment he decided to give the Tarnish soldiers his meat to his return to the Clan. The clanspeople listened, spellbound, to his every word.

When he finished his story, he formed a sphere of light over the camp and watched his people stare at it in rapt silence. He wondered what they were thinking. Were they terrified of his new power? Awestruck? Disbelieving? He felt all of that and more. One question kept repeating itself in his thoughts—why him? What purpose did Amara have in sending him back to life with the ability to wield magic? Was it simply gratitude or something more? He snuffed out his light.

"What do we do now?" someone said in the darkness.

The question voiced Valorian's own doubts. He really didn't know what to do now. The family was in serious trouble because of the killing of four Tarns. If Tyrranis found out, he would slaughter every man, woman, and child without mercy. They would have to move quickly. He rubbed his hand, which was still numb from the lightning strike, and tried to think. Whatever reason the goddess had for returning him to life would probably be revealed in time. Meanwhile, he still had the elusive mountain pass and his determination to find it. Amara had said nothing about his request for a new life for the Clan, so he proposed to seek it himself.

"It would be wise to leave here immediately," he said as if to himself, "so we will go to Stonehelm. I must talk to Lord Fearral." He lapsed into silence, his gaze lost in the dying embers of the fire.

Sensing his brother's exhaustion, Aiden rose to his feet. "Ranulf, since you were the one who fell asleep and let the Tarns slip by, you can come with me to dispose of their bodies." Shamefaced, the young man nodded as Aiden went on. "The boys can bring in the rest of the herds. Jendar, you and two others tear down the corrals. If we all move fast, we can have this camp obliterated by tomorrow afternoon."

Nods and murmurs of assent moved around the campfire.

With a great effort, Valorian pulled himself to his feet and put his hand on Aiden's shoulder in thanks. He felt Kierla's strong arm take his. To a sincere chorus of good-nights and blessings from his family, Valorian followed his wife to their tent.

He would have thought he was too exhausted for passion in the warmth of their blankets, but Kierla's closeness brought a new strength surging from his innermost being. They made love with a desire and yearning that surprised them both and left them gasping and giggling in the tangle of covers.

Later, in the dark of the night, Kierla put her hand on her lower abdomen. It had happened at last. She did not need the midwifery of Mother Willa to tell her—she knew. As surely as she had recognized her husband, she now recognized the son who had been conceived in the dizzying heights of their love. Her heart sang. Praise to Amara, she wanted to cry. The goddess had given her husband a gift; now she had given one to her. The greatest of all blessings.

Kierla felt hot tears trickle down her cheeks. Whatever purpose the gods had for returning Valorian, it had to be for the good. Only that would explain why, after fifteen years of emptiness, she had conceived a child on the night of his return.

Kierla smiled in wonder before she snuggled closer to her sleeping husband.

"Thank you," she whispered into the night.

6

or the second time in his life, Valorian slept past noon the following day. He woke slowly, luxuriously, on his pallet of furs to find his wife had left a bowl of meat and some hard bread by his blankets. He ate ravenously, washing down the food with long swallows of ale until the bowl was scraped clean.

When he rose to dress, he discovered his clothes had been cleaned and mended and left for him by the sleeping curtain. Outside, he could hear the noisy activity of the clanspeople breaking camp. He dressed quickly, for there was one more thing he wanted to do before he went to work. He wanted a shave.

Valorian stretched his right hand and fingers, wondering if he could handle a shaving knife. He felt better than he had in days, but his hand was still rather numb and difficult to use. He wondered if he would ever regain the feeling in his hand or shake the strange heat that warmed his body. Now that he could remember the lightning strike, he knew where the strange injuries to him and the burn on Hunnul's shoulder had come from. He was sure it was only because of Amara that the damage wasn't any worse. He also realized how his sword had been ruined.

Out of curiosity, he found his sword hanging in its customary place on the center tent pole. He drew it from the sheath and studied it carefully. On closer examination, he noticed that the point wasn't completely melted. It was simply rippled, and the metal itself seemed to be stronger and more pliable. With some careful polishing and sharpening, he thought perhaps he could save the weapon. It would look strange, but anything would be better than a Tarnish blade.

Valorian was about to return the weapon to its sheath when Kierla came in with a bowl of warm water. She smiled in delight. "Good day, my husband."

He stared hard at her, for she seemed different somehow. Her step was lighter and her eyes glowed with a new light of bliss and triumph that he had never seen before.

She saw him staring at her and surprised him by blushing. She had wanted to wait to tell him until there was proof of her pregnancy, but she couldn't contain her joy before him. With a quick step, Kierla stood before her husband.

"I cannot prove to you yet that what I say is true," she said breathlessly, her wide-mouthed smile radiant, "but after last night, I am carrying your son."

Valorian was dumbfounded. After so many years of disappointment, he had never imagined she would tell him this. "How—how can you know so soon?" he asked.

"Amara told my heart."

Amara. Valorian felt happiness and gratitude well up inside him until he grabbed his wife by the waist and whirled her around the small tent. Of course, Amara. The goddess had wrought this miracle in thanks. If he had received nothing else, this gift of a child alone was worth the journey into Ealgoden.

Valorian set Kierla down, hugging her in his powerful embrace.

With a laugh, she pushed him away. "Your beard scratches. It has to go!"

She picked up the warm water, took out her knife, steered Valorian to their small stool, and proceeded to shave off the dark growth of beard. When she finished, he rubbed his jaw in appreciation and kissed her firmly.

Kierla pulled him off the stool. "That was my time alone with you. The rest of the camp needs you now." She hesitated a moment, her eyes downcast. "Valorian, I have told you my secret because I knew you would believe me, but I would rather wait to tell the rest of the family when Mother Willa confirms it."

He understood and agreed. The Clan was going to find the news hard to believe, even with proof. At least this would silence the skeptics who advised him to turn her out. He chuckled. It was too bad he couldn't tell his father.

Still grinning to himself, Valorian left Kierla to pack their belongings and went outside to help tear down the camp. Two of his dogs sprang up to greet him at the tent entrance. He rumpled their ears as he looked around at the noisy activity. A great deal had been accomplished while he slept. Most of the tents were already struck and loaded on the two-wheeled, horse-drawn carts. The goat pens, the larger corrals, and the baking ovens had been dismantled and the bare patches of earth covered with loose dirt, leaves, and pine needles. Several of the older boys stood guard in the meadow over the small herd of horses and another herd of sheep and goats. Valorian could see his grandmother, Mother Willa, stirring the coals of the big central fire while her youngest grandson dumped dirt on the dying embers. Adults hurried through the disappearing camp, trying to get organized, and children and dogs ran everywhere.

The clansman heard a nicker close by and turned to see Hunnul beside the tent. The stallion's shaggy winter coat had been curried to a shine by someone who had also combed his mane and tail and treated his burn. He had been fed, too, for a few telltale wisps of hay hung unheeded from his mouth.

Valorian scratched the stallion's neck lovingly. He decided not to ride Hunnul today—the horse deserved a rest. Instead, the black could guard the brood mares while the family moved camp.

Hoofbeats caught Valorian's attention, and he watched Aiden and Ranulf come riding into camp, looking dirty, sweaty, and tired. Both riders spotted him and rode to greet him.

"It's done," Aiden announced, sliding off his mount. "If the Tarns ever find the bodies, they'll think the fools got caught in a rockslide." He slapped some dust off his leggings. "We got rid of the horses, too. We had to bury one with the soldiers for authenticity, but we turned the others loose high in the mountains."

"What about Sergius?" Valorian asked quietly.

His brother grimaced. "We had to bury him somewhere else. There was no disguising the burn on his chest."

Valorian barely nodded, his face set and unreadable.

"Unfortunately," Aiden went on, "we couldn't find his horse. I'm afraid it bolted for home."

"Then we'll have to take our chances that the Tarns will assume Sergius fell off and got lost."

"The sooner we put some distance between this place and ourselves the better." Aiden tipped his head in a thoughtful manner and asked, "But why Fearral's camp? That old dotard won't help us with anything."

Valorian's jaw tightened. This was a running argument he had had with Aiden for years. "He is our lord chieftain. Give him the respect his title deserves."

"When he earns it," muttered Aiden.

Valorian ignored that and added, "I don't want to ask for help. I need to talk to him."

"About the pass?"

"Yes."

The younger man threw up his hands in disgust. "Why waste your time? He'll never listen. That old man would rather die and take the Clan with him than ever risk leaving Chadar. His feet have turned to stone! Why, he hasn't even bothered to move camp in three years. He just drinks his wine, hides in his tent, and grovels twice a year to General Tyrranis."

While Valorian listened to his brother's impassioned words, his attention had fallen on Ranulf, who was standing silently and bashfully behind Aiden. Ranulf was Kierla's cousin, a shy, withdrawn young man who preferred solitude to the busy camp. Valorian knew he had been horrified by his negligence on guard duty and would do anything to help erase his shame.

"I know Lord Fearral's weaknesses," Valorian said sharply to Aiden. "But I'm going to try to convince him anyway." He turned to Ranulf. "Of course, I could use some help." The young man started in surprise. "I know the pass is somewhere south of here. Someone should go look for it so we can tell Lord Fearral exactly where it is."

Ranulf leaped on the dangled opportunity. "Please let me go, Valorian. My horse and I can find it and be back before you reach Stonehelm."

"I doubt that," Valorian said, pleased nevertheless by Ranulf's willingness. "The journey will be long and difficult, but if you are willing to try, I would be deeply grateful."

Ranulf whooped with relief and sprang on his horse to go gather his gear before everything was packed.

Aiden watched him go. "Even if Ranulf finds that pass, it won't change Fearral's mind. Then what?"

Valorian clapped his brother on the back. "One step at a time, Aiden. That's how you climb mountains." With that, he strode off.

Sometime later, when the afternoon sun was slanting through the trees, the clanspeople gathered for the last time in the meadow. The priest and priestess for the Clan deities recited the prayers for the breaking of camp and blessed the entire caravan. As soon as they were through, Valorian rode to the front of his family, where he turned to face them. He held up his hand for silence.

"All of you heard my tale last night," he began, "and some of you may even believe it. You have also seen the power Amara granted to me and the deadly effect of its force. It is a power that could do great good for the Clan or great damage. Until I know why the Mother of All has given me this gift, I ask all of you to swear to silence. When the time comes that my duty to Amara is understood, I will reveal the power as it was intended." He looked around at their faces and was satisfied. He knew he didn't need to say anything about the killing of the four Tarns. For the sake of their own lives, no one would breathe a word anywhere about that.

"In the meantime," he continued, "we have a chance to escape this land of oppressors and find a realm of our own. To do that, I must convince Lord Fearral to accept my plan to leave Chadar once and for all. He wouldn't be very cooperative if he thought I had had dealings with gorthlings."

The clanspeople chuckled at that remark, for Lord Fearral was notorious for his superstitious nature. Although the family members themselves were leery of Valorian's new power, they couldn't help but be proud that one of their own seemed to be in the light of Amara's grace. Those who understood the implications of Valorian's belief in a new life for the Clan also understood the nearly impossible task he faced of persuading Lord Fearral to agree. Most of Valorian's group accepted his desire to leave Chadar and were willing to follow him wherever he chose to go, but the rest of the Clan didn't know of his plan, and they would be hard to budge without Fearral's approval.

With loud voices, Valorian's family swore on the light of the sun and the honor of the Clan that they would not speak of Valorian's experiences until he was ready. Their leader nodded his head in thanks.

Drawing his sword, Valorian galloped his horse to the head of the caravan and gave a shout to start the wagons on their way. The people echoed his cry; dogs barked, horses neighed, and children yelled until the valley meadow rang with noise. Flanked by armed riders, the wagons followed a narrow trail upstream several leagues to a place where the valley broadened and a wide, treeless hill offered an easy way out. More guards, other riders, and the herds of stock brought up the rear.

By evening, the camp in the meadow had vanished. Only a close observer would have noticed the faint rope marks on trees, the disguised bare patches where the tents had stood, or the tracks leading out of the valley.

* * * * *

For nine days, the caravan traveled north through the Bloodiron Hills at a leisurely pace. Now that they were safely away from their old camp and a possible search by the Tarns for the four missing men, they took their time moving their herds and wagons along trails only the clanspeople knew.

Spring went with them in all her warmth and delicate colors. The days were dry and pleasant and breezy, making the journey a joy. Only the nights were still cold enough for cloaks, furs, and fires.

Kierla had repaired an old cloak to replace Valorian's lost one, but he rarely used it. It seemed to him that when he was struck by the lightning, some of its intense heat had remained in his body. Even when the winds blew cold from the snow-capped mountains, he was still comfortable in merely a tunic. He hated to think how he would feel in the heat of summer if this strange condition didn't wear off.

Late in the afternoon of the ninth day, Valorian's caravan spotted Stonehelm, the huge, rounded dome of white granite that sat like an upside-down bowl in the midst of the meadows, hills, and scattered woods. They, in turn, were seen by one of Lord Fearral's sentries. A long note from the guard's horn signaled the camp on the outcropping, and by the time the caravan reached the edge of the fields surrounding the stone hill, people were coming down to welcome them.

Because of its position on top of the natural fortress and Lord Fearral's status as lord chieftain of the Clan, the camp at Stonehelm was different from the camps of the other nomadic family groups. It looked much like a fortified village. It had a wide variety of huts, wooden sheds, stalls, workshops, and stables, all surrounded by a ring of palisades. Near the back of the town was the only permanent temple to the Clan deities and the natural spring that supplied the town with water. A small, crude market sat by the gate, and in the center of town stood Lord Fearral's wooden hall.

The population of Stonehelm was much larger and more diverse than the other groups, too, since it tended to draw in the smaller families and unattached people who desired the safety of numbers. Unfortunately the greater number of people in one place put a heavy strain on the natural resources of the area, and some clanspeople, for the first time, were attempting to plant crops in the fields at the base of the hill—a time-consuming occupation the nomadic people had never tried before.

Valorian shook his head when he saw the changes Lord Fearral had been making. It had been a long time since he had seen his wife's uncle, and in that time, the roots of Stonehelm had spread deeper and wider. This growing permanence wasn't going to make his task of moving the Clan any easier.

He helped settle the caravan in an open, grassy field not far from the road to town. As was customary in the Clan, their hosts brought firewood and offerings of food to welcome the visitors to their camp. Valorian set up his tent and tended to Hunnul. Then he, Kierla, and Aiden went to pay their respects to the lord chieftain.

They found Fearral in his hall, sitting in judgment over a man caught stealing a horse. The newcomers gaped in surprise at the large hall while they waited for Fearral to finish.

"What is he trying to do?" Aiden hissed to Valorian. "Compete with General High and Mighty Tyrranis?"

Valorian had to agree. The wooden hall was larger than anything the clanspeople had ever built, and he wondered if Fearral had brought in Chadarian craftsmen for the job. The design of the building certainly looked suspiciously similar to Chadarian architecture. The raftered ceiling had the typical timbered construction of lowland houses, the row of pillars down the center of the hall used the same popular fluted carvings, and Fearral had even hung weapons, cave lion pelts, and a Tarn-made tapestry on the walls.

"How did he pay for all of this?" Kierla whispered.

Aiden curled his lip in contempt, crossed his arms, and glared at the ceiling.

The three clanspeople had to wait a long while to see Fearral. The case against the accused horse thief wasn't clear, and since the punishment for guilt was death, the chieftain wanted to be certain of the facts. A number of people came forth to stand up for the man, but in the end, too much proof was piled against him.

"Guilty," Lord Fearral finally pronounced, and over the sudden wailing of the man's relatives, he ordered the customary sentence. The man was to be taken to the fields at dawn, where he was to be staked out on the ground and trampled to death by a stampede of horses.

Valorian nodded once in agreement. The sentence was harsh, but in a society whose survival depended upon horses, the animals had to be protected for the good of all.

Slowly the large hall emptied of the clanspeople there for the trial. Lord Fearral's two daughters and several other women began to set up trestle tables for the evening meal while a boy lit the fire in the central hearth. The smell of roasting meat wafted in from an outside kitchen.

Valorian waited until Lord Fearral was finished talking to two men before he approached the old chief. When he drew closer, he was surprised at how much the chieftain had aged since he had seen him last. Fearral's long hair was totally white now, and his beard was thin, gray, and stained around the mouth. His eyes were rheumy and bloodshot; his hands trembled noticeably. Red patches high on his cheeks and on his nose colored his weathered skin. In the midst of the new changes, Valorian was also rather surprised to see an amulet bag hanging around Fearral's neck. The bag was an ancient Clan custom that most people had given up. Keeping his expression bland, Valorian greeted his wife's uncle with grave respect.

"Valorian!" Fearral greeted him warmly. "How good to see you." The chief kissed Kierla on the cheek with affection and accepted Aiden's negligible salute. "You're moving early this spring. We haven't held our Birthright yet."

"Neither have we, Lord Fearral, but I—"

Fearral cut him off brusquely. "Oh? Well, then, stay and celebrate with us." He glanced over Valorian's shoulder at the doorway as if he was in a hurry to get away.

"My lord, I really need to talk—"

"Be glad to," the chieftain interrupted, unable to stifle his anxious expression. "We'll be having our evening meal soon. Stay and we can talk later."

Before the three clanspeople could say another word, the chief hurried out the door.

"Drunken old goat," Aiden muttered. "He's probably going to his nearest wineskin."

Valorian made a sound of irritation deep in his throat. "Whatever you think of the man, Brother, he is still our lord chieftain. We must give him our support and obey our vow of fealty, or what's left of the Clan will fall apart." He grunted. Who was he trying to convince, Aiden or himself?

"I know, I know," Aiden replied. "But Fearral makes it very difficult."

The three began walking to the entrance.

"What I would like to know," Kierla said, stopping by the wide double doors, "is how he got all of this." She pointed to the Tarnish tapestry on the opposite wall behind the chieftain's big carved chair. "And did you see his clothes? Lowland weave with ivory buttons. How could he buy something like that?"

"Easily," a new voice answered her from just outside the door. Mordan, one of Lord Fearral's personal guards, stepped in to join them. "First he sold off all our excess stock animals and suggested we take up farming." He laughed at the grimace on Aiden's face. "Then our lord began selling our breeding stock: goats, sheep, the few cows we had, even the horses. Do you know," he added, leaning against the doorframe, "that we have no pure-blooded Harachan horses left here? Our last stallion went to pay for that tapestry and the Chadarian craftsmen who finished this hall." His narrowed eyes watched the other three for their reactions.

"That's outrageous!" Kierla cried. "What is he going to do when there are no more animals?"

An ironic smile twisted Mordan's rugged face. "We wonder the same. The only things of value we have left are the women and children. I suppose we could borrow from some of the other families. Unfortunately, everyone has already paid his chieftain's gifts for the year and won't have anything else to spare until next year."

Valorian remained silent while Mordan talked. He was stunned by the suggestion of such a betrayal. The Harachan horse was the only true Clan-bred horse in existence and was one of the finest, most sought-after animals in the Tarnish Empire. The Clan had survived as long as it had by hoarding its remaining stock of purebreds and selling or trading the foals for taxes. Without good breeding animals, the Clan families wouldn't be able to pay their tribute to General Tyrranis, who was looking for the slightest excuse to be rid of the Clan once and for all. For a lord chieftain to deliberately betray his people like that for his own comfort was unbelievable.

Mordan must have seen the disbelief in Valorian's face, because he straightened up and touched his chest with two fingers, a sign that he was swearing to the truth. "Valorian, we don't know each other well, but I have been watching you for the past few years, and I know you seek what is good for the Clan. Look around this camp. Study the people. Ride through our empty fields. Then come talk to me." He nodded to Kierla and stalked off, his dark blond hair swinging like a horse's tail under his helmet.

Valorian watched the stocky warrior disappear among the huts and tents. It was true that he didn't know the guardsman well, but he thought he should change that. Although Mordan was his age, about thirty-five summers, he was one of the youngest of the chieftain's guards, a rank earned by proven skill and courage. If Mordan was willing to talk so openly to him about the problems of the camp, it was possible he could be looking for ways to change things. Mordan could be a good ally and a good ear in Fearral's camp.

"This is incredible," Aiden said forcefully. "Why would—"

Valorian held up his hand. "Let's follow Mordan's advice first. We'll look things over before we judge. Remember, Aiden, if we anger Fearral, he'll never listen to us."

The younger man subsided with a surly glare. "All right, but I'm going back to our camp. I won't share meat with our chieftain tonight."

"No," Valorian said, thoughtfully rubbing his jaw. "I think you'd better not. Just to be safe, I want you to take Hunnul and the brood mares to pasture in the mountains. Take some of the older boys with you and go up to Black Rock."

Kierla gasped. "Surely you don't think Lord Fearral would sell *our* horses."

"Right now I don't know what he would do. But his tribute is due, just as ours is, and I don't want to risk our breeding stock."

An appreciative glint warmed Aiden's gray eyes. "For how long?"

"Until I feel it's safe," Valorian said.

"Done! We'll leave tonight after dark." He saluted his brother and dashed away to make his preparations.

Kierla took her husband's arm. "I can hardly believe this," she murmured.

"It's worse than I feared," Valorian agreed. He turned to look at the big hall from the raftered ceiling to the stone floor. "Nothing short of a miracle is going to shake Lord Fearral out of this."

They stayed to share the evening meal with the chief, his two unmarried daughters, his guards, and a host of other bachelors, visitors, and drop-ins. The meal wasn't fancy, but compared to what Valorian and Kierla were used to, it was a feast. They ate roast venison, boiled mutton, and duck with slabs of bread, bowls of dried fruits and berries, cheese, and flagons of ale. The food was eaten mostly with the fingers from platters at the big trestle tables.

The only problem Kierla complained of was the serving of the meal. Sitting on a bench at a table to eat was a Chadarian custom, not a practice of the Clan. Tables and chairs were too difficult to move from one nomadic camp to another, and most Clan meals were eaten sitting on the ground. Valorian took this new habit of Fearral's as another sign that the chieftain was abandoning the ancient nomadic ways and setting his feet too firmly on the ground.

Although he tried several times to talk to Lord Fearral about moving the Clan out of Chadar, he was unsuccessful. Fearral's eyes were glazed all evening, and his speech was slurred. He drank ale all evening, then staggered out to his quarters before anyone could stop him.

The following days were much the same. No matter how often Valorian tried to speak with Fearral, the old chief either changed the subject, ignored him, or avoided him completely. Valorian's anger began a slow stew.

One afternoon seven days after their arrival at Stonehelm, Valorian invited Lord Fearral to his camp in hope of getting the chief to talk in the quiet privacy of a tent. Short of insulting a close family member, Fearral could hardly refuse.

He came late, with his guard Mordan at his side. His face was red—with exertion or drink, Valorian couldn't tell—and his hands twitched nervously.

Kierla welcomed him with a soft cushion to sit on and a cup of fermented mare's milk. For a while, the four people merely sipped their drinks and exchanged pleasantries. Finally Valorian plunged into his arguments. He gave a brief explanation of his hunting trip and the meeting with the five Tarnish soldiers, leaving out his journey to Ealgoden, and tried to detail his reasons for leaving Chadar.

Fearral listened, growing more agitated by the moment, until he could stand it no longer. "Absolutely not!" he cried. "I will not allow it."

"My lord," Valorian said, trying to keep his voice calm, "the pass is there. I know it. All you have to do is gather the

Clan, and we can leave these barren hills."

"Leave!" Fearral looked aghast. "And go where? Over a
pass you can't find? To a land you've never seen? You have
no proof that any of this exists, only the words of a few
drunken Tarns. No, Valorian, I will not leave. Our home is
here."

Valorian's hands tightened around the horn cup; his blue
eyes were snapping. "Our home is gone! There is nothing
for us in this place but starvation and death."

"That's ridiculous. Look around you. Look at this town
I've built. *Here*"—Fearral stabbed his finger at the ground—
"is where we will find our survival. Not out there in the
mountains."

Valorian leaned forward and studied his chieftain's face in
the afternoon light. He didn't notice Mordan watching him
with equal intensity.

The problem was that Lord Fearral was convinced he was
right. He had traded away the old ways for stability and protection, not realizing that the people's only defense from
General Tyrranis was their life-style. The family groups were
small and nomadic, forming no dangerous armies or fortified
settlements. They raised livestock to help feed the Tarnish
garrison at Actigorium and horses to enrich Tyrranis's purse.
As long as the Clan fulfilled these obligations, they were left
alone.

But now Fearral had organized a semifortified, permanent
camp, and he had sold off all of the best breeding stock and
most of the lesser animals to do it. Worst of all, the people
who lived here hadn't had time to replace their herds with
any marketable skills. The crops were meager, the artisans
were too few, and there were no natural resources such as
gold or iron to trade. There was little to support the camp
and nothing to appease the Tarns. Before too long, General
Tyrranis could decide that the village posed a threat to his
authority and have it destroyed. The inhabitants were
already growing uneasy. Only Lord Fearral didn't seem to
see the danger.

"My lord uncle," Kierla said, "we have looked at your town. Given time and good fortune, it could possibly succeed. But Valorian and I feel there will be no time. We have talked to the people and they are hungry and restless. They're afraid of General Tyrranis."

Fearral slammed his cup down and glared at her. "If they're afraid now, how will they feel if we pack our belongings, gather our herds, and try to leave his jurisdiction? How will they feel when they see his soldiers gathered on the skyline ready to sweep down on us? And how will they feel when Tyrranis has us slaughtered for our foolish attempt to test his authority? Oh, no. As long as we stay here he will not bother us."

"My lord, I don't think—" Valorian began.

The chieftain cut him off. "I've heard enough. The answer is no." He rose to go. "Do not bother me again with this ridiculous idea of yours." With a grunt, he stomped out of the tent.

Mordan followed close behind, then at the tent flap, he paused. "If you haven't done it already, you could send out a scout to find that pass," he suggested quietly.

Valorian looked up, and for a moment, the two men stared at one another with understanding and a growing respect. "I have already done so," Valorian replied.

"Good. Many people in this camp are talking about your plan, and not all of them agree with Lord Fearral." He waved a hand to Kierla and ducked out to catch up with the chief.

Sighing, Kierla bent to pick up the horn cups. "I never realized my uncle could be so hardheaded. He didn't even try to understand," she said sadly.

Valorian leaned back in the cushions and stared morosely at the tent flap. He hadn't really expected Fearral to agree with him, but the chieftain's total refusal depressed him. "At least he heard me. Maybe the words took root and he'll think them over for a while. I'll stay out of his way for a few days, then try again."

In hope that Fearral was mulling over the possibilities of

his plan, Valorian put off seeing the chief for six days. While he waited, he hunted and fished to help feed the family, aided Mother Willa with the births of the spring crop of stock animals, and kept his patience on a tight line.

On the evening of the sixth day, Ranulf came bursting into Valorian's tent. The young man was filthy, exhausted, and half-starved, but his face was lit with the success of his mission.

"I found it!" he shouted. "It's there, just as you hoped. About five days' ride into Sarcithia, and it's perfect for wagons."

"Sarcithia! No wonder we'd never heard of it," exclaimed Kierla.

Valorian felt a deep wave of relief and satisfaction wash away much of his worry. Sarcithia was south of the Chadarian province, and clanspeople were not permitted to go there. The country was unfamiliar to the Clan, but Valorian wasn't worried about that. There would be time to work out a path later.

"So," he said, his voice ringing with pleasure, "Wolfeared Pass does exist."

"Maybe this news will change Fearral's mind," Kierla said hopefully.

Valorian clapped Ranulf on the shoulder. "I'll ask him tomorrow."

Although Valorian tried several times to find Lord Fearral the next day, it wasn't until midafternoon that he rode his horse down the path from Stonehelm and saw the chieftain riding up the same path with several of his guards. Valorian stopped his mount in the middle of the road at the base of the stone hill and waited with a pleasant greeting ready.

Lord Fearral wasn't rude enough to just go around without acknowledging the clansman, but he didn't try to stifle the grimace of irritation that settled on his face.

"My lord," Valorian bowed slightly. "A scout of mine returned last night with good news. He found—"

Valorian got no further. Two long, strident notes from a

sentinel's horn sounded across the fields, freezing everyone who heard them in their tracks.

"Tarns!" Mordan snapped.

Even as he spoke, the men saw a cloud of dust kicked up by a troop of horsemen coming up the eastern road.

Lord Fearral went deathly pale.

There was no time to seek the meager safety of the hall, so the chief and his guards gathered in a tight ring on the road. Valorian stayed with them, although his eyes strayed to his camp across the field by a copse of trees. He could see the women scurrying with the children into the woods and the men drawing their weapons to defend the camp if necessary. Then there was no more time for worrying.

A tax collector and a contingent of ten Tarns under the command of a sarturian came galloping up the road to Stonehelm. They brought their horses to a halt a scant six paces from the chief's group.

"Lord Fearral, I presume," the tax collector said, his upper lip curled in distaste. He urged his mount to stand directly in front of the chief.

The man was shorter and older than Sergius, Valorian noted, but he seemed to be of the same ilk: well dressed, well fattened, and arrogant with his authority. The clansman kept his hands firmly clamped to the saddle pommel.

"Where is Sergius Valentius?" Lord Fearral asked weakly. His hands were shaking.

The tax collector shrugged. "Who knows? Probably skipped with some tribute due to our general. He will be found."

Valorian fervently hoped not.

"In the meantime, Fearral," the man continued irritably, "I am your new collector of taxes, tributes, and gifts. Your yearly tribute is due to help maintain the glorious Tarnish Empire that defends and cares for you. Do you have it ready?"

Fearral shifted in his saddle, his face haunted. "Not exactly. I—"

The tax collector snapped his fingers. The soldiers immediately cantered down to the meadows and began rounding up everything they could find. Horses, sheep, cattle, and goats were all driven into herds beside the road.

"Now," said the tax collector, unrolling a piece of vellum. "Fearral, twenty-five horses, fifty head of cattle, and fifty head of sheep or goats."

Valorian suddenly jerked forward in his saddle. The soldiers were sweeping through the fields, rounding up every animal they found, including those from his family's herds. "No!" he shouted. "Wait! Some of those are our animals." He turned to Fearral, expecting the chieftain to support him and explain the error, but to his horror, Fearral merely stared at the ground.

The tax collector lifted his tight, narrow eyes to Valorian. "And who are you?"

The clansman hesitated. He hadn't wanted to draw attention to himself. Now it was too late. "Valorian," he growled.

"Valorian," the collector mused. "Hmmmmm. Sounds familiar. However, I haven't had time to study all the tax records. If you have already paid your tribute, then consider this a donation for the good of your lord chieftain."

Fearral stiffened and remained silent. Mordan shot Valorian a look of apology.

Valorian had to try one more time. "My lord, please. We cannot spare those animals. They're all we have left."

His words fell on deaf ears. Fearral continued to stare at the ground. The collector laughed and signaled again to his men. Systematically the soldiers cut out the required number of animals, a good many of which were from Valorian's herds. Sick at heart, the clansman could only watch. He didn't dare protest or fight back for fear of attracting more attention to himself and his family.

"That should do it," said the tax collector at last. "For now. Fearral, you must be more prompt with your payment. I don't like having to gather it myself." He yanked his horse around, then turned his head. "By the way, General Tyrranis is not pleased with your little town up there. The palisades must go."

His horse cantered down the road to join the soldiers, and the whole troop began herding the livestock away.

Valorian didn't bother to wait for an apology or an explanation he knew would not come. In cold anger, he sent his horse galloping back to his camp. "Round up what's left of the herds!" he shouted to the men. "Pack the camp. We're leaving."

A short while later, Valorian and his family left the granite hill and its village behind.

From the gateway of his struggling town, Lord Fearral watched the little caravan disappear into the trees below, then he turned away, feeling cold and utterly sick at heart.

7

ow many did we lose?" Aiden asked two nights later. He settled comfortably into his cushion and watched his brother. For once, Valorian was the one who was pacing angrily.

"More than we can afford," Valorian said between clenched teeth. "Twelve mares and geldings; eight goats, including our last breeding male; and sixteen of the best wool sheep *and* their lambs." He walked faster, but he could only go a few paces in the tent before he had to turn around.

Aiden whistled. The loss cut deeply into the family's already meager resources. He took a sip of wine and waited for Valorian to cool down.

Aiden, Kierla, and Valorian were gathered in the tent in the cool spring evening. The caravan had arrived that afternoon at the high alpine meadow of Black Rock, so named for the single spire of black stone that rose like a spearhead out of the meadow grass. Aiden and the boys had been glad to see them and pleased to report that Hunnul and the brood mares were well. Many of the mares had already delivered their foals; two others, the Harachan mares, were due anytime. Unfortunately the good news had done little to abate Valorian's sense of betrayal.

"It wouldn't have bothered me so much," Valorian continued, his voice sharp, "if he had asked in the beginning for help in gathering his tribute, or if he had protested to the tax collector. But he just sat there and let them steal our herds."

"Didn't he have enough of his own?"

"Yes, barely."

Kierla took his arm and pulled him to a stop. "You're wearing holes in the rugs," she chided gently. "Perhaps you could look at this another way."

He crossed his arms and lifted an eyebrow. "What way?"

"As helping the Clan. If the Tarns had taken only the town's herds, would the people there have had enough left to hang on awhile longer?"

The clansman studied his wife for a long moment while the sense of her words became clear. His anger trickled away. "Probably not," he finally agreed.

"Then you gave them some time. Yourself, too. We still have enough animals to rebuild our herds, and so do they. With the goddess's grace, by next tax time we will not be here to pay it."

Valorian suddenly let out a laugh. He sat down on the cushions beside Aiden, stretched out his weary legs, and gave his wife a grateful half-smile. "All right. I'll quit stewing over spilt wine. You're right, of course." He reached for a bowl of nuts and thoughtfully cracked several. "We still have Hunnul and the brood mares," he went on between bites. "And Linna had those long-haired goats of hers in a pen at camp. They weren't taken. Isn't one a male?"

Aiden nodded. "The black and white one."

"We could cross-breed him to our remaining females. Could be an interesting mix."

"I could get a few males from the lowlands," Aiden suggested.

Valorian chopped his hand down. "No. I don't want you anywhere near the towns, the Chadarians, or anyone that even looks like a Tarn. We must not do anything more to attract their attention. Fearral is right about one thing. If Tyrranis hears even a hint that we're trying to leave, he'll do anything in his power to stop us." He subsided into his cushions and stared out the open tent flap.

The two men were quiet for a time, each busy with his own thoughts. Outside, they could hear the noises of the camp slowly settling down for the night: the voices of parents calling in their children, the sleepy yapping of dogs, the soft clop of the mounted guards as they rode around the camp's perimeter, and far in the distance, from a windy point, the sad howling of a wolf.

Kierla shivered when she heard the wolf. She had never liked wolves since she was little and her cousin had told her that wolves were the children of the goddess Krath, who ate little girls as punishment for disobedience. She pushed her feeling away and decided that a pot of Mother Willa's herb tea would help chase away the shivers. Carrying her glazed teapot and a small stone bowl, she slipped out of the tent.

Aiden finally broke the silence. "So what are we going to do now? Fearral has bought himself some time with our herds, but he still won't budge until Tyrranis burns the camp down around him."

When Valorian didn't answer immediately, Aiden suggested, "We could leave on our own."

"No!" Valorian said, his tone implacable. "I will not leave a single clansperson behind to face the Tarns. We will all go." He watched Kierla come back in with her pot of water and a hot coal from the fire outside. She fetched her copper brazier and the box of tea.

"But how are you going to drag Fearral out of his hall?" Aiden asked, growing exasperated at his brother's lack of an instant answer.

"Well . . ." Valorian began, his eyes still on Kierla. She was on her knees bent over her brazier, trying to light the dead coals with the live ember from outside. She had forgotten to bring some tinder and wasn't having much success.

An idea popped into his mind. "Kierla," he said, "stand back from the brazier."

She looked at him curiously, then shrugged and moved away. She and Aiden watched as Valorian's eyes closed. He lifted his hand in a small gesture, and suddenly a tiny bright flame leaped over the dead coals.

Kierla gasped, a sound between surprise and laughter.

"How do you do that?"

"I don't know exactly." He came over to look at the little fire, almost as surprised as she was. In the realm of the dead, things had been so strange and different, a magical power hadn't seemed so unbelievable. But here in his normal life, it was mind-boggling. He still wasn't really sure what to do with it. He carefully set Kierla's teapot on the grate and shrugged. "Lady Amara didn't explain much of anything when she sent me back," he said.

All of a sudden, Aiden clapped his hands. "That's it!" he shouted, bouncing to his feet. "That's what the power is for! Valorian, it's so simple. *You* are to lead our people out of Chadar, not Fearral."

Kierla's eyes widened. Her hand went instinctively to her belly, where the seed for the continuation of the family continued to grow. "Of course! Why else would Amara send you back with this magic?"

Valorian shook his head at their excitement. "I've thought of that," he said quietly. "But I don't think that's the reason. Fearral is our rightful chieftain. It's his duty to lead the Clan, not mine. My duty is to help him all I can in that effort."

Aiden threw his arms up and cried, "Oh, for Surgart's sake! That old relic isn't going to lead anyone anywhere. He wants his little town and his little hall, and the rest of us can either join him or die by the roadside. He doesn't care, but you do! Challenge him, Valorian. You become chieftain and gather the Clan yourself!"

A brief image of Sergius's smoking body flitted through Valorian's memory, making him wince. "No," he said forcefully. "I made my vow of fealty to Lord Fearral, and I will not go back on my word. The Clan would never follow me anywhere if I killed the chieftain in a duel for my own benefit." He went back to his cushion and sat down cross-legged. "If we can't get Fearral to move the Clan, maybe we can get the Clan to move Fearral. After the last foal is born and we celebrate the Birthright, we'll go see Gylden. Then Karez. We'll talk to everyone."

Kierla said, "That might work. Lord Fearral could hardly say no if the entire Clan was packed and ready to leave."

"Maybe," Aiden stated. "And maybe the Clan will drag its heels as much as Fearral, or maybe Fearral will sit on his rock and forbid anyone to leave. Then what?"

Valorian dropped onto his back and glared up at the tent roof. "I don't know, Aiden! All we can do is try. We'll leave Fearral to the gods. Maybe they can change his mind."

The young man threw his blue woolen cloak over his shoulders, preparing to go. "Think about what I said, Valorian. Amara chose you to be her champion. Not Fearral." With a wink to Kierla, he strode out of the tent, his cloak swirling behind him.

Valorian watched the tent flap swing down behind his brother. For the rest of the evening, he drank some of Kierla's tea and thought about Aiden's words.

Early the next morning, when the meadow was still clothed in a cold veil of mist and the sun had not yet risen over the mountains, Valorian went to find Hunnul. Aiden's words were still on his mind, and he wanted to leave the bustling distractions of the camp for a little while to think. He found the black stallion grazing protectively near the small group of brood mares not far from the camp. After a wave to the guard, he put his fingers to his lips and whistled.

Hunnul was in a fine fettle that morning. The stallion threw his head up with a snort and came galloping to his master, bucking and bouncing, full of good spirits.

Valorian laughed at his antics. He was pleased to see that Hunnul had recovered completely from their journey. The days of slow travel, fresh grass, and rest had worked wonders on the horse. For the first time since his arrival at Black Rock, Valorian closely examined the jagged lightning burn on Hunnul's shoulder. He was glad to see the wound had already healed. There was only one thing that puzzled him. Hair was growing back on the skin, and it was coming in white. Usually hair didn't reappear on a new brand or burn, yet this hair was not only growing in thick and soft, but it was also a different color.

Valorian stood back to appraise the results. When the whole burn had grown over, he decided the mark would be quite striking against Hunnul's black body. It looked exactly like a lightning bolt.

"The Mother Goddess has put her mark on him," a quiet voice said behind him.

Smiling, Valorian turned to greet his grandmother, Mother Willa, who was walking toward him through the long grass. She held a basket in her hand, and the hem of her skirt was wet with dew. She was a thin, wiry, small woman whose strength and energy belied her age. She served as the family's midwife for the women and animals alike, and she had helped deliver every child and most of the adults in the family. The clanspeople adored her. They knew she held a special place in Amara's grace, for no other woman had lived as long or brought so much life to a successful beginning. When she spoke of the Mother of All, her people listened.

Valorian listened now, glad for her wise words. "Is that what you think? This is not just a lightning burn?"

"Of course not! This horse rendered you and Amara a great service. The goddess left that mark as a sign of her favor." The old woman gently slapped Hunnul's neck when he tried to snatch for her basket of herbs and wildflowers. She held it out of his reach. "I have spent too long this morning gathering these for my medicines. You do not need to eat my labors, even if you are the beloved of Amara." She looked up at her grandson, her wrinkled face beaming. "Amara has blessed you, too, I see. Kierla will deliver a child by winter."

"Did she tell you?" Valorian asked in surprise.

"She didn't have to. It's written all over her face."

Valorian rocked on his heels. He was constantly astonished by the intuition of this tiny woman.

Mother Willa suddenly took his hand into hers and looked earnestly into his face. "My dearest child, you have seemed troubled since you came back to us. *That* is written all over *your* face."

He nodded once, but didn't say anything. She was right, of course. Ever since he had returned to life, he had felt as if he were galloping through a wall of mist. His journey from the realm of the dead had subtly changed his self-perspective and left him with an incredible power he didn't know what to do with. None of his old dreams and goals were steady or defined anymore.

"Then let me tell you something," she said forcefully. "I have seen much in my life that has saddened me; I have seen our people defeated and crushed under the Tarn's heel. I have seen them reduced to living in ragged tents, with poor stock and no food. But never once did I believe that the gods had abandoned us. Now I am certain they are weaving our destiny. The Clan will live! They have sent you to us. You will lead us to our freedom."

He ground his heel deep into the grass. "I have already had a similar discussion with Aiden. I will not displace Fearral."

"I did not say you had to. There are other ways to lead. The gods gave you a great mission to test your skills, and you passed, so they sent you back with signs for us to believe. You can unite this Clan with those signs, Valorian." She stabbed a finger at Hunnul. "That mark, your wife's pregnancy, the tale of your journey, and greatest of all, your power. Use those to convince the people that your dream to leave Chadar is the will of the gods."

He snorted. "How do you know it is? They didn't exactly carve it in stone."

"Because they chose *you*. You are the one in this Clan with the belief in a new land. If Amara had wanted us to build towns, she would have sent for Fearral!"

"Aiden said much the same thing," Valorian replied with a dry laugh.

"Huh. That boy shows some sense sometimes." She let go of his hand, her bright eyes twinkling. "Well, I've had my say. I've wanted to tell you that since we left Stonehelm, but there never seemed to be a moment."

"Things have been confused lately," he agreed.

"Well, don't look for them to get better any time soon," she chuckled. "By the way, I think Tala will deliver her foal tonight."

Valorian smiled in admiration. She was always right about those things. Tala hadn't looked different to him that morning, but if Mother Willa said the mare would go into labor that night, it would happen.

She patted Hunnul and walked back toward camp, leaving Valorian alone with his horse and his thoughts. The clansman sprang to Hunnul's bare back. They trotted past the black pillar of rock in the meadow, then went up a high-backed ridge just as the sun broke over the wall of mountains. Valorian stopped Hunnul so he could look down at the camp of his family nestled into the sheltering edge of a copse of trees. He studied the poor, ragged camp for a long while.

Although he would never admit it aloud, Valorian had to confess to himself that he was uncertain about his desire to take the Clan to a new land. How could they survive the trip? They had few animals left, their tents and gear were old and worn, and the people were ground down by misery. How could they survive a long, hard journey over the mountains to a land they knew nothing about, where they would have to start all over again? And most important, could they escape from General Tyrranis?

Drawing a deep breath, Valorian turned Hunnul and headed east, deeper into the mountains. Perhaps Fearral was right, he pondered. Perhaps Clan survival depended upon adapting to fit the changes, not running away from them. Was there some way to adjust to the demands heaped upon them and still flourish? The Clan had been trying to do that for eighty years without much success.

Valorian looked up at the great snow-capped mountain range that filled his vision. These mountains were a good example of the problems the Clan had had adjusting. Although his people had lived in the shadows of the Darkhorns for three generations, their tales and traditions, their dreams, their religious ceremonies, and their habits still reflected their old life on flat grasslands. These mountains were strangers— hard, merciless, unknown entities that dominated Clan life but were not a beloved part of it. The range had belonged to some other race of ancient people who worshiped the peaks as gods and vanished, leaving behind only a few ruins and some legends. The nomadic Clan belonged to the open grasslands, where horses could run with the wind, stock could graze, and tents didn't have to be erected on stone. If there was a chance to find a more suitable home, why shouldn't they take it?

Valorian felt as if his mind was running in circles. He went back to his thoughts about adapting. Could the Clan adapt to its present situation, given a little more time? It was possible, he reasoned. If the Tarnish provincial governor were anyone but General Tyrranis. If they could get more livestock. If Fearral paid more attention to long-lasting solutions. If the gods were willing. . . . That was a lot of "ifs," and too few of them were likely to change.

That left the gods. What did the deities want for their people? The Mother of All hadn't bothered to explain, but gods rarely did. They simply gave mortals the tools and let them find their own way. Could Mother Willa be right, then? He would expect Aiden to jump in and suggest that his brother lead the Clan out of Chadar, but Mother Willa was close to Amara. She wouldn't say anything that she felt contradicted the goddess's will. Perhaps this power to wield magic *was* his tool to take the Clan to the Ramtharin Plains.

The more he considered it, the more uses he could see for magic. He had been reluctant to think about it until now because Sergius's death had horrified him. He had seen all too clearly how destructive and powerful magic could be. But if he taught himself to use his power properly, there wouldn't be any more murders. He could use the magic to give his people heart. If they chose to follow him, they would not only be taking a physical journey, but also a spiritual journey as well, out of defeat and bitterness to a new hope. They would need all the help they could get.

"Is this what you want of me?" Valorian asked quietly to the arch of blue sky. He hoped for a sign or some sort of answer, yet the heavens remained unchanged and the mountains were still.

Maybe it was a good thing that he did not receive an answer, Valorian decided. The last time he asked something of the gods, he got struck by lightning. This time, he would just have to have faith that his journey to Ealgoden and back hadn't been just a whim of the gods and that bringing the Clan to the Ramtharin Plains was the right thing to do.

He came back to himself with a start to find Hunnul had stopped and was grazing contentedly on a patch of last year's sun-dried grass. Valorian swung his leg over and slid to the ground. He was surprised to see that they were high in the mountains, just above the tree line on the flank of one of the tallest peaks. Hunnul had apparently climbed that far with little effort or guidance. The stallion was feeling very good, Valorian thought.

Patting his horse, the clansman looked around. Although stubborn patches of snow still hid in the shadows, most of the ground in that area was bare, and the rocks glistened with moisture. The thin air was warm with sunlight despite a cool, fitful wind that blew from the north. Valorian grinned, stretched his arms, and left Hunnul cropping grass. He walked up the slope toward a small plateau where he could have an excellent view of the range. He had never been to this particular place before, and it looked like a good spot to continue his thoughts.

As soon as he reached the edge of the plateau, he realized he wasn't the first man to come this way. There at the opposite edge, overlooking a sheer cliff, was the ruin of an ancient temple. It was really nothing more than a foundation of stones skillfully laid into a ceremonial platform about waist-high and ten paces wide, with a large, flat stone in the center to represent an altar. Valorian had seen similar ruins on another peak to the south. The old platforms were all that remained of a race of people who had been there before the Clan, the Tarns, and the Chadarians. They had lived and died in the hearts of the mountains they had worshiped while the clanspeople were still learning to ride. Valorian knew little about them other than a few old tales passed on from the Chadarians.

Curious, he walked over to the platform. It was still in good condition in spite of its age and the harsh weather, so he clambered up to the top and stared out over the edge of the mountain. From the platform's vantage point, he could see the summit of the mountain he stood on and the peaks of two other mountains. Together the three summits formed a triangle with its points to the east, west, and south. Valorian wondered if there had been any significance to that placement in the minds of the platform builders. He felt a stab of sorrow for their disappearance and a deep respect for the remains of their culture.

And yet they *had* left something behind. The ceremonial platforms might not be significant in the course of men's lives, but they were reminders to all that saw them that their builders had lived and cared enough to worship their gods. Could the clanspeople say as much? If they dwindled and died, would anything of their creation be worth remembering?

Valorian didn't think so. Not at this time. Too much of their culture had been destroyed or lost; too much was impermanent. The village at Stonehelm would rot in a few years if abandoned, and too many of the best Harachan horses had passed into the hands of others. No, if the remnants of the Clan faded, no one outside of the Bloodiron Hills would notice.

The realization made Valorian bitter. His people deserved better than an ignominious extinction. They should have a chance to live and renew their culture in any realm they chose. Amara was the goddess of life. She would certainly understand that!

Raising his hand to shoulder level, he fired a blue bolt of magical energy into the mountain air and watched as it seared toward the cool blue sky and finally fizzled out. A bright, hot feeling of excitement, exultation, and even nervousness jolted through him, and its heat burned away the last of his doubts.

"If I'm going to learn to use my power," Valorian suddenly shouted to the peaks, "this is as good a day as any to begin!"

From the top of the ancient platform, Valorian hurled more blue blasts of energy harmlessly into the air. He experimented throughout the remainder of the morning and the afternoon with the power, trying different intensities and speeds. He practiced his aim on the stone face of the peak and pushed himself to learn the limits of his strength while the sensations of magic's power coursed through his body and became more and more familiar. By dusk, he was exhausted and elated by his success. Without a word to anyone, he returned to camp, sat up late with Mother Willa, and helped her deliver a beautiful Harachan filly.

The next day he came back to the platform and worked on other skills. Keeping in mind the lesson he had learned in the cavern of Gormoth, he focused his mind on the magic and practiced making his spells as exact and concise as possible. He tried making protective shields of various sizes and thicknesses, spheres of light that glowed in different colors, and fires that could light a candle or incinerate a tree. He also learned what could happen if he let his concentration slip and the gathered magic go awry.

He was sitting in a small dome-shaped protective shield when a large golden eagle came gliding on the warm updrafts between the mountain peaks. Enthralled by the sight of the rare and sacred bird and by the beauty of the sun shining on its feathers, Valorian's mind began to wander. The next thing he knew, the shield's red energy had ruptured, and the uncontrolled magic was swirling around him into a vicious red whirlwind that trapped him in the center of its fury.

The clansman staggered to his feet. His ears ached in the shriek of the whirling energy, and his skin tingled as if covered with ants. Desperately he pressed his hands to his ears. He had to do something to disperse the tornado, for he could feel it feeding on the magic around it and building to an explosive level. Yet it was hard to think or act in the maelstrom.

With a great effort, he gathered his thoughts into a single purpose and forced his will into the center of the magical vortex. Bit by bit, he slowed the frenzied whirl of broken magic and spread it apart until it dispersed into a mist on the afternoon wind. When it was gone, he sank down on the stone and wiped his sweating forehead in relief and chagrin. "That will teach me to be complacent," he said aloud to the stones.

Valorian didn't make that mistake again. Over the next few days, while his family hunted for food, cared for the livestock, and waited for the Birthright, he went to the mountain to practice his magic. He let his imagination help him and tried whatever came to mind. He learned many things about the natural power, including its limitations. He found that he could not create life or something out of nothing. He could alter forms or images, move objects, and shape the magic into the deadly blue blasts and protective shields, but he couldn't conjure something out of thin air or give life to something inanimate. He also discovered that he had to be very careful not to overextend his power. If he became too weak to command the magic exactly as he willed, it could turn on him and destroy him. He realized from his mistake with the shield that if he hadn't had the strength to bring the magic back under control, he would have died in the release of unspent energy.

Late one evening, ten days after he had begun his self-training, he rode home to Kierla. With a mischievous grin, he borrowed one of her wooden bowls, and before her mystified eyes, he filled it full of small rocks. He covered the rocks with a scrap of cloth, closed his eyes, and murmured something to himself. After a moment, he whisked off the cloth and presented the bowl to Kierla. Her mouth dropped open and her eyes popped. The bowl was full of her favorite black grapes.

"I've worked all afternoon on that spell," he said, his pride shining on his face. "What do you think?"

She tasted one. "It's delicious!" she gasped. "Can you do that again?"

He nodded.

"Into anything?"

"Anything I can visualize."

Her wide-mouthed smile burst open like a flower. "We won't ever have to worry about starving now!" she cried. She grabbed the bowl of grapes and raced off to share them with the rest of the family.

Pleased at her reaction, Valorian followed and spent the rest of the evening transforming mounds of rocks into all the grapes the family could eat.

The family's pride and awe in Valorian doubled after that night. Unfortunately, so did their demands on his time. Nearly everyone besieged him with requests for his magic until he wore himself into exhaustion trying to help.

Finally Kierla gathered the family members and made them promise to save their requests for emergencies. Valorian, for his part, explained exactly what he could and could not do and described the consequences if he let his power get out of control. His talent was still limited, he told them, and he didn't want to overextend himself.

He looked around at the circle of faces, at the children, at the old people, at his and Kierla's aunts, uncles, cousins, brothers, sisters, in-laws, and friends—at all the people who were dear to him—and he made them the promise he had been thinking about since the murder of Sergius.

"I vow to you," he said loudly so everyone could plainly hear, "that I will never use my power against the people of this Clan, nor will I use the killing blasts against our enemies."

A murmur of surprise arose, and Valorian held up his hand for quiet.

"I believe this ability to wield magic was given to me for a good purpose. I will not abuse it! It is not for wanton destruction and murder."

"What about self-defense?" Aiden called out.

Drawing his sword, Valorian hefted it so they could all see the blackened blade. "If I cannot defend myself against mere Tarns, I am not worthy of Amara's trust."

His relatives cheered, and after that evening, their requests for his magic virtually stopped. Valorian was a man of his word, and no one wanted to incur his wrath.

Several nights later the entire camp was awakened by Mother Willa's joyful cry. The last foal had been born alive and well, and now the family could get ready for the Birthright celebration. For two days, the men and women hunted and gathered food for the feast and made the necessary preparations for the religious ceremonies.

The Birthright was an important celebration in the lives of the clanspeople. It was their gift of gratitude to the goddess Amara for all her blessings, and a supplication to her for the continued fertility and well-being of the animals and people for the coming year. Hoping to take advantage of Amara's attention, most betrothed couples were joined during the Birthright, and pregnant women were blessed.

The ceremony itself occurred at dawn beside a running stream. Water was a symbol of fertility and the neverending flow of life, and it played a major role in the rites. Men, women, and children gathered at first light to the beat of a solitary drum, then proceeded with chanting and songs to the bank of a nearby creek. There the priestess of Amara began her ritual of prayers to the goddess as the sun slowly lifted from behind the mountains.

When the great orb crested the peaks and sent its light pouring onto the meadow, the clanspeople cheered wildly. They made their offerings of milk and flowers and honey into the water, which they believed the stream would carry to the goddess. Next an unblemished lamb was brought forth. Amid the prayers of the people, the priestess drowned the lamb and slit its throat to let its life's blood flow on the waters. Its small body would be roasted and the sacred flesh given to the newly wedded couples to ensure the success of their marriage beds.

When the rites of thanksgiving were over, two betrothed couples came forth to be joined. Valorian watched with pleasure as Aiden and Linna took their vows. He wished Adala could have been there to see the joy on their faces. He thought his mother would have liked Linna. Linna was a strong woman who would stand up to Aiden's willful charm, and he obviously adored her.

Mother Willa stepped forward after the joining to call the names of the pregnant women to come forward to be blessed. Five women left the onlookers and came to kneel before the priestess. When Kierla went proudly to join the others, her face was radiant with joy. She didn't see the stunned looks on the faces of her people or the eyes that swiveled from her to her husband.

"Praise to Amara!" an aunt cried, and the shout was taken up by everyone.

By the time the day's religious celebrations were over, the afternoon was well advanced and the clanspeople were ready to eat. The food was brought forth in great abundance to represent the bounty the people hoped for in the year to come. They feasted and danced late into the night to the music of pipes and drums, until even the strongest young men and women were happily exhausted.

The celebration of birth was now over. Summer was working its way into the mountains with its hot days and short nights, and the season of nurturing was about to begin. The sleepy clanspeople rose at dawn, gathered their herds, and broke camp. In the cycle of life they had followed for generations on the lowlands, they would spend the summer visiting other families and moving their herds from pasture to pasture to fatten them for the winter to come.

Valorian watched from Hunnul's back as the carts and
horses began to leave Black Rock to take the trail to the
west. He was planning to visit the camp of his friend
Gylden, who had long been receptive to the idea of abandoning Chadar. If all went well this summer, they would
never again need to seek this high pasture. Valorian took a
last look around at the meadow that had served them well,
then he kneed Hunnul into a trot and, without a backward
glance, left Black Rock behind.

8

ur lady goddess stood before me and raised her arms," Valorian said to the listening crowd. He copied the gesture for emphasis. "She cried, 'By the power of the lightning that brought you here, I name you magic-wielder!' At that moment, she threw a bolt of lightning directly at my chest."

The crowd *ooh*ed with excitement.

Pausing, Valorian looked all around at the large circle of spellbound faces. They were sitting in a natural amphitheater near the camp of his friend Gylden. Valorian's family had arrived three days before to a happy welcome, and already there had been one betrothal, two fights, some trading, and countless horse races—a typical visit for clanspeople.

What had not been typical was Valorian's tale. He had told it once already, and Gylden's family had enjoyed it so much they had besieged him to tell it again. Valorian knew not many of his listeners believed the story was true, and he could understand how they felt. The tale *was* rather incredible! So he intended to tell it as often as he had to until the entire Clan believed. That evening, though, he had a surprise for his audience.

"The bolt didn't hurt," he continued. "Instead, it tingled and warmed and strengthened every part of me. I saw a blue aura covering me like a cloak, and I asked, 'What is it?' Lady Amara told me that I now had the power to wield magic."

Murmuring voices filled the bowl, and Valorian smiled at

their disbelief. " 'Magic,' I said. 'There is no such thing,' but the goddess explained that there is an ancient power of magic in all the world around us and that I now had the ability to use that power. 'The magic is here, clansman. Concentrate,' she said to me. So I closed my eyes, focused my will on this strange power I felt and . . ."

Valorian lifted his hand to the darkening sky and formed a bright blue bolt that shot up into the night sky. The crowd gasped and cried out. Some leaped to their feet, but Valorian had them so captivated with his story that, as he pushed on with the narrative, the people slowly subsided back into their seats.

He told them everything he had the night before of his journey to Ealgoden and the caverns of Gormoth, except this time he continued to use his magic to bring the story to life. Out of the smoke of the torches, he brought the images of the Harbingers and the mighty peak of Ealgoden; he showed his people the field of grass in the realm of the dead and the souls who came to greet him. He even heard several exclamations from the crowd when some of the dead faces were recognized. Step by step he led the audience up the side of the mountain and into Gormoth to face the gorthlings. At the sight of the hideous, wizened creatures, some of the women screamed, and even the men looked horrified. With wide eyes they watched as Valorian fought off the beasts with his magic, passed the lava river, and captured the little gorthling. He repeated each spell he had used to show his watchers how the magic worked and how he had finally attained the cavern of the whirlwind and rescued Amara's crown. Then he told of the four deities and how Amara had returned him to life with his power intact.

Knowing he had the rapt attention of his people, he went on to explain his vision of a new life for the Clan and why he felt it was the will of the gods that the clanspeople leave Chadar to find the Ramtharin Plains. He formed an image of a wide landscape of grass and rivers and horses running free, then he slowly let it fade. A profound silence filled the bowl.

After several long moments, Gylden stood and asked, "How far is this Wolfeared Pass?"

Like a bee nest hitting the earth, the silence burst with a swarm of questions from every quarter.

"You mean we have to leave Chadar?" a woman cried.

"But what about our herds and the other families?" someone else wanted to know.

"Are you sure the Tarns have left the Ramtharin Plains?"

An older man asked, "What makes you think we can do better there?"

"Why should *we* leave," another man demanded. "You have this power from Amara. Make the Tarns leave!"

"What does Lord Fearral say about this?" Gylden's father shouted over the noise.

The questions buzzed around Valorian, and he tried to answer them all as honestly as he could. By the time the people had subsided into a thoughtful silence, the night was quite late. In ones and twos, they stood and made their way back to camp.

Valorian watched them go. He wasn't disturbed by their vociferous reaction, because he knew he had shaken them deeply. Even his own family had been impressed. He could only wait now to see if the seeds he had planted would take root.

*   *   *   *   *

"Valorian, I have heard some fabulous tales in the past, but I have never heard one to top the story you told last night."

Valorian glanced at his friend Gylden, cantering his horse beside Hunnul, then looked back at the three hunting dogs coursing through the grass ahead. He kept his expression unreadable as he asked, "What did you think of my 'fabulous' tale?" Gylden was one of his few good friends, and his opinion meant a great deal.

Gylden's eyes crinkled with merriment. "Either you have

one fantastic imagination, or the goddess holds you in her favor. I'm choosing the goddess. It's probably safer."

The two men were out hunting together in the early hours. They had decided to go alone, with only the dogs and the horses, so they could talk freely. The morning was partly cloudy and cool, with the hint of rain to come. Valorian was glad to be away from the crowded camps and the curious people for a time.

"What about the rest of your family?" he asked.

Named for his bright gold hair, Gylden pulled thoughtfully on his long mustache. He was a handsome man, or so Kierla liked to say, a hand shorter than Valorian and broader in the chest, with small hands and a ready smile. "I'd follow you in a moment," he replied. "You know that. But my father respects Lord Fearral and won't budge without his orders. As for the rest of my family, well, my mother is ready to pack now, my brother wants to know more about the Ramtharin Plains, and my cousin doesn't know what to think. I imagine the rest of the family, and probably the rest of the Clan, will have the same mixed reactions. You've dropped a big, live snake in our laps, Valorian. This may take time."

"We don't have much time. I was hoping to cross Wolf-eared Pass by autumn."

"There's little chance of that. Spring thaw is probably the earliest you'll get this Clan to make a decision."

Valorian said nothing, although a part of him had to reluctantly agree. It would be much safer to get the Clan out of Chadar before winter snows blocked the pass or General Tyrranis got wind of their intentions, but he was beginning to see that uniting the families and getting them to Wolf-eared Pass before autumn would be extremely difficult. The only advantage he could see with spending one more winter in the Bloodiron Hills was that the Clan could cross the pass in the spring and have the summer to find a place to live on the plains. *If* they could keep this secret from the Tarns.

He stifled a sigh of exasperation and went back to watching the dogs. The three big spotted hounds seemed to be on the trail of something. Their tails were whipping with excitement as their noses swept over the ground.

Suddenly one dog bayed. All three instantly leaped after the scent of their quarry, drawing the men after them. Whooping with delight, Valorian and Gylden kicked their horses into a full gallop after the dogs just as a large buck sprang up out of his cover. The deer took one look at the dogs coming toward him and leaped away across a broad field. The big, long-eared deer in these hills were fleet and strong, and the hunters knew the buck could outrun his pursuers given enough lead. The dogs bayed wildly when they saw the deer. They sprang after it, their long, sleek legs bounding over the uneven ground, but they couldn't catch up with the running buck.

Both men drew their bows. It would take extreme skill and luck to shoot a deer from a galloping horse, yet that was half the fun. Valorian was not very accurate at such a long distance, so he pressed his heels into Hunnul's sides to urge him a little faster. To his astonishment, the black lunged forward as if he had been catapulted. His stride lengthened into a blistering run that carried him over the ground like a projectile, past the startled dogs and right up beside the buck. Valorian held on with all his strength. The ground was a blur beneath Hunnul's hooves, and the wind of his passing whipped his mane into the man's face. The big stallion came so close to the fleeing deer that Valorian could have reached out and touched it. Instead, he had the presence of mind to draw his bow and fire an arrow. The deer staggered and fell in the grass with the arrow through his ribs.

Thunderstruck, Valorian eased back in the saddle to slow Hunnul down. The stallion promptly obeyed. He snorted as if in satisfaction and trotted back to the fallen deer, his neck arched and his tail held high. The clansman slid off, quickly pulled off the excited dogs, and slit the throat of the dying deer. When he was finished, he drew a long breath and stood back to stare at his horse.

Gylden came cantering up, his mount in a sweat. "Good

gods, Valorian," he shouted as he jumped off. "What have you been feeding that horse?"

Valorian threw up his hands. "Grass!" He was as mystified as Gylden. Hunnul was fast, but he had never shown signs of that much speed.

"Look at him! He's not even breathing hard."

Amazed, Valorian ran his hands down Hunnul's long, powerful legs. Gylden was right. Hunnul was breathing normally, and his legs looked perfectly well. He hadn't even broken into a sweat. The man studied the black thoughtfully, and his fingers unconsciously traced the white lightning mark on Hunnul's shoulder.

"Valorian."

Gylden's voice startled him out of his reverie.

"I have some mares about to come into season. Would you consider allowing me to breed them to Hunnul?"

Valorian was pleased and a little surprised. Gylden was passionate about his horses and had painstakingly built over the years the largest and finest herd of Harachan horses left in the Clan. It was an honor that he wanted to mingle Hunnul's bloodline with that of his beloved mares. There was only one problem. Valorian rubbed his chin and said apologetically, "You know he's not a full Harachan. I, uh, borrowed Tyrranis's stallion one night."

Gylden burst out laughing. "You mean that big, mean bay he brought from Tarnow? I wondered why your horse was so tall. I don't care if he's half-cow. I've never seen a horse run like that."

The clansman glanced up at the sky as if something had occurred to him. "That trait may not be something he could pass on to his foals."

"I'll take my chances," Gylden replied. "He's a fine horse."

"Then you may breed him to every mare you have . . . on one condition."

"What?"

"Talk to your father. Talk to your family. Be my ally in your camp."

Gylden grinned. He would have done that anyway for Valorian. "Done!"

The two men clasped hands to seal the bargain and went to work butchering their catch.

Later that evening, Valorian brought Hunnul into camp and tethered the stallion just outside his tent.

"I wish you could have seen him run, Kierla," he said to his wife while he curried the horse's black hide. Hunnul was shedding his winter coat in great handfuls, and he leaned into the scratchy brush with pleasure.

"Could Amara have given him more than a white mark?" Kierla asked. She enjoyed watching her husband care for his horses. He took such care to thoroughly clean them, scratch their itchy spots, and treat them like friends. She marveled at how his hands could be so gentle and yet so strong at the same time.

"That's the only explanation I can think of," Valorian answered. "He's never run like that." He finished his work and leaned thoughtfully against a tent pole. "Gylden wants to breed Hunnul to his mares. We have some in foal heat, so I think when ours come into full season, we'll breed them to Hunnul, too."

Kierla chuckled, low and throaty. "He's going to have a busy summer."

The man laughed with her, but his thoughts followed another notion that had been growing in his mind all day. Tomorrow he intended to try it out.

After sharing the morning meal with Gylden and his father the next day, Valorian mounted Hunnul and rode into the wooded hills near the camp. He wanted to find a secluded place where he could use his magic away from prying eyes. It wasn't long before he found what he was looking for in a narrow canyon watered by a shallow creek. He rode upstream for a time until they came to a wide bend shaded by trees and scented with the smell of honeysuckle.

There Valorian slid off Hunnul's back and left the stallion free to wander while he settled under a tree to think. He knew what he wanted to do, but he wasn't sure how to go about it or whether he should even attempt it. He had never used magic on a living creature—except Sergius, and that had been a disaster—so he didn't know what to expect. The spell he had in mind could easily cause irreparable harm if it went wrong. He would never forgive himself if he injured Hunnul in any way.

Still, there was no other horse he wanted to use. Hunnul was already a highly intelligent animal who had complete trust in and love for his master. He and Valorian had developed a strong rapport in the six years of the stallion's life, and Valorian was counting on that attachment to help his magic complete the transformation he wanted to make.

The clansman sat for a little while longer, with the spell slowly forming in his head, then he called Hunnul.

The big stallion was in the creek, having a luxurious roll in the sandy, cool water when Valorian summoned him. He came willingly to his master's side and promptly shook himself. Water and sand sprayed over the man in a shower, soaking his clothes and covering him with sand and loose horse hair. The black looked at Valorian through his long forelock, and the clansman swore he saw a glint of laughter in the dark, liquid eyes.

Trying not to laugh or curse, Valorian brushed off his clothes as best he could. He should have known better than to call Hunnul in the middle of a wet roll. When most of the sand and hair were gone, he led the stallion to a large, flat boulder where he could sit at about eye level with Hunnul while he called forth the magic. He paused a moment and scratched the stallion's neck, feeling the bone and brawn and silk that formed his magnificent horse. This is going to work, he said firmly to himself. It has to!

With that thought firmly in mind, Valorian sat cross-legged on the rock to begin the spell. He took Hunnul's soft muzzle in his hands, closed his eyes, and reached out with his mind to draw on the magic around him.

The stallion shifted his feet restlessly a time or two at his master's strange behavior, but he trusted Valorian and didn't try to pull away. Gradually, though, a change came over the big horse. He stilled to an unnatural motionless pose, his breathing slowed, and his eyes stared straight into the clansman's face. He didn't make a sound or flicker a muscle, nor did Valorian. They remained locked together by touch, by magic, and by the unseen link of their thoughts as, ever so gently, Valorian probed into the mind of the horse.

The deeper he went, the more he was amazed by the complexity of the stallion's mind. There was far more to the horse's feelings and awareness than the primal desires for food and self-protection. He also learned for the first time the full extent of the gifts Amara had given Hunnul by the power of the lightning: greater speed, strength, endurance, and, most interesting of all, a heightened desire to learn.

Valorian immediately focused his magic on the last gift. He wanted to find a way to communicate with Hunnul, to teach the horse a comprehension of human language and a way of transmitting thoughts. Horses obviously couldn't talk like humans, but Valorian thought that, through magic, he could teach Hunnul how to speak to him. He wasn't trying to turn the stallion's equine intelligence into human intelligence, and yet as he manipulated the magic in Hunnul's mind, he unconsciously imprinted some of his own experiences, thoughts, and his understanding of human emotions onto Hunnul's brain. In the process, the man and the horse formed an inseparable bond that would never be broken as long as they both survived.

It was dark when Valorian came out of his magic-induced trance. He blinked in surprise and would have fallen off the boulder if he hadn't caught Hunnul's mane. His body seemed petrified from sitting so long in the same position, and he was completely and utterly exhausted. Very carefully he eased himself off the rock and leaned against the stallion for support while he stretched his aching legs and arms.

"By Amara's crown, I'm tired," he said aloud. Gently he patted Hunnul's neck, wondering if his magic had done any harm or good. The stallion seemed sluggish, and it was difficult to see his eyes in the darkness to know whether the horse was alert.

He was about to lead Hunnul to the creek for a drink of water when something incredible happened.

The black stallion poked his nose at Valorian's chest, and clear and strong in the man's mind came the words, *I'm hungry.*

* * * * *

Kierla knew something extraordinary had happened the moment her husband burst into their tent. His entire body was tense with excitement; his eyes shone brilliant blue in triumph. Without a word, he took her hands and danced her a few steps around the tent.

"It worked!" he chortled. "The spell worked like a prayer."

"What spell?" she asked, mystified by his boyish behavior. "What have you been doing?"

"Hunnul! He can talk to me!"

She pulled him to a stop. "What?"

"Well, not exactly talk. But he can send his thoughts to me, and I can understand him. He's unsure of his words at the moment, but he'll get better in time, I know it!"

Kierla put her hands on her hips and said, "Valorian, if I didn't know what you'd already been through, I would think you were sunstruck. Can he talk to me?"

"I don't know. Come on. We'll find out." He pulled her out of the tent to where Hunnul was standing nose deep in a pile of hay. "Hunnul, would you say something to Kierla?" he asked.

The stallion lifted his head, his mouth full of hay. Valorian heard him in his mind say carefully, *Good evening, Kierla. I like the way you brush my coat.*

"Did you hear that?" Valorian demanded excitedly.

Kierla shook her head. "I didn't hear anything. He just looked at me."

"Oh." Valorian's excitement receded a little, and yet he was rather relieved. He didn't really want to share this unique experience for a while or be asked to repeat the spell on other horses. The magic had worked on Hunnul because he and his master were so close. Valorian didn't think he could accurately perform the spell again on a strange animal.

"Perhaps you can hear him because you worked the magic," Kierla suggested.

Valorian grinned again. "Perhaps that's it. He said he likes the way you brush his coat."

The woman stepped up to the big horse and threw her arms around his neck. "Take good care of him," she whispered to Hunnul.

In complete understanding, the stallion curled his neck around and gently embraced her with his head.

*   *   *   *   *

Valorian didn't have much time after that to go out alone. Summer was coming to the hills with all its heat and flies, keeping the clanspeople busy fattening their herds and engaging in the daily tasks of survival. The weather grew warmer by the day, and with the afternoon heat came scattered thunderstorms.

Valorian found that his dislike for lightning had deepened to a real fear. He flinched every time lightning crackled and thunder boomed, and it was all he could do to stifle a strong urge to run for cover whenever the thunderheads built up to the west. The damage done by his last encounter with the deadly streaks of energy was still too fresh for comfort. Fortunately the sensation of heat within his body had eased enough so he could tolerate the summer temperatures, but full feeling had not yet returned to his right hand.

For a while, though, he didn't have to use his hand for dangerous or delicate work. Much of the time he was helping Aiden and Gylden breed Hunnul to many of the mares

that came into season. Often a stallion was simply allowed
to run with the herd of mares and mate as he desired, but
the two families didn't want their herds or some of the
Harachan bloodlines mixed, so the men had to supervise
every mating. As Valorian watched each mare come to Hunnul, his imagination wondered how many of Hunnul's traits
would be passed on to the foals.

When he wasn't busy with his own family or horse breeding, Valorian took every opportunity to talk to Gylden's
father and other family members. Gylden's assessment of
their reactions was correct. Some people could hardly wait
to leave, while others couldn't comprehend abandoning
their ancestral home of Chadar. Valorian spent days arguing,
cajoling, and encouraging everyone who would talk to him
until slowly he began to sense they were swaying toward his
position. At the first swelling of the summer moon, he knew
it was time to move on to another camp. He had said all
there was to say to Gylden's people. It would be up to them
to make their decision about whether to join his exodus
when the time came.

On a hot summer morning, Valorian's and Gylden's families bade farewell, broke camp, and went their separate
paths. Valorian and Gylden promised to meet again in the
autumn. Then they clasped hands and followed their caravans on to other pastures.

Valorian's family traveled slowly southeast toward the natural springs called Amara's Tears. The springs were a popular stopping place for the Clan families, and Valorian hoped
to find at least one other group there. They arrived on a sul-
try evening and made camp by the clear, bubbling springs in
the light of a full moon. Valorian was disappointed to see no
one else was there, but the feeling didn't last long.

A few days later, as he was watering Hunnul at one of the
stone wells built around the spring pools, the black lifted his
head and pricked his ears. The clansman looked to the hills
and saw one of the guards lift his horn. A high, ringing note
sounded on the wind, bringing the clanspeople running. A

second caravan, much larger than Valorian's, appeared over
the rim of a slope to the east, led by a burly, heavily bearded
man on a big white horse.

You do not like this man? Hunnul asked in Valorian's
mind.

The clansman started, surprised by the words and the per-
ception behind the question. Although he had shaped the
spell that gave Hunnul the power to communicate, Valorian
was not yet accustomed to the slow, deep voice that spoke
in his head without sound. Hunnul's use of his new talent
was growing every day, and it could be very disconcerting,
especially when he was right.

"How did you know?" Valorian asked softly.

Hunnul snorted. *I remember this man's smell. He is sour,
and you are not pleased to see him. Your hand has tightened
on my mane.*

With a chuckle, Valorian released the black hairs and
swung onto the stallion's back. "No, I do not like Karez. He
is . . . unpleasant. He is also the leader of the second largest
family and someone I must convince if we are to succeed in
uniting the Clan. So I will be polite."

In only a matter of moments, Valorian's good intentions
were put to the test.

"Valorian!" Karez's voice boomed out to span the distance
between them. "What in the gods' names are you doing
here?" He guided his horse toward the largest spring and
made an angry gesture toward a small herd of goats grazing
near the clear, bubbling pool. "Tell your people to move
those ragged-looking beasts!" he bellowed without any further greeting.

Resignedly Valorian ordered several boys to move the
goats out of Karez's way, and he watched as the big clansman directed his caravan to the biggest camping area and
settled in as if the springs were his alone.

Aiden, his entire demeanor stiff with outrage, came galloping over to where his brother was mounted on Hunnul.
"That bullheaded Karez just had his men drive our horses off

the east meadow!" he shouted furiously. "He's moving in his own herd."

Valorian didn't react. His own anger was tightly clamped by the knowledge that he didn't dare alienate Karez before he had a chance to talk to the man. He only said grimly, "Karez hasn't changed much, has he?"

Aiden nearly choked. "Aren't you going to do anything about it?"

"No, and neither are you," Valorian replied as calmly as possible. "Keep a civil tongue in your head, or I'll be forced to banish you from the springs."

The younger warrior slammed his fist on his saddle pommel, but he subsided under Valorian's ferocious glare and watched sullenly as Karez made himself comfortable under an awning. The other family began to set up their camp. They seemed genuinely pleased to see Valorian's family, yet they made no attempt to greet the other clanspeople until their work was completed.

"Karez obviously still thinks he's going to be lord chieftain," Aiden muttered. "He's already acting like one."

Valorian barely nodded. Karez had made it common knowledge for years that he wanted to be chieftain someday, but he hadn't yet tried to challenge Lord Fearral or make any serious move to claim the title. He simply made himself obnoxious to everyone by behaving as if the chieftainship were already his.

To Valorian's dismay, Karez's brutish and unpredictable temper didn't improve over the next few days. It took all of Valorian's willpower to remain polite to the heavy warrior and keep relations pleasant between the two families.

After three days of the two families keeping their distance, Valorian talked Karez into joining the groups for an evening of music and stories. The people mingled and danced and enjoyed the company long into the night. Then Valorian rose to tell his story. He told the tale as he had before, in words and magic, and his own people thrilled to his adventure. They never grew tired of hearing it.

The other family, however, grew quieter and quieter. Quite a few worried looks were cast at Karez, who sat with some of his strongest men around him. As soon as Valorian revealed his power, Karez's face abruptly turned red. By the time Valorian reached the end and began talking about the Ramtharin Plains, Karez was livid. It had never dawned on him that Valorian had any serious ambitions to the leadership of the Clan, yet here he was talking about the will of the gods and leading the people out of Chadar. Jealousy and resentment surged within him.

Before Valorian could finish, Karez climbed to his feet. "Valorian," he said with heavy sarcasm, "you should get a position as storyteller in Tyrranis's court. You could make enough denair to buy yourself a new tent or maybe a woman who could bear you sons."

Valorian's family broke out in angry cries of protest. Valorian coolly crossed his arms. His eyes were hooded in the shadows, but there was no mistaking their glittering scorn.

"You do not think the tale has merit for the Clan?" he asked, choosing to ignore the insults. Karez wasn't going to incite him into a fight now.

"Merit?" Karez laughed; his belly shook beneath his tight leather vest. "Your tricks of so-called magic might entertain the Tarns, but *I* see no use in them. As for your idea that we leave Chadar for some pitiful land even the Tarns don't want, don't waste your breath. No one will go."

"I will!" Mother Willa shouted. The old woman rose from the log she was sitting on, marched forward, and shook her fist under Karez's nose. No one in either family smiled or ridiculed the little woman glaring up at the burly man. They respected her too much for that.

"It is the will of Amara that we leave, Karez, not Valorian. Are you willing to risk denying the goddess of life?"

Every eye fastened on Karez to see his reaction. His red face paled several shades, but he knew he had to hold his position if he were going to keep a grip on his people. He stepped back from her—not even he dared lay hands on

Mother Willa—and looked over her head.

"You let women talk for you now?" he said to Valorian with contempt. He quickly moved to counter Mother Willa's influence by demanding, "What does our lord chieftain have to say about this?"

Valorian didn't move a muscle. "He is not in favor of it," he answered truthfully.

"Huh!" Karez gestured fiercely to his people and they hurried to leave the gathering. "Neither am I!" he bellowed, and he stomped off, leaving Valorian and the rest of the clanspeople looking slightly dazed.

Aiden curled his lip. "He is as bad as Fearral."

"Worse," Mother Willa replied sadly. "He's jealous, too."

In spite of Valorian's best efforts to talk to Karez some more, the man would have nothing to do with him. The big clansman made it clear to all that he had no intention of going anywhere with Valorian and would not set foot out of Chadar without Lord Fearral's command. The rest of his people wouldn't talk to Valorian either, for fear of angering their leader.

Mother Willa sought out Valorian one afternoon and told him, "I've talked to a few of Karez's family, and they seem to be interested in leaving Chadar."

"But?" he asked, knowing from the tone in her voice that there was more.

She sighed irritably. "But . . . they won't make a move without Karez's direct order."

A shadow of anger passed over Valorian's face and was gone. "Well, there's nothing more I can do with Karez if he won't listen. We'd better move on. The sun has already passed its solstice, and we have four more families to visit."

His grandmother glanced up at him, her eyes twinkling under her rough-woven sun hat. "You knew it wasn't going to be easy."

He suddenly grinned at her. "Of course. I won't give up on Karez entirely. Even he doesn't deserve being left to the Tarns." With a shake of his head, Valorian went to find

Aiden. The following day the family packed their caravan and left the springs without a word of farewell.

Karez watched them go from under the shady awning of his tent. His heavily lidded eyes narrowed as Valorian crested the hill on his black horse and disappeared from view. He had a bad feeling about that man. It was obvious to him that Valorian wasn't going to give up his ridiculous scheme easily. He sounded too fervent, too convincing. And those strange tricks of his . . . Karez didn't believe for a moment that Valorian really had the power of magic, but more gullible people could take those tricks very seriously. Valorian could cause some real trouble in the Clan. Something would have to be done, or Valorian could maneuver his way into the chieftainship before anyone could stop him and actually try to take the Clan out of Chadar.

Perhaps, Karez thought to himself, General Tyrranis should hear about this—in a circuitous way, of course. The governor might be very interested in hearing what Valorian was doing. Karez settled back on his stool, and a gap-toothed smile slowly creased his dark beard.

9

y summer's end, Valorian knew his hopes to cross Wolfeared Pass by autumn were dead. It had taken most of the summer to find and talk to every family in the Clan, and even then he couldn't persuade everyone to agree to go. The reasons for refusal were not many, but they were common throughout the scattered clanspeople. Many of those who didn't want to attempt the journey were afraid of General Tyrranis and his troops, and some were reluctant to disobey Lord Fearral or apprehensive about leaving Chadar for a new, unseen land.

Valorian had to agree their fears were valid, but not insurmountable. About half of the clanspeople *did* agree with him, either out of belief in the will of the gods or a fierce desire to escape the Tarns. He knew his inability to convince the other half wasn't for lack of trying. He had done everything he could think of, from revealing his power of magic to extolling Hunnul's gifts from the goddess and offering him as stud to any family in need of a good stallion. There simply had to be something else he could do, something he hadn't thought of yet, that would convince the rest of his people. Particularly Lord Fearral.

Unfortunately there wasn't much time left. Valorian knew if the Clan didn't leave Chadar by the next summer at the latest, they would probably lose any chance they had of escaping. The tribute to General Tyrranis would be due again, and many of the clanspeople admitted to Valorian that they wouldn't be able to pay the crippling tax by the next season. If they didn't pay, the Tarns would confiscate everything they could get their hands on or sell the people as slaves.

There was also the problem of Stonehelm. Lord Fearral had ignored the general's order to tear down the palisades and had made little effort to replenish the herds or strengthen the town's economy. Many people believed the Tarns would put the village to the sword within the year.

Secrecy was also a major problem. Valorian knew it was only a matter of time before word of his activities reached the ear of the general. Tyrranis would not be pleased to learn a clansman was trying to persuade his people to go to a new land. Knowing the general's reputation, Valorian was well aware that Tyrranis would not sit idly by while he tried to convince his people to leave.

Therefore, by some means or another, Valorian had to secretly unite the Clan, convince Fearral to change his mind, and slip the people out of Chadar after the snow melt but before the Tarns could catch them. The whole thing was enough to make him groan.

Yet through all the disappointments and setbacks, his faith in his mission never faltered. After the first doubts and confusion when he returned from the realm of the dead, his belief in a new home had turned into a bright, steady flame that burned in his heart with unquenchable zeal. The exodus would happen—he knew it. Its execution was merely a matter of effort and timing. Somehow the will of the gods would help him fit everything into place.

* * * * *

Leagues to the west, in the garrison town of Actigorium, General Ivorn Tyrranis drummed his long fingers thoughtfully on a windowsill in his large, airy dayroom. Several of his aides and officers watched him silently from the back of the room, and two guards stood motionless by the door.

"Tell me this rumor again, merchant. Leave out no detail," Tyrranis said. His voice was glacial.

The Chadarian merchant, on his knees before the general, swallowed hard. "I—I've been hearing rumors, Your Eminence," he stammered.

"Yes, yes," Tyrranis said testily. "We know that." He turned to face the fat old Chadarian, and the edge of his sword clanged against the stone.

The merchant winced. Tyrranis, as usual, was dressed in the full regalia of a Tarnish officer, although he had retired from active duty to serve the emperor as a provincial governor. He felt the gleaming brass breastplate, the black tunic edged in gold, and the sword were intimidating to those beneath him.

He was right in part, but what intimidated most people was his demeanor. The general was a man of medium height and gigantic ego. He kept his body strong and lean and his mind dagger quick. His jaw was clean shaven, and his hair was cut very short, which left nothing to distract from his cold, sharp features. His eyes had the merciless, deadpan stare of a cobra, and he used them to their full effect by staring at people with his thin lips pulled tight and his expression contemptuous. When General Tyrranis turned his cold gaze on someone, there was no need for him to shout or demand.

Now he stared, unblinking, at the merchant. The Chadarian had brought him news and rumors from the marketplace before, but the man was getting old, and his news was often unreliable. Tyrranis wanted to be certain that this rumor wasn't a mere fable the merchant had brought in for gold.

The old man cast his eyes down, unable to meet the general's dark stare. "I've heard several times of a clansman named Valorian," he managed to say. "He has been going around the hills trying to talk the clanspeople into leaving Chadar."

"Are they listening?" Tyrranis inquired.

"Some of them are, but I think their chieftain refuses to leave his camp, and many of them won't go without him."

"Wise decision," muttered one of Tyrranis's aides.

The general crossed his arms, his chiseled face unreadable, his unwavering gaze still pinned on the Chadarian's sweating face. "Has this Valorian given up on his ridiculous quest?"

The merchant's jowls swayed in the motion of his shaking head. "Not yet, General. He is still wandering after the other families, trying to convince them to follow him." The man hesitated and cleared his throat.

Tyrranis studied him through blank eyes. He could tell the merchant hadn't told everything he knew. "If you have more, then out with it!" he demanded.

The old man shifted nervously on his knees, his hands twisting behind his back. "I—I don't know if I believe this myself, Your Eminence. You might not—"

"Tell me!" Tyrranis hissed.

"I've also heard," the merchant said hastily, "that this clansman claims he was struck by lightning and now can use magic."

General Tyrranis didn't twitch a muscle, nor did he blink or gasp or outwardly change in any way. But in his mind the spark of interest flared to a bonfire at the word "magic." "Has he shown any signs of such a power?" he asked, his excitement buried under layers of careful control.

"There have been a few tricks, General. Bolts of blue fire, images in smoke . . . nothing extraordinary."

"Hmmm." Tyrranis turned on his heel and strode to the carved wooden table that served as his desk. He drew a handful of coins from a box, tossed them at the kneeling merchant, and jabbed a finger at the door. "You may go."

The Chadarian lost no time. Scooping up his money, he bowed to the ground, then struggled to his feet and hurried out.

No one watched him go.

A heavy silence fell on the room while everyone waited for the general to speak. Even though the topic of magic was never discussed in the general's presence, all the men there knew of Tyrranis's fascination with the elusive force, and they wondered how he was going to react to this strange news of a clansman with alleged magical powers.

The general remained motionless by his table for a long while, his thoughts busy behind his cruel face.

Finally one of the waiting men cleared his throat in the tense silence. Tyrranis's gaze immediately snapped to the man's face. It was the tax collector.

"My lord general," the man said silkily, "I seem to remember something about this Valorian from my records. Do I have your permission to withdraw so I may check on this?"

General Tyrranis jerked his head at the door, and the tax collector bowed and quickly left. Wordlessly the other men waited while the general found his chair and sat down. The only sound in the room was the soft drumming of Tyrranis's fingers on the tabletop as he resumed his thoughts. The other men looked at one another uneasily. They had seen these silent moods descend on their commander before, and it usually boded ill for someone.

After a long time had passed, the general stirred slightly in his seat. "I want this clansman brought before me," he said to them all.

His aides knew the statement was not a request.

"On what charges?" asked the commander of the army garrison whose responsibility it would be to find Valorian.

Tyrranis slammed his palm on the table and snapped, "I don't care! That's your problem. Just bring him to me."

The commander glanced at his adjutant and shrugged slightly under his armor. "We could probably arrest him for inciting rebellion."

Tyrranis waved a hand. "That will do." Even though he was angry at the thought of a miserable clansman trying to undermine his authority in his province, the feeling was almost lost in his desire to get this man into his private workroom and study his use of magic. The clansman's rumored powers were the first strong lead in Tyrranis's search for magic since his posting to this province, and he wasn't going to let it slip away.

Just then the tax collector hurried in, looking pale and nervous. "Your Eminence," he breathed. He was praying silently to himself that the information he had found would distract Tyrranis from his own negligence. "I finally remembered the man Valorian. He was at Fearral's camp at Stonehelm at the time I began my duties for you. He protested that we took some of his stock animals when we collected Fearral's tribute."

"So?" Tyrranis demanded.

The tax collector swallowed hard. "I went back in our records, and I cannot find my predecessor's marks for Valorian's family. I don't believe they have paid their tribute for this year."

The general glared at him. "Why didn't you collect it?"

There was a long pause while the collector tried to wet his dry mouth. "Sergius Valentius left the tax records in a shambles, General. It took days to straighten out his scrolls and notes. I thought he had collected all the Clan families' tributes but Fearral's before he disappeared."

At the word "disappeared," the Tarnish commander snapped his fingers and said, "General, four soldiers of mine went with Sergius that day. They never came back either."

Tyrranis looked thoughtful. "Where were they going?"

"Sergius never said. That's why it was so hard to look for them. We finally assumed the men had deserted."

"I remember that now," the adjutant put in. "We looked for several days; never even found their horses. But Sergius's horse appeared at his home with an empty saddle."

"Maybe the soldiers killed Sergius and took off with his taxes," another officer suggested. "It has been known to happen."

The commander waved that away. "Maybe if he was collecting gold, but the clanspeople are too poor to pay in coin. Their tribute is in animals. I can't believe four Tarnish soldiers are going to risk their lives for a few measly horses or goats."

"Interesting," murmured the general. He stood up. "There

are your charges, Commander. Enough to crucify the man. Inciting rebellion, failure to pay the tribute, and suspicion of murder. Now, *get him!*'

All the Tarnish officers saluted the general. He returned their salute and gestured to his other men to leave. They all hurried out, the tax collector drawing a quiet sigh of relief. In a moment, the room was empty except for Tyrranis. He returned to the window and leaned on the stone sill to look out over the courtyard of his house. Far beyond the roofs of his estate and the walls of Actigorium, he could see the purplish peaks of the Darkhorn Mountains. Somewhere in their shadows hid a man who could hold the secret to magic, a secret Tyrranis would sell his soul to attain. With magic, he believed he could gather the greatest army in the known world and expand the Tarnish Empire into every corner of civilization. He could ride in triumph into Tarnow bearing the riches of a thousand realms. He could sweep away the ineffectual man on the emperor's throne and wear the royal diadem himself. He was already setting his myriad plans in motion to usurp the Tarnish imperial throne, but magic would assure him of the conquest.

Tyrranis's fingers curled around each other and tightened until the knuckles turned white. First he had to get his hands on Valorian.

* * * * *

On a cold autumn night, Valorian was taking his turn at guard duty and trying to keep his anger under control. Aiden had left early in the day, to go hunting he had said, and as yet hadn't returned. Usually that wouldn't have bothered Valorian. His brother was a capable woodsman and could have easily gone too far to return to camp by nightfall. But this time, Linna had told him in a mixture of tears and anger that Aiden's Chadarian clothes were missing, and his hunting bow was still hanging in the tent.

Valorian realized immediately that Aiden had gone down

to the lowlands. He knew it was impossible to curb his brother's impulses, but he had fervently hoped Aiden had seen the sense of staying out of the Tarns' way. So far, the Tarns hadn't tried to find the family to question them about Sergius or their late tribute, and Valorian hoped they had gotten lost in the tangles of bureaucracy. However, if Aiden got himself caught, that could all change.

He rode Hunnul along the edge of camp to exchange a word or two with the other guards, and then he headed out to check the herds. The family was camped in a small meadow in the lower foothills of the mountains to take advantage of the warmer weather. Snow had already fallen in the higher elevations, and no one was looking forward to returning to winter camp.

That was another problem that worried Valorian. He didn't know where to take the family for the winter. He didn't think it would be safe to return to their usual valley because the Tarns had already found it. They needed to go to some out-of-the-way place the Tarns didn't know about where there was protection from the winter weather and enough fodder for their animals. There weren't many such places left in the Bloodiron Hills.

Hunnul walked slowly around the open field where the animals grazed. The night was frosty clear and quiet. The only sounds came from the slight wind that brushed the grass and bracken, and the sleepy animals as they shifted in their resting places. Not far away, the soft clank of a bell indicated the presence of the bell mare and the brood mare herd.

Valorian sighed in the peaceful night and tilted his head to look at the glittering swath of stars. Automatically his eyes picked out the shapes of the Drinking Gourd, the Bowman, the Eagle, the Twin Sisters, and the Great Snake, whose starry outline curled along the eastern horizon. Each figure seen in the stars was an important part of the Clan's ancient legends and a practical part of daily life. By knowing the movement and position of the stars, the clanspeople kept track of the time and the seasons and could find their way in the darkest night.

Valorian fixed his eye on the big red star that hung like a jewel in the southern sky. The star was sinking rapidly to the west, and the night was getting late. He hoped Aiden was out there somewhere following the stars back home. He rode Hunnul to the top of a nearby high hill that overlooked the flatlands, hoping to catch some sign of his brother.

The wind was blowing from the east, bringing the smells of newly harvested fields, ripe grapes, and curing hay to the sensitive nostrils of the stallion. At last, to Valorian's vast relief, the stallion lifted his head, his nostrils fluting to catch the familiar scent on the breeze.

He comes, Valorian. He smells strange.

"What? Has he been hurt?" Valorian demanded.

No. It is something like your wine, only different. Sharper. More bitter.

"He's probably been drinking Andor liquor again," Valorian said irritably. He patted Hunnul in thanks and urged him down the slope toward the camp. They stopped at the edge of the tents and waited to meet Aiden coming up from the direction of Actigorium.

The young man whistled loudly to alert the guards of his identity, then kicked his horse into a canter toward the camp. "Valorian!" he shouted even before he saw his brother waiting at the edge of the tents.

The camp was dark and shadowed. Valorian had forbade fires and torches after dark to avoid easy detection. Aiden didn't see the black horse and its rider until he was almost on top of them.

"Valorian!" he shouted again.

"I'm here."

Aiden had to rein in sharply to keep from running into Hunnul. "Good gods, where did you come from?" Without waiting for an answer, he plunged into his news. "Valorian, you've got to hear—"

"Aiden," Valorian said sharply, cutting him off, "what did

you think you were—"

But Aiden was too agitated to listen. With a frantic gesture toward the lowlands, he interrupted Valorian. "Yes, I know, I know. I shouldn't have gone to Actigorium. I could have endangered the family." He saw the look on his brother's face and added contritely, "Or myself. I'm sorry to have worried you." He put a finger in his ear and jiggled it around. "Unfortunately I had this terrible tickle in my ear for news. I had to go!" He finished with his charming grin.

Valorian rolled his eyes. It was impossible for him to stay angry at Aiden when he was back safely and bursting with news. He decided to let it drop. Linna would probably be angry enough for the both of them. He sighed. "So what did you find out?"

"I went down to Actigorium to some of the drinking houses I know, and Valorian, they're talking of nothing but you!"

That was a nasty jolt. Valorian's mouth tightened into a grim line. "Why?"

"Magic mostly. Not paying the tribute. Some people are even discussing the missing Tarnish soldiers and Sergius." Aiden's voice rose as his anger flared. "It's easy to guess. Someone has been talking about you down there, someone from the Clan, because the Chadarians and Tarns know almost everything we've been doing this summer."

A sick feeling of betrayal rose in Valorian's stomach. He knew rumors of his activities would eventually reach the lowlands, but the clanspeople were usually so reluctant to talk to Tarns or Chadarians that he had hoped it would be a long time before the Tarns knew. Now, if Aiden was right, it seemed a clansperson was deliberately trying to sabotage his efforts.

"Any idea who it could be?"

Aiden shook his head. "Whoever it was was too clever to reveal his Clan identity. But that's not the worst of it." He hesitated and cleared his throat. "General Tyrranis has issued orders for your arrest. The Tarnish garrison is sending detachments up to look for us."

"On what charges?" Valorian asked quietly.

"Failure to pay the tribute, insurrection, and . . . suspicion of murder." Aiden's voice hesitated. "Do you suppose they found the bodies?"

"I don't know. Maybe. Or maybe the Tarns are just guessing," Valorian answered.

Aiden tried to see his brother's expression, but Valorian was turned slightly, and his face was lost in the darkness. He was very still. "I heard some good news you might like," Aiden offered. When Valorian didn't say anything, he went on, "It's been confirmed that the Twelfth Legion crossed over Wolfeared Pass this summer. They're in Sar Nitina, waiting for transport downriver to the gulf. The Ramtharin Plains are abandoned."

Valorian smiled then. He reached out and clasped his brother's shoulder. "Thank you," he said. Then he turned Hunnul and disappeared into the night to finish his watch.

*   *   *   *   *

Ten days later Valorian's family was still on the move and still uncertain of where they would go. They had traveled higher into the hills every day, setting up camp in a new meadow each night and staying one step ahead of the numerous scouts and Tarnish detachments that were sweeping the lower hills for some sign of Valorian. The family realized the danger they were in, but they were growing disgruntled and worried. Snow mantled the mountain peaks, flurries had already dusted the lower hills, and the nights were growing cold. The time was well past for the family to establish their winter camp. If they waited too long, they would have a very cold, hungry, and miserable time ahead. Yet no one, not even Mother Willa, could think of a suitable place to go that would be safe from the Tarns for the entire winter.

Valorian had toyed with several ideas, including wintering

at Stonehelm, but although he knew Lord Fearral was too honorable to be the one responsible for spreading the rumors of his activities, he didn't trust the people of the town. The village was too open and vulnerable.

In fact, he didn't know who to trust anymore, outside of his own family. Anyone in the Clan, for any number of reasons, could have gone down to the Chadarian villages and spread tales, and that same person could easily reveal Valorian's location. He decided that once he got his family settled somewhere, he would keep moving. He could visit the camps, continue talking to the clanspeople, and, with luck, keep the Tarns guessing over his whereabouts. He could even go south and see Wolfeared Pass for himself before the snow clogged the hills. Staying on the move would also help keep the soldiers away from his family.

Early one afternoon, when his thoughts weighed heavily in his mind, he slowed Hunnul to a walk beside the cart carrying his tent, his few possessions, Mother Willa, and Kierla.

Kierla was over six months into her pregnancy by now, and the bulge of the baby was becoming quite evident under her bulky skirts. She smiled at her husband until a hard jolt from the cart knocked the smile from her lips. He watched her worriedly as she tried to settle herself more comfortably on the cart seat.

Mother Willa irritably slapped the reins on the rump of the old mare pulling the cart and pursed her lips. "You know we can't go on much longer like this," she said tartly to her grandson. "Kierla needs rest before her confinement, not all this jouncing around."

He agreed. Kierla was past the prime age to bear children, and he was already deeply worried about her.

Kierla laughed at them both. "I'm fine!" she cried. "I've never felt stronger or happier in my life, so don't waste your worries over me. Just think of a place to go so we can set up some ovens. I have the strongest craving for some freshly baked bread."

Valorian chuckled at her. He had to admit that she did

seem to be in excellent health. So, by the gods, if it was
bread she wanted, then somehow she would have it!

Just then a shout went up from the head of the caravan.
Ranulf came galloping over to Valorian and called, "A rider
coming. A clansman!"

Hunnul cantered forward past the carts, horses, and people to meet the approaching rider. Valorian recognized with
pleasure the rider's bright hair. It was Gylden.

The rider waved his arm and hallooed at the caravan in
obvious relief and happiness. He cantered up to Valorian,
his red cloak snapping in the cold wind, and greeted his
friend. "Valorian! Am I glad to see you! I've been looking for
you for almost seven days. No wonder the Tarns can't catch
up with you."

"You know about that?"

"Everyone does. Word spreads fast. That and the fact that
the Tarns have stopped every family they could find. They're
really anxious to catch you." He studied Valorian intently
before he said, "Something about a suspected murder?"

For a long breath, Valorian hesitated. His first reaction was
to keep quiet and not extend his trust any further than he
had to. Only his family knew the circumstances of Sergius's
death, and it would be safer if no one else learned the truth.
Then he felt ashamed. Gylden was his oldest friend. How
could he gain the Clan's respect and trust if he couldn't
extend the same to those around him?

"That part is true," he explained to his friend. "Sergius
Valentius was trying to take Kierla. I struck him with a bolt
of magic before I remembered I had the power. We hid his
body up in the mountains."

A cloud fell away from Gylden's handsome face, for he
realized how much Valorian was trusting him with that information. He was both relieved and pleased. It made his news
for Valorian that much more gratifying. "That isn't murder,"
he snorted. "That's just snake killing."

"Not to the Tarns," Valorian replied dryly.

Aiden and several of the other men on horseback joined

them at that moment, and Gylden brought up the reason that had sent him chasing after them.

"We knew you might be in trouble when we heard about the charges brought against Valorian, so Father had an idea. He wants you to come winter with us."

Valorian chuckled with a mix of surprise and disbelief. "Your father? I thought he would have nothing to do with me without Lord Fearral's approval."

Gylden didn't take offense. His father was known to be set in his ways. "I've been talking to him," he said with a grin. "I had to do something to earn all those pregnant mares. And gods' truth, Valorian. He knows a place deep in the Gol Agha that he says will shelter both of our families through the winter. He wants you to come."

"Gol Agha?" Aiden questioned. "The canyon of the winds? I didn't know there was any place in there worth camping for a day, let alone several months."

"I didn't either. But Father swears it's there. He sent several scouts out to check on it while I came to find you." He tugged at his mustache and glanced at Valorian. "Will you come?"

"You realize that we could be putting your family in great danger," Valorian said.

Gylden didn't hesitate. "Of course."

The clansman looked to his brother and the other men around him. The hope and relief on their faces melted the last of his reservations. If Gylden and his family were willing to risk hiding them, then he wasn't going to argue further. He felt relief lift the weight of worry from his shoulders. "We'll come," he said. Then he trotted back to Kierla and told her the news.

"Praise Amara!" she cried in delight. "We'll have bread by the Hunting Moon."

And she was right.

By the time the next full moon, or "the Hunting Moon" as the clanspeople called it, swelled over the Darkhorns, the two families had joined and traveled south of Stonehelm deep into the mountains to the canyon called Gol Agha. The wide canyon mouth, aptly named the Place of the Winds, faced the northwest, catching storm winds and the winds of winter like a giant funnel. The reddish brown canyon was never still or silent from the winds that surged down its long length. They keened and whined and howled and sang, sometimes so strong a man couldn't stand upright in their passing.

Further along, however, the canyon made several bends that took the force out of the winds, and between the protection of high walls was a long, narrow, flat place, green with grass and scattered trees. It wasn't ideal, but it was safe enough. Only a few clanspeople had ever bothered to explore beyond the Place of the Winds; one of those had been Gylden's father in his younger days.

Happily the old man's memory was as sharp as ever, and after three days' traveling with the winds howling at their backs, the two families found the sanctuary within the canyon. They immediately set about building the more substantial camps that were used for winter, including the carefully constructed ovens for baking bread. Two days before the moon was full, Kierla ate her fill of the warm, fragrant, freshly baked bread.

The rising of the Hunting Moon was another day of celebration for the clanspeople, this time for the god Surgart, the god of war and the hunt. They spent the day dancing and reenacting famous hunts, and when the full moon sailed over the canyon wall, the men set out on foot to hunt the fiercest predator in the mountains, the cave lion. After his horses, a cave lion pelt was the most respected and treasured possession a clansman could own. To kill one of the big cats during Surgart's celebration was a feat of great honor and a good omen for the year to come.

Valorian himself had never had a successful lion hunt, but this year, Kierla wasn't surprised when the men returned two days later filthy, exhausted, and laden with the pelt of a huge lion.

In front of both families, Gylden's father stretched the pelt out flat for all to see. "Before the eyes of Surgart," he shouted to the gathered people, "Valorian threw his spear straight and true into the chest of the springing cat. It is to him that we give the pelt for the honor of the killing blow!"

The crowd cheered as Valorian gathered up the pelt, and pride and gratitude burned in his heart. He gave the fur to Kierla to tan and prepare as she wished.

Several days later, on a windy, frostbitten morning, he kissed her good-bye, and, leaving her in Mother Willa's care, he set out with Gylden, Ranulf, and Aiden to see the Wolf-eared Pass.

10

t wasn't difficult for the four clansmen to elude the Tarnish soldiers still searching the hills. Unencumbered by herds and carts, they were able to travel fast and on paths known only to wild animals and the Clan. Before too many days were gone, they passed the ridge where lightning had struck Valorian and headed into country only Ranulf had seen.

The young man was thrilled to be the guide for the other three, and he led them south down the long length of Chadar over ridges, hills, and valleys they never knew existed. Not far from Valorian's ridge, Ranulf had to lead them out of the foothills and down to the plains to circumvent a vast, deep canyon that sliced through the mountains and forced its way through high bluffs into the lowlands. The steep gorge formed an insurmountable barrier across any mountain path going north or south, and Valorian grimaced when he realized that if the Clan came this way, they, too, would have to risk going down to the plains to avoid that canyon.

Several days after passing the canyon, the clansmen crossed the Bendwater River into Sarcithia. They worked their way south along the flanks of the mountains for five more days until they reached a wide valley carved out of the hills by the swiftly flowing Argent River.

When all four men saw the old scars of wagon ruts left on the trail by the retreating XIIth Legion, Valorian felt his excitement grow. To the east, he could see where two peaks rose from the same summit, forming a shape similar to a wolf's prick-eared head.

Ranulf nodded when Valorian pointed to it. After all that time, Valorian was finally able to see Wolfeared Pass for himself. Following the legion's trail, they rode up the long and often steep path to the snow-covered summit of the pass and sat on their horses to gaze on the land beyond. They were silent for a long time as their eyes slowly traveled down the rumpled mountain slopes, past steep granite faces powdered with snow, to the pine-covered foothills and the purplish vistas of the far distant plains.

Hunnul stretched his neck to snuff the wind from the east, and his pleasure sang in Valorian's mind. *I smell grass down there. More grass than I have ever seen. That is a good place.*

Grinning widely, Valorian patted the stallion in agreement. He could tell by looking at his companions that they thought so, too. He was encouraged as never before. Until that moment, the dream of going to the Ramtharin Plains had been something only he had truly believed in. His friends and family had thought about it, accepted it, and wished for it, but none of them had passionately believed in its possibilities. Now the dream had been passed to others. Valorian could see it ignite and begin to glow in the three men beside him. They stirred, straightened a little, and glanced at one another like conspirators in a wonderful secret. Ranulf was grinning. Gylden's brown eyes were wide and brimmed with excitement, and Aiden's fingers drummed on his knee as he imagined the vast potential of such a land.

Valorian nodded to himself. Now he had three dedicated disciples who would help him carry the dream to the Clan. The people had to understand! If he could only bring them all here to this mountaintop to look down on the far plains, he knew they would come to believe in hope and freedom just as his three companions had. Unfortunately he couldn't bring the Clan here just for a look. He had to instill enough trust in the people for them to make a mighty leap of faith. When they ascended this mountain, it would be for the first and last time.

With a quiet sigh, he turned Hunnul away from the pass and the tantalizing view and led his friends back down the mountain. The weather was still mild and dry for late autumn, so Valorian decided to use the opportunity to scout for trails passable by carts. The other three men agreed. No one in the Clan was familiar with the land this far south, and it would be very helpful to know the fastest way to reach the pass.

They began at the Argent River valley and methodically worked their way north, exploring every trail through the rugged hills—the small valleys with rushing streams, the deep canyons, and the open meadows of sun-cured grass. They looked for watering places, areas that could accommodate a large number of tents and herds, and smoother paths for the carts. They didn't try to keep a map or write down any of the information they learned. None of them knew how to write, beyond a few basic names and symbols, and maps were for Tarns. After generations of traveling from place to place, the clanspeople were adept at memorizing landscapes and distances. When the Clan finally came that way, Valorian knew he and his companions would be able to lead the caravan unerringly along the ways they had chosen.

Before too many days had passed, however, Valorian began to feel his nervousness for Kierla increasing by the moment. They had been gone for a full passing of the moon, and her time was coming quickly. He wanted to be there with her when their child came into the world. He didn't admit it aloud or even to himself, but he also wanted to be with her in the horrible event that she did not survive childbirth.

The other men, too, were getting anxious to see their loved ones and be sure the camp was still safe, so they pushed a little faster and reached the Bendwater River at the border of Chadar and Sarcithia by the end of autumn.

The four men made camp that night on the southern bank of the Bendwater under an evening sky that was clear and dazzling with stars. When they woke the next morning, the sky had turned to a solid, unmarred roof of gray. A damp, chilly wind stirred restlessly through the brown grass and rattled the bare trees.

Valorian studied the sky worriedly as they packed their gear. Everything under the lowering roof of cloud looked dull gray and cold; it was difficult to see the far horizon to the west and the north, where the land and sky blended together in a dark, dismal haze.

"We'd better look for some real cover today," Aiden remarked, coming to stand by Valorian.

The tall clansman nodded. There was snow in those clouds, probably a lot of it, and he didn't want to spend a night out in a storm if he could help it.

The clansmen had already found a suitable ford on the wide, shallow river, so they hurried down to the water, glad to be going back to their own homeland.

Valorian watched the pleasure on his friends' faces while Hunnul waded through the water. That was the sad incongruity of his dream to leave Chadar. The clanspeople loved their own country. They didn't want to tear themselves away from a land that had nurtured them for generations. He felt the same way. Given half a chance for survival, he would drop his plans for an exodus in a moment and strive for a better life in Chadar. But it was too late. What most of the clanspeople did not want to accept was that the Tarns had already taken away their homeland. Chadar was no longer home, no matter how deeply the people cared about it. The time had come to move on, just as the clans had done long, long ago when they came out of the west to settle in Chadar. Once again they must follow Amara's rising sun to the east.

Valorian was so busy mulling over his own thoughts, he didn't notice Hunnul's ears suddenly swivel forward or the stallion's nose test the breeze. They were nearly to the bank on the Chadarian side of the river when Hunnul started to tell him, *Master, I think there are* . . .

He didn't get a chance to finish. At that instant, there was a loud yell from a clump of birch trees close to the water, and six Tarnish soldiers sprang out of hiding, their bows drawn and aimed at the riders.

"Stop right there!" their leader ordered.

Valorian cursed inwardly. It was just their luck to run into a border patrol now. He wondered if they could bluff their way past the soldiers. Perhaps these Tarns didn't realize who he was.

Before he could get a word out, the idea was driven from his mind by the clan war cry. The three men beside him clapped their heels to their horses, yanked out their swords, and charged directly at the six archers. Valorian cursed aloud this time. Tarnish soldiers were good bowmen and unlikely to miss three men riding at them at such short range.

Unbidden, Hunnul leaped after the three. Valorian saw the Tarns take careful aim, and he raised his right hand. The arrows flew from the bows faster than the eye could follow, but Valorian's spell was just as fast. He flicked his hand, and a gust of wind suddenly swirled between the two groups of men, knocking the arrows in every direction. The surprised Tarns scattered along the bank as Aiden, Gylden, and Ranulf charged into their midst with swords swinging.

Valorian, however, didn't want a fight now. He wasn't going to break his vow by killing these six Tarns with magic, and there was nothing to gain by fighting them. "Keep going!" he bellowed to his men as Hunnul galloped up the riverbank, flinging water in all directions. The clansmen reluctantly broke off the attack and raced toward the hills to seek cover, with Hunnul close at their heels.

It took a moment for the startled soldiers to gather their wits, then five of them ran for their horses to give chase to the fleeing clansmen. Only their frustrated leader paused long enough to draw his bow and quickly fire two arrows at the escaping men before turning away to get his mount. He didn't wait to see where the arrows went.

The powerful composite bow favored by the Tarnish army did its work well. It fired its arrows at a speed faster than a galloping horse, in a perfect trajectory that caught up with the group of clansmen near the end of the long flight. The first arrow fell to the grass. The second, like a slender bird of prey, dropped out of the leaden sky and slammed into Valorian's back.

The clansman suddenly felt himself knocked forward over Hunnul's neck from an agonizing pain that burst through his upper back and left shoulder. He grabbed frantically for the black's mane to keep himself from falling.

Hunnul felt his master's agony stabbing into his mind. He neighed a stallion's scream of rage, which brought the other riders' heads snapping around to see what was happening. Distraught, the big horse slowed down, but Valorian managed to push himself back into the saddle.

"No," he gasped through clenched teeth. "Keep going."

Behind him, Hunnul could see the Tarnish patrol galloping their horses up the hill in pursuit. He bared his teeth, stretched out his neck, and ran as he had never run before to put as much ground as possible between his master and the men who had hurt him. He passed Aiden, Gylden, and Ranulf like a black streak.

Aiden barely caught a glimpse of the shaft sticking out of Valorian's back and the spreading red stain on his cloak when Hunnul flashed by. His heart dropped to his stomach. "Oh, gods!" he cried. "Valorian's been hit!"

The three men bent frantically over their horses, their bodies molded to the animals' movements. The Clan-bred horses, raised and trained on the rough terrain of the foothills, sped over the earth with the speed of deer and soon left the Tarns behind. But they couldn't keep up with Hunnul. The last the three men saw of him was his streaming tail disappearing over a far hill.

"We'll never catch that horse," Gylden finally yelled. The Tarns were far behind and out of sight by that time, and the men's horses were sweating heavily, so they pulled their mounts to a walk and followed Hunnul's trail through the sparse, dried grass as best they could. The tracks were fairly easy to see, since the gentle hills to the north of the river were treeless and smooth. But it was a nerve-racking search. At any moment, they expected to top a slope and see Valorian's body lying dead in the grass.

They had only ridden a league or two after Hunnul when the first snowflakes began to fall in light, swirling patterns. In moments, the fall turned into a blizzard, and the fitful wind that had been blowing took the bit in its teeth and bolted, driving the snow before it in blinding white horizontal sheets. The cold became a vicious, sucking thing that snatched at their breath and stole the heat out of their bodies.

Aiden stared desperately into the snow for some sign of his brother or Hunnul. The tracks were gone in the blinding snow; there was no way to tell where Hunnul had gone. What was the stallion going to do, carry Valorian all the way back to the winter camp? Valorian would bleed to death by that time. Or freeze. His hope sinking, Aiden pulled his hood up over his head and pushed his horse closer to Gylden's and Ranulf's mounts. Together they pushed on into the storm.

Far ahead of the three men, Hunnul was racing across the flatter slopes at the edge of the foothills, racing as if all the gorthlings of Gormoth were on his heels. His eyes were rimmed with white, his nostrils flared wide, and his long black legs were a blur against the brown landscape. Every instinct within the frantic horse told him to go home, to take his master back to the place where there was food and warmth and care. He didn't know how far it was or how badly Valorian was hurt, he only knew to run north, where help could be found.

Yet something was bothering Hunnul. He felt an unfamiliar nagging sense that something was not right with his actions. There was more to this that he should try to understand. The stallion's pace began to slow, and he neighed in frustration.

Valorian was lying along Hunnul's neck, grimly clutching

the mane with his right hand. His eyes were screwed shut, and his teeth were clenched against the pain. As the stallion slowed down, Valorian managed to gasp, "We can't leave them!"

Hunnul came to a complete stop. He knew Valorian meant their companions, and as he thought about them, he slowly came to understand what was wrong. His horse instincts had told him to go home, but the greater wisdom and understanding of humans that Valorian had given him helped him to see that he shouldn't leave Valorian's companions behind. They were much closer than the family camp. They would have the knowledge and ability that he did not to heal his rider. As quickly as he had raced north, the big black turned on his heels and galloped south the way he had come.

He had only run a few minutes when the storm broke loose around him. Hunnul was forced to slow to a trot. Very warily, his head stretching into the darkening wind and snow to search for the scent of the three men, the stallion continued on his way.

To Aiden, Gylden, and Ranulf, the morning seemed to be an endless nightmare. They hunted in the dense snow like blind men while their hope trickled away and their bodies grew sluggish in the cold.

It was Aiden, peering into the snow, who heard a neigh and saw a black shape materialize out of the blowing snow. With a glad cry, he urged his mount forward to meet the horse. "Valorian!" Aiden cried.

The clansman was slumped over his saddle, his right hand clenched in Hunnul's mane, his left arm hanging uselessly, and his face was deathly pale. Somehow he managed a weak smile. "I'm . . . still here," he said weakly.

Hunnul came to a stop, and the other horses huddled around him. Man and horse alike were thoroughly miserable.

Aiden knew he and his friends had to find shelter out of the deadly wind for Valorian as quickly as they could. However, finding their way in the blizzard would be virtually impossible. They couldn't see more than a few feet ahead of them and could easily fall off a sheer cliff, wander in circles, or lose each other entirely in the storm.

"Did anyone see any kind of shelter?" Aiden cried over the howling wind.

The others shook their heads. They were in an area of the foothills that was fairly smooth and had few trees. There were no caves or deep valleys or big windfalls that anyone could remember.

"Rope your horses together," Valorian croaked, still lying against Hunnul's neck. "We'll find something."

The others nodded mutely and quickly bundled themselves with every scrap of clothing they had, strung ropes from saddle horn to saddle horn, and struck out into the teeth of the storm.

To Hunnul, Valorian whispered, "Find someplace out of the wind."

The stallion took the lead. Step by step he led them east through the whipping storm toward the rising hills. He didn't really know where to go, but he realized that his beloved master and the others wouldn't survive for long in the frigid blast of the blizzard. Before too many hours passed, they wouldn't be able to fight the cold any longer. Their smaller bodies would slip into death long before he grew tired. He had to find someplace closer where they could rest. His nostrils searched the wind, his keen eyes looked into the endless white and gray storm, yet even he found nothing.

The big stallion plowed on. Behind him, he sensed the three smaller horses were beginning to falter. The rope on his saddle jerked more frequently as the horses stumbled through the gathering drifts. Hunnul became worried. Valorian had put his complete trust in him to find what the humans with their weaker noses and eyes could not. If he didn't find something soon, his master would die.

Then, on the dim edge of his range of smell, the black

caught the faintest scent of something familiar: hay. His ears perked. His head swung around to follow the smell and he hurried to catch up with the elusive scent.

Valorian had no idea where they were or where they were going. Numb and weak from loss of blood and the cold, he was barely conscious. Gradually, though, the change in Hunnul's gait attracted his hazy attention. He lifted his head and tried to focus on the snowy gloom.

He was staring ahead into the shifting walls of snow when something moved. He had the impression of a large, upright figure standing there, but then he blinked and it was gone. "Hunnul, what was that?" he whispered.

I do not know. They seem to be leading us somewhere.

"They?" gasped Valorian.

Yes, there are at least three of them. They have been out there for a short time now.

"Why are you following them?"

They have food, master, and I do not sense any threat from them.

"What if they're predators?" Valorian mumbled.

Hunnul snorted as if insulted by his rider's lack of faith. *They do not smell like meat-eaters. They smell like stone.*

Valorian was startled. Stone? What were these creatures? he wondered. Hunnul seemed to think they weren't dangerous, but how could he be sure?

Valorian thought he saw the creatures several more times, each glimpse just a quick view of a large, dark shape against the shifting snow shadows. The beings made no noise or any movement toward the four riders. In fact, they seemed to be very elusive of human contact.

Time passed slowly as they plodded wearily through the snow. For once, Valorian was grateful for the vestiges of the heat left in his body by the lightning. It was probably one of the few things keeping him alive. He could feel the intense cold slice through his clothes and his boots. His hands and feet were numb, and his face felt like ice. The only blessing in the cold was that it stopped his bleeding and eased the pain in his back. His breath was coming in shuddering gasps that shook the arrow at every movement. His consciousness began to waver again, slowly slipping away until the world rolled before his eyes and went dark.

He didn't stir when Hunnul suddenly neighed. Somewhere, not far ahead, a guttural cry answered his call. The stallion surged forward, pulling the other horses with him. He went around several boulders and up a steep, slippery slope. All at once a wide, dark entrance opened up before them, and Hunnul plunged into the blessed shelter of a cave.

The next several hours were a blur to Valorian. He was only vaguely aware of Aiden, Ranulf, and Gylden moving around him. Someone must have lit a fire, for he saw a vague, flickering light on the ground, and someone else pried his fingers from Hunnul's mane. It took all three men to lift him from the stallion's back and carry him to some blankets by the fire. He felt their shaking hands and knew they were as cold and exhausted as he. He wanted to get up and help them. They needed water and food, and someone had to take care of the horses, but when he tried to rise, a brutal pain in his back pinned him to his pallet. His senses reeled, and for a while, all light and awareness faded from his mind.

He woke briefly to see Aiden bending over him with a bloody cloth in his hands, then the pain abruptly lanced through him again, and he passed out once more.

It wasn't until late that night that he returned to consciousness. He woke in fits and starts to the sound of strange voices.

"Live will he?" a deep, rumbling voice said near his head.

Valorian opened his eyes. He was lying on his stomach, facing the fire. His vision was unfocused, and the only light in the big cavern came from the feeble embers of the low fire. All he could make out were the shapes of his companions under their blankets and Hunnul's front legs standing close by his arm.

"The Mother said he would," another strange voice replied.

Valorian couldn't see the speakers because they were behind his head. When he tried to move, his exhausted body would only stir.

The second speaker spoke again in a voice that sounded much like rocks being ground together. "See, he wakes. Poultice we must give him. Amara asked."

Strangely the clansman wasn't afraid. Even though he had no idea who these speakers with the odd voices could be, he sensed they only wanted to help. Hunnul didn't seem to be upset by their presence. At the mention of Amara's name, he relaxed back into his blankets. The Mother Goddess would watch over him.

As he drifted off to sleep again, he felt something warm and heavy laid across his back, and the gravelly voice said softly, "Peace, magic-wielder. When our home you leave, follow the little blind fishes under the mountain. Shorter will be your way."

Something large and ponderous moved slowly toward the back of the cave. Valorian roused himself just long enough to lift his head. There at the flickering edge of the firelight he thought he saw two upright, bulky creatures step into the dense darkness. He sighed once, and his eyes gratefully slid shut.

Another voice woke Valorian abruptly early the next morning, and this one he recognized. It was Aiden.

"Gylden, Ranulf!" he heard Aiden cry. "Come here. Look at this!"

The three men gathered around Valorian on his blanket.

"By all the holy gods!" Gylden exclaimed. "What is that?"

"Is he dead?" Ranulf asked worriedly.

"No," Valorian said before anyone else could speak. He opened his eyes and saw Aiden kneeling by his side, worry and confusion plain on his face. Valorian wondered what all the fuss was about. Surprisingly the pain in his back was completely gone. Only a heavy lassitude kept him on his bed; he was still too tired to move and just holding his eyelids open was an effort.

"Valorian," Aiden said hesitantly, "there is something on your back."

"I know," he replied.

"What is it? It looks like a blob of cooled stone."

Stone? How interesting, Valorian thought. "It's a poultice," he told his friends. "Someone put it there last night."

The three men exchanged glances.

"Can you take it off?" Gylden suggested.

Very carefully Aiden hooked his fingers over the edge of the blob. The poultice, or whatever it was, was smooth, gray, and heavy. It covered Valorian's bare upper back from shoulder to shoulder, as if it had been poured directly onto his skin and left to harden. It felt warm under Aiden's fingers. Gently he peeled it off and laid it aside.

All three men gasped. They had cut the arrow out of Valorian's back the night before; they had all seen the bloody wound and the damage to Valorian's shoulder. This morning it was virtually healed. The deep puncture and the cuts were no more than lines of new pink skin.

"Carrocks," Gylden said suddenly.

Aiden and Ranulf looked at him as if he had lost his mind. Carrocks were supposed to be manlike creatures of living rock who made their home in the dark roots of the mountains. But everyone knew the beings were only myths.

"Carrocks," Gylden repeated, and his eyes lit with wonder. "That has to be it. The Carrocks helped us."

On his blankets, Valorian nodded. "Of course. Amara sent them," he whispered.

"That's impossible," Aiden said. He stared down at his brother's back. "Carrocks don't exist. They're only legends."

Ranulf picked up the stone poultice and turned it over in his hands. "But what if they're real? I mean, look at this thing. Only the Carrocks in the tales had the healing stone. They lived in caves like this one." He waved a hand at the enormous cavern that sheltered them.

Gylden rocked back on his heels. "*Something* brought us here, that's for certain. When we got here, there was firewood, hay for the horses, even cut pine boughs for our beds."

The three clansmen stared around the cave at the dark corners and crevices, perhaps hoping for some glimpse of the mythical Carrocks.

Valorian remembered something Amara had said. "Magic is responsible for creatures that you have never seen and know only in legends," he repeated softly. His eyelids gave up the effort and fluttered shut. Carrocks, he thought with pleasure. The stone people who had sprung from the loins of the earth when drops of Amara's blood fell from the sky and spattered on the newly formed mountains. No one had ever clearly seen a Carrock, and no one really believed anymore that they existed. Until now. He wished he could have seen his benefactors, perhaps spoken to them and thanked them, but he realized they wouldn't be back. Their duty was done. He was healed, his friends were safe, and it was time for him to go home.

Two days later, Valorian stood at the mouth of the cave and looked out at a world transformed by snow. The blizzard had finally blown itself out, leaving behind brilliant blue skies, towering drifts, and a dazzling white landscape. It was incredibly lovely, and it would be incredibly difficult to travel through.

Sleep and the Carrocks' poultice had done their work well. Valorian felt stronger and fitter than he had in days. He just wasn't happy about continuing their journey through that deep, drifted snow. Traveling would take longer, be very difficult, and would be hard on the horses. Because it was an early storm, it was probable that warmer weather would be back soon and melt most of the snow. They could wait until then to leave, but Valorian didn't want to sit any longer than he had to. Kierla was waiting, and he wanted to get back to her.

He glanced around at the cave that had sheltered them for

three days, and the last words of the Carrock flitted through his memory: "Follow the little blind fishes." His eyes looked down at the small stream that flowed through the cavern. The water was shallow and perfectly clear. He couldn't see anything that looked like fish, so he walked upstream deeper into the cavern.

The cave was the result of massive long-term erosion in the side of a huge cliff. It had smooth walls, a floor of bedrock and gravel bars, and a towering ceiling that gradually dropped down toward the back. Valorian had assumed the cavern was nothing more than a large chamber with a stream that bubbled up from a spring or some underground river. Now, as he explored farther back into the cave, he wasn't so sure. There was a distinct draft that grew stronger the closer he approached the back wall. Still following the little stream, he discovered that what looked like the back of the cavern was actually a short slope and a rockfall. He scrambled up the rocks, and there at the top, where the ceiling arched down toward the floor, was a broad tunnel leading down into the mountain. A shiver crept up his back at the memory of other dark tunnels and the cold evil that had lurked there.

He paused in the dim remains of the light from the cave mouth and peered into the black depths where the stream came bubbling along its rocky bed. There was no movement or noise or any sign of life down there that he could see, and no indication that the tunnel led anywhere but underground.

Yet the Carrocks would know where it went. Would they save his life only to lead him astray on a fool's path? He wondered. If it wasn't for the pink scar just below his left shoulder blade, he would have thought he had dreamed the whole thing.

Valorian glanced down at the stream by his feet. There they were, barely visible in the weak light, a school of small white fish feeding on the graveled bottom. When he stepped closer to see, they flashed in unison and swam upstream into the lightless waters. He saw them just long enough to note they had no eyes. The little fish settled his mind. He would go into the tunnel.

Convincing the others wasn't as difficult as he had imagined. They were all loath to travel in the snow and willing to try something different if Valorian thought it would work. Aiden's only suggestion was to mark their trail as they went along so they could find their way back if the going got too rough.

The men saddled their horses and, out of habit, wiped out the signs of their camp. Valorian left the stone poultice sitting in plain view near the faint scorch mark of their fire. Perhaps the Carrocks could use it again. As a last thought, he dug through his saddlebags and found a small green chunk of jade he had once carefully carved into the shape of a horse. It was rather crude, he knew, but it could serve as a small token of thanks. He left it sitting beside the poultice.

One by one the four men led their horses over the rockfall and into the tunnel entrance that sloped gradually down deep into the roots of the mountain. They paused together to stare down into the black passage. No one seemed willing to be the first to go into that underground hole.

"Where does the tunnel go?" Aiden wondered aloud.

Valorian shrugged slightly. "The creature didn't say. It only told me that our way would be shorter."

"I'm for that!" Gylden replied, trying to sound hearty. He was about to urge his horse forward when Valorian held out his hand.

"Wait a moment. We need some light." And before his friends' startled eyes, he formed two small spheres of bright light that dangled over his head like obedient stars.

Aiden laughed, a hint of relief in his voice. "I'd forgotten you could do that. Bless Amara and her gifts!"

The others echoed his sentiment, and in single file, they followed Valorian down the stone tunnel. To their amazement, the broad passageway remained high, wide, and fairly straight. Its floor was smooth and level and ran parallel to

the little stream. It was very much like a road delving under
the hills to faraway, unknown destinations.

Although the passage was a natural formation, the men
noticed a great deal of work had been done to enlarge and
smooth the trail. Legends said that the Carrocks were incom-
parable miners and crafters of stone, and from the appearance of their tunnel, the legends were right. Skilled miners
had removed obstructing rock, chiseled away rough spots,
even constructed stone bridges where needed. They had
also apparently tried to preserve the natural beauty of the
caves. The occasional stalactites and stalagmites were carefully preserved, veins of gold or crystal were exposed and
polished to reveal their beauty, and colorful mineral forma-
tions were kept clean of debris and dust. A few passage-
ways, equally as large and well tended, joined or intersected
the road.

Once the riders rode by a stone statue of a squat, manlike
figure standing like a guardian by the side of the road. The
four men passed by wordlessly. They were awed by the
statue, the spacious passageway, and the tremendous
amount of labor that must have gone into the creation of
both. They never knew anything like this existed.

"What are all of these passages?" Aiden mused when they
passed another road intersecting their own.

Valorian peered down it into the impenetrable darkness.
Then he looked up at the high ceiling and walls illuminated
by his lights. He couldn't see anyone or anything, but he
had the strong feeling that he and his party were being
watched. He wondered if they were the first humans to have
ever passed through the Carrocks' domain.

"I don't know," he replied, "but I wouldn't want to come
this way without the Carrocks' permission."

Aiden stifled a shudder that had nothing to do with the
cold, damp air. "Neither would I," he said.

Time passed without measure in the strange, black tunnels. The men began to grow anxious. They stopped twice
to eat and rest the horses before exhaustion finally forced

them to make a brief camp. They fed the horses a little grain and lay down on their blankets and tried to sleep. Unfortunately none of the four men could sleep well. The immense weight of the earth over their heads, the confining stone around them, the stifling darkness, and especially the unseen Carrocks played too heavily on the clansmen's minds. After only a short while, they saddled up and pushed on. Even the thought of fighting snow drifts began to look better than much more of this underground road.

Just as Valorian was about to call another halt, Hunnul nickered. *I see light.* The clansman stared up the passageway until he, too, saw it: the faint, whitish light of day. He whooped with relief. Out went his spheres, and the four men trotted their delighted horses up the road to the mouth of another large cave.

The land was blinding with snow and afternoon sunlight, forcing the men to halt until their eyes grew adjusted to the light. True to the autumn season, the air had turned warmer, and the snow was melting rapidly into puddles and rivulets.

"Where are we?" Gylden called from where he stood outside the cave.

Valorian didn't respond immediately. Instead, he turned and looked back the way they had come. "Thank you!" he shouted into the blackness. There was no reply, nor did he expect one. He simply wanted to voice his gratitude and hoped the Carrocks would understand.

"I know where we are!" Ranulf cried suddenly. His usually serious face shone with excitement as he said to Valorian, "We're in that valley that comes out near the ridge where you were struck by lightning. If we spent two days underground, then that road cut off nearly twenty leagues from our original trail. We even went by that canyon!"

"And it was so much easier," Aiden added. The men grinned at each other. Their anxiety of the underground had vanished in the light, the air, and the pleasure of being so much closer to home.

Four days later they were joyously welcomed back into

the camp by both families. This time it was Gylden and Aiden who fascinated the clanspeople with the tale of the journey, and for many days, the people could talk of nothing but Wolfeared Pass and Carrocks.

Kierla was delighted and relieved to have Valorian back. As a gift, she gave him a cloak she had made from the lion pelt. It was heavy, warm, and silky soft, with the hood made from the lion's head. Valorian hugged her fiercely in gratitude.

The winter settled in in earnest after the first big storm melted away. Kierla's time quickly approached. The end of the year was quietly celebrated on the dawn of the winter solstice, and the clanspeople began to look forward to spring.

Shortly after noon, five days after the new year began, Kierla went into labor. In Clan custom, she retired to a special tent set aside for lying-in, with only her sister and Mother Willa in attendance. Valorian was left to pace and worry outside. To everyone's surprise, Valorian's father's prediction that Kierla would be a good breeder turned out to be accurate. Despite her age, Kierla easily gave birth to a healthy, kicking boy just as the sun set beyond the canyon walls.

Clan law dictated that she had to remain in the lying-in tent for ten more days. The baby, however, had to be blessed and named immediately so the Harbingers could find him if he died. Mother Willa brought him out, tightly bundled against the night air, and proudly presented him to his father.

Valorian was overwhelmed. With trembling hands, he took his tiny son into his arms, then carried the infant to the priestess of Amara, who was waiting with the water and salt to bless the boy. People from both families crowded around to watch.

As soon as the blessing was over, Valorian raised the baby over his head and shouted to his people, "I, Valorian, accept this child as mine. His name shall be Khulinar, beloved of Amara. Welcome him into the Clan!"

The noise of the cheering penetrated the walls of the tent where Kierla lay waiting for her son to be returned to her. Joy and triumph brought her smile shining to her face. Khulinar's birth had been a wonder to her, but even more marvelous had been the warm, comforting feeling of Amara's presence that had stayed with her through the hardest hours of labor. Kierla knew now with certainty that her son's birth was only the first of many.

11

he winter that year held on with a stubborn determination. The snow fell deep in the mountains,
blocking the trails, covering the meadows, and
keeping the clanspeople close to their camps. The
cold remained steady day after day until everyone wondered
if spring would ever come.

Eventually, though, little by little, subtle changes began to
happen to the land. The clanspeople, being tied so inti-
mately to the natural cycles of their world, recognized every
change and rejoiced in it. Each day the sun rose a minute or
two earlier and lingered a while longer in the sky. The bitterly cold temperatures gradually lost their grip on the snow
and ice. On sunny days, melting snow sent rivulets of water
flowing over the canyon walls to join the small creek at the
bottom. In the lowlands, the rivers began to swell and the
roads turned to mud.

Valorian watched all of these changes with a sense of
mingling worry and happiness. The time to make plans for
the move to the Ramtharin Plains was upon him, and that
gave him great joy, but no one else seemed to be paying
attention. *That* deeply concerned him. Everyone, even Kierla
and Aiden, was involved in his or her own responsibilities
and plans, with little time to discuss leaving Chadar. He rode
out a few times to talk to other families but met with little
success. Most of the people were leery of having a wanted
man in their midst and were in no frame of mind to discuss
an exodus. It was very frustrating. Valorian didn't give up,
though. He knew he had to keep trying. Perhaps when the

weather warmed and the clanspeople felt the urge to travel
again, he could grab their attention.

In the meantime, the unusually heavy snows and cold
weather had kept the Tarns in their homes and made life a
little easier for Valorian and his family. That, he knew,
would change with the first big thaw. He imagined Tyrranis
was not pleased with the soldiers' lack of success in finding
him. By spring, he was afraid Tyrranis's search for him
would be renewed with a vengeance.

*   *   *   *   *

"Not pleased" was putting Tyrranis's mood mildly. In fact,
he was enraged. For three months, his servants, aides, and
officers had stepped very carefully around the volatile general. One wrong move, one imagined slight or mistake could
send a person to the dungeon cells beneath the old Chadarian garrison tower—or worse. Tyrranis railed against the stupidity and incompetence of his soldiers and threatened
executions if Valorian was not brought to him by early summer at the latest. He wasn't going to lose this man through
the blundering of his underlings.

As soon as men and horses could travel through the snow
and mud of the lower foothills, he started sending scouts out
to search for the winter camps of the Clan. He knew the
families couldn't leave their camps until the trails dried
enough to allow carts and herds to travel, so he hoped to
find some clue or information that would lead him to the
elusive clansman.

To make matters more interesting, he had it announced all
through Chadar that he was offering a large reward in gold
for the capture, or information leading to the capture, of Valorian. Tyrranis hoped the lure of gold would loosen the
tongues of the impoverished clanspeople.

Then, late one windy night in the fourth month of the
year, his offer of a reward reaped results. A Tarnish scout
came galloping into the courtyard of Tyrranis's palace with

another man clinging behind his saddle. He demanded to see the general immediately, and the officer of the guard, seeing the ragged clansman with him, escorted him to Tyrannis without hesitation.

As usual, the general was working late on the endless details necessary to running the large province. Tyrranis was a ruthless man, but he drove himself as hard as he drove others, and his great pride lay in his enormous ability to govern. He glanced up irritably when his officer of the guard pounded on the door and announced himself.

At the general's command, the three men entered, the two Tarns nearly dragging the reluctant clansman.

"What is it?" snarled the general. His fastidious side hoped the smelly, filthy clansman wasn't the Valorian who had reputed magic powers and had eluded his best men for so long.

"I found him coming down out of the hills, sir," the scout said breathlessly. "He says he has information and wants to claim the reward."

Tyrranis pinned his dark stare on the clansman. It was impossible to tell the man's age because he was so ragged, bearded, and covered with mud. He was probably one of those foul exiles even the clanspeople couldn't stand in their midst. "Let's hear what he has to say," the general said to the scout. "Then we'll decide if he has earned the reward."

The clansman smiled a gap-toothed grin and shuffled a step forward. "Oh, I've earned it all right, Yer Highness. I know where Valorian is!"

Tyrranis didn't deign to reply. He sat at his desk, his arms crossed, his face haggard-looking in the light cast by the oil lamp on the table. Outside, the wind gusted to a roar, rattling the shutters and blowing tiles off the roof.

There was a long pause while the clansman stared nervously around him until the thought of the gold in his hands shored up his courage.

"I know Valorian, you see," he finally muttered. "Big man. Son of Daltor. Daltor didn't like me. He arranged it so I was exiled seven years ago. The stinking—"

"Get on with it!" growled General Tyrranis. He was growing impatient with this fool.

The clansman started with fear and stumbled over his next words in his hurry to be away from there. "I, uh, saw him—Valorian that is—five days ago, riding that big black horse of his. Hard to miss that horse. So I followed him. At a distance. He went into Gol Agha and rode up the canyon for a long way. They're camped in there, General. The whole family. Valorian's with them." He stared eagerly at Tyrranis, but if he was hoping for some sign of excitement or praise, he was disappointed.

The general only turned to the scout. "Can you find this Gol Agha?"

"Yes, General," the scout answered.

"Good." Tyrranis shot a quick glance over the clansman's shoulder to the guards standing by the door and barely nodded.

"What about my reward?" the exile demanded, holding out a grubby hand. "Isn't my news worth something?" He was so anxious to get his gold he didn't see the guardsman slip up behind him.

There was a quick flash of steel and the sound of a thud, and the clansman slowly sagged to the floor, a dagger buried between his ribs.

"Now he cannot go back and sell a warning to Valorian," Tyrranis said with heavy contempt. He gestured to the body. "Remove that."

Just as the guards were dragging the body out the door, the garrison commander hurried in and saluted his general. He didn't give the corpse a second glance. The commander was a very anxious man these days, for he was responsible for the success or failure of the search for Valorian.

"Did he have any news?" the commander asked, trying not to appear too hasty.

"Gol Agha," Tyrranis replied. He rose to mask the sudden excitement that filled him and strode to the fireplace. The

light of the flames flickered over his harsh face. "Go there,"
he ordered the scout. "Find the camp." He turned to the
commander. "Now, as for you," he snarled, "do as we discussed, and do not fail me again."

Both men saluted and hurried out. While the scout went
to find a fresh horse, the commander went to rouse the garrison. The officer wanted every man he could find for this
duty. He didn't intend to let a single clansperson escape
from that camp.

*   *   *   *   *

That same night, the early spring winds were streaming
down the canyon of Gol Agha with the strength of a gale
and the voice of a howling madwoman. The lone rider who
rode its length could hardly believe that any Clan family in
its collective right mind had chosen to camp in this wild
place. It wasn't until he trotted his horse around the curves
and into the comparative peace of the back canyon that he
saw its advantages. He was around the last bend with the
campfires in sight when two guards rode up beside him.
One of them was Valorian's younger brother.

"Mordan!" Aiden cried with pleasure. "What brings you
from our lord chieftain's side?"

"Believe it or not, Lord Fearral sent me," the stocky
guardsman replied jovially. "He wants to talk to Valorian."

"Oh? Another warning? Another dithering?"

Mordan laughed. He had long ago given up being insulted
by the behavior of their chieftain. "I'm not sure. Our lord has
had a rough winter, and he's getting very nervous about
spring."

"He should be!" Aiden grinned and pointed toward the
camp. "Valorian's in his tent."

Mordan was about to ride on when he paused and suggested, "You might want to extend your guards out beyond
that bend in the canyon. If I can find this place, so could
others."

Aiden nodded negligibly, waved, and rode on with his

companion. Mordan's comment was quickly forgotten in the excitement of Lord Fearral's summons.

Mordan found Valorian's tent at the edge of the big camp without too much difficulty. He dismounted and left his horse to munch hay with Hunnul in the shelter at the side of the tent. For just a moment, he stopped to pat the black stallion's neck. The big horse lifted his head, his dark eyes shining, and snorted lightly as if in greeting.

"Mordan!" Valorian called from inside the tent. He stuck his head out the flap. "What are you doing here? Come in out of that wind."

The chieftain's guard gave Hunnul a strange look. How had Valorian known it was him? He shrugged and returned the man's greeting. Following custom, he wiped the mud from his boots and left his sword by the entrance before he entered Valorian's home. He stepped into the warm and pleasant interior. Outside, the wind was blowing in cold, damp gusts strong enough to make the tent walls heave and dance. Inside, rugs on the floor, light-colored wall hangings, and three or four small lamps combined to create a welcoming and snug living place.

Kierla was there, gently rocking her baby in the swinging cradle that hung from the tent poles. She made their guest comfortable with hot spiced wine and pillows and returned to her rocking without missing a step.

"I see the rumors of Amara's blessing are true," he said to her with a pleased grin.

Kierla surprised him by blushing. She looked at her husband proudly. "True and true again," she replied.

Valorian, who was sitting down again polishing tack, chuckled. "The dam has broken, Mordan. There'll be no stopping her now."

The guardsman was nonplussed for a moment until the significance of what they had said sank in. "You're expecting another?" he asked in astonishment. "Already?"

"I have years of childbearing to catch up on," she said, her voice smug with satisfaction.

"Valorian," Mordan said to his host, "you really do have the favor of the Mother Goddess." He went straight to the point then of his message from Lord Fearral.

Kierla looked up excitedly, but Valorian merely nodded and said, "I will come."

The chief's guard hid a smile of satisfaction. He was pleased to see that Valorian wasn't greeting the news with wild expectations. Lord Fearral had had all winter to think about Valorian's plan, but he hadn't explained his reasons for the summons. Valorian was wise not to get carried away by hope that Fearral had changed his mind.

The two men talked for a long while of Lord Fearral, the deteriorating conditions at Stonehelm, and Valorian's journey south to Wolfeared Pass. Valorian explained in detail about the route he and his companions had planned, and he told Mordan everything he could remember about the pass and the land beyond. Unknowingly, his eyes glowed vivid blue with enthusiasm, and his hands fanned the air with excited gestures.

While he talked, Mordan avidly watched his every move and expression. What he saw in Valorian finally satisfied his own lingering doubts. The Clan needed a new leader, of that he was certain, and this tall, quiet clansman had a greater strength and vision than he had ever seen in any man before—a strength that drew Mordan like a hawk to the lure. It didn't hurt, Mordan thought, his eyes straying to Kierla, that Valorian had the blessings of the Mother Goddess as well. Silently and knowingly, Mordan switched his allegiance to Valorian. He would continue to serve Lord Fearral for a while longer to fulfill his promised service. But when Valorian headed south, Mordan vowed he would go with him.

Early the next morning Valorian kissed his wife and son, swung up onto Hunnul's back, and rode with Mordan back down Gol Agha canyon. Gylden and Aiden went with them, since Valorian felt two extra swords and a small show of support wouldn't hurt his image. They left early enough so that by the time they reached the mouth of the canyon the next day, the Tarnish scout had not yet arrived from Actigorium. They rode out of the Place of the Winds and turned north for Stonehelm, unaware of the Tarn who came shortly thereafter.

The scout, weary from several days of constant travel, didn't attach much significance to the fresh tracks he saw in the canyon. Tyrranis had told him to find the camp, not follow a few stray riders, so he cautiously began his search, not knowing the prey had already slipped out of the trap.

Valorian and his escort rode into Stonehelm a few days later only to find that Lord Fearral had been stricken ill. His daughters had confined him to his bed and refused to let anyone talk to him until his fever broke and he was stronger.

Valorian was annoyed by the delay, but since there was little he could do about it, he spent the time walking around Stonehelm and talking to its inhabitants. He quickly saw that Mordan's assessment was accurate. The little village had deteriorated since his visit nearly a year ago. Most of the small pens and corrals were empty; the fields were only partially plowed, and some of the huts and shops were abandoned. The whole place looked neglected and forlorn.

"There's little enough food," one woman told him while her thin little boy clutched her skirts. "We're herders, not farmers."

One man, an old shepherd who loved his sheep as most clansmen loved their horses, put it more forcefully. "That flybrained chieftain sold everything we had and left us nothing to start over. What does he think he's going to do when the tribute comes due again? I say let him sell that precious hall of his. What does a Clan chieftain need with a hall anyway? He's as bad as a Tarn!" he finished gloomily.

When Valorian mentioned leaving Chadar, the old shepherd brightened considerably. "I'd go with you, son. So would most of the people here, with or without Lord Fearral. We're getting tired of staying put and starving. You get the chief to give his permission and the whole town would pack and leave by sundown. I'd wager my last lamb on that."

Other people were not as outspoken as the shepherd, yet their feelings were still evident in their grim faces and their willingness to listen to Valorian. They were tired of pouring their sweat and labor into things that were immediately taken away from them. They were tired of despair and lean bellies.

Their plight saddened Valorian and strengthened his resolve. It also made him more anxious to talk to Fearral and learn what was on his mind. To Valorian's irritation, it was nearly six days before the chieftain was well enough to meet with him.

When his daughters could no longer keep Fearral down, he sent Mordan to bring the three clansmen into the hall shortly after the noon meal on a delightfully warm spring day. The old lord was sitting in his carved chair, moodily sipping a steaming mug of tea. When the men stopped before him and lifted their hands in salute, he eyed Valorian and the three men with him for a long, speculative pause. He noticed immediately that Mordan did not make a move to leave Valorian's side.

Valorian, for his part, returned Fearral's scrutiny. He was rather surprised to see that the lord chieftain actually looked better than he had last spring, in spite of his illness. His eyes were more alert, his hands were steady, and his shoulders were straight, as if a weight had been removed.

The chieftain seemed to read his thoughts. He lifted his mug and smiled dryly. "As you can see, I am not drinking wine or ale. My daughters and a few other people," he said with a significant glance at Mordan, "prevailed upon me to get my head out of the wineskin and look around. It has been difficult, to say the least."

Valorian said nothing, although his heart began to pound. Even Aiden was silent, watching the chieftain with a mingled look of disbelief and hope.

"I asked you to come," Fearral continued, "because I want

to hear about your plan for this exodus you have been talking so much about." He chuckled wearily. "Everyone has heard about you and your journey to the realm of the dead except me."

Fearral's daughters brought chairs and mugs of tea for the chieftain's guests, admonished him not to wear himself out, and left the five men alone in the big hall.

With pleasure, Valorian launched into his tale, complete with full magical effects. This time, though, to Aiden and Gylden's surprise, he went on to include his second journey south to Wolfeared Pass and the trail back over Carrocks Road. His magical visions were so vivid his audience saw the splendid vistas of the Ramtharin Plains, felt the cold of the blizzard, and were awed by the dark beauty of the Carrocks' caverns. When he was finished with his story, he bowed low to his lord and sank wearily into his seat. He had done the best he could to present his case, and he breathed a silent prayer to Amara that it would be enough to convince Fearral.

There was a long moment of silence, then the hall erupted with cheering and clapping. Valorian turned around, startled, and saw the hall filled with clanspeople who had slipped in to hear his story. Fearral's two daughters sat near the front of the crowd, clapping wildly.

Lord Fearral watched the people, his wrinkled face torn by conflicting emotions. He knew what he had to do, but he wasn't sure that he had the strength to go through with it. He was about to rise, when a stunned, faraway look suddenly crossed Valorian's face.

"No!" Valorian shouted fiercely. The people quieted and muttered among themselves at his odd behavior. He bolted to his feet, his face white with a strange fear.

"What is it?" Aiden asked, alarmed.

At that moment, Hunnul charged into the hall, neighing in agitation and scattering people left and right.

"Ranulf is coming," Valorian cried to his brother, and he ran to the doorway.

It was then that they all heard it, a loud despairing wail coming up the road through the town. "*Valorian!*"

"I'm here!" the clansman shouted. He ran outside to meet the young rider, followed by everyone in the hall. The people gasped aloud when Ranulf reined his jaded, staggering horse to a stop by Valorian and both mount and rider fell to the ground.

Valorian sprang forward to help him. He hardly recognized Ranulf under the dirt and soot and splattered blood that covered his face and clothes.

"Valorian! Thank the gods," Ranulf choked out. His hands grasped at Valorian's tunic. With Aiden's help, he was pulled out from under his half-dead horse and laid gently on the ground. He shoved away an offering of water. "Valorian," he cried in a voice drenched in tears, "they're gone. All of them!"

"Who is gone?" Valorian prompted gently, though his stomach was sick with dread and his hands were trembling.

"Everyone! The Tarns came. The whole lousy garrison. They knew where we were. They came looking for you, and when we told them you were gone, they tore the camp apart. We tried to stop them, but they killed anyone who argued. Then they burned everything, drove off the herds, and took everyone who was left."

"What do you mean they took them?" demanded Aiden frantically.

Ranulf's haunted eyes shifted back and forth like a trapped animal's. "The Tarns chained all the clanspeople together and herded them down to Actigorium."

"Why?" Lord Fearral cut in.

"As bait," Valorian said coldly. His face had gone rock hard.

Ranulf nodded. "The commander let me go to find you. He said to tell you they would let everyone go if you would turn yourself in." He clutched Valorian's sleeve in sudden panic. "You won't do that, will you?"

Something suddenly snapped in Valorian's mind. Hunnul

came quickly to his side and waited only a moment for Valorian to spring to his back before he leaped forward down the road, heading for the town gates.

Mordan started to grab the reins of a nearby horse to follow him, but Gylden put his hand out. "You'll never catch that horse," he said sadly. "I know where he's going."

For the first time since they returned from the realm of the dead, Valorian witnessed the full power of his stallion. From the moment he broke into a gallop just outside the gates of Stonehelm until they reached the rocky mouth of Gol Agha, where he had to slow to a jog, Hunnul ran at a constant, ground-eating pace. He didn't slow down, break into a sweat, or show any indication that he was tired. He simply kept going over the leagues of hills and fields like a creature possessed. Numb with unanswered fears, Valorian held on to the black's mane and watched the land streak by while the wind roared through his ears.

It was night when they reached the mouth of Gol Agha. A full moon swelling above the mountains showed Valorian the first sign of the devastation to come. A deep, muddy trail, black in the silver moonlight, marked the passage of the Tarnish troops and their long lines of prisoners. Off to the side of the new trail, in the grass, lay the body of a little girl from Gylden's family. Her clothes were stained with smoke and mud, and her pale face was turned lifelessly toward the starry sky. Valorian swallowed hard.

Hunnul raced on deeper into the canyon. They saw more bodies, some older people, some children—all Valorian recognized—strewn along the way, tossed to the side with broken weapons, abandoned personal belongings, and an occasional dead animal or wrecked cart.

Finally, in the early afternoon, they rounded the bend in the canyon and found the ruins of the winter camp. Its blackened remains were an ugly sore against the warm sunshine and the newly budding trees. The sight sickened Valorian.

"Kierla!" he shouted. Even though he knew if she were there, she would be beyond answering, he couldn't stifle his frantic desire to see her. Hunnul clattered up the trail through the burned and trampled tents to the site of Valorian's tent. The clansman threw himself to the ground. He staggered, his legs stiff from the long ride, and made his way to the ruins of his tent. The entire thing was burned to the ground; everything in it was destroyed. The baby's cradle, Kierla's favorite tea box, their clothes, everything was gone. His only consolation was that there were no bodies among the charred ashes.

For the rest of the day until the evening grew too dark, Valorian searched the camp. What he found left a hard, cold lump in his chest and a rage that settled deep into his bones. The Tarns had left nothing for the survivors to salvage. They had swept through the camp with ruthless, deadly efficiency, destroying every tent and cart, pulling down the corrals and pens. The meager food stores were gone, the horses stolen, and the dogs and the livestock were either slaughtered or driven off.

Worst of all were the murdered clanspeople lying among the ruins of their homes. Valorian found Gylden's father by his tent with an old, rusty sword in his hand and a spear through his chest. The Tarns hadn't been particular about their victims; they had killed anyone who had stood in their way: men, women, and children. Valorian saw his elderly uncle, several of his cousins, Kierla's younger sister with her baby, and numerous other friends and members of both families—perhaps thirty people in all. The ones he did not find were Kierla, Khulinar, Linna, and Mother Willa.

That night he lit a huge bonfire and stood guard over the bodies. They had been dead for five days and already torn by carrion eaters, but Valorian wouldn't let another vulture or wild dog near them before they were properly buried.

Aiden, Gylden, and Mordan found him the next afternoon carefully hauling the bodies to a large bier that he had built in the center of the camp. Wordlessly they looked over the faces of the dead, then bent to help him as he laid the bodies side by side. No one said anything to Valorian. His eyes had a strange, distant look, and his expression was anguished. He didn't greet them; he merely nodded in acknowledgement when they joined him in his heartbreaking task.

When their duty was done, the four men stepped back from the big bier. Gylden chanted the prayers for the dead until his voice grew tight and stumbled to a halt as he looked on his father's face for the last time. Aiden and Mordan finished the prayers in his stead.

Valorian at last raised his hands. He spoke a command, and the entire pile burst into towering flames. He watched the fire burn for a long, long time before he finally broke his silence.

"The Harbingers were busy that night," he said to no one in particular. The other three turned to stare at him, realizing perhaps for the first time that only he among living men really knew what it was to die. He went on, unmindful of their looks. "But I know where they went and how they will fare. We will see them again."

His companions knew he was speaking of the dead, and they all took comfort in his words.

They waited until the smoke had faded and the fire had burned to ashes before they mounted their horses and left the demolished camp. Valorian didn't look back. His thoughts had already moved on to the future and the survivors who were waiting for him in Actigorium.

"Tyrranis has gone too far!" Aiden burst out when they were halfway through the canyon. "It's bad enough that he drives us into poverty and keeps us imprisoned in these forsaken hills. But now he has stooped to murder, pillage, and kidnapping!"

"But what can we do about it?" mourned Gylden. The death of his father and the loss of his beloved family and horses had devastated him.

Mordan glanced thoughtfully at Valorian, but the clansman said nothing. He had turned inward to secret places in his own heart and mind.

When they reached the open mouth of the canyon where the walls fell away to open hills, they came upon something that brought even Valorian up short. Lord Fearral was camped and waiting for them with every man, and some of the women, of fighting age in the Clan. They were all heavily armed and fiercely angry. In a noisy, turbulent crowd, they met the four returning clansmen at the edge of the temporary camp.

Valorian scanned the faces of the men gathered around the chieftain, and his heart leapt with hope. Even Karez was there, looking surly. Solemnly Valorian saluted his lord chieftain. "Word spreads fast," he commented.

"It does when I spread it," Fearral responded, returning the salute. "We saw the smoke two days ago. Were there many?"

"Thirty-two too many," said Valorian.

Fearral winced. "And the rest of them have been taken to Actigorium?"

"It appears so."

The chief lifted his head. "We cannot leave them there. We will work out a way to free them," he promised.

"I have already done that, my lord," Valorian told him softly.

"Oh? And what is that?"

Valorian smiled then, the feral grimace of a hunter about to pounce. "I will turn myself in."

12

alorian, you can't be serious!" Aiden insisted. "That would be suicide."

"And it's not necessary. Every clansman here has sworn vengeance against the Tarns for this hideous attack. We can free the survivors together," stated Lord Fearral.

Valorian didn't reply at once to their pleas. Instead, he gauged the faces of all the men and women around him, from his brother and friends to Karez and people he barely knew by sight. He could judge from their expressions that Fearral was right. They were furious, furious to the point of finally turning on the Tarns. But did they realize the possible consequences of their actions if they went ahead with their plan to attack Actigorium? Tyrranis would have no compunction in retaliating by slaughtering the rest of the Clan. The fate that so many clanspeople had tried to avoid by staying in Chadar could happen anyway.

But would that realization make them change their minds? Valorian doubted that now. The people had been pushed and prodded like caged animals until at last they were beyond reason. All they knew now was that the hated Tarns had dared attack two families, killing or capturing over one hundred people—people who had relatives in every other part of the Clan. No clansperson could stand by and let that mortal insult go unpunished.

What Valorian found ironic was that in one fell blow Tyrranis had succeed in doing what Fearral and Valorian had not—uniting the Clan under a single cause. Valorian immediately saw in this tragedy an opportunity. If he could rescue the prisoners and maintain this fragile unity of the people in the process, they would be much more willing to accept his plan for leaving Chadar. Especially if the Tarns were breathing furiously on their heels.

Deliberately he drew his sword and handed it hilt first to Aiden. "I do not intend to throw myself away on Tyrranis's false promises," he said loudly so all could hear. "We all know he will not keep his word."

Tucking his hands in his belt, Aiden demanded, "Then why go?"

"Because we need to have someone within Actigorium to find out exactly where the prisoners are being held. We will also need several men to infiltrate the city and cause a distraction while others hold the gate." He lifted his head to address the entire crowd. "This will be a dangerous raid. We will be outnumbered and fighting heavily armed men in a city they know well. But we can succeed! The only things we need to free our people are surprise, speed, teamwork, and the will of the gods. Who is with us?"

The entire crowd lifted their weapons in unison. The Clan war cry filled the hills and hollows and rode on the winds of Gol Agha to echo around the ruins of the dead winter camp.

They sat down then, Fearral, Valorian, and the leaders of the other families, to work out the details of their plan. In the end, Aiden reluctantly took Valorian's sword for safekeeping. The night was late, so the clanspeople settled down for a few restless hours of sleep. By the time dawn painted the mountains with its golden light, Valorian was ready to go.

He had washed the soot, dirt, and old bloodstains from his hands and face and shaved his scraggly stubble. He had nothing left but a few weapons, his lion pelt cloak, and a few odds and ends of clothes, all of which he had left behind in Stonehelm, so he brushed off his filthy tunic and leggings and left them as they were. He bade farewell to Lord Fearral and Gylden.

He clasped Mordan's hand and said, "I will see you tomorrow night."

Mordan's fingers tightened around his own. "I will not fail you," the warrior replied.

Last of all, he hugged Aiden with a fierce embrace. The older brother in him couldn't forget one last remonstrance. "Be careful, little brother. Linna will never forgive us if you do anything stupid."

Aiden laughed. "You'll never know I'm there. Just take care that you do not annoy the high and mighty Tyrranis."

"Is it wise to take Hunnul?" Gylden asked worriedly as Valorian swung up onto the stallion's broad back.

"Absolutely." He winked at his friend. "Someone has to rescue our mares."

With a ringing neigh, Hunnul reared, his front hooves slashing the air. As he came down, his powerful hind legs thrust him forward into a gallop, and in moments, he was gone out of sight beyond the crest of a slope.

In the camp, the warriors began to pack and ready themselves for the ride to Actigorium.

The day was bright with a warm wind and scudding clouds, allowing Hunnul to make good time down to the pastured lowlands. His fast canter brought Valorian to the outskirts of Actigorium long before the man was ready. In spite of his brave facade before the men of the Clan, Valorian was apprehensive about meeting the notorious General Tyrranis. He guessed the real reason behind the general's desire to capture him was to learn more about his magic, but Valorian had no intention of revealing any part of his power until the time came to free the hostages. What he was afraid of most was that Tyrranis would resort to torture if he didn't learn what he wanted. If that happened, Valorian couldn't be certain he'd be strong enough to help the surprise attack on the Tarnish garrison. Or even still be alive.

Well, he thought as Hunnul trotted along the stone-paved road toward the main gate of the city, he would have to take his chances. He only had to survive Tyrranis's hospitality until tomorrow night. He looked toward the high city walls, where the late afternoon sunlight glinted off the helmets of the guards walking along the battlements, and he wondered how long it would be before someone realized a clansman was riding into their midst.

The road Hunnul was on was an old one, a major thoroughfare between Actigorium, Sar Nitina, and other cities to the north and south. Dating back to the days before the Tarnish Empire, the road crossed the Miril River and established the town as a busy Chadarian trading center. The invading Tarns had immediately seen the benefits of the town and its intersection of road and river. They had thrown out the Chadarian ruler who occupied the city and proceeded to strengthen and modernize it with fortifications around the city limits, paved roads, aqueducts, improved port facilities, and a large Tarnish garrison of five hundred men, or half a legion, under the command of the provincial governor.

The day that Valorian walked Hunnul along the road was an important one for Actigorium because a big caravan had just arrived from the provinces in the north, and a large market was planned for the next day. The road was crowded with wagons, carts, hawkers, livestock, riders, palanquins, and pedestrians, all making their way to the city to be on hand for the market. Although the rough-looking clansman on the big black horse drew many glances, the Chadarians were too busy with their own prospects to worry about a stray clansman. The other people—the merchants, Sarcithians, travelers, businessmen, and the inevitable thieves and riffraff who gathered at a big market—did not know who Valorian was and couldn't have cared less.

Thus he was able to ride up to the very gates of the city before anyone tried to stop him. The gateway of the main entrance into Actigorium was wide enough for two large freight wagons to pass through side by side, and high enough to allow the tallest hay wagons, banners, or stilt walkers to pass underneath. But it wasn't big enough to avoid traffic jams at market time. The heavy crowd flowed well enough until it reached the narrow bottleneck of the gate, but then it swirled into a tangled, noisy, often angry mob of people and vehicles jostling for position to enter the city. The five Tarnish guards tried their best to direct the crowd through, but they were overwhelmed by the late afternoon rush. They didn't see Valorian until he was already past the walls and through the open gates.

"Sarturian!" he heard one of the soldiers shout. "There's a clansman. He's got a black horse!"

"Hey! You!" a different voice yelled at him over the noise of the traffic. "Stop!"

Valorian pretended he didn't hear. He rode on, leaving the soldiers caught behind in the press of the crowd. There was a sudden blare from a horn at the gate. Three times it sounded, loud and resonant, over the hubbub of the city. Probably a prearranged warning signal, Valorian thought idly. He had come to give himself up, but he wasn't going to make it *that* easy for the Tarns.

Hunnul followed the road on through the city, past crowded tenements, bustling shops and alehouses, stables, private homes and businesses. Valorian wasn't familiar with Actigorium, so his brother had told him the basic layout of the city. In the center, like the hub of a giant wheel, was the huge, permanent open-air market. The main Tarnish garrison was housed in the old Chadarian tower to the north, near the river. The tower was actually a sprawling stone edifice that held an armory, barracks, and dungeons. Near the garrison along the river were the wharves and warehouses. The affluent residential areas, as well as Tyrranis's palace and personal estate, were to the west of the city. The main gate Valorian had just entered was in the south with the major business districts. Valorian knew he had only to follow the road to the market and turn left. If he wasn't accosted along the way, he would eventually reach Tyrranis's heavily guarded front door.

Valorian was rather hoping he could escape the soldiers' vigilance long enough to knock on Tyrranis's front door.

Unfortunately the warning signal from the front gate had alerted the city patrols, and they finally caught up with him in the market. Three separate detachments came cantering along different roads, scattering people in all directions.

"You there, clansman! Stop where you are!" the commander yelled.

Valorian noticed six or seven drawn bows pointed in his direction and the same number of swords in the hands of the men riding down on him. Sighing, he told Hunnul to stop, and he waited for the soldiers to catch up.

In short order, the Tarns had him off his horse, his arms tied behind his back, and his legs in chains, even though Valorian did not offer any resistance. The clansman paled with anger and humiliation.

Hunnul was furious at his master's treatment. He lashed out with his hooves and teeth at anyone who came too close. Valorian managed to shout at the horse to stop before the soldiers shoved a gag in his mouth. The big horse squealed in fury, but he settled down and allowed himself to be roped and haltered.

One night! Valorian heard the stallion call in his head. *That is all I will wait. Then I will get my mares and come for you!*

The clansman was glad for Hunnul's feelings as he watched his horse being led away. The proprietary instincts of the stallion combined with his enhanced intelligence made him a surprise weapon the Tarns wouldn't expect.

Just then the soldiers tied a blindfold over Valorian's eyes, rendering him virtually helpless. This is going too far, he thought as they picked him up and slung him painfully over the back of another horse.

It wasn't easy bringing his temper and composure back under control while bumping like a sack of grain on a pack-horse through crowds of jeering people, but through sheer willpower, Valorian was calm by the time the troop of soldiers trotted their horses into the spacious courtyard of Tyrranis's palace. He managed to retain his control while they dragged him off the horse and shoved him, stumbling and blind, toward the porticoed front entrance.

The next thing he knew, he was in what sounded like a large room full of the noises of running feet, shouted orders, and excited voices.

Suddenly slow, measured footsteps came toward him, and the room fell silent. The blindfold was yanked off Valorian's eyes. The first thing he saw was a hard, bony face of harsh angles and menacing, deep-set eyes staring at him from only a handspan away. He forced down an urge to shudder and met the eyes glare for glare.

"Remove the gag," the face said, "but keep your weapons on him."

The soldier to Valorian's right tentatively pulled the gag out of his mouth. The clansman glanced around at the ten or eleven soldiers clustered around him and was startled to see how tense they all seemed. Rumors of his magic had obviously spread.

"Who are you?" snarled the man in front of him.

From his full armor and his commanding attitude, Valorian guessed this was General Tyrranis. "I am the one you have been seeking. I understand you wanted to see me," Valorian replied, his voice level.

"We have wanted to see you since last autumn," Tyrranis said sardonically.

"Why didn't you just ask? It wasn't necessary to slaughter my family."

"But it worked."

Valorian curled his lip. "Yes. So now I am here, and if you would be so kind as to honor your word and let go the people you hold, I would be grateful."

"I'm sure, but I did not give my word. My commander did, and I feel no need to keep *his* promises."

Valorian didn't expect anything else, but he knew he had to react or the Tarns would grow suspicious. He struggled against his bonds. "What do you mean?" he cried. "I came in good faith to exchange my family for myself, and now you will not free them?"

"Exactly." Tyrranis smiled like a snake. "I still have need of them."

Valorian lunged forward, his face twisted in rage, but he got only about a foot before the soldiers dragged him down and gagged him again.

Tyrranis hadn't moved. "Take him downstairs," he ordered. Four men grabbed Valorian by the arms and legs and hauled him unceremoniously out of the big room, through several corridors, down two flights of steps, and into a much smaller, darker room. At Tyrranis's order, they chained the prisoner, hand and foot, spread-eagled against the cold stone wall. Then they left him alone with Tyrranis.

For once in his life, Valorian was sorry to see Tarnish soldiers leave. He watched Tyrranis suspiciously as the general went slowly around the room, lighting thick candles on sconces along the walls. Slowly the room grew brighter until Valorian was able to recognize it as some sort of workroom. There was a floor-to-ceiling cabinet of shelves and drawers on the left side of the room, a large table in the center, and a wooden chair and writing desk on the right. Over every available surface lay piles of scrolls, sheets of vellum bound or loose, writing instruments, and intricate tools Valorian did not recognize. The shelves were full of racks of vials and bottles of colorful liquids, wooden boxes of every size, bags, bowls, a mortar and pestle, and more instruments of unknown function. Strangest of all was a curious design someone had drawn on the floor under the space where Valorian hung. It was an eight-sided star surrounded by a red circle.

"You see my artwork," the general said, pointing to the floor. His expression was gloating. "It is an ancient ward against evil magic. You cannot use your power while you stay within its bounds."

That was nonsense, but Valorian wasn't going to disillusion the general this soon. Instead, he widened his eyes and tried to look surprised.

Tyrranis very deliberately removed his sword belt, the

breastplate, and his military cloak and laid them carefully aside. Then he brought out a pair of leather gloves and slowly began to pull them on, one finger at a time. "Now," he said with cold malice, "let us discuss magic."

Valorian's mouth went dry. "What do you mean?" he managed to ask.

The general picked up a short, heavy club and came to stand in front of his prisoner. His muscles were tense, as if his body were tightly coiled beneath his knee-length tunic. "Magic," he hissed. "The power of the immortals." Without warning, he brought the heavy club smashing down on Valorian's upper right arm.

The clansman stiffened in pain; his jaw clamped shut. The blunt instrument hadn't broken his arm, but it felt as if it had. Valorian strained vainly against his chains, but the soldiers had pulled them tight, leaving him stretched flat against the wall with no room to escape Tyrranis's attentions. Queasy with fear, he stared as the general raised the club again.

"We have all night, clansman," Tyrranis informed him. "You will tell me the secret of your magic, or it will be a long night indeed." And the club swung down viciously once more.

* * * * *

Through a black haze of pain, Valorian heard new sounds intrude into the deathless silence. There was a faint click and a grind as someone opened the door into the room. He didn't try to look up. He didn't dare move for fear of setting off the seizures of agonizing pain that swept through his arms, legs, and abdomen every time he so much as flinched.

"General?" he heard someone say tentatively.

"What is it?" that hated voice answered.

"You asked to be called for the opening ceremonies for market day. They're about to begin. The dignitaries are waiting."

"Fine." The general rose from his chair where he had been brooding and came to stand in front of Valorian. Deliberately he pulled off his gloves finger by finger.

The clansman risked the onslaught of spasms again to raise his head and glare at Tyrranis through battered eyes. For a long moment, the two clashed eye to eye before Valorian's muscles rebelled against the abuse they had taken and seized into uncontrollable, frightening waves of pain. He arched in his chains, his teeth clenched, his fingers clawing at the walls.

Tyrranis watched him impassively until the agony gradually loosened its hold and Valorian was still.

Behind the general, the Tarnish commander swallowed hard to hide his pity. "What about him?" he asked.

"This man is a fraud," Tyrranis snapped irritably. "Take him to the other prisoners. Tomorrow we'll provide some entertainment for the market crowds. A slave auction and perhaps some wild animal baiting. See if the beastmaster has a few wolves or lions who could use a good meal." He leaned forward to snarl at Valorian, "Our friend here will be the guest of honor at my side. He can watch until the end. Then nail him to the city wall."

When Valorian didn't react, Tyrranis grunted in annoyance, turned on his heel, and strode out of the room.

The commander called in several guards, and together they unfastened the shackles around the clansman's bloodied wrists and ankles. Valorian would have liked to have stayed on his feet and walked from the room, but his bones buckled and he sagged to the floor, moaning.

"Better get a litter. The man's not fit to walk," the commander ordered.

While the two men hurried to obey, Valorian lay on the cold floor, thankful that Tyrranis was gone and that he was still alive. He remained as still as he could and willed his muscles to slowly relax. He had never hurt so much in his life. He made no protest when the soldiers came back and lifted him onto the litter. To his surprise and gratitude, they were gentle and careful not to jar him.

Quickly they carried him up the stairs, out of the palace, and into the bright morning sun.

Morning? The fact burst on Valorian as bright as the sunlight. He closed his eyes against the glare and groaned. He had been in the room with Tyrranis all night. It had seemed like a hideous eternity.

After a time, the motion of the litter and the knowledge that he was away from Tyrranis for a while lulled him into a state of lethargy. He was cold and nauseated. His wrists and ankles were cut and bleeding from the chains, his limbs were battered, his muscles were torn and bruised, and he ached everywhere. He hoped if he could just lie motionless for a time, the racking seizures would not return. He didn't look to see where they were going; he didn't hear the busy racket from the crowded streets as the Chadarians gathered in town for the market. Nothing penetrated his daze until all at once, a familiar voice yelled something in Chadarian near his head.

Surprised, he opened his eyes and stared into the face of a drunken Chadarian farmer, holding a flagon of ale in one hand and a chicken leg in the other. The man was gesturing rudely at the clansman with the chicken leg and staggering alongside the litter while shouting something at the top of his lungs. It suddenly sank into Valorian's befuddled mind that he knew that man. It was Aiden. He had just enough time to give his brother a slow wink and see the slight nod of relief before the guards shoved Aiden back toward an alehouse and hurried on their way. Valorian's eyes closed again and he relaxed, reassured by his brother's presence.

A short time later they reached the tower on the high banks of the Miril River. The fortified complex was an old, hulking mass of stone that had seen better days. Its walls were pitted and worn, and its roof was in need of repair. A square, squat tower, the one that gave the building its name, guarded the front entrance. There were no windows on the first floor of the large edifice and only four doors. The main

entrance was the only one wide enough to allow the men
and the litter to pass through.

Valorian heard the sound of horses as he was carried into
the forecourt of the tower. He opened his eyes to see if he
could find Hunnul, but there was only a stable close by that
housed mounts for messengers and scouts. There had to be
corrals near the garrison for other horses, he reasoned.
Maybe Hunnul was there.

He kept his eyes open while they went through the tower
and entered a long, narrow hallway. The place was quite
busy with soldiers passing back and forth, sentries at their
posts, officious-looking civilians hard at work. Doors and
other corridors opened onto the hall, revealing offices, a soldiers' mess, and other rooms foreign to Valorian. The soldiers carrying his litter followed the main passage to a
heavily barred door at the end guarded by a stocky watchman. The watchman took a look at Valorian and impassively
drew a key to let them in.

Down they went on a long, echoing stone staircase dimly
lit by torches. The air was heavy and oppressive with cold,
damp, and the smell of rot. The dungeons of the old tower
were dug deep into the foundations, where the light of day
couldn't penetrate. Because of the proximity to the river, the
walls seeped with moisture, and the floors were often slick
with slime and standing puddles.

At the bottom of the stairs was a short passage with
barred doors lining both sides. Valorian could see the cells
weren't large, but he guessed from the volume and variety
of noise that the entire group of nearly one hundred hostages
was crammed into those foul rooms.

Except for a few meager torches along the walls, the
dungeon was miserably dark. The sound of footsteps and
the arrival of new torches drew everyone's attention. Faces
crammed into the barred doorways, and voices whispered
nd muttered in the gloom. "Who is that?" they asked each
other.

Then someone yelled, "Kierla! It's Valorian!" and the

whole dungeon filled with cries, shouts, and pleas.

"Shut up, you dogs!" shouted the commander.

His order did little good. The people were desperate, and Valorian was their first sign of hope. By pure chance, the guards opened the last cell door where Kierla and perhaps twenty others were imprisoned. They shoved the clans-people back, dumped the litter on the floor, and beat a hasty retreat away from the uproar, the stink, and the darkness.

Valorian felt his beloved's arms around his shoulders and her fingers gently probing his face and limbs. He knew he was safe with her. Sighing once, he closed his eyes and let sleep steal him away.

The day passed slowly for those in the dungeon and those who waited scattered around the city or hidden in the fields beyond the walls. The sun crept with nerve-racking slowness past noon, midafternoon, and finally into evening. In the cells, the people didn't see the sun sink below the horizon, but their bodies sensed it, and their stomachs cried with hunger.

It was the clang of iron pots that brought Valorian out of his healing sleep. Guards were bringing big kettles of soup to each cell. Kierla felt him stir, and her heart leapt with relief. She brought him a bowl of the soup, lifted his head, and carefully fed him the entire helping. He would have liked more, despite its watery taste and the lack of anything in it resembling food, but the pots were already empty and being carried away.

Ever so slowly, Valorian sat up on the litter. The rest, the food, and his natural strength had worked together in a small miracle of recuperation. He could move again with only stiffness and aching accompanying his motions. The agonizing muscle spasms were gone, and he was fortunate that nothing was broken. He wondered if General Tyrranis was finicky about blood. That might explain why the general was so adept at causing pain without drawing blood, and why he wore gloves.

"What happened to you, Valorian?" Kierla whispered.

"What are you doing here?"

He chuckled in the darkness. "I turned myself in so Tyrranis would let all of you go."

Kierla sucked in her breath. Her fingers tenderly touched a swelling on his cheek. "Tyrranis did this? That monster! He must have beaten you half the night."

"About that."

"Well, why did you turn yourself in?" one of his cousins said gruffly. "You should have known Tyrranis would never keep his word to a clansman."

"I knew that."

"They why are you here?" someone else asked. Valorian lay back down on his litter. "Just wait," he said softly. "Wait for the red star to rise above the mountains."

The people around him grumbled a little about cracked heads and settled down as best they could to sleep. No one took him seriously.

Valorian didn't mind. He took his own advice and waited. Kierla gave him Khulinar to hold while she tried to rest. He held the infant close to his side on the litter, letting his battered muscles rest. He had no sky to watch or anything other than his own ingrained ability to mark the passage of time, yet when the hours had passed into late night, he knew the time had come. The red star was rising.

He gave the baby back to his wife and very carefully sat up. Kierla wrapped the infant in her sling and, without question, helped Valorian to his feet. He swayed for a moment, then steadied himself on Kierla's arm and took a step. His body felt heavy and unwieldy, and every muscle protested as he moved, but everything worked. With Kierla at his side, he painfully made his way over the dozing prisoners to the barred door. The cell was too dark to see what he was doing, so he formed a small globe of light.

The effect was galvanizing. Every person in the cell sprang to his feet, his mouth wide open. Without looking at his companions, Valorian studied the door a moment. He placed his fingers against the lock, formed his spell, and used the magic to turn the lock into a small pile of rust. He pushed the door open with one finger. Only then did he turn to the stunned people behind him and say, "Time to go."

One by one, he used his spell to open all the cell doors wide until every clansperson and a few stray Chadarian prisoners were crowded into the passage. The people were startled by their sudden freedom, and they crowded close to Valorian as he led them quietly up the stairs. Near the top, he motioned them to stop. Through the large, iron-bound door, he could hear sounds that made him smile. He had timed it perfectly. The garrison was in an uproar of running feet, shouting voices, and blaring horns. Aiden and his men must have begun their diversions on schedule.

Valorian made the clanspeople wait until the noise beyond the door had dropped to a more normal level. As soon as it was quiet beyond the door, Valorian gently turned the lock to rust and eased open the door a crack. The watchman on the other side stood looking down the corridor. He never saw the door opening or felt the spell that put him to sleep. As his body sagged to the floor, Valorian stepped into the passageway.

The hall at that moment was empty, and there was no sign of other guards. A few torches flickered along the stone corridor, sending shadows dancing along the walls.

Frightened, elated, and nervous, the clanspeople hurried along the passage toward the front entrance. Because of the alarms in the city, only the usual sentries were roaming the building and the grounds. Valorian used magic to put every guard he saw to sleep, giving them no chance to sound an alarm. He was grateful there weren't many Tarns to deal with, for the beating he had taken the night before had left him with little strength to control the magic. Even the simple spells he had used on the locks and the guards had seriously weakened him.

As soon as he and his people were out the front door, Valorian pointed to the garrison stables. "Some of you get those horses. Hitch them to any wagon you can find. Hurry! The rest of you stay here. Lord Fearral will be coming any moment."

The younger men obeyed with alacrity. The few Chadarian prisoners chose that moment to take to their heels. No one tried to stop them.

"Look!" someone shouted, pointing toward the center of the city.

Not far to the south, a ruddy gold glow illuminated the city's outline against the night sky, revealing a great column of smoke that billowed toward the stars. Valorian grinned. Aiden and his men had planned to light a fire in the city as a diversion for the Tarnish garrison. From the intensity of the ruddy light, the fire must be a big one.

At that moment, there was the sound of shouts and fighting from the stables. Before Valorian could get there, though, the noises quickly died away and several harnessed pairs of horses were led out of the stable by some of the clansmen. The men were carrying Tarnish swords and looking satisfied.

"We ran into a patrol," one called cheerfully to Valorian as they headed for some wagons parked by the stable wall. Rapidly the horses were hitched, and the first of the women, children, and elders were lifted into the vehicles. Other horses were brought out and saddled until the stable was empty. Still there was no sign of Tyrranis's troops or Lord Fearral's men.

Valorian was growing anxious. There wouldn't be much time before the garrison began to realize something more than just a chance fire was happening. If they got the slightest warning that the clanspeople were trying to flee, they would seal Actigorium like a trap. There would be no escape for anyone.

Then everyone stiffened to listen. They could hear the sound of a large party cantering toward the tower from the north gate road. Valorian ran forward to head off the horsemen. He whistled three times to signal them, and to his intense relief, they whistled back. Lord Fearral himself led the party of men, extra horses, carts, and wagons into the forecourt of the tower.

The people of the Clan cheered to see each other. Without further ado, the rest of the prisoners were placed in wagons or mounted on horseback. In a matter of only a few minutes, the entire party was ready to leave.

There was only one thing left for Valorian to do. Concentrating all his will in one call, he shouted at the top of his voice, "Hunnul!"

Loud and strong, the call went out, and to the surprise of everyone, it was answered from far, far away. A neigh, triumphant and proud, came in reply on the wind, and after it came a distant, muffled thundering. The clanspeople waited expectantly, although they weren't sure what they were waiting for.

Then their answer came on the flying hooves of a large stampede of horses. With Hunnul at their rear, driving them on, the entire herd of horses from the Tarnish army corrals came careering along the road. The stolen Clan mares were there as well as army mounts and workhorses. Neighing wildly, their eyes rolling in fear at the fierce black stallion at their heels, their manes tossing in the wind, they swept by the waiting people in a tumbling wave of browns, blacks, and ghostly whites.

Hunnul charged up to Valorian, halted, and threw himself upward in a mighty rear, his hooves high over the man's head. He came down with a thud and paused just long enough for Valorian to mount.

"Let's go!" shouted Lord Fearral. The excited horses surged forward after the disappearing herd. The entire cavalcade of horses, riders, and vehicles galloped headlong on the stone-paved road through the city toward the northern gate. They were passing through an area that was predominantly storehouses and open lots, but the loud rumbling of their passing still drew the attention of people scattered through the area. Shouts rose up behind them, and from somewhere in the night, a signal horn sang out a warning. The fleeing clanspeople paid little heed. They held on for dear life and urged their horses on as fast as the animals could go.

The northern gate wasn't far from the garrison tower, and it was as large as the gate to the south. Unfortunately Valorian knew it would still take a little time to get the wagons and horses through. He prayed to the gods that Mordan and his men still held the gate and that the Tarns were too busy elsewhere to organize an attack.

A loud cheer came from ahead as the city walls loomed before the stampeding horses. The gates were wide open, with Mordan, Gylden and ten men standing to either side. Three dead Tarnish legionnaires lay in the shadows of the gate.

Valorian urged Hunnul over to where his friends were waiting. Both men were grinning at the stream of horses pouring past them. They saw Valorian and waved in evident relief.

"Better hurry," Mordan shouted, his sword in hand. "We killed the sentries, but I've heard signal horns in all directions. There'll be Tarns swarming all over this place in a moment." He took a closer look at Valorian and winced. "Good gods, what happened to you?"

"Tarnish hospitality," replied Valorian over the thunder of hooves. He pointed to the blood on Mordan's tunic. "What about you?"

"Not mine," came Mordan's terse reply. "Go on and get those wagons out of here. We meet at Stonehelm, right?"

"Yes! Everyone!"

"Until then!" Mordan shouted, and Hunnul dashed away.

Although the clanspeople tried to maintain an orderly retreat, it took time to sort out the wagons, carts, and riders in the darkness and keep them moving in a steady flow through the exit. It wasn't long before Tarnish soldiers appeared on the battlements above and in the streets behind them. There weren't enough men to dare a charge against Lord Fearral and his mounted warriors standing as the rear guard, so they hid behind walls and corners and began to pepper the fleeing wagons with arrows. People screamed and shouted as several arrows scored hits, and the remaining wagons crowded toward the exit on the verge of panic.

Valorian rode back to join Fearral in the rear. He felt terribly sore and tired, and he had no weapons, but he still had a little strength left. As soon as Lord Fearral pointed out the scattered Tarnish warriors lurking in the shadows, Valorian aimed several bolts of magical energy into the walls and stonework near the soldiers' heads. The Tarns were so stunned by the sight of the brilliant blue bolts and the explosions of sparks, they ducked out of sight.

Even the clansmen who saw the bolts gasped with shock. Everyone had seen Valorian's magic in his tale, but few had accepted its real power.

Meanwhile the rest of the clanspeople hurried through the gateway in a steady stream of wagons and riders. The rear guard drew in behind them, and Mordan and his men retrieved their mounts and joined Lord Fearral. At last Valorian saw the final hostages pass through the gate, and he breathed a silent prayer of thanks.

Just as he and the rear guard were about to withdraw, a small troop of Tarnish horsemen came galloping along the north road in response to the earlier signal horns. Torchlight flickered on the tips of their spears and the polished metal of their light armor. They didn't hesitate at the sight of the slightly larger force but lowered their spears and charged out of the darkness head-on into the clansmen. Their attack was so sudden, Valorian had no chance to use his power in defense.

Two Clan warriors fell to the spears before the others closed in furiously with sword, axe, and shield. The gateway turned into a struggling, writhing mass of fighting men and frantic horses. Without a weapon, Valorian could only hang on while Hunnul used his hooves and teeth to keep the enemy away from his rider.

Angrily Valorian searched his mind for some spell he could use against the Tarns, only to realize that his magic would be too dangerous. The Tarns and clansmen were too close together for simple explosive bolts, and Valorian knew he was too exhausted to manipulate any spell more complicated. All he could do was hang on while his companions fought for their lives. He saw Gylden close by, struggling hand to hand with a stocky legionnaire. Mordan was by Fearral's side, defending his lord's back.

All at once Lord Fearral gave a great shout, and the officer of the Tarnish horsemen fell, the chieftain's axe in his crushed skull. The soldiers faltered.

Valorian sensed an advantage and raised his hand toward the night sky. A brilliant, sparkling ball of magic soared into the air to explode overhead in a shower of golden red sparks. Everyone instinctively ducked, and the Tarns, outfought and without a leader, fled into the safety of the night.

The clansmen cheered wearily. Quickly they gathered their dead warriors and trotted toward the gate, but they had forgotten about the Tarns on the battlements. The sentinels, armed with the army's powerful composite bows, ran to the arrow loops that looked down on the arched entrance and hurriedly loosed every missile they had.

The flight of arrows swarmed down on the rear guard as they passed underneath. Most of the bolts fell harmlessly behind the horses, and a few whizzed past Fearral's men to stick in the dirt. Only one flew straight and true toward the last four clansmen to leave the city. Out of the darkness, the shaft came as if guided by an unseen hand. With deadly vengeance, it flew past Mordan's head and struck deep into Lord Fearral's neck.

13

alorian and Mordan saw the chieftain lurch sideways on his horse. Sick with fear, the guardsman reined his mount over and caught Fearral just as he was about to fall. Valorian came up on the other side, taking the reins from the chieftain's motionless hands.

Fearral was still alive for the moment, but all three men knew he wouldn't survive for long. A steady stream of blood flowed from the wound where the arrow had nicked an artery. The arrow itself, still lodged in his neck, kept the blood from spurting out. Fearral couldn't talk; instead, he jerked his hand to motion the men away. The two ignored him. Neither of them would abandon their lord while he was still alive.

They trotted the horses forward through the gate, both men supporting Fearral. In a final gesture, Valorian half-turned just outside the city walls and launched a blast of magic at the top of the gateway. The stonework exploded under the powerful blow and came tumbling down into a massive heap of rubble and debris where the gate used to be. Silence and dust settled over the wreckage. Mordan stared at the wall in awe before Valorian hurried him away with the chieftain.

Fearral's other guards and a few warriors had slowed to stay with them. The main body of the clanspeople had galloped on ahead. As planned, the people were to follow the Miril River east for a few leagues, then split up into smaller parties and scatter into the hills to confuse the Tarnish troops who would surely follow. If all went well, the entire

Clan was to meet at Stonehelm to plan their next move.

The night was growing late by the time the last of the rear guard left the river and rode for the hills. Valorian glanced back once at the distant city. He could still see the faint glow of a fire outlining Actigorium's horizon. It was unlikely, but he hoped with all his heart that General Tyrranis was roasting in those flames. A shudder shook his frame at the memory of that horrible, helpless night in Tyrranis's room. He didn't think he could ever go through anything like that again. He thought, too, of Aiden down there somewhere. Aiden and three other men had volunteered to infiltrate the city, set the fires, and slip out in the confusion. They had obviously been successful with the first two objectives, and Valorian could only pray that Aiden would succeed in the third.

Weary and aching, he turned back to the task of helping Lord Fearral. The old chieftain was failing fast. Blood covered his side, and his skin was deathly pale. He could no longer hang on to his horse.

Near daybreak, the warriors with Fearral found a thick copse of trees in the fold of a hill. They took their lord into the sheltering grove, gently lifted him from his horse, and laid him on his cloak. Valorian, Mordan, and the others gathered around him. They didn't try to remove the arrow, since that useless gesture would have only caused more pain.

He lay motionless as his life's blood slowly trickled into the cloak. His eyes flickered once when the sun pierced the dawn sky and lit the trees with gold and green. One of Fearral's hands groped out for another human hand, and Valorian clasped it tightly.

"The Harbingers will come soon," he said softly in Fearral's ear. "Do not fear them. Go in honor, my lord."

A fleeting smile touched the old man's mouth, and he was gone.

Valorian tilted his head. Somewhere on the furthest edges of his senses, he fancied he heard the faint pounding of hooves from the Harbingers' steeds as they came to escort Lord Fearral to the realm of the dead.

Wordlessly the Clan warriors wrapped the body of their chief in his cloak and tied him to his horse. There was now one more dead man to take home to the Clan. Without a conscious decision, they automatically fell in behind Valorian as he and Hunnul led the way back into the Bloodiron Hills.

At noon, the sad entourage approached the massive granite dome of Stonehelm. News of Fearral's death had obviously been passed along by the sentinels, for the entire population came out to the meet the riders. All of the raiding party and the escaped hostages, except for Aiden and his men, had arrived ahead of them, and most of the Clan families had also come to Stonehelm. They all lined the road, their faces stricken at the loss of their chieftain and awed at the sight of the man with the incredible power who had helped two families escape from a fortified city and the entire Chadarian garrison.

Fearral's two daughters ran down the trail, their faces white with fear. When they saw their father's body, they broke into wails of grief that were taken up by everyone present.

Through the lamenting voices, past the town he had tried to build, to the hall that was his pride, the warriors escorted their dead chieftain. They laid him out on a trestle table in front of his carved chair with his cloak spread beneath him and his weapons at his side.

Customarily the Clan buried its chieftains in burial mounds, but this time Fearral's eldest daughter stepped up to Valorian and suggested something different.

The men around her looked shaken.

"Burn him in the hall?" Valorian asked. "Why?"

The woman lifted her chin. She was a plain, forthright young woman who had chosen to care for her widowed father instead of marrying. Her intelligence was equal only to her pride. "The hall was my father's choice, not the Clan's," she answered honestly. "Now that we must leave Chadar with you, I do not wish to abandon the hall for anyone else to claim."

"Leave Chadar!" someone exploded. "Who said anything about leaving Chadar?" Karez pushed his way through the gathering of men and thrust his bulk at the woman, as if to shove her aside.

She glared at him, refusing to budge. "It is obvious, Karez," she said impatiently. "Our time here is over. We must move on before the Tarns finish what they began with our grandfathers."

"Don't be ridiculous, woman," he bellowed. The raised voices had drawn clanspeople into a large crowd in front of the hall. They were worried, upset, and fearful of the future, and now they had no chieftain to guide them. Karez decided this was an excellent time to make his move. He pushed in front of Valorian and raised his hands to placate the anxious people.

"There will be no leaving Chadar. The Tarns are angry now, but they'll come to their senses and see that it would be wiser to let us remain as we are," he said.

"Why?" Valorian asked calmly. He stood, his arms crossed, his bruised and battered face impassive. He was nearly shaking with fatigue, yet he could see now very clearly where his path lay. Aiden had been right. In order to take his people to a new land, he had to become the lord chieftain—which would certainly mean confronting Karez. He had known for a long time that Karez had ambitions to be chieftain, but the reality of such an occurrence hadn't been important until now. If Karez declared himself chief, Valorian would have to challenge him to the traditional duel. Unfortunately Karez hadn't gone to Actigorium. He had stayed behind with a small contingent of men to help protect the families. He was rested, healthy, and as strong as a bear.

Valorian, on the other hand, had had little rest or food for over seven days. He had been severely beaten, his muscles were pulled and strained from the chains, and his strength was depleted by the magic he had used to escape from Actigorium. He knew too well that he was in no condition to fight a physical battle. Yet nothing on earth would make him back down now.

"Why?" repeated Karez, snorting at the ludicrousness of the question. "We grow the meat that feeds them and raise the horses that serve them. In our own way, we are important to them."

"I'm tired of feeding *their* bellies," a man yelled from the crowd. The others muttered among themselves, and several agreed loudly.

"We have nothing to worry about from the Tarns. This little incident will blow over," Karez declared. "We will pay our tribute, and they will be placated."

"Little incident!" Valorian bellowed. He came around from behind the big, burly clansman, his eyes crackling and his expression furious. "You call the murder and imprisonment of two families a 'little incident'? What would you call the massacre of the whole Clan, a small setback? Open your eyes, Karez. Tyrranis will never let us get away with that raid on Actigorium. We've outlived our usefulness. We're worth more to his prestige dead!"

"It's *you* he really wants," Karez shouted in return. "As lord chieftain, I will see that you are turned over with our tribute to General Tyrranis—dead or alive. There is no reason to sacrifice the Clan for one man."

"What did you say?" Valorian demanded, his voice deadly cold.

Karez did not reply. Instead, he faced the people, drew his sword, and lifted it hilt first toward the sky. "Before Surgart, I claim the honor and title of lord chieftain. Let all who would challenge my claim step forward and answer before the gods."

All eyes swiveled toward Valorian, and he didn't disappoint them. Mordan wordlessly handed him a sword, and with equal intensity, Valorian stabbed it point down into the ground at Karez's feet. "In the name of Amara, I challenge your claim," he cried.

The people were startled. Men didn't usually call on Amara, the Mother Goddess, to help in a matter such as this.

But Kierla and Mother Willa weren't surprised. Amara had supported Valorian from the day of his encounter with the lightning. They realized his challenge was just another step in his unfolding destiny.

Karez's lips pulled back in a malicious smile. His teeth gleamed against his dark beard. "You have a strange power, Valorian. How can we be sure that you won't use it against me?" He deliberately paused, as if something had just occurred to him. "How can we ever know that you won't turn your power against the Clan? What if you already have?" He pointed dramatically into the hall. "Was it Tarnish luck or your magic that sent that arrow into Fearral's neck?"

The onlookers gasped. Kierla drew a long, painful breath and clenched her fingers together. Valorian didn't move.

But Mordan did. He took stepped forward beside Valorian, his stocky, muscular figure like a bulwark at the man's side, and he touched his fingers to Karez's chest. "You weren't there, Karez," he said loudly, his tone scathing with contempt. "You couldn't know. But we who were there saw the magic that Valorian wrought. He saved our lives and was responsible for the success of our raid. There was nothing but the hands of the gods in Fearral's death. He died with honor, Karez. Do not stain that honor with your own selfishness and stupidity."

The rest of the chieftain's guards, Gylden, and several other warriors who had been in the rear guard came to stand by Valorian to show their support.

Karez's face flushed with anger. This wasn't a good beginning for his leadership. He hadn't anticipated the chieftain's guards siding with Valorian.

Valorian hadn't expected that either, and he was grateful for their acceptance of him. If he was killed and Karez became chieftain, Karez could easily dismiss them with dishonor from their favored positions or even have them executed. They were taking a big risk supporting him when he was in such poor shape, and now he knew he would have to make their risk even bigger.

He raised his hands to the sun, the light of the Mother Goddess, and he swore for all to hear: "I made a vow when I returned from the realm of the dead that I would never use my power against our people. Today I reconfirm that vow before Amara and all the gods, and before you. I give you my word that I will not use magic against my opponent. We will fight in the honored tradition of swords. Will you accept the victor as your lord chieftain?"

"Yes!" every voice answered him.

Valorian lowered his arms, satisfied. He was taking a terrible chance to fight a man like Karez with only a sword, but if he could defeat his challenger, he would win the respect and trust of the entire Clan.

By this time, nearly all the clanspeople had gathered in the large open space before the hall, almost six hundred men, women, and children of all ages. Quickly they backed up to form a big ring where the challengers would fight.

Duels to decide a new chieftain were traditional and quite practical to the minds of the clanspeople. If several men desired to be lord, they fought with only swords until all but one surrendered. That one was then considered to be the Clan chieftain, chosen by the god Surgart, until he died or was too feeble to lead his people. There were few rules for the duel. The opponents couldn't leave the ring of battle until the duel was over, and they couldn't have help from the spectators. They were on their own, with only the gods for their allies.

Mordan pulled his sword from the ground, cleaned the point, and was about to hand it to Valorian when Gylden came up with Valorian's own sword. "Aiden left this with his clothes and weapons," he said briefly to his friend. His strong, even features were dark with concern as he handed Valorian the sword and went to stand by Kierla and Linna in the crowd of spectators.

Valorian hefted the blade, pleased to have his own weapon back with its strange blackened blade. Its weight felt good to his arm; its hilt fit comfortably in his hand.

Mordan nodded, satisfied. He gripped Valorian's arm. "Your only chance is to wear him down. Let him do the chasing, and keep the sun to your back as much as possible."

Valorian inclined his head. He returned Mordan's grip, pleased to have this man's concern and friendship. After a second thought, he decided to remove his tattered, filthy tunic and fight in nothing but his pants to give his opponent less to grasp. As he stripped off his shirt, he heard startled exclamations from the people around him. He saw why when he looked down at his upper body. It was a mass of bruises, purple, blue, and red—Tyrranis's own signature of pain.

Soft fingers touched his arm, and he saw Mother Willa standing beside him, a cup in her hand. She was breathing heavily, as if she had been running. "Drink this," she ordered and thrust the cup at him. Gratefully he drank the proffered liquid. He didn't recognize its tart flavor, but it warmed his stomach and spread into his body with invigorating strength.

"I grow impatient, Valorian!" bellowed Karez from the center of the circle. He, too, had stripped to his coarse leggings and stood waiting, his heavy body already glistening with sweat.

Valorian strode to meet him. They rapped their sword points together in salute, and without further ceremony, the combat was joined. Valorian saw Karez's sword rise and fall even before his own had moved into a defensive position. He managed to parry the wicked blow and duck out of Karez's way by a hairbreadth.

The big man bulled by him, carried by his own momentum, then quickly turned with a grunt and brought his sword around in a murderous arc that would have cut Valorian in half.

Valorian dodged sideways and leaped back, every muscle protesting. He noticed immediately that Karez was using his sword more like a club, swinging great hammerlike blows at Valorian's head and torso with little thought of skill or finesse. The man was relying on his larger bulk and brute strength to overwhelm his weaker opponent.

Like a bull ready to crush his foe, Karez roared and stamped after Valorian again. His sword flashed in the sunlight. Valorian gave way before him, his own blade his only shield from Karez's violent slashes.

Valorian knew he couldn't hope to meet Karez's attack blow for blow, so he deliberately lured the big man along and enticed him to make the powerful moves and the mighty swings with his heavy sword, while Valorian moved only as much as necessary and did little to push an offensive attack.

The duel settled into a steady sort of rhythm of thrust and swing, swipe and dodge. Time and again Karez charged at Valorian, and each time Valorian just barely slipped out of reach at the last moment. When their two blades did meet, the clash was heard all through the village. Back and forth the two men moved across the ring, their fierce struggle fought in the deadly silence of concentration. The crowd, meanwhile, yelled and cheered and offered advice, but the combatants didn't hear a word.

Gradually Valorian's breathing grew heavy and labored. His movements began to drag. It wasn't long before his muscles had turned to liquid fire. He couldn't move his sword without shooting pains in his arms, and he had to hold it with both hands just to ward off Karez's violent swings. His legs, too, were weakening fast and slowing his reactions.

He tried grimly to force his limbs to keep moving, but then he stumbled trying to parry one of Karez's jabs and the passing edge of the sword caught his ribs. The blade slashed through the skin to the bone in a long, jagged line.

Karez grinned maliciously as Valorian staggered and nearly fell. The big clansman lunged forward to press his attack. With a sudden spurt of desperate strength, Valorian regained his feet. Instead of dodging out of Karez's way, he slipped under the hacking cut of the sword and jabbed his own weapon blindly toward Karez's big body as he went by. The keen blade cut deep into fleshy thigh.

Karez roared in pain and fury. Both men fell back, breathing hoarsely and shaking with their exertion. Their blood mingled with the sweat and dirt on their bodies to form muddy rivulets down their skins.

Valorian leaned forward a moment to prop his shaking hands on his knees. His breath burned in his lungs, and he had never been so exhausted. A troubled doubt rose in his mind at his ability to endure much more of this. He knew he could defeat Karez with one simple spell, but the price of such a betrayal was too high. On the other hand, he couldn't fight like this much longer. He had gone beyond the reserves of his strength and was relying on sheer willpower alone. Mother Willa's drink had helped for a while until it, too, had worn off. If he kept on fighting as he was, the price of his honor would surely be defeat or death.

He could tell the battle was finally taking its toll on Karez as well. The man's movements had slowed considerably, his body was drenched in sweat, and his face was flushed dark red. And yet it wasn't enough. Karez had started fresh and healthy; he still had stamina to burn.

Then another thought intruded into Valorian's mind. It began like a tiny seed that takes root and grows into a magnificent flower. It was a vision of the Ramtharin Plains, green with spring grass and blue with open sky. The vision was so clear he could see the yellow butterflies in the wildflowers and smell the freshness of the wind that swept from a distant sea.

A sudden, powerful desire swept through him to see that land and claim it for his sons. He wanted to ride Hunnul forever over its rolling hills and pitch his tent beside its clear-running streams. He wanted that land with every fiber in his being, and the only thing standing in his way was that fat, glistening man with the ugly face.

Valorian straightened slowly, his expression a mask of ferocity. From some buried place in his mind, a final reservoir of strength poured into his arms and legs. A challenging roar of fury burst from his lips.

Karez looked startled at the change in his hitherto half-dead adversary. He lifted his sword just as Valorian launched himself across the space between them.

This time Valorian didn't try to stay away from Karez. He threw himself into the fight like a berserker, using every ounce of skill he had to thrust and parry past Karez's heavy swings. He knew he couldn't beat down the bigger man, but the fury of his offensive was enough to keep Karez's weapon from inflicting serious injury and to force the man to give ground. Valorian was nicked and cut on his arms and thighs, while his own sword drew blood from Karez's arms, shoulders, and chest.

The burly man was beginning to look dumbfounded, and under his heavy lids was the rising shadow of fear.

Valorian pressed harder. He couldn't overpower Karez's stronger defense, so he tried to outmaneuver the bigger man. Stroke after stroke, he forced Karez around until the sun was behind his back. He felt its warmth on his skin, as if Amara herself were standing behind him, looking on with approval.

The bright light shone full into Karez's eyes. Valorian saw him squint and saw his sword falter for the briefest moment. His teeth bared, Valorian struck. Before Karez realized what was happening, Valorian drove his sword past Karez's guard, slashed his arm, and knocked his weapon flying to the rocky ground.

A cold, bloody point pressed into Karez's throat. Trembling, the warrior stared into Valorian's ice-cold eyes and saw the fierce, merciless glare of a hunting eagle. For a moment, his own bearlike pride refused to admit defeat, and his lips pulled back in a snarling grimace.

Valorian pushed the point of his black sword against the skin of his antagonist's neck until blood dripped down the tip. "Well?" he growled.

Karez's eyes bulged. "I surrender," he finally said bitterly, his words heavy with disappointment and defeat.

"Who am I?" hissed Valorian.

Painfully Karez knelt on the rocky ground and paid his homage. "Lord chieftain of the Clan," he muttered.

Valorian raised his sword to salute the sun. The Clan roared its approval. He staggered slightly, for the surge of strength that had brought him this far was beginning to fade, leaving him dizzy and sick. Then he felt a warm, soft muzzle touch his shoulder. Hunnul had trotted through the crowd and was standing there, waiting for his master.

It took every vestige of Valorian's willpower to hoist himself onto the black stallion's back. Once he did, however, Hunnul's own vast warmth and energy sustained him. The stallion pranced around the ring, his neck arched and his muscles flowing under his black coat. Valorian straightened, threw his head back, and shouted the Clan's ancient war cry until it echoed throughout Stonehelm. His people picked up the cry and sent it soaring through the Bloodiron Hills.

At last he drew Hunnul even with Fearral's daughters, and he dismounted before them. "We will do your will," he said simply.

Taking her sister's hand, the eldest marched into the big hall. Together they removed some important items: several old relics, a few personal belongings, and the banner of the lord chieftain, piling them safely outside the hall. The clanspeople watched them for a few moments before, one by one, they moved to help. Only Valorian and Karez stood back while the hall was emptied of its few valuables and the wooden walls were soaked with oil.

The Clan priests began to chant the songs of the dead. At the request of relatives, the fallen warriors brought back from Actigorium were laid by Fearral's side. His daughters carefully laid the Tarnish tapestry over his body, then everyone left the hall to stand outside.

Fearral's daughters lit the funeral fire by touching burning brands to the oil-drenched walls. The fire surged up toward the roof, and in a short time, the hall was a roaring inferno.

As Valorian watched the flames destroy the hall and the bodies of the honored dead, Kierla gently touched his wounded side. Looking at his pinched face, she said softly, "It will be evening before that fire burns down. Come. Rest while you can."

Valorian felt his exhaustion down to the bone. Without a second thought, he nodded and left with her to find a place to sleep.

* * * * *

It was very dark when Valorian came awake. He woke slowly, dragged out of his rest by an urgent hand. With him woke his memories, so he wasn't confused to see the interior of Mordan's tent where he had come to sleep or have the odd feeling of exhilaration and nervousness that sparked in his mind when he remembered the events of . . . when?

His senses told him it was late night, but of what day? He felt as if he had been asleep for months.

"When?" he mumbled to the hand that kept shaking him. "What day?"

"It's almost dawn, Lord Valorian. I'm sorry to awaken you, but you've got to see this." It was Gylden's voice, and he sounded strangely elated.

Valorian smiled to himself. Even in his excitement, Gylden had easily and naturally called him lord. It was an incredible feeling to hear that. Stiff and sore, he hauled himself off his pallet and pulled on the clean tunic Kierla had retrieved from the belongings he had left at Stonehelm those many days before. His wife was awake beside him, so she bundled the sleeping baby into her carrying sling and swiftly rose to join the men. The three hurried out of Mordan's tent. Valorian stifled another pleased grin when two of the chieftain's guards fell in behind him.

Gylden led them to the road out of town and down the smooth stone slopes of the outcropping to the fields below. The camps of the Clan families were scattered around the open grassy areas, their tents like dark, hulking animals curled up asleep in the night. In the east, a pale rim of light tinted the horizon and heralded the coming of Amara's sun.

Gylden went on through the grass heavy with dew to the pasture where the brood mares had been separated from the herd recovered at Actigorium and left to rest and graze.

Valorian was surprised to see a large crowd of people gathered on the gentle hill and staring down at something in the herd.

"You're not going to believe this," Gylden resumed breathlessly. "I found them just a little while ago."

"Found what?" Kierla asked. She felt her own anticipation flutter in her stomach, for she could see by Gylden's smiling face that something wonderful had happened.

"It must have been the excitement of the run from Actigorium that started them. They're just a little early," Gylden replied, without actually answering her question. He reached the crowd, and the people made way for their chief. At the front of the curious onlookers stood Mother Willa, looking down the hill as if in a daze.

The herd of mares was just a short distance away, the horses scattered along the base of the hill, peacefully grazing. Valorian didn't see anything remarkable at first, but then Kierla made a small exclamation and pointed. There, in the brightening dawn light, he saw them by their dams' sides. There were three of them, newborn, still slightly damp, all long legs and heads and wispy tails. One of them was lying down, while the other two tottered about their mothers. They were obviously healthy, well-formed foals, but the most remarkable thing about them was that they were all black—and all had a white lightning mark emblazoned on their right shoulders.

Valorian clenched his jaw to fight down the intense joy and wonder that threatened to overwhelm him. He looked inquiringly at Gylden, even though he already knew the answer.

His friend nodded, beaming. "They are all Hunnul's foals." He gestured to the big herd and added, "I've never seen anything like this. Three identical foals from the same sire!"

Mother Willa suddenly started and flung open her arms to

the eastern sky where the rising sun gleamed behind the mountain peaks. Her face was bright and her voice sang in a prayer of thanksgiving. "Oh Mother of All, in your gratitude and graciousness, you sent your champion back to life with a great gift to lead his people out of tyranny. By your blessings, he has prospered, and now his beloved stallion is blessed as well. By his seed will a new breed of horse be granted to the Clan, a horse that will always bear his color and his lightning mark of honor. May they forever run with the wind of your grace!"

The people in the crowd around her heard her words. Their stares swung over to the new lord chieftain, and their voices rose in murmuring excitement at the incredible possibilities. A new breed of horse, from one stallion.

"Praise Amara!" Kierla said, and her hand came to rest on her abdomen where her second son waited for his chance at life. In her sling, Khulinar woke with happy gurgles. His hand reached out of the leather sling, groping for his mother's long, unbound hair.

Valorian looked from the foals to his son, and his heart echoed Kierla's words of praise. Even with his magic, he couldn't see into the future, yet he didn't need to, to recognize the union of the destinies of these black horses and his sons. Through the Mother Goddess's grace and benediction, they would ride together as he rode Hunnul to be leaders of the Clan's new future.

He would have stayed to watch the foals and daydream all morning if a sharp, cold gust of wind hadn't suddenly brought him out of his musings. He laughed ruefully at himself. The distant future was still a long time away, and what was to come was not yet born. He had to deal with the immediate future if he were going to save something for his offspring.

He turned to the people beside him. "Come," he called to everyone. "Bring your families to the gates of Stonehelm. It is time we decide our destiny."

14

y the light of a clear dawn, the people of the Clan gathered at the gates of their one town to hear the words of their chieftain. Most of them expected him to stand before them and demand that they pack immediately to leave for his new land. But he surprised them.

Instead, he looked out over the faces gathered before him—at the Clan priests and priestesses, elders, and leaders of the families in the foreground, the other men, women, and children in a quiet mass behind—and he said, "Through the summer, fall, and winter, I have tried to convince you all to leave your homes in Chadar and seek the new realm of the Ramtharin Plains. You have heard my reasons time and time again, and I still believe in them with my whole heart. But now that I'm in the position to command you, I realize that it would be wiser for you to make the decision yourselves. This journey cannot be a success if you as a whole do not accept the change and work together to bring it about.

"So, do we go or do we stay? You have heard Karez tell you that the Tarns will be placated by tribute and time. Perhaps that is so, and we can stay here as we are. However, I have met General Tyrranis. I know him to be obsessive, ruthless, and cruel beyond measure. *He* will not let us off so easily. The journey itself will not be easy either, and I believe Tyrranis will try to stop us. But if we can reach Wolf-eared Pass, we will be through with the Tarns and their tributes forever."

Valorian drew a deep breath before he went on. "I must ask you now to make your choice. There isn't much time. Talk to your priests and elders and send them to me when you're ready. I promise you that whatever decision you reach, I will do my best to defend and preserve this Clan." Without a further word, he stepped back and withdrew to the open space by the charred ruins of Fearral's hall to wait.

The clanspeople looked at one another, surprised by his move. It wasn't a typical gesture of a Clan chieftain. Hesitantly at first, then in gathering volubility, the men and women turned to one another and talked. It was the first time in many years that the entire remaining Clan population had been together, and they had a great deal to discuss.

Mother Willa made her way out of the vocal groups of men and women. She had nothing to say to any of them, for she had made up her mind months ago, and someone else needed her more. She went instead to find her grandson, who was sitting on the ground, staring morosely at the few charred beams still standing in the ruins of the hall. He was totally alone; his guards were with the rest of the Clan, and even Hunnul was out grazing. Her faded blue eyes softened when she saw him. He looked so vulnerable at that moment, with his hands clenched together and his normally straight back slumped. His new authority was weighing heavily on his shoulders.

She walked across the stony ground where the two men had fought the day before and slowly bent her stiff joints to sit down beside him. The air was still sharp with the smell of smoke and burned wood. "Amara will be with them," she said quietly.

His smile welcomed her words, and his back seemed to straighten; only his eyes remained pensive and distant. The two sat together in silent companionship while the morning sun grew warm and the indistinct murmur of distant voices hummed on the air around them.

All at once, a dearly familiar voice called to them from the road, and a dusty bay horse came jogging through the tents and shops. It was Aiden, still in his Chadarian clothing, his face beaming through a mask of soot and stubble. Once again he had two small goats tied in a bag behind his saddle.

Valorian bounded to his feet, and this time, it was Aiden who was nearly knocked over when he dismounted to greet his brother.

"By all the holy gods, Valorian," Aiden asked incredulously, "what happened around here?" His gaze went flying from Valorian's battered face to the hall's burned remains and back again. "What's going on? Why is everyone at the gate? I saw Linna, but she said to come talk to you."

Valorian didn't answer Aiden's questions immediately. He had too many of his own. "Where have you been?" he demanded, his voice made sharper by joy, relief, and the anger of pent-up frustration. "What took you so long? Are the others with you?"

The excitement of his answers temporarily distracted Aiden, and his face lit up with a mischievous grin. "Yes, they're with their families. We didn't lose one. Oh, gods, Valorian, you should have seen that fire! It was spectacular!" He clasped his brother's arm, his gray eyes clear and sparkling through the grime on his face, and the two men sat down beside their grandmother.

Aiden rushed on. "It was the most magnificent fire I've ever seen! We found an old warehouse built of wood and full of bales of wool. We waited until dark, then set it alight. Whoosh!" He threw his hands up in the air and chuckled appreciatively. "It went up like an oil-soaked torch. There were people and soldiers everywhere trying to fight that blaze with buckets and shovels. They might as well have spit on it, for all the good their buckets did. The fire got so hot, it spread to several other buildings nearby."

Valorian's eyes narrowed. "You were there? You were supposed to leave as soon as the fire began."

Aiden laughed outright. "I helped in the bucket lines," he said, showing Valorian his ash-covered clothes. "Actually, we couldn't get out right away. The gates were kept shut until nearly midday, and when they finally opened, everyone who went through was searched from head to boot. We didn't try to leave until last evening. Gave me some time to find some new goats for Linna. Besides, I also wanted to see General Tyrranis's reaction." There was a long hesitation, and the merriment died from his eyes.

"I imagine he was angry," Valorian said to prompt the younger man.

"Tyrranis goes far beyond angry," Aiden replied in slow and worried tones. "I really think he has gone over the edge of sanity. He had every sentinel at the north gate hanged in the market and has nailed the commander of the garrison to the city walls. A *Tarn!* Nailed up with a murderer and two cattle thieves. In front of the whole city." He shook his head. "It was eerie in that city yesterday. Everyone was holding his breath and sidling into shadows whenever Tyrannis came near. He personally tore the city apart looking for you or anyone who even looked like a clansman. He hacked down one poor traveler wearing a cloak before he realized the man was only a pilgrim going south to Sar Nitina."

"That doesn't bode well for Karez's hopes," Mother Willa murmured.

Aiden looked at her curiously, then resumed his tale. "That's not the worst of it. When we left last night, he had put out a call for all able-bodied men to report to the tower for temporary duty. He's ordered the garrison to arm and stand by and he stripped the city of all available horses. As soon as he has enough men, he's going to march up here and, in his own words, 'Wipe out the vermin once and for all.'"

"Huh!" Mother Willa snorted indelicately. "Vermin. I like that, coming from him."

Aiden cast a speculative glance at Valorian and saw that his brother was sitting motionless, his neck muscles drawn tight in unspoken tension and his head slightly cocked, as if he were listening to something far away. Aiden suddenly noticed what Valorian was listening to—the silence. The distant voices had stopped.

A slow, satisfied smile lit Mother Willa's seamed face from the knowledge of certainty. "They have done it," she said softly to Valorian.

"Done what?" Aiden demanded, irritated now by the lack of answers. "What *is* going on here?"

No one replied. Valorian straightened his back a little, his eyes on the road from the palisade.

"They understand now," his grandmother went on. Her voice became gentle and singsong, and she swayed slightly as if she were repeating the images of a vision. "The goddess Amara has walked among their thoughts today, reminding them of her gifts to you, her champion. At last they believe."

Aiden was staring at her now, amazed, while Valorian watched the road. For a moment, no one moved. Then Valorian suddenly rose to his feet. Aiden turned to look, too, and saw the entire Clan walking up the road toward them. Mordan, Kierla, and Gylden were in the forefront, their faces shining. But it was Karez and the leaders of the other families who came to stand before the tall clansman and bow low before him.

"We will go, Lord Valorian," the oldest man said.

Aiden's jaw dropped open. "*Lord* Valorian?" he cried. "Since when? Will someone please tell me what has been happening around here?" And with great pleasure, Mother Willa told him.

From that moment, Valorian took command. He explained to the gathered Clan about Aiden's news of General Tyrranis's plan to march into the hills, and impressed upon them the urgency of a rapid departure.

"We must leave no later than tomorrow," he ordered. "Every family will be responsible for packing their tents and belongings and gathering in their herds. If any of you know of someone who isn't here, please send that person word immediately. We will not leave any clansperson behind to face the wrath of the Tarns." He went on, issuing orders and answering questions until everyone was satisfied with the immediate task ahead.

And the task was monumental. Although most of the Clan families were already prepared to spend the summer on the move, the families of Gylden and Valorian had lost all their tents, gear, and personal possessions; the people of Stonehelm had to pack the contents of a town, and none of the groups had traveled as a whole for as long as anyone could remember. The tact and work involved in supplying, organizing, and forming the large caravan was more than Valorian could have handled alone.

Fortunately he didn't have to. Mordan worked tirelessly to organize carts, wagons, and horses for baggage and supplies. The extra animals that Hunnul had brought from the Tarnish corrals were a godsend, Mordan told Valorian. Gylden helped the clanspeople mark their horses and stock animals not already branded and organize the herds. Everyone contributed from his own meager supplies and belongings to help the survivors of the raid of Tarn, and Aiden served as Valorian's spokesman, easing ruffled feathers, soothing fears, and encouraging young and old with his optimistic smile.

By the time the sun lifted its rays over the mountain peaks the next day, Valorian began to believe they would be able to leave on time. Every person in the Clan was accounted for and doing what needed to be done to get ready to go. A caravan was taking shape in the fields below Stonehelm, where wagons and carts jostled for position and the herds waited in nervous expectation. People hurried everywhere, looking for lost children, fetching forgotten belongings, running for last-minute items. Dogs scurried underfoot, and the children were wild with excitement.

Valorian rode Hunnul from one end of the forming caravan to the other, helping wherever he could, full of calm and courage. He lifted the hearts of all his people and spurred them on to greater efforts.

At noon, Mordan, at the front of the long caravan, sounded a deep, undulating signal on a ram's horn that soared over the fields and meadows and swept through the empty buildings of Stonehelm. The Clan priests and priestesses gathered together with Valorian to call on the gods for protection and goodwill.

When the prayers were finished, Valorian stepped forward, raised his arms to the sun, and cried, "Amara, Mother of All, lead us into the hills with your truth and your light. Guide us on the path of our destiny."

Every clansperson's eye automatically lifted to scan the sky or the horizon for some omen that the gods were listening. Every breath was held, and the only movements in the caravan were the restless shifting of animals.

Then the omen came on the wings of a pair of rare golden eagles—the birds of Surgart, the color of Amara. They came from the west and slowly soared on the upper air currents until they were over the line of wagons. The two birds flew lazily side by side, their gleaming heads seeming to look down on the people below. In unison, the birds wheeled over the procession of carts, wagons, packhorses, and herds. When they reached Valorian, they seemed to swoop lower to let the light of their wings shine upon his face. Finally the eagles turned south, and the clanspeople watched them until the pair vanished in the distance.

"The gods have sent their oracles to point the way!" a priest shouted into the awed silence. An uproar of cheering, whistling, and shouting broke loose from the entire Clan.

In the next moment, whips cracked, reins popped, horses neighed; gradually the train of animals and vehicles began to move. They headed south after the eagles, slowly at first, then faster as the people and the animals settled into a steady pace.

Valorian had long before decided what path they would take, should the Clan ever decide to leave, so he and a group of armed warriors rode to the front of the caravan and led the long string of herds and wagons deeper into the

Bloodiron Hills. He knew it would have been easier to take the Clan to the flatter lowlands and skirt the foothills, but the Tarns would expect that and search for them there. By using the rougher, lesser known paths, the caravan would move slower, but they would stand a greater chance of evading Tyrranis and his soldiers.

As the wagons one by one crested a ridge and Stonehelm fell behind, it seemed every person turned to take one last look at the abandoned town and the large blackened spot in its center where Lord Fearral and his men rested in the ashes. In the rear guard, Aiden, too, paused to bid a silent farewell. Wordlessly he raised his hand to salute his dead chieftain. Without a regret, he turned his back on the forlorn town and followed his new chief over the ridge toward a future known only to the gods.

* * * * *

A haze of thickening clouds obscured the sun two days later when General Tyrranis led his mounted soldiers up the road toward Stonehelm. They made no effort to hide their approach, trotting in fully armed ranks up the hills to the town. Some resistance from the clanspeople was expected, but not enough to worry the Tarnish troops, who had superior arms, training, and numbers.

What worried the soldiers more was their leader. After summarily nailing the garrison commander to the city wall by his hands and feet for his abysmal failure to prevent the Clan raid, General Tyrranis had taken over direct command of the troops himself. Before roll call the day before, he had made a vitriolic speech to the regular troops and the new draftees, telling them that they were charged with the duty of washing the hills with Clan blood. Not a single clansperson of any age was to be spared anywhere in Chadar.

Some of the men didn't like the idea of slaughtering innocent women, children or elders, but no one could look into the brutally cold darkness of Tyrranis's eyes and suggest

otherwise. They would rather face a cornered pack of clansmen or a murdered pile of corpses than draw the attention
of his merciless fury.

The troops were silent as they rode, unchallenged, into
Stonehelm. Their eyes flicked nervously from the empty,
abandoned buildings to their general's face, and they waited
in ranks, holding their breath for his reaction.

Tyrranis said nothing at first. Irritably he looked over the
burned ruins of Fearral's hall, the lifeless paths, and the empty
corrals before reining his horse around. He rode to the gate of
the palisade, pulled off his helmet, and studied the churned-
up fields below. His skin seemed to tighten across his hard
face as his mouth tightened into a grimace of anger.

"So," he murmured under his breath like the hiss of a
snake, "the quarry has flown." With his eyes, he followed
the trail of hoofprints and wagon ruts leading out of the valley. "No matter. They cannot go far."

A sudden, violent feeling of hatred and rage stabbed
through his self-control at the thought of Valorian and his
people. Never in his successful and perfectly ordered career
had Tyrranis ever been so deceived and humiliated. A worth-
less clansman had tricked him and ruined his prestige throughout the provinces. When word of this got back to Tarnow and
the emperor's ears, his reputation could well be stained
beyond redemption. He would never be able to gather the
support and funds necessary for his bid for the throne.

His only hope of repairing the damage and taking his
revenge for this insult dealt to his self-respect was to slaughter the clanspeople to a man. They were useless anyway;
their tribute was pitiful, and their horses could survive just as
well without them. Only their deaths had any value now.

Tyrranis's hands tightened unconsciously on the reins
until his horse jigged its head in pain and shied sideways to
escape the brutal pressure on the bit in its mouth. The general angrily lashed it to a trembling standstill. When the
horse was quiet again, Tyrranis slowly forced his emotions
back under control. Fury and hatred were exhausting if

allowed to burn freely. He would save his strength for the day that his troops cornered Valorian and the people who followed him; then he would release his rage and cool it in Clan blood. Only Valorian would live, just long enough to impart the secret of his magic. Tyrranis had no idea how Valorian had suffered through the night of torture without revealing his power, but the general swore that wouldn't happen again. If he had to tear apart every member of Valorian's family with his bare hands to get the man's secret of magic, he was prepared to do so.

"Maxum Lucius!" he snapped.

The man now second-in-command of the Actigorium garrison rode forward hurriedly and saluted.

"Raze this pitiful village to the ground. I want nothing left of it!" ordered the general. "Then dispatch scouts to all the known Clan camps. Search every hiding place in these hills until you find those people. The rest of the force will come with me to follow their trail." His eyes suddenly narrowed, and the veins bulged dangerously in his neck. "If any of those clanspeople escape, I will personally send you to the copper mines of Scartha. I will not tolerate any more incompetence. Is that understood?"

Keeping his face unreadable, the Tarnish officer saluted and moved to obey his commands. After a few brief orders, the ranks of legionnaires broke into groups and set about their duty with a vengeance. With ruthless efficiency, they tore down every standing building, corral, shed, shop, and pen, and piled the debris on the blackened remains of the burned hall. They scattered salt over the plowed fields and small gardens, demolished the shrine to the Clan gods, poisoned the well, and killed every stray dog and abandoned animal they found. The palisades were broken to pieces and heaped on the growing pile of shattered ruins. Nothing was left standing.

When the town was completely leveled, the soldiers stood back while several of their number soaked the huge heap with oil and set it aflame. The fire burst into light with a hungry roar, consuming the remains of the Clan village in a searing bonfire that sent clouds of black smoke billowing high over Stonehelm.

Tyrranis looked on in grim satisfaction. When nothing remained but a few bare patches and the blackened stone where the coals of the pile were still smoldering, the Tarns remounted and rode down from Stonehelm. They, too, trotted over the ridge and disappeared to the south on the trail of the Clan.

*　*　*　*　*

The last rays of sunlight were streaking the pink western sky when the Clan finally reached the meadows below the ridge where Valorian had been struck by lightning a year before. The wagons creaked to a halt, the footsore animals fell to grazing, and the clanspeople heaved a mutual sigh of relief. They had been traveling almost constantly for six days, and they were exhausted.

Valorian had been pushing them hard over rugged terrain, for he knew Tyrranis's troops could move faster than laden wagons and herds of livestock, and he wanted to put as much distance between them and the Tarns as possible.

This night, however, he allowed the caravan to stop a little early. He had sent out scouts several days before, and they were to rejoin the Clan here at what everyone had started calling Lightning Ridge. He didn't really want to wait, but he badly needed the scouts' information, and the weary clanspeople needed the rest.

Through the dwindling daylight hours, the people bedded down the herds of horses and livestock, set up shelters, and found food for everyone before collapsing on their blankets for some much needed sleep.

Valorian thought several times about riding Hunnul up to the top of the ridge, but there was no real reason to do so and too much to do to get the Clan camped for the night. Being responsible for about six hundred people was quite different from leading a small family of fifty.

In the past few days, Valorian had come to truly appreciate the awesome responsibilities of his position as lord chieftain. Not only did he have to lead a large caravan over difficult trails, but he also had to elude the Tarns, see to the people's everyday needs, settle minor disputes, and make countless decisions about everything from whether to send someone to search for a lost goat and how to punish a young woman who stole food, to which men should ride in the rear guard. In order to preserve his strength, he refused to use his magic for anything but emergencies, and he delegated some of the duties to Mordan, who was increasingly becoming his invaluable friend and right-hand man, and to the other heads of the families. But the brunt of the work and the ultimate responsibility were still his.

Despite it all, Valorian wouldn't have exchanged places with anyone. He relished his new authority and gave his people his full attention. His constant optimism and his evident pleasure at being on this journey were infectious to all who were with him. He gave hope and purpose to everyone during the long and difficult days of travel.

Perhaps because of their new hope and anticipation, the people had traveled faster and harder than Valorian expected. They had put aside their major differences and were working together to achieve their common goal. No one knew for certain if Tyrranis and the Tarnish soldiers were coming after them yet; they only knew their decision to leave Chadar had been irrevocably made, and they were on their way to a new home.

Late that night, however, the first of the scouts returned, and the Clan learned the truth that Valorian had feared.

"They've found our trail again," the young man wearily told Valorian and the few other men who had awakened when he arrived. "We lost them for a while, but they're catching up now. About a day behind."

Valorian nodded, hardly surprised. "Is Tyrranis with them?"

"Yes, lord. But not the full garrison. I only counted about two hundred men."

"Interesting," Mordan said, stifling a yawn. "Either the Tarns are incredibly arrogant, or they're not going to try to stop us."

The chieftain scratched his jaw thoughtfully. His expression was unreadable in the darkness. "I can't believe . . ." he said half aloud, then he paused and said to those around him, "We'll wait to see what Ranulf has found. But with the Tarns so close behind us, we cannot wait here for him. We will have to leave at daybreak."

The others agreed.

Valorian didn't go back to his blankets after that. Worry weighed heavily on his mind, so instead of futilely trying to sleep, he went to check the brood mares. All of the Clan's precious brood mares were together in one herd, faithfully tended by Gylden and a flock of enthusiastic boys. In the past seven nights, twenty more black foals had been born, all with the white lightning mark of their sire. To the delight of everyone, Hunnul's foals were already showing signs of being stronger and more intelligent than the other new foals born on the trail. No one had the slightest doubt that the black foals were another blessing and omen sent by the goddess Amara.

Valorian stopped to speak to Gylden, who was taking his turn at guard duty, and sent him back to bed. Then he rode up the slopes among the peaceful horses. Hunnul found a quiet place near the herd and stopped to watch over his mares. Stiffly the chieftain rubbed a healing bruise on his arm and leaned back on the stallion's rump. He spent the remaining hours until dawn wondering what Tyrranis was planning to do and how long he would have to wait to hear from Ranulf.

It turned out that Valorian didn't have to wait long at all. The young man sent to scout the trail ahead for Tarnish patrols came galloping into camp at dawn as the clanspeople were harnessing their horses and packing their gear. Disheveled and worried, he was met by Valorian, Mordan, Karez, and several other men at the head of the forming caravan.

His words came tumbling out even before he saluted the chieftain. "There's a big force of Tarns, Lord Valorian," he cried excitedly. "They're *ahead* of us on the trail around the great canyon."

The chief's mouth tightened into a grim line. "How many?" he asked.

"About four hundred, as close as I can count," Ranulf replied. "They just arrived there yesterday. They must have force-marched down the lowlands to cut us off."

Mordan folded his arms. "Tyrranis probably knows where we're going by now. I'd say he's going to try to trap us between a sword and a shield."

"He's picked a good place to do it," Valorian said, his concern plain on his face.

The other men with him looked mystified by their chief's grave reaction to the news. Few clanspeople had ever traveled this far south, so they weren't familiar with the territory. "Why can't we just go around through the hills?" asked a Clan priest.

Picking up a stick, Valorian scratched a crude map of the lands just to the south of their position. "The Darkhorns run in a fairly even line north and south of Lightning Ridge, except right here," and he stabbed the stick at the place in his drawing. "The mountains bulge out there in high bluffs on either side of a very deep canyon. We can't take the wagons and carts across the canyon and we can't go around it to the east because the canyon is too long. We can only drop down to the lower hills to the west to pass around it—"

"And the Tarns are waiting for us there," one of the men finished for him. The truth of their predicament became all too clear.

"By Surgart's sword," Karez suddenly snarled. He jabbed his bandaged arm at Valorian. "You're the one with the magic in your grasp. Use it to wipe out our enemies once and for all!"

Mordan rolled his eyes. "Don't you pay attention? Lord Valorian will not use his power to massacre other men."

"I say that's ridiculous!" Karez roared in reply. "What about us? Are we to be slaughtered because our chief is too squeamish to slay a few Tarns?"

Several of the listening clansmen nodded in agreement and watched Valorian expectantly.

The new chieftain felt his anger flare at the big clansman. Karez hadn't changed a bit after his defeat. He was as arrogant and abrasive as ever. Volarian bit off a sharp remark and decided he shouldn't lose his temper now. "Ridiculous or not, that is my vow," he said adamantly. For the benefit of his other companions, he added, "Even with my power, I cannot defeat half a legion alone. We must get past Tyrranis's army to reach the Bendwater River. Once we're over that, we're out of his jurisdiction. He wouldn't dare bring his armed troops into Sarcithia without Governor Antonine's permission."

Karez spat at the ground. "And just how do you propose to elude the Tarns? Do we fly like birds?"

Something in Karez's snide words triggered a sudden inspiration. "No," Valorian said in a voice tinged with satisfaction. "We'll tunnel like Carrocks!"

The effect of that statement was everything Valorian could have wanted. Karez was effectively silenced with surprise, and the others stared at their chieftain as if he had suddenly lost his sanity.

"Tell the people to make torches and to gather all the firewood they can carry. Fill the water bags, too. If all goes well, we should be underground about three days." He turned on his heel and quickly mounted Hunnul to hide the shadow of doubt creeping into his own face. "I'll ride ahead to the cave entrance to contact the Carrocks. Aiden, you and Ranulf bring the caravan as soon as it is ready."

Hunnul cantered away before they could respond and headed toward the valley and the cave not far away where Valorian and his friends had come out of the Carrocks' underworld last winter. The chieftain groaned inwardly as they left the Clan behind. He had blurted out his nebulous idea without any consideration, and now he was stuck with it. He hadn't thought about how he was going to contact the Carrocks or how they would react to an invasion of people and animals into their realm. What if they didn't agree? Then what would he do?

If his plan worked, however, the Clan would save several days of travel and come out of the caverns south of the Tarns' position, only a day or two from the Bendwater River. That alone would be worth the risk of taking such a large caravan through the subterranean passages. But only if the Carrocks agreed. Without their willingness to tolerate the intrusion, the clanspeople would be in even worse trouble.

Hunnul slowed to a trot over the rocky trail and passed by a huge old pine with a double trunk. Valorian remembered that tree, and he counted five hills to the valley where the cave opened out of the mountains. They topped the slope of the fifth hill to drop sharply down into a valley strewn with small trees and early spring flowers. The cave opening was about half a league into the valley, disguised by a grove of scrub oak, cedar, and pine. Valorian found its entrance by memory and sent Hunnul clattering into the cool, dim interior.

How will you find the Carrocks, master? Hunnul asked in Valorian's mind. The sound of the stallion's hooves echoed in the hollow spaces.

"I don't think I can," Valorian answered. "They will have to find me."

They rode deeper into the cavern until the light from the entrance was a mere pinprick and Valorian was forced to form a sphere of glowing light. In its pale illumination, he stopped Hunnul and let the silence settle around them. After a thoughtful pause, he drew more magic to his bidding, formed a spell, and raised his hands to his mouth. Loud and strong, carried on the power of his magic, his call rang down into the depths like a pealing bell to summon the denizens of the eternal rock and endless night.

He waited for a long time while his hands and feet grew cold and his doubts hardened. After what seemed an endless wait, he called again and continued to listen in the darkness. Hunnul relaxed a hind leg and let his neck droop. Only his ears pointing toward the black passage indicated his alert awareness.

Valorian was considering riding deeper into the tunnel when Hunnul raised his head, his nostrils flaring at a familiar scent. *They come,* he told his master silently.

Somewhere deep down in the passage, a heavy grating sound grumbled out of the darkness. Valorian's stomach lurched, and his hands tightened on Hunnul's mane. He could see only the small area lit by his sphere, but he sensed several large beings moving slowly along the tunnel toward him.

They stopped somewhere out of his sight. "Us you called, magic-wielder. Come have we," a strange, hard voice said.

Valorian sat back in relief. "Thank you!" he cried. "I did not wish to disturb you, but I must ask for your help." He quickly explained the Clan's danger and his wish to travel through the Carrocks' caverns. "I would not ask this of you if it weren't desperately important. We are seeking to leave this land, and if we are successful, we will never bother you again."

A different stony voice responded, "And if successful you are not?"

Valorian gave a dry chuckle. "There won't be any of us left to worry about."

There was a lengthy pause. No sound or movement disturbed the earth's silence. Then the first grating voice said, "Come, magic-wielder. For the sake of the Mother, pass may your people. But beware you must! Stray not from the path nor touch the works of the Carrocks. Watch we will!"

The heavy sound of stone moving on stone came again and vanished, leaving the tunnel in emptiness.

Valorian leaned his arms on Hunnul's neck as his breath slipped away in a ragged sigh. There was barely time to savor his relief before Aiden, Ranulf, and the vanguard of armed warriors came trotting into the cave. Valorian turned back to meet them.

He was surprised to see the afternoon sun shining into the valley, for he hadn't realized so much time had passed. The long procession of wagons, carts, and riders was already winding its way up toward the cave entrance.

"We have permission to pass," Valorian called to Aiden. His triumphant smile spoke more than words to his young brother, who raised his fist in a victory salute.

The chieftain quickly joined his leaders and explained the length of the trail, a brief description of things to expect, and the reasons for his drastic plan. "Pass on my words," he commanded, "but don't let anyone slow down to think or balk. Keep the wagons and herds moving! Also warn everyone not to stray from the trail or touch anything beside the trail. We must obey the Carrocks."

One of the family leaders rolled his eyes at the dark tunnel and exclaimed, "Gods above! The Carrocks really exist?"

"Yes!" Aiden replied, the respect from his previous experience with them still strong in his voice. "Believe me, you do not want to anger these beings."

At that moment, the first of the laden wagons rolled into the entrance, and the driver automatically hauled back on his reins, confused by the idea of entering a cavern.

"I'll keep them moving," Aiden said to Valorian.

The chieftain nodded his thanks, and with the vanguard at his side, he grinned at the wagon driver, grabbed the bridle of the harnessed horse, and personally led the first wagon into the cave and down into the buried gloom.

15

n a long, single file, the wagons, carts, riders, and herds of animals reluctantly entered the cavern and followed their chieftain under the mountains. He led them along the same broad road that he and his companions had followed before. He thought the wagons and herds would be slower in the dark passages, but the Clan had no desire to dawdle.

It was a measure of the clanspeople's growing trust in Valorian that they went into the caves at all. Once inside, though, it was their fear of the strange, dark tunnels that kept them moving, the cold and dampness that made them reluctant to stop, and the half-sensed presence of the mythical Carrocks, always out of sight, that kept them all on edge.

They ate their food on the move and stopped only long enough to water the stock at the ice-cold stream that trickled beside the road.

As they worked their way along the underground passages lit only by torchlight and several of Valorian's spheres, the clanspeople stared in awe at the stalactites, the guardian statue, and the crystal walls that sparkled in the unnatural light. They also heeded their chieftain's warning implicitly. The ancient tales of the Carrocks' legendary strength and possessiveness were more than enough to discourage any thoughts of exploring or souvenir hunting.

When at long last Ranulf trotted down the line passing the word that the exit was just ahead, the entire caravan breathed a heartfelt sigh of relief and pressed forward toward the open air. Beyond the cave mouth, Valorian saw that the sun was sinking in the west. He realized his estimate of the time the Clan would be in the tunnels hadn't been quite accurate—they had been underground for only two days, not three. He hadn't taken into account the speed lent to the animal's feet by nervousness or the willingness of people to push past hunger and weariness when they were apprehensive.

As soon as he had escorted the first wagon out into the cool twilight and given instructions for the Clan to make camp in a meadow farther down the valley, Valorian turned Hunnul back into the cave. He passed by the herds of live-stock and the horses neighing at the smell of fresh grass. He went by the creaking wagons and carts, the tired riders, and the woebegone dogs. When at last the rear guard came up the slope toward him, he waved them on and waited while the noises slowly died away. The passage at last was empty, and he and Hunnul were alone.

Valorian heard nothing in the tunnels below nor saw any movement or sign of life, but he knew they were there. He flicked out his spheres of light, letting the darkness the Car-rocks craved surround him.

"Thank you," he called to the lightless depths. "May Amara bless your people and guard your caves forever!"

From far away out of the subterranean night came a single deep voice. "Go in peace, magic-wielder."

Hunnul nickered softly. Moving slowly in the darkness, the black horse walked up and out of the caverns and trot-ted gratefully out onto the soft earth and green grass.

The Clan camped that night near the mouth of the valley, where a stream dropped in a silvery fall to a clear pool below. The Bendwater River and the relative safety of Sarcithia were only a day or two away, and the people hoped that Tyrranis and his soldiers were now behind them. Weary from the long two days under the mountains, the people settled down for the night.

On a razor-backed ridge high above the valley, a Tarnish scout peered down on the camp in surprise. There was just enough light left for him to recognize several features of the big encampment before night threw its shadows over the mountains. Excited, the man mounted his horse and rode north as fast as the animal could carry him.

*   *   *   *   *

"General, I swear on the honor of the Fourth Legion, I saw them last night! They're south of us, not more than twenty leagues from the river. The commander is certain it is the Clan, and he is awaiting your orders." The scout who was speaking touched the emblem of the crescent moon on his tunic as a sign that he was swearing to the truth.

General Tyrranis hardly noticed. As quick as a cobra, his hand reached out and clamped around the soldier's throat, skillfully cutting off his breath and sending pain stabbing into the man's head. "That's impossible!" he hissed. "They couldn't have passed around us so quickly without being seen."

"But . . . I . . . saw them," the terrified scout choked out past the merciless fingers. He tried to pull at the hand, but he might as well have tried to remove steel claws. The other soldiers around him looked everywhere but at his red, mottled face.

Tyrranis eased his grip a fraction and demanded, "Exactly where? How many? How do you know it was the Clan?"

The scout gasped for breath before he answered. "They had Clan carts and a few of our freight wagons. It was a big camp, maybe five or six hundred. In a valley past the bluffs. There was one man with a lion-pelt cloak and a big black horse."

Suddenly the general's fingers let go, and the soldier fell back, clutching his throat. "So," Tyrranis said venomously. "Perhaps he has found a way to get around me." His fingers unconsciously found the amulet around his neck that protected him from evil magic.

"His magic must be powerful," one officer said, then immediately regretted his words when Tyrranis's frigid glance fell on him.

The general chose to ignore that remark and continued to speak, as if to himself. "He will still not escape. We will catch him before he crosses the river." He turned to his officers. "I should execute every scout and guard who failed me, but I still have need of every man. Mount up!"

An orderly brought Tyrranis's big bay stallion and held the stirrup for the general to mount. Viciously the stallion tried to lash out with a hoof at his master, but Tyrranis stepped out of the way and cracked his whip across the horse's soft muzzle. While the stallion flung his head around in pain, the general adroitly mounted and spurred him forward. The orderly sprang out of the way to avoid being trampled.

In frantic haste, the small troop left their makeshift camp behind and galloped south to the larger camp at the edge of the towering bluffs by the canyon. Tyrranis thundered in among the tents and surprised the soldiers with a face darker than a storm cloud, then lashed the men into action.

"Mount your horses," he shouted. "You will catch that caravan before it reaches the river, or I will drown the lot of you!"

The commander and his officers scrambled in their haste to salute their general and obey his orders. Quickly the Tarnish legionnaires and draftees made ready to leave. Horns blared on the morning breeze, calling the ranks to order; horses neighed in excitement.

In a matter of minutes, the Tarnish camp was empty, except for a few cooks and orderlies who were to tear down the abandoned tents and bring the provision wagons behind the troops. The rest of the army was thundering south to pursue the elusive clanspeople.

* * * * *

The late afternoon sun was beginning to dim behind gathering clouds when the foremost scout of the Clan caravan spotted the line of trees and the silvery band of water that marked the location of the Bendwater River far in the distance. Whooping, he rode back to tell Lord Valorian and the Clan. Word spread swiftly down the line of wagons. Drivers sat up straighter and slapped their reins to urge their horses faster; riders kicked their mounts into a trot. The thirsty herds smelled the water and picked up their pace.

At the same time, a lone scout far to the rear of the caravan saw something else come over the top of a far rise that froze his blood. He waited for a few heartbeats to be sure he was seeing correctly through the dust and haze, and then his eyes bugged out in recognition. A large column of horsemen was rapidly approaching from the north, with what looked like blood-red banners at its head.

His stomach roiling in fear, the clansman clapped his heels to his mount and streaked madly back toward the Clan.

"Tarns!" he bellowed at the rear guard. "Tarns behind us!" The swelling call of a signal horn followed him up the line of animals and wagons toward Lord Valorian at the head of the caravan. Heads turned toward him and eyes followed him in sudden fear.

The scout brought his horse skidding up beside Hunnul and blurted out to Valorian, "General Tyrranis is coming!"

Valorian didn't hesitate. "Get the Clan to the river," he ordered Aiden and Mordan, then told his guards to stay with the wagons.

"Where are you going?" Aiden shouted in alarm when he saw Valorian wheel Hunnul around.

"To slow them down!" the chief replied as the black leapt forward. Like a thunderbolt, Hunnul raced past the Clan, back toward the north and the oncoming Tarns. Frightened faces watched him for a moment before the entire caravan broke out in a wild gallop down the long, smooth, treeless slope toward the river.

Racing over the thick grass, Hunnul stretched out his neck and legs in a run no other horse could rival. He flew over the ground along the Clan's trail toward the top of a long, low ridge. Valorian had made a vow that he wouldn't use his awesome force to murder humans, but that didn't mean he wouldn't use it to hinder them.

As the black slowed at the crest of the ridge, Valorian scanned the land to the north and immediately saw the Tarnish column advancing at a full canter. In fact, at the rate they were coming, Valorian estimated they could easily catch up to the slower-moving caravan long before it reached the river. Unless they ran into a little trouble, that is.

Hunnul came to a stop on the bare ridge top. Drawing a long breath into his lungs, Valorian forced himself to relax and wait. He would hold his place there until the Tarns were closer. He glanced at the sky and noticed an angry blue-gray line of clouds building in the west into a towering white peak of violent energy. He winced when thunder rumbled in the distance. A gust of wind dashed over the slopes, unfurled Hunnul's tail, and sent Valorian's lion-pelt cloak flapping.

The chieftain hardly needed his cloak in the warm afternoon, but he wore it now to draw on the lion's courage intrinsic in its pelt—and for effect. He watched silently while the Tarns drew closer. He could see the crescent moon emblem on their banners and the weapons in their hands; he recognized Tyrranis at the head of the long column. Very deliberately, he pulled the lion's head down over his eyes like a helmet visor and stared out through the empty eyeholes. He could tell the Tarns had recognized him, because their leaders pointed his way and their speed increased. The pounding of the horses' hooves drowned out the distant rumble of thunder.

Valorian waited until the soldiers were just within arrow range, then he raised his hand and gathered the magic around him to his bidding. He felt an unfamiliar mild surge of energy in the magic, but his spell was already forming, and he didn't want to let go of it to find out about something so small. He concentrated instead on the power building within him.

The Tarns were raising their weapons when four balls of blazing blue energy seared from Valorian's hand in rapid succession and slammed into the ground in a line just in front of the foremost riders. The subsequent explosions sent huge fountains of blue sparks, dust, clods of earth and rock, torn grass, and shattered shrubs flying in all directions. The front line of riders collapsed into a mass of neighing, bucking, falling horses and shouting men.

Valorian saw General Tyrranis's panicked mount throw the general to the ground and bolt in terror back the way he had come. The whole column disintegrated into turmoil.

Valorian thought it was time to fall back. As Hunnul turned away, the chief caught the faintest mental impression of something like a chuckle from the big stallion before he broke into a gallop after the fleeing caravan.

General Tyrranis picked himself up out of the dirt in time to see the horse's black tail disappear over the slope. "Get him!" he screamed at his second-in-command, who was trying to bring his own horse under control. "Or I'll have your head!"

The man cast one wild look at his commander and decided it would be safer to chase a magic-wielder than stay and argue with the general. He rounded up all the men still on horseback, reformed the troops into a charge formation, and led them up the gentle ridge. From the top, they could see the retreating form of Valorian and, beyond him, the main body of the Clan running pell-mell for the river. The trumpeter sounded the charge. In unison, the mounted troops sprang forward.

Valorian heard the clear notes of the Tarnish trumpet with a stab of surprise. The column had reformed faster than he had expected, and he could see ahead that the caravan had already run into trouble. Several wagons had broken down during the frantic run and lay in the dust with their drivers working desperately to fix them. The brood mare herd was off to the side of the line of wagons and carts, but while the other herds of horses and livestock were moving well, the pregnant mares and mothers were forced to go much slower. They were already well behind the caravan.

Meanwhile, the head of the long train had reached the river and it, too, had run into problems. The shallow ford was too narrow for everyone to cross at once, and the Clan wagons were starting to slow down as they reached the bottleneck.

Hunnul came to the first wrecked wagon and stopped at Valorian's command. The driver, a lone woman with a daughter and two nearly grown sons, looked up gratefully as the chief slid off to help. Valorian was relieved to see the problem was only a broken axle. One quick spell repaired the wagon, then he and Hunnul quickly hurried the little family toward the next broken-down cart.

This one had hit a large rock, shattered its wheel, and sent its contents and occupants flying. The two people were still trying to deal with their injuries when Valorian arrived. Once again he fixed the wagon with magic, but there was nothing he could do with the broken arm and the cuts and abrasions. The woman and her children helped the driver while the chieftain returned the belongings to the cart with a spell. In moments, they were off after the caravan.

Twice more Valorian stopped to help until he had four carts and wagons with their passengers and several stragglers, a warrior with a limping horse, four dogs, and Gylden with the boys and the brood mare herd in his company. Just ahead, the rest of the Clan was rumbling down to the riverbank, while behind, the Tarnish soldiers were drawing dangerously close.

Valorian decided it was time to slow the Tarns down again. He waved on the wagons, then turned Hunnul to face the oncoming troops. He had to pause for a moment to draw a deep breath and steady his thoughts. He was growing weary from using magic, and he didn't want to lose control of the power when the Tarns were bearing down on him. When he was ready, he formed a spell that crackled into the grass before the charging horses. In a blinding flash,

the grass burst into towering flames. Horses suddenly
screamed in terror and fell back; their riders shouted with
fear as a wall of fire rose high above their heads and formed
a great circle around them. Smoke billowed up in great,
blinding clouds.

Valorian, his expression bleak, turned back to follow the
caravan, leaving the fire to hold off the Tarns. Another crash
of thunder from the approaching storm rolled over the hills,
and the chief hoped fervently that his flames would last long
enough to allow the Clan to cross into Sarcithia.

He was pleased to see that the repaired wagons had
caught up with the tail end of the caravan. The rear guard
was urging everyone and helping the stragglers as best they
could, so Valorian galloped Hunnul on past the remaining
wagons to the ford.

The scene there was chaotic. The heavy vehicles and
numerous hooves had churned the banks of both sides of
the river into knee-deep mud that clung to legs and wagon
wheels. Several conveyances were bogged down, and one
terrified team was balking and blocking the way for those
behind it. Mordan was trying desperately to bring order to
the uproar of cracking whips, squealing animals, and shouting people. He nodded with relief when Valorian came to
join him.

Once more the chieftain drew on his power and used a
magic spell to help free the mired wagons. As soon as they
were moving again, he and Mordan led the frightened team
across the river. Together they sorted out the tangle of vehicles and animals and directed them across until the flow of
traffic settled into a steady, reasonably calm crossing to the
woods on the other side. Somewhere on the trail ahead,
Aiden was leading the wagons deeper into Sarcithia.

At the same time, Valorian kept a cautious eye on the
storm clouds filling the west and the black, soaring clouds of
smoke to the north. He prayed that the wind wouldn't shift
and blow the flames toward the caravan and that the storm
wouldn't break too soon and put out his fire. As if to taunt

him, thunder boomed nearby, and the wind gusted noisily through the trees along the river.

At long last, the final wagon surged into the river. Behind it came the brood mares and their foals, sending sheets of water flying as they trotted across the ford. At the rear of the herd, Gylden waved a weary hand to indicate that these were the last horses to cross. Valorian watched the mares walk up the muddy bank into Sarcithia, and he felt relief like a sudden ease of pain. The Clan was safely across.

Only a moment later, the relief was driven from his thoughts by a flash of lightning and a tremendous crack of thunder. Valorian flinched. Once again he felt that odd surge of energy, as if something was increasing the magic around him, but before he had time to think about it, the sky opened in a deluge of rain.

"Get across!" he bellowed at the rear guard. The men spurred their horses into the water, followed closely by Valorian and Mordan. They had just reached the Sarcithian bank when a faint rumble of horses' hooves came to them over the noise of the storm. Valorian half-turned to look and saw that the smoke of his fire was quickly dissipating. The heavy rain was dampening the flames, and the Tarns had apparently broken through.

Valorian and Mordan glanced at one another in weary triumph, then wheeled their horses around to follow the caravan into the woods.

By the time the Tarnish cavalry reached the river, there was little sign of the Clan. All they could see were the churned and muddy banks, the empty river, and the trees on the far side, dripping with rain. Then one man pointed toward the distant forest, and they all saw a large, dark shape, indistinct in the heavy rain, standing in the wind-tossed shadows of the undergrowth. The figure seemed to watch them for a moment before it moved and the Tarns recognized it as a black horse and its rider. There was a flash of lightning overhead, and the rider was gone from sight.

The commander paled. He looked up and down the river, as if seeking an answer, but in his own mind he knew General Tyrranis would never forgive him for his failure.

"We could cross over," a young officer suggested.

The commander shook his head with bitter frustration. "General Tyrranis ordered us to stop them before they crossed the river. He said nothing about invading Sarcithia. You know we cannot enter another province under arms without permission from the ruling governor."

"Well, why can't we just slip over there and drive the Clan back into Chadar?" another officer asked.

"Not without General Tyrranis's direct order."

A third man grimaced. "Who are you more afraid of," he muttered under his breath, "Tyrranis or that magic-wielding clansman?"

But Commander Lucius heard him, and the grain of truth in the man's remark stung deeply. "It is our general's responsibility to decide if we break the emperor's law, not mine!" he said harshly. "It is Tyrranis who would have to face the emperor's punishment if Governor Antonine ever found out we chased after the Clan into Sarcithia. I will not be accountable for that!"

The younger Tarn looked appalled as he realized the full import of this fiasco. "But surely the general will understand."

Commander Lucius sagged in his saddle. His eyes followed the muddy trail of the caravan into the trees on the far bank, and he said hollowly, "The general never understands failure."

*   *   *   *   *

General Tyrranis closed his fingers tightly around the hilt of the sword at his side. His basilisk eyes burned into the trembling gaze of the commander who was trying to make his report.

The officer was standing in the mud with his back to the

river while the last drops of rain fell from the thinning clouds. "He started a fire, sir, that completely surrounded us," he was saying. "We couldn't escape without serious injuries to the men and the horses, and by the time we—"

Before Commander Lucius could finish his sentence, Tyrranis whipped his sword around and brought it slashing into the man's neck. Blood splattered over the general's armor as the commander's head came loose and thudded to the ground. The body remained upright for just a moment, as if it couldn't accept what had happened, then it, too, toppled into the mud and lay twitching at Tyrranis's feet. In an instant, the bloody sword point was poised at the throat of a second officer.

"Tell me something useful so I do not do the same to you!" the general snarled.

The officer held very still, desperation plain in his face. "General, sir! Sar Nitina is not far from here. With a small honor guard, you could ride there in two days. You could visit Governor Antonine and receive permission for our troops to pass. We could still make it to Wolfeared Pass before the Clan."

"How do you know that is where they are going?" Tyrranis demanded, the bloody sword still pressed against the officer's neck. Cunning began to glow in his eyes as new possibilities emerged through his anger.

The officer swallowed hard and stared straight ahead, encouraged by the general's slight hesitation. "They are moving south, sir, and we have heard rumors that Valorian wants to go to the Ramtharin Plains. Wolfeared Pass is the only pass near here low enough to allow wagons."

Tyrranis's eyes narrowed to slits as he considered the officer's words. The man made sense. Valorian did seem to be in command of this exodus, so it was quite likely that he was trying to lead the Clan out of the Tarnish Empire. Not that it mattered. They were never going to reach their destination.

That is where Governor Antonine would be useful. Most provincial governors got very nervous and irritated when a neighboring governor asked to move into their jurisdiction with a large, heavily armed force. Antonine, the governor of Sarcithia, however, was a young, impetuous man who had come to his power through wealth, connections, and bribery. He had no real experience dealing with crises, so it should be possible to talk him into allowing a hunt for the Clan over his province.

The officer beside Tyrranis shot a quick look at the body of his commander lying in the mud nearby before he offered his final bid to save his life. He cleared his throat. "There is also the Twelfth Legion, sir. It is still stationed in Sar Nitina. If you remember, last winter they received word to remain there to help guard the new borders."

A strange expression, a cross between a snarl and a smile, altered Tyrranis's bloodthirsty grimace. Slowly he handed his sword to an orderly. "You are the commander now," he said to the officer. "Pick five men to ride with me to Sar Nitina."

The new second-in-command saluted Tyrranis's back as the general whirled and strode to his horse. He tried to feel relieved and pleased by his reprieve and the unexpected field promotion, but the position of commander under Tyrranis seemed to be dubious at best and definitely not a guarantee of honor and long life. Perhaps he had merely postponed the inevitable.

Leaving the main body of his army camped on the banks of the Bendwater, General Tyrranis and his men rode late into the night through mud and darkness, following the river until they were ready to drop. He allowed them only a short rest before he pushed them on again at dawn. By noon, they had reached a newly paved road called the Tartian Way, one of the roads that united Chadar and Sarcithia. The Tartian Way crossed the Bendwater River, then followed it south and west. The road eventually ended in Sar Nitina's huge public square in front of the governor's palace and the barracks of the XIIth Legion.

Sar Nitina was a river port nearly as big as Actigorium, a popular stopping place for pilgrims, and a city of artisans.

While Actigorium was a large agricultural center, Sar Nitina was a resort town catering to tourists, wealthy visitors, and a large stream of pilgrims who came through from all parts of the empire on their way to visit shrines throughout the south.

When the Chadarian governor arrived at the river port city in the afternoon two days later, Governor Antonine met him at the gates of his small but elegant palace. He noted with a qualm the soldiers' battle armor, their full complement of weapons, and the look of cold determination on Tyrranis's face, but he put on a pleased expression and offered them his hospitality. The knowledge that he himself had a full legion at his beck and call gave him a greater feeling of confidence and generosity, even in the face of an unexpected visit from the infamous General Tyrranis.

The two governors retired to the palace, to a large, airy garden room that Antonine had had built for the pleasure of his numerous mistresses. Servants brought cooled wine, sweet cakes, and fruit for the two men and discreetly retired. Antonine and Tyrranis settled themselves comfortably in a pair of couches to talk and sample the fine wine.

Yet neither of them relaxed. They had never met one another before, and their characters were too different to be compatible. They spent the first part of their visit taking each other's measure.

Tyrranis wasn't impressed by what he saw in Antonine. The young governor hadn't won his position through ability or service; it had been given to him, along with plenty of intelligent secretaries, aides, and legion officers to help him run the prosperous, peaceful country. The lack of any real effort in his life showed in Antonine's every indolent movement, in his lazy gaze, and in the pudgy roundness of his body. He was a handsome young man, in a soft way, with wavy blond hair, nondescript blue eyes, full lips, and broad, uncalloused hands. Tyrranis thought to himself that Antonine's hands probably spent more time fondling women than handling a sword.

He drowned out his contempt with friendly politeness and graciously accepted another glass of wine.

"It is such a pleasure to meet you at last," Antonine was saying between bites on a small sugared cake. "But I must admit I was surprised to see you." He lifted an eyebrow inquiringly.

Tyrranis hooded his reptilian eyes under half-closed lids. "You have heard of the Clan?" he asked mildly.

Antonine looked puzzled. "The Clan? Hmmm . . . Oh, you mean that disreputable pack of thieves and herdsmen that hide up in the Bloodiron Hills?" He shrugged. "What do they have to do with a provincial governor leaving his capital and province for an unannounced visit to Sar Nitina?"

"They have been causing some trouble," Tyrranis replied, trying not to be irritated by Antonine's question or his bored tone. "They have banded together and are fleeing Chadar."

"Banded together? Indeed. How inconvenient." The full meaning of Tyrranis's words suddenly occurred to Antonine, and he blinked several times before he asked in mild alarm, "Have they caused many problems?"

Tyrranis nodded. "They are heavily armed and very dangerous." He decided not to mention Valorian's magic until he had to, for fear of terrifying Antonine out of his ineffectual wits. He would merely stir up the young man's sense of duty. "They pillaged and burned their way down the length of Chadar."

His cake forgotten, Antonine straightened in his seat and asked suspiciously, "And where are these renegades now?"

The Chadarian general sighed sadly, steepled his fingers, and answered, "They crossed into Sarcithia two days ago."

"What?" Antonine lifted his chin and sat straighter. "And you did nothing to stop them?"

Tyrranis didn't move. "I was unable to be with my men when they chased the Clan to the Bendwater River. The commander who let them escape has been dealt with, but by law, I could not simply charge my troops into your province after those outlaws."

"No. No, of course not." Antonine shook his head in agitation. "Where are these clanspeople going?"

"We believe to Wolfeared Pass and the Ramtharin Plains."

The young man's face cleared. "Oh! Well, that changes things. If they want to go to the other side of the Darkhorns and starve on those empty plains, let them." He sat back, relieved, and helped himself to another cake.

General Tyrranis waited until the cake was eaten, then stared thoughtfully at the ceiling and said, "Unless, of course, they decide to stay in Sarcithia and raid your villages and farms, or rob caravans and travelers."

The Sarcithian governor paled. "They wouldn't dare do that with the Twelfth Legion here," he cried. "That would be folly."

"Whoever said clanspeople were intelligent? As you said, they are thieves. Greedy, violent thieves." Tyrranis slowly leaned forward to stare unblinkingly at the younger man. "And what if they do escape the Tarnish Empire? Do you want to be the one who explains to the emperor why you refused to help me capture these outlaws who are endangering the peace and security of two of his most profitable provinces?"

Antonine sagged back on his seat and was silent for a long time while he tried to think of ways to squirm out of this onerous duty. He wanted no part of chasing a pack of bloodthirsty barbarians around the countryside. Annoyingly he could think of no way to get out of it that would leave his public image intact. Tyrranis was right: They had to bring these people to heel. However, Antonine knew he couldn't simply let the Chadarian general march freely through Sarcithia with such a large force. Nor, Antonine swore angrily to himself, was he going to allow Tyrranis to take any part of the Twelfth Legion without him.

"Thank you for bringing this to my attention, General Tyrranis," he said at last, trying not to be surly. "If you wish to accompany me, we will take the Twelfth Legion. *They* will have no trouble dealing with these brigands."

Pleased, General Tyrranis ignored the insult. His mouth tightened into an unpleasant smile, and his eyes glittered like a predator's. "That will do," he murmured, as if to himself.

Antonine looked away, stifling a shudder at the brutal light he saw in Tyrranis's face. "Have you a plan of action in mind?" he asked sarcastically. He had no use for tactical maneuvers, but knowing Tyrranis's past reputation in war, the general had probably planned his strategy even before he arrived in Sar Nitina.

"Of course," the general replied coldly. "We send a fast messenger to my men waiting on the Bendwater. They will force-march south to meet us at the Argent River near Wolf-eared Pass. The Clan travels on the mountain paths, so we should easily reach the trail to the pass before they do and have time to arrange a small welcome for them."

Antonine didn't bother to argue, criticize, or debate the general's plan. "So be it," he said resignedly, and he sent for General Sarjas, the commander of the XIIth Legion.

By early evening, the legion was on the march.

16

he Clan wanted to celebrate after their successful crossing of the Bendwater, and for one day, Valorian allowed them relief and rest. They found a broad meadow ringed with trees late that evening and set up camp there. They were awake half the night talking, telling stories, and singing, still energized by the effects of the wild race for the river and the crossing into Sarcithia. The only thing Valorian forbade was fires. The caravan was still in Tarnish territory, he warned the people, and too close to Sar Nitina for comfort.

Although the Chadarian garrison hadn't crossed the Bendwater River, the chieftain had a strong suspicion the general hadn't given up. Tyrranis was too tenacious, too obsessed by vengeance and a desire for power, to let a mere thing like a border or jurisdiction thwart him for long. With Sar Nitina within marching distance and Governor Antonine likely to help him, Valorian knew it would only be a matter of time before the Tarns were after the Clan again . . . and there was still a long way to go to Wolfeared Pass.

So Valorian gave his people one day to rest, hunt, gather food in the hills, dry their clothes and gear, tend their stock, and enjoy their respite. Then he moved them on once more. They followed without too much complaint, since even the dullest among them could see the sense of Valorian's reasons and knew the fear of General Tyrranis's legionnaires.

Nevertheless, Valorian worried about his people, especially the children, the elders, and the pregnant women. The journey had been hard on everyone, and while no person, other than Karez, voiced any bitter objections, Valorian could see the strain on the faces of young and old alike. He wished there was an easier way to find peace and freedom; he wished he didn't have to put his people through this ordeal.

But when he voiced his concern to Mother Willa, his grand-mother laughed. "We chose this journey, as you well know!" she reassured him. "We'll make it. Just look at your wife. Look at me or Linna. Do we appear to be on our last legs?"

Valorian had to admit they did not. Kierla, Linna, and Mother Willa shared a cart on the trail, and all three women were healthy. Even Kierla, with her baby and her growing womb, was glowing with well-being.

"Yes," Mother Willa went on, "we are tired and hungry. People have been hurt and some animals lost. But, Valorian, look how far we've come!" She gave him a bright smile intended to boost his flagging confidence. "Don't worry about us. Worry about that awful Tyrranis and how to get us over those mountains. We'll have plenty of time to complain when we get to the Ramtharin Plains."

Valorian appreciated her words and took strength from her wisdom. In the back of his mind, he knew she was right, yet it helped sometimes to hear another person tell him.

For seven more days, the Clan worked its way south along the flanks of the mountains toward the valley of the Argent River and the trail up to Wolfeared Pass. They saw very few people in these hills. Most Sarcithians lived along the coast or in the river valleys to the east. Up in the higher elevations, there were only some scattered shepherds, a few mountain men, and an occasional band of outlaws. One small gang followed the caravan for a half a day hoping to pick off some animals or a straying wagon until the rear guard drove them off. Nobody seriously threatened the large caravan, and there was no sign of any Tarnish soldiers.

In the meantime, the weather remained clear and warm, the trail stayed dry, and the caravan made good progress. On the seventh day into Sarcithia, the people clearly saw for the first time the strange twin peaks they had heard so much about. It was there, they said to one another; the pass was truly there! It was still several days' journey away, but just to see the peaks gave every man and woman a thrill of confidence.

Ten days after leaving Chadar, the Clan arrived at the Argent River valley, where the trail from Wolfeared Pass wound down out of the mountains. Valorian had forgotten how beautiful the valley was, made prettier now by the verdant green growth and burgeoning wildflowers of spring.

The valley floor was broad and grassy, its walls steep, rocky, and overgrown with trees. The river, a bouncing, noisy, white-rapid stream nestled into the valley floor, flowed in a ribbon of silver through groves of broad-leafed trees, willows, rushes, meadows, and stands of evergreens. Behind it all, like an omnipotent guardian, stood the white-capped ramparts of Wolfeared Peak.

The clanspeople paused when they saw the breathtaking view. They stared in appreciation and excitement and hoped that the land beyond the mountains was equally as beautiful. Contented, they angled their wagons down to the river, turned east, and headed into the mountains for the final climb to the pass.

The next day dawned clear and mild, with a slight breeze and the hint of heat to come in the afternoon. The clanspeople broke camp early, eager to be on their way. Valorian, his guards, and the men riding in the vanguard took their places at the head of the caravan. At the sound of the signal horn, voices shouted, whips popped, wheels creaked, and the procession was on the move once again.

They traveled without incident through the morning, moving deeper and deeper into the valley. Gradually the valley floor narrowed, and the walls steepened and rose higher. The day turned warm as the morning breeze died to a whisper.

Valorian was riding Hunnul ahead of the cluster of guards and warriors when a great white-headed eagle abruptly launched itself out of a tall pine to the right of the trail. Its piercing screech filled the valley with its warning. Hunnul stopped in his tracks. His head went up, and his nostrils flared to search for a scent of danger on the light breeze. Suddenly he snorted.

The angry word "*Tarns!*" had barely registered in Valorian's mind when a dense flight of arrows rose out of the rocks from the right and dropped out of the sky into the midst of the unsuspecting vanguard. The quiet morning burst into bloody, yelling confusion. Hunnul wheeled back as another flight of arrows swarmed among the Clan warriors before Valorian could react. Several whizzed by his head, forcing him to duck, and he saw a dozen men fall, pierced by the Tarnish shafts. Three other men were wounded and clinging to their horses. The chief felt a sickening surge of rage.

"Ambush!" someone screamed, and the word was flashed down the line of wagons and carts. Simultaneously a force of about a hundred Tarnish soldiers rose from their hiding places among the clustered rocks and trees of the steep valley slope and came leaping down to attack the vanguard.

Valorian didn't move for a moment while he tried desperately to decide what to do. The vanguard was too disorganized by the sudden attack to form an effective defense, and there wasn't enough time for him to reach them to help. He had to act immediately or the Tarns would overwhelm the smaller force of clansmen. Then his eyes fell on the large clumps of boulders that rested on the slope above the trail.

He rose to his full height on the back of his great horse. His eyes snapping with fury, he pulled the magic out of the earth itself, shaped his spell, and sent it hurtling back as a barrage of powerful bolts that exploded into the ground beneath the piles of tumbled boulders. The section of the slope lurched from the force of his power; the rocks slid out of their resting places and began to slide downhill. Their growing momentum jarred others loose until the slide became a grinding monster of rock, earth, and gravel. The soldiers stopped, staring at the approaching landslide with horror. They tried to run, but it was too late.

"Get back!" bellowed Valorian to his men.

Terrified, the clansmen grabbed their wounded and scrambled back out of the way as the landslide came rolling and thundering down the hill in a great cloud of dust. It caught the Tarnish soldiers and dragged them down into the churning mass of rock. The slide rumbled all the way to the riverbank before its impetus slowed and the roaring noise of its passage slowly grumbled to an end.

Valorian stared balefully at the settling dust and the strip of land laid bare. All along the ground below him, the trunks of trees and the bodies of men lay broken and twisted among the rocks. He saw that some of the soldiers were struggling to get out of the rockslide's debris or to help others who were trapped or wounded, but he doubted from their slow movements or stunned faces that they were going to offer any more trouble to the Clan.

The chieftain turned away to assess the condition of his own people. He hadn't had time to realize who had been killed or wounded, and his heart was in his mouth as he hurried back to the caravan.

The lead wagons had stopped during the aborted ambush, which had brought the entire caravan to a halt. Some of the clanspeople were helping the wounded men, while others were coming up to join the vanguard and keep a close watch on the broken Tarnish force.

Valorian gave the wagons only a cursory glance before he slid off Hunnul and went to help the wounded. His heart was pounding with dread. When he saw Aiden alive and uninjured, his fear and anger eased, then it soared again when he saw the dead faces of two of his guards, who had ridden with him from the gates of Actigorium and had stood by him before the duel with Karez. One of his other guards was slightly grazed, and there were five other warriors who were wounded. But there was still one face Valorian had not seen yet.

He hurried from group to group, helping where he could, loading the wounded into wagons, and searching. He used his power to dissolve arrows lodged in men's bodies and to transform scraps of cloth into clean linens for bandages.

Finally Valorian yelled to his brother, "Where is Mordan?"

Aiden shook his head and pointed to a wagon several vehicles back. His face grim, Valorian hurried over, and there he found his friend lying on a pile of blankets hastily thrown over the contents of the wagon. Mordan stirred slightly when Valorian climbed up beside him, but the chieftain went cold. It was immediately obvious why someone had put Mordan there without trying to bandage his wound. In the bloodied mess of Mordan's torn tunic was an arrow lodged between his ribs.

Valorian felt sick. Mordan's lids were open, his eyes dark pools against his deathly white skin. He was breathing in shallow, rapid breaths, and his hands were clenched against the pain. He saw his chieftain and attempted a feeble smile.

Very carefully Valorian used his dagger to cut away part of Mordan's tunic. He probed the edges of the ugly wound and studied Mordan's face. Usually an arrow buried in a clansman's chest spelled death. The clanspeople had very simple surgical practices and only herbal medicines. Removing the shaft and barb would kill him as quickly as leaving it in his chest.

But Valorian's hopes rose a little as he examined the muscular warrior. He didn't think the barb had pierced Mordan's lung or heart, for there was no blood on his lips and his pallor wasn't gray with approaching death. Perhaps, with magic, he would be able to help his friend. He could not heal; he could only remove. But maybe that would be enough to give Mordan a fighting chance to live.

Gently Valorian touched a finger to the red-dyed feathers. Mordan stared up at him, totally trusting. There was a pause while Valorian concentrated, then a brief word and the arrow vanished, shaft and all, into mist, leaving only the wound of its entry.

Mordan's fingers slowly uncurled. "You have a habit of disappointing the Harbingers," he whispered gratefully.

"They can argue with Amara," Valorian said, hiding his own intense relief behind the task of bandaging the bleeding wound. He clasped Mordan's shoulder and was about to leave him when the warrior's hand clamped on his arm.

"Lord," Mordan said, his voice hoarse with worry and pain. "That was only a small force trying to slow us down. They knew we were coming. Look to the rear!"

Valorian jumped to his feet with a sudden jolt of apprehension. Mordan's words made too much sense. The caravan, stopped in place, was open and vulnerable to attack, and it wound down the valley for a long way through trees and open spaces, making it impossible for Valorian to see the end of it. If the attack on the vanguard was meant to stop the train of wagons, then it was likely that the rear was in danger, too. A powerful sense of urgency boiled up inside him.

He whistled for Hunnul. "See you at the pass," he said softly to Mordan and jumped from the wagon to Hunnul's back. He shouted to his brother, "Aiden, get the caravan moving now! Get them to the pass!" and he was gone, racing along the file of wagons toward the rear.

"Get moving! Go, go!" he yelled to the Clan drivers as Hunnul galloped by. "Don't stop. Keep going!"

He and the stallion were halfway back along the length of the caravan when the frantic blast of the rear guard's signal horn sounded through the valley, followed almost immediately by Tarnish legion horns signaling the attack. Fear swept up the stalled wagons. The drivers, already nervous and tense from the ambush in front, began jostling their vehicles and teams and shouting at one another. The drovers pushed their herds into motion again.

Perhaps thirty mounted men and boys riding beside the wagons saw Valorian racing back toward the rear guard and rode after him to help. Screaming broke out from the end of the train of vehicles, mingled with the clash of weapons.

Hunnul plunged into a patch of trees and out the other side in two strides, just in time to see the warriors in the rear

guard close into hand-to-hand fighting with a troop of Tarnish cavalry wearing the crescent moon of the IVth Legion.
The men were too close together for Valorian to use his
magic, so he slowed Hunnul just long enough for the other
riders to catch up with him. Then he drew his sword and
shouted a piercing war cry. The small force of clansmen
charged into the skirmish.

Hunnul plunged into the midst of the Tarnish horsemen
with hooves kicking and teeth snapping. Valorian fought with
desperation and cold anger, laying about him with his black
sword as if every man who faced him were Tyrranis himself.

Shouts of rage, cries of pain, and the deafening clash of
iron on iron filled his ears. The clansmen around him were
fighting like wolves with every weapon they could lay their
hands on. They weren't as well trained or armed as the
legionnaires, but they stood to lose everything if they failed.
Every clansmen knew there would be no surrender.

Valorian parried a heavy blow at his head from a beefy
Tarnish officer, avoided a second blow, and swiftly jabbed
his blade at the unprotected spot between the man's jaw
and his breastplate. Blood spurted from the wound, and the
Tarn toppled from his horse. Hunnul pushed forward
through the struggling mass of horses and men.

"For Surgart and Amara!" Valorian yelled over the uproar,
and his men, hearing his rally cry, responded with yells of
their own.

Slowly the Tarns began to give way before the ferocious
defense of the Clan warriors. The soldiers had expected to
meet weak, cowardly clansmen who would flee at the first
strong attack. They weren't prepared for the fierce-eyed men
and boys who fought back with a strength born of desperation.

Suddenly the melee seemed to lurch as the Tarns hesitated.
"Withdraw!" a soldier yelled, and the Tarns broke off, turned
their horses, and galloped away, leaving the clansmen gasping in relief. The beleaguered rear guard raised a cheer when
they saw the legionnaires fleeing back down the valley.

"Lord Valorian, you're a welcome sight," called one of the warriors with a tired grin.

The chieftain hung on to Hunnul, who was prancing in excited circles, and asked, "What happened here?"

"They came out of those woods up there," the warrior responded, and he pointed to a large strip of trees growing along the edge of the valley. "Just as we passed by, they charged out at us. There must have been almost a hundred of them! If you hadn't come when you did, they would have overrun us for sure."

"Did you see General Tyrranis with them?"

The man shook his head. "No."

Valorian stared worriedly down the valley where the Tarns had disappeared. If there had been about one hundred soldiers in the front ambush and the same number in the rear, where was the rest of the garrison? Where was Tyrranis? The general would never let the Clan get away this easily!

The chief swiftly urged his men to the task of gathering their dead and wounded and loading them into the back wagons. At last the tail end of the caravan began to move again, and the rear guard fell in behind it. More mounted men from the caravan rode back to join Valorian until there were over one hundred men, boys, and a few women of all ages gathered in ragged ranks behind the wagons.

There was now a strong body of men in the vanguard with Aiden and a larger force in the rear with Valorian. The chieftain hoped against all odds that that would suffice. There simply weren't enough fighting men to ring the entire caravan. On the other hand, he didn't think they had to worry about an assault in the middle of the line of wagons. If one had been planned to coincide with the ambushes at the head and rear, it would have occurred by now. The valley itself protected them, too, for with its river, it was too narrow to allow a large force to move up unopposed and attack the center. He thought Tyrranis had probably planned the ambushes to stop the caravan so the larger remaining force could sweep up and overwhelm it. But his plan hadn't worked, and now the Clan was on the move again.

Valorian glanced back over his shoulder and wondered what Tyrranis would try next.

He didn't have to wait long to find out. The Clan passed the place of the first ambush without any more trouble. Disregarding the dead and wounded Tarns, they traveled on as quickly as the rough terrain would allow. They had only gone a short distance up the trail, though, when a shout brought the rear guard whirling around. One of the warriors pointed down the valley, and everyone saw the full remaining forces of the Chadarian garrison coming into sight along the crest of a low slope near the river. Red pennons fluttered on their spears, and their armor sparkled in the afternoon sun.

As the Clan warriors watched, the Tarnish cavalry wheeled into position, forming seven widely spaced lines that stretched from the river to the high valley walls. Valorian felt his apprehension grow. The soldiers seemed to be trying something different in hopes of thwarting his power. Their ranks were much thinner and farther apart than usual, perhaps to prevent him from focusing his spells on a single mass.

To his dismay, they were right. His power was great, but he was only one man facing hundreds, and his strength and concentration were limited by his body's weaknesses. If the Tarns were determined enough and could distract or kill him, they could easily sweep over the entire caravan.

Valorian's mouth went dry. Slowly he sheathed his sword and tried to calm himself so he could think clearly. Under his breath, he said a prayer to all four deities to watch over the Clan. The Harbingers had already been busy in this valley today, and he didn't want to give them more to do. He glanced at his companions and saw that they were all as nervous as he. He recognized, with a start of surprise, Karez sitting on his big white horse in the rank just behind him. The big clansman must have joined them just a few moments before. Valorian felt uneasy under the uncharitable thought that perhaps he ought to watch his back, also.

Karez noticed his chieftain looking at him and he grinned, his teeth flashing in his dark beard. As if he guessed what Valorian was thinking, he waved his sword at the enemy.

Just then, the Tarnish trumpets blew the charge. The blaring notes soared through the valley, accompanied by a great shout and the sudden thunder of hoofbeats.

The clansmen automatically surged forward, but Valorian called them back. "Hold your places!" He held on to Hunnul's mane as the stallion half-reared and leapt forward to the front of the meager Clan lines.

The caravan behind them rumbled on up the trail, faster and faster. The herds of horses and stock animals broke into panicked flight.

The Tarnish charge approached at a terrifying speed. Their lines grew ragged as the horses galloped over the uneven terrain. There was another loud blast from their horns, and the horsemen's spears lowered in unison, point first toward the waiting rear guard.

Valorian took only a moment to wonder where General Tyrranis was before he lifted his hands and launched his first attack. He fired six large spheres of blue energy in rapid succession, spaced out along the lines of galloping horses. The fusillade landed with terrible force among the riders. Explosions rocked the ground and blew dirt and rocks in all directions, frightening some horses and knocking others off their feet.

But it wasn't enough. The Tarns were expecting the magical bombardment, and they continued their charge.

Valorian hesitated while he racked his mind for another idea. He didn't want to try a fire again since the line of soldiers was too long and the wind was blowing up the valley from the east. Nor could he use another rockslide over an area so large. He needed a new tactic.

Suddenly a possibility intruded into his thoughts that seemed so crazy he decided to try it. He couldn't create life, but he could create the image of life, as he had done when he told the story of his journey into Gormoth. He would use the same sort of image, only make it larger and see how brave the Tarns really were.

He closed his eyes to remember the small, ugly forms of the gorthlings and shaped the spell in his mind. Using dust and bits of gravel, dirt, and leaves to give his image substance, he molded the magic into a gigantic animated form. He knew it had worked when he heard his own men yell in fright.

The chieftain opened his eyes and surprised even himself with the huge realistic creature that now stood between the charging Tarns and the Clan. It was fearsome! A monstrous, bestial figure of a gorthling that towered above the nearby trees and blocked the valley trail. The Tarnish cavalry saw it and brought their horses to a rearing, sliding stop.

It was difficult to tell the creature wasn't solid and could do no real damage, but before the horrified Tarns could realize that, Valorian set his creature into motion. It screeched terribly and reached out as if to grab the horses. The Tarnish lines disintegrated. Horses bolted in panic, taking their riders with them. Other soldiers yanked their mounts around and fled from the hideous monster back the way they had come.

"Stay put!" Valorian shouted to his own men. "The beast is only an image."

The clansmen stared from him to the creature in amazement, their eyes popping, yet they stayed in rank.

"Now back away slowly," he ordered and gestured to them to follow the caravan. They went gratefully. Valorian stayed where he was to maintain the image of the giant gorthling for as long as he could.

At the same time, on an overlook in the valley downriver, General Tyrranis and Governor Antonine watched the retreat of the Chadarian garrison with very different emotions. Tyrranis was rigid with anger at the cowardice and foolishness of his men.

Antonine was so shocked at this second display of magical power that he could hardly contain his rage and fear. He rounded on Tyrranis, his intense dismay momentarily blocking out his fear and hatred of the general. "Why didn't you tell me of this magic-wielding clansman?" he screamed at Tyrranis. "We cannot defeat a sorcerer of such power! We should have let them go. This whole journey was a waste. I will not allow my legion—"

He got no further. Tyrranis's hand lashed out and caught the young governor across the right cheek and nose, nearly knocking him from the saddle.

"Silence, you fool!" hissed Tyrranis. "His power isn't invincible."

Antonine glared ferociously and mopped the blood from his nose with a scented handkerchief. He was furious not only at the Chadarian governor, but at himself as well for not daring to retaliate. A stronger man wouldn't have stood for such a personal insult. "Not invincible!" he repeated, hiding his anger behind incredulity. "Look at that creature he has summoned. None of our soldiers will go past *that!*"

Tyrranis scoffed. "It's a fake, an image. Magic cannot create life. Look at it carefully. You can see light through it."

"I don't believe it. General Sarjas, surely you don't want to risk your troops against such a beast." Antonine appealed to the commander of the XIIth Legion, who was sitting on his horse behind them, tight-lipped at the actions of the two governors.

"He won't have to," Tyrranis snarled before the commander could speak. "I'll take my own garrison against the rear guard. You attack the Clan. Surely your legion will have no trouble dealing with women and children."

Stung by the insult in the repetition of his own earlier words, the young governor's face turned fiery red. "But what if there are more—"

"There are no other magic-wielders!" Tyrranis stabbed a finger toward the disappearing caravan. "There is only him, and he is mine!"

For just a moment, Antonine accidentally looked full into Tyrranis's dark eyes, past the icy glare into the seething rage in the general's mind. In that brief glimpse, he thought he saw the growing shadows of madness. A shudder overtook him, and he wrenched his eyes away from that awful face. "All right, all right," he said sullenly. "We will do it." Anything to finish this dreadful task and be rid of Tyrranis.

Without another word or gesture, Tyrranis drew his sword and whipped his horse into a gallop down the slope to cut off his retreating troops. The officers pulled up in front of him at the bottom of the hill, shamefaced and frightened, their horses lathered and their tunics dust-covered.

"Cowards!" he screamed at them. "You are not fit to be Tarns! Stop those men at once and reform your ranks before I cut you down myself."

None of the officers disobeyed him. As quickly as possible, they stopped the fleeing legionnaires, rounded up the panicked horses, and brought the troop back under control. All the while, the gorthling image roared and howled from its place on the trail.

When the IVth Legion detachments were regrouped, the general rode past the lines of white-faced soldiers. "What you see is a fake!" he yelled, shaking a fist toward the gorthling. "You ran from an image, you fools! *Those* are real." And he gestured to the rear guard and the tail end of the Clan caravan they could see disappearing up the valley. "Destroy them!" he bellowed. "Destroy them *now*. Prove that you are men, not rabbits."

The troops gave a ragged cheer. With the speed and skill that had always been his strength in battle, Tyrranis reorganized his men into a new attack formation.

But even his best plan or his worst threats wouldn't have convinced the legionnaires to attack that hideous screaming monster if Tyrranis himself had not led the charge. Raising his sword over his head, the Tarnish general bellowed the order to charge and spurred his horse into a gallop, straight toward the fearsome gorthling. The soldiers followed, rather reluctantly at first as they watched their general approach the monster, then with gathering confidence when they saw the gorthling could not lay its hands on the man.

Before the Tarns' startled eyes, Tyrranis forced his horse to run directly through the beast's legs. With a thunderous shout, the Chadarian forces spurred after him.

Valorian watched the general with dismay. He had to admit that Tyrranis had courage, but the general made things very difficult. Valorian's strength was flagging from the heavy use of magic, and now the Tarns were attacking again. He instantly blanked out the image of the gorthling to save his energy and sent Hunnul cantering back to catch up with the rest of the rear guard. The Clan warriors turned one more time to face the enemy while the caravan rumbled away as fast as it could go over the uneven ground.

This time the Tarns didn't charge in a straight line. They split into three groups that attacked the rear guard from several different directions. One group galloped up the slope above the valley and fired a black rain of arrows down into the lines of Clan warriors. The other groups, one led by Tyrranis, spurred their horses toward the front and the right flank of the rear guard.

Valorian tried desperately to duck the falling arrows behind his small shield and at the same time keep the Tarns at bay with missiles of blue energy, fireballs, and smoke screens. Yet the Tarns faced his barrage and kept coming. He felt his strength slowly draining away and his spells becoming weaker. Despite his power, he was only one man against determined, overwhelming forces who were coming at him from several different directions. None of the other clansmen could help him fight off the Tarns until they came into arrow range, and by that time, it was too late.

The Tarnish charge swept into their midst, their swords smashing into their defenses. Valorian and his rear guard tried to hold their formation, but the clansmen couldn't maneuver or fight the running battle they excelled at. They had to stand in the open and defend themselves. All too quickly their thin ranks crumpled under the overwhelming onslaught. The warriors fell back around their chieftain in a last attempt to make a stand. Everything was in a bloody tangle of horses wheeling and colliding, men struggling and falling, and over it all was the sickly smell of blood and fear.

In moments, the superior Tarnish forces had ringed in the rear guard and cut them off from the rest of the Clan. The end of the caravan was now left open and helpless.

Seeing their danger, the drivers urged their horses frantically and drew their own weapons to try to defend their lives and their families. Strangely, the Chadarian forces didn't move to attack the line of wagons. Instead, they concentrated their ferocity on the rear guard.

Valorian saw all of this with a horrified clarity. He couldn't defend the entire caravan when it was strung out along the trail, and now he was too busy fighting for his own life to defend the warriors around him. They were trapped in a desperate battle of hand-to-hand combat. Valorian knew if he didn't do something fast, the entire rear guard would be slaughtered, leaving the Clan virtually defenseless. He saw Tyrranis fighting his way toward him, and he began to urge Hunnul forward to meet the general.

Then he heard something that froze his blood. A new fanfare of trumpets blasted through the sounds of shouting, neighing, and clashing weapons. The chieftain jerked his head around to look down the valley. What he saw stunned him with an appalling feeling of utter despair.

There, in solid ranks of cavalry and infantry moving up beside the river, was an entire legion—one thousand of the emperor's finest men—heading rapidly after the fleeing Clan. Sick, Valorian recognized the black eagle emblems on their tunics. It was the XIIth Legion from the Ramtharin Plains.

Tyrranis cut down a young clansman in his way and saw the hopeless look on Valorian's face. "Yes, magic-wielder!" he shouted at the chieftain. "Your Clan is about to die!"

And for one moment of eternity, Valorian believed he was right.

17

ike an indestructible war machine, the legion's ranks marched in solid phalanxes past the surrounded rear guard. Their black pennons fluttered in the breeze like crows' wings. The tramp of their feet and the rattle of their armor sounded like a death knell to Valorian. He watched helplessly as they increased their speed to a quick jog to catch up to the Clan caravan.

The Chadarian garrison, encouraged by the sight of their comrades, tightened the ring of fighting relentlessly around the remaining warriors. The chieftain risked one last glance after the legion before he was forced to fend off another attacker. He gritted his teeth. He could taste the dust and smell the blood of his failure. If only he had more strength, more ability to wield his magic, more power. There just hadn't been enough of those within him to save his people. A stab of resentment burned through him. If he was Amara's champion, if he had risked everything to face the gorthlings for her, why was she letting him lead his people into this slaughter? Why had she turned her back on him?

Heartsick, he hefted his weapon and was about to rally his men when small fragments of his own thoughts came back into his mind with startling clarity. More power. Gorthlings.

Of course. That was what he needed, a gorthling. With a gorthling in his control to enhance his power, he could still use his magic to sweep away the Tarns and save his people. But, by the gods, how could be get one of those creatures out of Gormoth to help him here in the mortal realm? Would a gorthling's enhancement be effective outside of Ealgoden?

Valorian had no answers to his questions yet, and very little time left to learn them. His small force was being cut to pieces, and Tyrranis was closing in on him. Only two warriors stood between himself and the general, who was fighting ferociously to reach him.

Valorian made up his mind then and there. He had little left to lose at that point, and for good or ill, he was going to try it. He turned Hunnul away from the edge of the fighting to a small clear space in the center of the beleaguered ring. "Pull in, pull in!" he yelled to his men. "Fall back and stand by me!"

His cry went rapidly through the rear guard, and as fast as they could, the clanspeople obeyed. Some were still on horseback, some were on foot, and some were being held up by their friends. In all, there were only about half of the one hundred still alive. Together they formed a tight knot around their lord chieftain. The Tarns closed in after them.

Valorian realized he didn't have the strength to maintain a magic shield around his small force while he strove to capture a gorthling, but he could give them some shelter. Delving into the last of his strength, he focused his spell down into the ground to the rock beneath the soil.

Suddenly the earth began to rumble in a ring around the Clan warriors. The combatants paused in the midst of their fighting; the Tarns looked about nervously and began to back away. Only Tyrranis did not move. He was reaching for his protective amulet when all at once huge slabs of stone erupted through the ground at his horse's feet. The animal staggered backward out of the way. There was the sound of a great rending crash, and the slabs came together to form a circular wall higher than a man on horseback around the clansmen and their horses. A larger, opaque slab of rock rose higher than the rest and came down over the top with a thundering boom, forming a roof that would protect the men inside from the Tarns' arrows and spears.

A stunned silence fell over the battleground. The Tarns stared at the stone fortification in amazement and confusion.

Only General Tyrranis was not surprised. He was furious. "You cannot escape, clansman!" he shrieked. "You have just built your own tomb!" Then he turned to his men. "You have assaulted defenses bigger and stronger than this. Tear that thing apart—with your hands if you have to!" The soldiers hesitated, then reluctantly moved in toward the stone edifice.

Inside the round stone building, the clansmen were staring at the walls in equal amazement. "What is this?" one man murmured.

Valorian heard him and lifted his head to look at the men clustered around him. They were all weary, sweat-soaked, filthy with dirt and spattered blood. Several were wounded, and one man died even as his two friends laid him down to help him. Some of the riders were dismounting to calm their nervous horses.

The light glimmering through the opaque ceiling was dim with a strange yellow tint that cast a sickly hue over every man's face. The air was warm and growing stuffy with the smell of sweat and blood, but a slight breeze and some light were able to leak through the cracks between the slabs.

A harsh voice broke the silence. "Lord Valorian, what do you expect us to do now, set up camp?" It was Karez, snide as always.

Valorian ignored his tone and slid off Hunnul to the ground. His legs nearly buckled under him because he was so tired, and he had to catch Hunnul's mane to keep himself upright. "I'm going to summon help," he said hoarsely, "and I need time to do it."

"Time!" one of the warriors cried. "We have no time. Didn't you see the legion? They're going to slaughter the Clan! We have to stop them."

"We *will* stop them. But we are no good to our families dead."

"And they are no good to *us* dead!" Karez said belligerently. "You brought us to this disaster with your talk of escaping the Tarns. Well, they caught us anyway. Now what are you going to do?"

Valorian stifled the urge to weld Karez's tongue permanently to the roof of his mouth and said as calmly as he could, "I will do what I have to do. Now, be quiet! The rest of you keep a watch through those gaps in the stone."

The men and boys looked at one another uneasily, then did as he asked. The chieftain had brought them this far, farther than many believed they would ever get. Perhaps he could still save them.

Valorian went to stand beside the man who had just died. The man's two friends were still beside him, wiping the dirt from his face and laying his sword by his side. One man had tears in his eyes. The chieftain sagged to the ground and sat cross-legged beside the dead warrior. He had known the man for years and keenly felt his loss. "The Harbingers will be coming soon," he said softly.

The man's friends glanced at him askance at the mention of Harbingers, but they didn't move away.

Without a word being spoken, Hunnul came to stand behind Valorian, his long legs lightly supporting his master's back.

"I need your strength, my friend. Will you stay with me?" Valorian asked the stallion quietly.

Gladly, Hunnul replied and lowered his muzzle until it rested gently on the man's head. The clansmen around them watched curiously.

Although Valorian was still uncertain of what he was doing, he had an idea—the only idea he could think of. He prayed it would work, because he was certain he wouldn't have enough strength left to try anything else.

He pulled off his gold armband and set it on his knee in easy reach, leaned back against Hunnul's front legs, and closed his eyes. He felt the magic begin to gather within him. The sounds of the world around him gradually faded to silence as his mind ranged outward to touch the stallion's being. Because of their earlier meld, his thoughts found Hunnul's very quickly and merged perfectly into the horse's consciousness.

Valorian felt Hunnul's vast strength surge through him as hot and vivid as lightning. He realized, with a start of surprise, that traces of the lightning bolt's power were still within his horse. He hadn't noticed it before because he had been concentrating on Hunnul's mind, but now as he drew energy from the stallion's muscle, bone, and blood he could feel the crackling touch of the lightning sizzle through his every fiber.

Borne on the power of the black stallion, Valorian sent his consciousness questing out of his body to find the soul of the dead warrior beside him. He didn't know what to expect by such an attempt, or if it was even possible to separate his mind from his body. Yet with the magic, it seemed to work. He felt himself become weightless and lose all sense of feeling as his conscious self stepped out of the mortal bonds of his body.

His eyes opened. It startled him to see his body sitting by the horse not more than two paces away, and for a moment, he was afraid he had performed his spell too well and perhaps separated his soul from his body. Then he noticed his chest was moving slightly in and out, and a small trickle of blood was flowing from a cut on his arm. He was still alive.

Elated, he looked about for the soul of the dead man at his side. The world he had entered looked much the same as when he was struck by lightning. The mortal realm was out of focus and bright with an unearthly diffused light. But unlike the time before, the world of the living was not vanishing before his eyes. Valorian soon found the dead man's soul close by, confused, angry, and frightened. The chieftain knew those feelings well. He reached out to the dead man to reassure him and together they waited.

In eternity, there is no sense of time, and while Valorian thought the wait was terribly long, in reality, the Harbingers came before his body had drawn another breath. There were two of them this time, as shining white and enigmatic as Valorian remembered. They had brought a saddled steed for the man's soul and invited him to mount. If they sensed

Valorian's presence, they paid no attention to it.

Swifter than eagles they flew out of the mortal world into the curtain of mists, while Valorian's mind followed, using his touch with the dead warrior as a guide. He was glad he had the warrior to accompany him, for the passage through the thick gray mist was longer than he recalled. Without the Harbingers and the soul for company, he could have become disoriented and lost forever in the eternal mists. He tried not to think how he was going to get back alone.

At last they broke through into the blessed light and touched down on the plains of the realm of the dead. With the mountain of Ealgoden in sight, Valorian's mind bade a silent, sad farewell to his companion and sped over the green fields to the massive peak. He wondered if the gods knew he was there. He hoped they didn't. Lord Sorh might not appreciate a mortal borrowing one of his servants. He pushed the thought aside when Ealgoden's peak loomed beneath him. This time he didn't need to search for a doorway. He went directly to the entrance he had used before and plunged through the black rock into the cold, dark tunnel.

An intense aura of hatred and malice immediately struck him like a physical blow from the small, cunning minds of the gorthlings. It was a powerful mental sensation that he hadn't picked up when his soul traveled through Gormoth, and it nearly smothered him in its depth and strength. He fought off the destructive aura with every bit of his and Hunnul's combined strength and concentrated instead on finding a gorthling as quickly as possible.

He knew they were there in the rocks and crevices of the tunnel walls, waiting for condemned souls to come down the road, but he didn't know exactly where to look, and he didn't want to alert them by poking haphazardly into possible hiding places. However, there was one gorthling he remembered vividly, plus the place in the tunnel where it had been hiding. Perhaps it was still there. His mind probed deeper and deeper into the black holes. He didn't need lights this time to find his way, but he wished for one if only to dispel the terrifying, devouring darkness. Like a wraith, he slipped along the trail, past the lava river, and down the long, twisting passages.

At last he came to the section of tunnel where the gorthling had tried to snatch his dagger. As he had hoped, the little beast was hiding in a crevice waiting to torment approaching souls. Valorian gathered his magic into a powerful kinetic force, channeled it through his mental link into Gormoth, and snatched the gorthling out of its hiding place before it realized its danger. It gave a furious screech of alarm.

In an instant, every gorthling was aware of Valorian's presence and came swarming to stop him. The chief sensed rather than knew that if they caught up with him, they could imprison his consciousness with their own powerful, cunning thoughts. Desperately he pulled his mind through the tunnels, taking the gorthling with him.

The other creatures ran furiously after him. Valorian pushed faster, holding the gorthling in his mental grip. He slowly forged ahead of the pursuers and reached the entrance before they could trap him. He didn't know if the magic command to open the door would work from the inside, but he tried it anyway and was rewarded when the door cracked open. The darkness and the furious cries of the gorthlings vanished into light as Valorian brought himself and his prisoner out of Gormoth. Before the other gorthlings could escape, he slammed the door shut again and came hurtling back across the realm of the dead.

Too quickly they entered the mists that were the barrier between the mortal and immortal realms before the man had a chance to get his bearings. Now Valorian had no guide. He wasn't sure how wide the mists were or which direction to turn. His mind became disoriented by the total lack of sight, sensation, or physical touch, and his momentum stumbled to a halt. He probed this way and that into the blank mists and found nothing. Fingers of panic began to clutch at his consciousness.

The gorthling in his grip cackled in glee at his predicament. Then it stiffened angrily.

Far away, on the edge of the mists came a voice, masculine, strong, and rich in timbre. *Master! We are here! This way.* It was Hunnul, his being reaching out to Valorian. The chieftain raced after the beloved voice, its touch like a light glowing in the darkness.

Suddenly he was back in the warm, dim shelter, with the noises of horses and men assailing his ears and the pressure of Hunnul's legs against his back. Startled, he blinked and felt something squirm in his hands.

Master, the armband! Hunnul reminded him urgently.

Valorian snatched the gold armband and shoved it over the head of the furiously struggling creature in his grasp. When the gold settled around its neck, the gorthling subsided in his hands. Its high-pitched squeal of rage brought everyone's attention snapping around to the chief.

"Gods above, what is *that?*" Karez gasped. They all stared in horrified surprise at the little, wizened beast crouched like a hairless, desiccated monkey on Valorian's arm.

Another warrior cried, "That's a gorthling! You've brought one of those things out of Gormoth?"

There was a collective exclamation of revulsion and horror, and everyone jumped back against the stone wall.

The chieftain climbed to his feet with the gorthling still clinging to his arm. Hissing, it sidled up to his shoulder and glared balefully at the clansmen. "Yes, it's from Gormoth," Valorian answered grimly. "And back to Gormoth it will go when we have destroyed the Tarns."

The gorthling suddenly cackled, showing its sharp pointed teeth. "That's what you think, dung-head. You'll never send me back!" The men edged even farther away at the sound of its raspy, malicious voice.

Valorian ignored the creature. In truth, he wasn't certain how he was going to return the gorthling, but he would worry about that later. "How long have we been in here?" he asked, striding to a slit in the wall to look out. The Tarns were busy running back and forth and trying to shoot arrows between the stone slabs.

The clansmen looked at him strangely. One shrugged and replied, "Not for long, lord. You were only sitting there for a few minutes."

The chief drew a long breath of relief. A few minutes. The journey had seemed interminable to him. Maybe there was still time after all.

"Mount your horses," he said tersely.

"Mount your horses, stupid mortals. You're about to die," repeated the gorthling, sneering.

"Be quiet," demanded Valorian, "and stay put, or I'll stuff that gold down your foul little throat."

The gorthling's mouth clicked shut and he clung to Valorian's shoulder, looking sullen, while the clansman mounted Hunnul. The chief ran his hand down the stallion's silky neck and said softly, "Thank you, my friend." Hunnul bobbed his head in reply.

When everyone was ready, Valorian nodded once. "Cover your ears and hang on," he warned. He closed his eyes to concentrate. Would the gorthling's enhancement work here in the mortal world? he wondered. Had his quest into Gormoth been in vain? He began to summon the magic, and his answer came at once in an incredible flow of power. He felt invigorating strength flowing through his mind and body, enough strength to gather the magic out of the mountains themselves.

"Amara!" he cried in exultation and threw his arms wide to initiate his spell. At his command, the stone room suddenly exploded outward. The blast shattered the stone slabs and sent splinters and fragments of rock cutting like scythes through the Tarnish soldiers close by. The force of the explosion slammed others to the ground in a wide radius around the spot and leveled the entire ring of stone. The bodies of the dead lay scattered in the dirt and broken rubble.

For a moment, the clansmen and their horses, the Tarns and Tyrranis were stunned by the powerful blast. No one moved in the settling dust. Then Hunnul leaped forward up the trail, and the Clan warriors followed close on his heels.

"Stop them!" Tyrranis yelled furiously. Drawing his own bloody sword, the general kicked his horse to cut off Hunnul's escape. His officers and a few of the men who were still mounted followed him with their own weapons drawn.

Valorian saw them coming and felt his hatred rise to choke him. He wanted more than anything to sear Tyrranis to a smoking ruin, but he wouldn't break his vow for the likes of that man. Instead, he raised his sword over his head with both hands, lifted his voice in a great cry of rage, and clamped his legs to Hunnul's sides. The black flattened his ears, gathered himself into a mighty leap, and plowed directly into the general's big bay horse.

The brown stallion staggered under the force of the blow, knocking the general off balance. In a frenzy, Tyrranis clutched his sword and grabbed for his saddle horn, his face masked in rage. He clung to the side of his saddle while his horse tried to regain its balance, and he looked up at Valorian's implacable face. His lips curled in a snarl of hatred.

The black sword came smashing down on the general's shoulder at the edge of the polished breastplate. The blow knocked Tyrranis further off balance. He slipped sideways, exposing his neck for a brief moment, and in that space of time, Valorian struck again. His sword slashed into Tyrranis's neck and hacked through to the spine. The general's head lolled sideways as blood poured over his immaculate uniform. He seemed to hang on for a heartbeat or two, then his body sagged out of the saddle and fell to earth. His horse bolted away.

The gorthling on Valorian's shoulder licked its lips.

Almost in an afterthought, Valorian hurled a whirlwind of dust, gravel, and flailing winds into the midst of the other mounted officers that blew them off their terrified horses. The remaining soldiers of the Chadarian garrison, demoralized, made no further effort to follow the rear guard as they broke out of the encirclement and galloped up the trail after the caravan.

A prayer was on the chieftain's lips that he and his men weren't too late. By the position of the noon sun, he knew they hadn't been separated for long, but the XIIth Legion wouldn't need much time to catch and massacre the Clan. He sent Hunnul racing over the rocky trail, deeper into the valley, with the rear guard trying madly to keep up.

At first, Valorian couldn't see the caravan through the groves of trees and the rocky outcroppings. He heard it first—an inarticulate roar of screaming, yelling, roaring voices, mingled with the neighing of panicked horses and the rattle of weapons and armor. The sound cut to his heart.

Valorian leaned low over Hunnul's neck, his fingers clamped to his sword, and his body automatically adjusted to the horse's violent movements. The black mane whipped his face, and the gorthling's claws sunk into his shoulder, but he didn't feel a thing. He saw only the trail before him that led to the legion he must defeat.

All at once the valley opened up into a flat, broad meadow of thick grass, flowers, and butterflies. The Tarns had caught the caravan there and brought it to a crashing halt.

Valorian saw it all in a flash when Hunnul broke out of the trees and crested a small rise. A force of perhaps two hundred soldiers were positioned between him and the caravan. They were there presumably to keep the clanspeople from turning back or escaping into the woods and hills. To Valorian, they were a cutting insult, a challenge thrown in his face to keep him from his family. Farther ahead on the trail, the wagons, carts, and herds were thrown together in a chaotic mass of terrified people and animals, and all along that crowded line were clansmen and women tangled in bitter fighting with the legionnaires.

The chieftain's jaw tightened. Once again he relied on the gorthling's touch to summon more forces of magic. His vivid blue eyes seemed to spark from the vast power he drew out of the earth, river, and trees. On his shoulder, the gorthling began to bob and weave in excitement, for it had never felt such power before. The other warriors were close behind them now, their expressions angry and grim.

In unison, they broke over the rise and galloped down on the force of Tarnish soldiers who were sitting patiently on their horses, watching the battle surge around the caravan. The Tarns weren't expecting an attack from their rear, since they thought the remains of the Clan rear guard were being destroyed by Tyrannis's men. It wasn't until they heard the hoofbeats close by and a few men turned to look that they realized their danger. Before they could set up any defense, the clansman on the big black horse raised his hand toward them.

Several bolts of crackling white-hot energy shot from Valorian's hand and slammed into the ground at their feet. To the soldiers, the white streaks looked like bolts of lightning. They had seen a little of Valorian's magic from a distance, but nothing prepared them for the powerful, jagged streaks in their midst or the thundering explosions as the energy hit the rocky ground. Men and horses were slammed to the ground; those that were still on their feet were quickly cut down by the clansmen behind Valorian.

The chief rode on without a backward glance. His men were hard pressed to catch up with him as Hunnul raced over the remaining distance to the embattled Clan. Valorian was so terrified by what he might find, he didn't search for Kierla's cart or look at any of the wagons. He focused instead on the clusters of tunics with the black eagle emblems. Those were his quarry. It would have been easier, he thought, if they had been separated from the clanspeople and formed in ranks. Unfortunately they were scattered along an entire line of crowded vehicles and livestock, intermingled with the clanspeople in a frantic struggle for survival. He couldn't drive them off with one final, magnificent blow. He would have to deal with them piecemeal.

Then he had an idea. If he couldn't fight them en masse, perhaps he could persuade them to retreat that way. He slowed Hunnul a little to allow the other men to catch up with him, and he waved them into several lines abreast with his position. Before their startled eyes, he began to form the images of mounted warriors. The images looked like clansmen with their homespun tunics, iron-bound helmets, and small round shields; they carried spears and swords and rode Clan horses, but their faces were hidden behind visors, and their movements were strangely lifeless. Rank after rank of the ghostly men fell in behind Lord Valorian until the troop looked and sounded as big as a legion. Banners floated over their heads, and the realistic noises of rattling armor, jingling bridles, and neighing horses filled the air.

At Valorian's command, the magical army burst into full gallop toward the caravan, with the chieftain at its head. He cast a quick glance back at his strange force and hoped it would look real enough to the Tarns. The speed of their charge and the dust kicked up by the horses seemed to help obscure the somewhat mechanical movements of the false warriors.

The first group of Tarns at the tail end of the caravan was scattered among the wagons. Some were fighting with the clanspeople, some were raiding the contents of the wagons, and a few were trying to cut loose the harnessed horses. They were so busy and so certain of victory that they didn't notice the charging clansmen until Valorian produced a ram's horn and blew a great, resounding blast that shook the valley and echoed off the peaks.

The Tarns froze in their tracks at the sight of the huge Clan force bearing down on them. Valorian smiled fiercely as the soldiers left their victims and drew together into a line of defense. He formed another whirlwind of dust and grit and sent it whipping into their midst. The Tarnish lines fell apart. Just before his warriors reached the legionnaires, Valorian banished the wind and drew his sword.

Half-blinded by the whirling dust and confused by the overwhelming numbers of clansmen coming at them, the soldiers didn't stand their ground for long. Valorian killed two men with his sword, and his living warriors claimed a dozen more before the Tarns pulled back and began to retreat up the line of wagons.

Valorian blew another long note on his horn, and the clanspeople close by cheered as he passed. He came to the next force of Tarns near the rear of the caravan, where they were struggling with a small knot of men and boys surrounded by what looked like a swarm of angry horses. With a start, Valorian recognized one man as Gylden. He was even more startled when he realized the horses around the small band were the brood mares with the Hunnul foals. The little black horses were biting and kicking the Tarns to defend their human friends. Their frantic mothers were adding to the confusion by trying to defend their babies. The soldiers were taken aback by the foals' deliberate attack, but they were still moving in on the clanspeople for the kill.

Hunnul neighed a warning, and his children scattered just as Valorian loosed a storm of sizzling bolts into the group of soldiers. Stunned, the Tarns turned to see a horrifying apparition of a man with lightning in his hands, atop a giant horse as black as night, leading a huge army of fearsome warriors. They, too, took to their heels. A few stragglers were cut down by Valorian's living warriors, but no one seemed to notice that the images hadn't harmed a single person.

The tide began to turn quickly against the Tarns. The retreat of the few in the rear started a ripple that worked its way up the caravan. Valorian and his army rode along the line of wagons and carts, driving an ever-growing number of Tarns before them. Strengthened by the gorthling, Valorian used his magic in a relentless barrage to keep the Tarns off balance. Whenever the legionnaires showed signs of slowing or gathering together to make a stand, Valorian would hurl blistering bolts of white or blue fire at their feet and force them on, while the warriors behind him attacked any Tarn who offered resistance.

The surviving clanspeople looked on in surprise that quickly changed to joy when they recognized their chieftain. Some still able to ride and carry weapons joined the charge and helped swell the ranks of living fighters.

At last the retreating Tarns and the Clan attackers neared

the front of the caravan, where several hundred soldiers had blocked the trail and were about to overwhelm the last survivors of the vanguard. Even from afar, Valorian could see the fighting was bitter. He sounded his horn a third time to tell the vanguard they were on the way and was rewarded by an answering call.

The fleeing Tarns ran past the last of the vehicles and milling animals, and with a terrified rush, overran the vanguard and its attackers. Suddenly Valorian lost sight of the Clan warriors in the tangled press of men. He looked frantically for Aiden in the mob, but all he could see was a struggling, chaotic mass of soldiers.

It was then that Valorian noticed for the first time a small group of Tarnish officers watching from their horses on a rise near the river to his left. From their armor and the standards that flapped lazily in the breeze over their heads, he recognized them as the commanding general of the XIIth Legion, his aides, and someone of importance from the Sarcithian government. With these men in his control, he could demand the surrender of the entire legion.

He could see that they were very upset and seemed to be arguing. Several of the men were pointing toward him; another was gesticulating wildly. The chieftain didn't wait to see if they would make up their minds. He forsook his attack on the milling legionnaires, kneed Hunnul to the left, and flung his ranks of warriors directly toward the officers.

Very few Tarns between the chieftain and the river made a real attempt to protect their leaders. They didn't have a chance. Those who tried to stand, Valorian knocked aside with violent gusts of magical wind, and those who actually tried to fight were hacked down by the real Clan warriors.

The men on the hill saw their danger too late. They tried to reach the rest of the legion massed at the front of the caravan, but Hunnul dashed past their slower mounts and cut them off. In a moment, the officers were surrounded by a ring of angry clanspeople with swords in their hands and bloodlust in their grimy faces.

Valorian brought his warrior-images to a halt in ranks behind the living men. His face expressionless, he examined his seven prisoners for a deliberately long time while they sweated and their horses pranced and shied. Finally Hunnul paced forward into the ring. The officers looked at Valorian with a mixture of belligerence, apprehension, and anger.

Only one, the man in the richest armor with the Sarcithian emblem, seemed terrified, almost out of control.

Valorian nodded curtly to the commanding general. "General Sarjas?"

The man inclined his head once and kept his eyes pinned on the clansman. At first he didn't see the gorthling, who was clinging unheeded to the back of Valorian's neck.

"I am Valorian, lord chieftain of the Clan. I demand the surrender of your legion immediately." He watched the muscles tighten in the general's neck and jaw and saw the play of emotions over his face. He knew what the man was thinking. The XIIth Legion had never surrendered in its history. To do so now against an inferior force would be a disgrace. Death would almost be better than such a dishonor.

But while the general hesitated, his companion did not. Antonine wrenched his horse around to face Valorian and with a sharp, frightened gesture, threw his sword to the ground. "Surrender, General Sarjas. We have no choice!" he croaked.

Sarjas visibly winced, as if the younger man had struck him, then bitterly he threw his sword down, too.

The chieftain bowed slightly to Sarjas and jabbed a finger at one of the general's aides, who was carrying a signal horn. "Sound the surrender. Call them in," he ordered.

Loud and final sounded the unfamiliar notes of the surrender call, soaring up and down the valley like a dirge. The men of the XIIth Legion didn't recognize it at first, but then, in twos and threes, the soldiers stopped in their places and unhappily laid down their arms.

For the first time in its history, the Clan had brought one of the emperor's legions to its knees.

18

 hideous cackle of glee from the gorthling startled everyone, including Valorian, who had forgotten it was there. It crawled out onto his shoulder again and curled its lips in a sneer. The Tarnish officers stared in revulsion at the ugly little creature and in bald amazement at the man who controlled such a thing.

"What are you waiting for?" the gorthling hissed in Valorian's ear. "Destroy them! Sear them to ashes! They don't deserve to live after what they did to your people."

The insidious voice touched the rawest nerve in Valorian's self-control. Suddenly he *wanted* to blast the Tarns where they stood, to slaughter every single man as they had tried to do to the Clan. It was the least they deserved for the eighty years of misery, poverty, and murder they had inflicted on his people—and for this last atrocity, the unprovoked attack on an inoffensive caravan. His hatred, contained for so many years, boiled up like acid, and the tension became a visible pain on his face.

"Do it!" prodded the gorthling again. "It would be so easy. You have the power. Kill them all!"

Imperceptively Valorian's hand began to lift; the magic seethed within him. He saw the faces of the officers in front of him staring at him in increasing alarm and fear. He saw the legionnaires gathering nearby, laying down their weapons. It would be so easy to kill every one of them. All he had to do was . . .

The gorthling chuckled in anticipation.

Suddenly Valorian's hand clamped down on his knee. He

shoved his sword back in the scabbard, and with every ounce of his willpower forced his hatred deep down out of sight in the most hidden chambers of his heart. How could he even think of abusing Amara's gift by slaughtering men who had already surrendered? Or breaking his vow before his people? It would have been a heinous thing to do, something better suited to a gorthling.

He cast a speculative look at the little beast on his shoulder. Valorian knew he wasn't so easily overcome by his own emotions. Could this creature somehow be influencing his thoughts? If that was so, he thought, he had better get rid of it as soon as possible.

"Keep quiet," he told the gorthling harshly. It subsided temporarily and hid behind Valorian's back again.

The chieftain spoke another command, and the clansmen around the Tarnish prisoners lowered their swords. Hunnul walked over to the small group where Lord Valorian relieved the standard bearer of the XIIth Legion's gilded eagle standard. He turned to face the Clan and held the tall standard high to catch the afternoon sun.

A loud cheer rose from the gathered Clan. It grew louder as the people began to realize that the danger from the Tarns was over and, in a stunning victory that boggled the imagination, the soldiers had become their prisoners.

General Sarjas glanced at the noisy caravan and back to the silent ranks of warriors behind the Clan chieftain. His brows knotted together. "Lord Valorian," he finally asked, puzzled, "where were your other men hiding? We saw no sign of another troop of warriors before the battle."

Valorian's face slowly broke open in a wide grin. With a dramatic snap of his fingers and a muttered command, the images of the warriors vanished, leaving the chieftain with only his battered, smiling rear guard. "What men?" he asked.

The Tarns stared, unbelieving, at the empty field. General Sarjas swallowed hard. How was he going to explain this to the emperor?

Valorian's grin faded and he turned brusque. It was time

to get back to the Clan. "General, we are going to the Ramtharin Plains as we had planned. If you leave your weapons and horses here, you and your men may leave peacefully. If you do not, we will keep this man as a hostage," and he pointed to Antonine. He still wasn't certain who the soft-looking young official was, but he recognized the man's ultimate authority over Sarjas.

The commander hesitated. To abandon their weapons and horses to the clanspeople was almost more than he could bear, but once again Antonine stepped in. "Do it, Sarjas! I'll buy you new horses when we get out of this!"

Sarjas's rough-hewn face was abruptly frozen by a powerful self-control. Tight-lipped, he dismounted and gestured to his men to do likewise. A Clan warrior came forward to take the reins of the seven horses.

Valorian was satisfied. He turned to Karez nearby and said, "Make sure the word is spread. Have them leave their weapons here and picket their horses by the river. They can take their dead and wounded if they like."

Karez nodded, rather surprised and pleased that Valorian would give him such an important task.

Then the chieftain turned back to the legion general and saluted him. "It is on your honor that the legion obeys the terms of surrender. Good day, sir!"

Sarjas returned his salute reluctantly, but with a measure of respect in the crispness of his motion.

At Valorian's touch, Hunnul trotted back across the field of grass toward the caravan. The chieftain groaned when he finally took a good look at the mass of carts, wagons, people, and animals. It was a shambles. There was so much to do he hardly knew where to begin. Wagons were tipped over, damaged, or jammed together; horses ran loose everywhere, and the herds of livestock were scattered all over the fields and slopes. Gear and belongings were strewn over the ground. People were milling around in confusion, and frantic children and dogs were scampering underfoot.

Worst of all were the dead and wounded lying scattered

along the trail, in the grass, and among the wagons. Many of them were clanspeople, but they had defended themselves fiercely against the Tarns, leaving quite a few soldiers among the numbers of the dead. They would all have to be dealt with—the dead buried and the wounded tended. Valorian could see it was going to be a long and difficult task to get the Clan back on its feet.

He began at the first group of people he reached, where he found the survivors of the vanguard trying to help the wounded around them. The retreating Tarns had actually saved the remnants of the vanguard when they rushed through the head of the caravan by throwing the remaining Tarnish forces into chaos and distracting the vanguard's attackers.

A jolt of relief hit Valorian when he saw Aiden sitting on a rock, feebly wrapping a rag around a bad slash on his leg. "Thank the gods," Valorian muttered fervently. His parents would have to wait awhile longer to see either one of them in the realm of the dead. He slid off Hunnul to help.

Aiden's normally cheerful grin and snapping eyes were dulled with pain and exhaustion, but the spark wasn't out entirely. The corners of his mouth turned up to greet Valorian, and his grip was strong on his brother's arm. He was about to say something when he saw the gorthling peeking over Valorian's shoulder and recoiled in disgust.

The creature snarled at him.

"Ignore it. It will be leaving soon," Valorian said.

"That's what you think," hissed the gorthling.

Aiden looked disgusted and puzzled, but then a comprehending light came over his expression. "Is that how you did it? You used a gorthling to enhance your power?" Valorian nodded. "Gods above! You'll have to tell me how you pulled that one off."

"Another time," the chieftain said, taking the rags from Aiden's fingers, transforming them to clean strips, and wrapping them carefully around the wound. "You rest now."

Aiden pulled himself to his feet. "Oh, no. There's work to

be done. I'll rest later."

"You need a healer," Valorian protested.

"Then find one. And while you're looking, I'll get the wounded set up over there." He pointed to a fairly smooth place under a cluster of trees by the river.

The chieftain frowned at his brother and reluctantly acquiesced. Short of tying Aiden down, there would be no stopping him, and the Clan needed all the help it could get.

"What do we do about the Tarnish wounded?" Aiden asked, looking at the bodies lying around them.

Valorian felt the gorthling stir and its claws pinch at his skin through the fabric of his tunic. It hissed softly in his ear. The hatred he thought he had buried suddenly rose again to choke him in thick, viscid clots, and he almost told Aiden to slit their throats. The intensity of the feeling shook him badly—he wasn't used to such powerful emotions. Was the gorthling doing this to him? He fought the feeling down again and said instead, "Take them to their officers. They can take care of their own better than we can."

Before he could go on, a strange voice said bitterly behind him, "I should have killed you when I had the chance."

Valorian whirled, drawing his sword, and scanned the people nearby. At first glance, he saw only the Clan warriors moving around to check the bodies. Then a Tarnish soldier lying close by moved in the dust. Painfully the man hauled himself to a sitting position and glared at the two clansmen. It took Valorian only a moment to see through the blood and the dirt to the man's face and insignia. He recalled the night a year ago when he had last seen this man in a wet, dark clearing with four other hungry Tarns.

"Sarturian," he said, sheathing his sword, "your chance is gone, but all of you seemed to enjoy the deer." He knelt down beside the older man and examined the bloody wound beneath the soldier's ribs.

The sarturian glared helplessly at him. Although he had been struck by a Clan arrow in the side and suffered cuts and bruises, he didn't appear to be in danger of dying. He was panting, though, and in great pain.

Valorian cautiously touched the arrow shaft and turned it to mist before the sarturian's astonished eyes. "That's for the reprieve you gave me that night." He twisted his mouth into a wry smile. "And for the information."

The soldier grimaced at the memory. "If you're still going to the Ramtharin Plains, you're making a mistake. Your people will probably starve by winter."

"It couldn't be any worse than the Bloodiron Hills," Valorian replied. He helped the sarturian to his feet and gestured to two other Tarns who were shuffling down toward the river. "Take him with you," he ordered.

Aiden tilted his head to watch the Tarns hobble away. "He'll never take a meal from a clansman again."

"Not if I can help it," Valorian said with hearty satisfaction. He was turning to mount Hunnul again when Aiden put a hand on his arm.

"Please, when you have a chance, will you find Linna and tell her I am well?"

The raw note of worry in his voice matched the same concern in Valorian. As chieftain, Valorian's first responsibility was to his people. He knew, though, that he couldn't give them his full effort until he had learned the fate of the rest of his family. He returned his brother's clasp and jumped onto Hunnul to go on with his difficult duties.

He left Aiden busily organizing the able-bodied to bring in the wounded, find the Clan healers, and set up a makeshift shelter. Slowly he made his way down the jumbled line answering a myriad of questions, organizing people to help with the most pressing problems, finding boys to round up the livestock, and helping the wounded whenever he could.

He found Mordan still in the wagon, half-buried under the body of a dead Tarn. He despaired for the warrior's life, until he hauled the body off and saw Mordan clutching his bloody dagger. The guardsman gave him a grateful smile.

"Have you been busy?" Valorian asked, relieved.

Mordan nodded once. "That Tarn thought I looked like

easy prey. But even wounded, I'm still a match for one of them," he replied hoarsely.

Valorian gestured to several men who came and lifted Mordan out of the wagon and carried him to the grove of trees.

The chief hurried on from one emergency or disaster to the next, lending his calm strength, optimism, and his enhanced magic wherever he could. There were many wounded among the clanspeople and more dead than he wanted to find. No age or group had been spared; men, women, and children had fallen to the merciless attack.

All of the Clan families had suffered casualties, but it wasn't until Valorian reached the section of the caravan where his own family had been traveling that the toll of the dead sank in hard. Quiet, loyal Ranulf would never go beyond the pass he had found, for he had died defending his sisters. Other relatives were also dead or dying, and more were hurt. They cried out to him as he approached, and even though he wanted to help, his eyes could only search the wreckage of carts and the confusion of horses and people for the four faces he desperately wanted to see most.

Then a voice called out to him over the hubbub. "Valorian! We're over here!"

He nearly threw himself off Hunnul to reach the speaker. Kierla ran through the carts to meet him, her dark hair loose and flying, her body sound and strong. She flung her arms around him, buried her face in his neck, and cried in joy.

Valorian was beyond words. He merely held her tightly while his heart sang a prayer of gratitude.

"We saw you go by," Kierla said between tears and laughter. "That was quite a cavalry you found."

"Not bad for a thick-witted mortal," the gorthling said, sneering. "Wait till you see what he can do when I give him some real training."

Kierla sucked in a sharp breath and stepped back; her eyebrows shot up over her widened eyes. She hadn't seen the gorthling until that moment.

"I'll tell you later," Valorian said hastily. "Are Linna, Mother Willa, and the baby safe?"

Kierla looked dubiously at the gorthling before answering. "Yes, they're all right. Mother Willa made us cut the traces and turn our cart over. We crawled underneath it just before the soldiers reached us."

"And that's not all," Mother Willa added. Valorian's grandmother and Linna, carrying the baby, came up to them. Mother Willa went on. "Kierla stabbed a Tarn in the leg when he tried to push the cart over."

The chief smiled at his wife. "The four of you seem to have handled things well."

"We were lucky," she answered and pushed her hair back out of her eyes with a sharp, tense gesture. "If you hadn't come when you did, there wouldn't have been much left."

Linna agreed, her fair face still shadowed with the memory of fear. Then she added, "I didn't see Aiden with you. Is he . . ." She couldn't finish the words.

"He's alive. He has a wounded leg, but it's nothing serious. He's over by those trees, helping the wounded."

"Then that is where I will be," Linna said firmly. She passed Khulinar over to Kierla.

Valorian hugged her in thanks. He knew with Linna there, Aiden wouldn't be able to overexert himself. "Take Mother Willa with you. They need all the healers who can help." When Linna was gone, Valorian kissed his wife soundly on the lips and forced himself to stand back. "Will you . . ." he began to say.

Kierla knew immediately what he was going to say and interrupted him. "We will be fine. Go! I will help here." She recognized as well as he the responsibilities of a Clan chieftain, and she gave him a gentle push.

By nightfall, some semblance of order had been restored in the valley meadow. The Tarns had marched down the valley just before sunset in sullen, silent ranks. Valorian had allowed them to bring in their teams and provision wagons to haul away their dead and wounded—as long as they left half of their foodstuffs and medical supplies behind. The clanspeople stopped what they were doing to watch the legion fall back, for it was a sight no one had ever expected to see. When the last file faded down the trail into the twilight, the people burst out with a cheer that followed the Tarns far down the trail. For the first time in three generations, the clanspeople were free to go, and they were jubilant.

Meanwhile, the survivors began to set up a camp of sorts beside the river. Gylden and some of the older boys, with the help of Hunnul, rounded up most of the loose horses and were slowly gathering in the scattered livestock. The dead clanspeople were placed in covered rows to be readied for burial, and a guard of honor was stationed to protect them from scavengers. The injured were lovingly tended in the shady grove; the able-bodied were fed. One by one, the young and the old put aside their grief, joy, gratitude, and pain and fell into deep, exhausted sleep.

Only Valorian could not find the rest he dearly needed. He still had to dispose of one small, tenacious problem. When the makeshift camp seemed quiet and a nearly full moon had risen, he rode Hunnul up the steep slopes to the top of a distant hill. The night was warm and muggy and undisturbed by any breeze. Far to the east, on the other side of the peaks, clouds obscured the stars, and a faint flicker of sheet lightning outlined the edges of the mountains.

Valorian paid little attention to the land around him. He simply stared for a long time over the scattered campfires in the dark camp below while the gorthling swayed soothingly on his shoulder.

Now that he had a chance to try sending the gorthling back, a strange reluctance overcame him, as intense as the hatred that had dogged him earlier. He knew he couldn't leave this evil creature in the mortal world; every sentient particle of his soul believed it would be hideously dangerous and wrong. The gorthling belonged in Gormoth.

But he really didn't know how to send it or take it back, and his mind was too tired to think. The effort would be so difficult. Maybe he could do this later.

The gorthling stopped weaving and softly stroked the dirty stubble on Valorian's jaw. The chieftain hardly felt it through the fog of his preoccupation.

There was nothing, he thought to himself, that required him to send the creature back now. He could wait until tomorrow. Perhaps even a few days. The gorthling's enhancement of his power would be useful to have while the Clan repaired their wagons and healed their wounded. There was so much more he could accomplish with the greater power at his fingertips.

Wearily he leaned forward to rest his forearm on Hunnul's mane. He had done enough for one day. The gorthling could wait, he decided, and he would think about a spell for a few days. Later, perhaps, he would send the creature back.

Under him, Hunnul stamped his hooves restlessly. His ears flattened as he sensed his rider's reluctance, and his tail was jerking back and forth in annoyance. *Master.* His voice broke into Valorian's thoughts. *Have you asked the creature how to send it back?*

The chieftain started violently. His sudden movement upset the gorthling and caused it to accidentally scratch his cheek. Irritably he swatted at it, forcing it to withdraw to the farthest point of his shoulder.

"How would it know?" Valorian demanded. "And for that matter, why would it tell me the truth?" He was cross at the interruption of his musings, even though a part of him realized Hunnul's suggestion was a good one.

The gorthling is cunning and knows more about the immortal world than we do. It could think of some way to go back to its home. Simply command it to tell you the truth.

Valorian's reluctance seemed to ease in the face of such a sensible idea. He plucked the gorthling off his shoulder and dropped it to his knee, where he could see it better in the moonlight. Now that the gorthling was away from his head, the strange hesitancy to send it back weakened even more.

Valorian's eyes widened in alarm and comprehension. So

the gorthling *was* trying to influence his mind with its own insidious thoughts. That was why he had wanted to slaughter every Tarn and keep the gorthling by his side. If the creature could alter his emotions so easily after just half a day, what control would he have had left of his mind if he had waited for several days? The realization washed away the last tendrils of his unwillingness. Valorian knew without a doubt that the gorthling couldn't be allowed to remain the night—for the sake of his immortal soul.

"Unless you wish to eat that gold ring, you will tell the truth to every question I ask," he informed the wizened creature on his knee.

The gorthling had no choice when it was under the power of the bright gold. It hunched down, its lip curled up in a silent snarl. "What do you wish to know, nag rider . . . the truth? You have seen it. Your power is sevenfold when I am with you. Nothing can touch you. Nothing can harm your family or your people when you wield such magic. Think about the possibilities!"

Valorian ignored the conniving tone and demanded, "Would I be able to use my consciousness and return you to Gormoth the same way I brought you out?"

"Yesss . . ."

Valorian caught the edge of smugness at the end of the reply. "But?" he prompted.

"Yes, you can go back. But there are dangers."

"Like what?" demanded the chieftain.

The gorthling's face wrinkled even more in its effort not to answer, but it couldn't fight the power of the gold around its neck. Its words came spitting out. "If you try to enter the realm of the dead without a Harbinger to guide you, you could become lost in the mists of the barrier, where there is no escape. If you do find a Harbinger to guide you and you make it through, Lord Sorh may not allow you to enter the realm of the dead while your body still lives. You slipped through once, but not again. And he's probably not happy that you kidnapped me!

"Nor will the other gorthlings let you into Gormoth. They have sensed your mind, and they know your presence. They would catch you the moment you opened the door." The gorthling suddenly broke off and smirked at Valorian. "Do you know what they would do to you? They might torment your mind for eternity or maybe just a few years. *If* your consciousness ever returned to your body, you would be . . . utterly . . . hopelessly . . . demented!" It chuckled at the whole idea.

In the back of his mind, Valorian had been afraid of something like that. The hatred and the malice he had felt in Gormoth had been focused too intently on him when he pulled the gorthling out. The others probably knew he would have to return his prisoner sometime, and they had all eternity to wait for him. He scratched his neck where the dried sweat itched and thought about other ways.

"Could the Harbingers take you back?" he suggested.

"No!" the gorthling rasped. "Those messenger boys only obey Lord Sorh." At the thought of the god of the dead, the gorthling began to grovel on Valorian's leg. "Please, master. Let me stay with you. I will wear your nasty gold and obey your every whim. Please let me stay," it wheedled.

Valorian wasn't moved this time by the gorthling's attempt to sway him. Beneath the whining voice and the pleading posture, there was an indistinct phosphorescent glow in the creature's eyes that sent shivers down the clansman's back. "Enough!" he snapped. "Tell me what other ways will return you to Gormoth."

The gorthling hissed its frustration, but it finally had to answer. "There is only one other way—the ancient way that Lord Sorh used to trap us in the mountain." It cackled suddenly with derision. "Not that it will help you. No simple, weak-handed mortal can wield the power necessary to return me!" Still cackling, it leapt into a mad dance on Valorian's knee, as if it had just conclusively proved its victory.

The chieftain had had quite enough of the gorthling's antics. Muttering an imprecation, he snatched it up by the

golden armband and shook it until it stopped its wild movements and hung there glaring at him. "Just tell me what it is!"
he insisted furiously.

"Yes, master! Nice master!" the gorthling crooned and
rubbed its tiny hands over the man's fingers. Valorian
dropped it in disgust back onto his knee. It giggled nastily.
"You have to make an opening through the barrier between
the mortal and immortal world and send me through it. If
you could do that, which you can't, your magic would
return me to Gormoth."

"What power do I need to make this opening?"

With a snicker, the gorthling replied, "There is only one in
the mortal world that will work, but it would fry you to
ashes and turn your nag into vulture bait."

"And that is?"

The gorthling waved a hand at the east, where a faint
flash illuminated the mountain peaks for the blink of an eye.
"Lightning."

Valorian went numb and cold all over. Oh, sweet, merciful
goddess, not that! he thought, terrified at the very suggestion. His one experience with lightning had been enough to
last him a lifetime and beyond. And the gorthling was right.
Even with the enhancement of his power, he didn't have the
strength to withstand the unbelievable energy of a white-hot
bolt of lightning.

Master, Hunnul's quiet, reassuring voice touched his
mind. *We could use it together.*

There was a long pause, then Valorian said, "Tell me." His
voice was unsteady as he tried to balance hope and fear.

*When we were struck by lightning before, you know the
bolt left some of its strength within me. In some way I do not
understand, it has made me invulnerable to its power. If you
are in touch with my body when you call the lightning, you
should be protected.*

" 'Should be'? Not 'will be'? " Valorian asked dubiously.

The stallion cocked his head to look back at Valorian out
of one deep, velvet eye. *We have never tried this before, so I*

cannot be certain.

Valorian considered Hunnul's words. The whole concept of using lightning as a fuel for a magical spell was completely beyond his experience or knowledge. He had only a horse's word that it *might* not incinerate him the second he touched it. That was hardly reassuring.

But it was intriguing. He had sensed the traces of the searing power in Hunnul and, if the stallion were right, it would be worth the attempt to create a spell that would send the gorthling back through the barrier alone.

There was only one other problem: There was no lightning close by. He was certain that even with the gorthling's help, he didn't have the skill to create the intricate and vast forces that birthed a thunderstorm. Nor could he form lightning out of thin air. Fires, bolts of magical energy, rockslides, or images of warriors were spells he could manage, but lightning was a power far beyond his present ability and knowledge.

The only hope he had was to use real lightning, but once again, there was none available. The existing storm was too far away to be of any use. It was probably somewhere over the Ramtharin Plains, and by the time he rode Hunnul there, it would be long gone.

Relief, disappointment, and frustration ran through his mind in turn. What were they going to do? "It won't work," he said morosely to Hunnul. "We have no lightning to use."

The gorthling sneered. "No lightning! Of course not, moron. The stars are out. And why are you talking to that creature? Did you think that worm-eaten grass biter was going to help?"

Hunnul gave a snort. *Actually, I think I can.*

Valorian sat straighter. "How?"

Lightning begets lightning. I think we can use our power to pull the storm close enough for you to draw on its energy.

"We?"

My foals and I.

"Oh, gods above!" Valorian murmured weakly.

There were no more excuses, no more reasons to hesitate.

He had pulled the gorthling out of its prison, and it was his responsibility to send it back by whatever means necessary—even lightning. He swallowed his terror and said softly to Hunnul, "Let's try it."

The gorthling leaped upright, its eyes glowing like coals. "Try it? Try what? What brainless thing are you going to do? Answer me!" it screeched.

Both man and horse ignored the creature. Hunnul lifted his head and neighed a long, ringing call into the night.

Out of the darkness, the little ones began to come in answer to their sire's summons. Small and as black as the night, they were ghostly shapes in the moonlight that gathered in a circle around the stallion at the top of the hill. Only their wide eyes and their lightning marks caught the faint gleam of moon and stars and threw it back with equal brilliance. They shifted noisily in their places like children at play until Hunnul nickered to them to be still.

By that time, there were over seventy Hunnul foals in the Clan herd, and every one of them down to the smallest, only a few hours old, was there to help their sire. Gently he told them what they were going to do, and they filled the night air with whinnies of excitement.

Hunnul quieted them again. As one, father, sons, and daughters raised their muzzles to the sky, where the stars sparkled across the ebony spaces, and joined their power to summon the storm. A deep stillness settled over the horses' motionless forms, and a silence as palpable as the darkness.

Valorian barely breathed, so rapt was he in the unmoving spectacle of the horses, the night, and the magic. Only the gorthling fidgeted, for it didn't understand what was happening, and its suspicions were beginning to burn.

Nothing seemed to happen for a long while. The ring of small horses and the stallion in the center remained held in the spell of their unseen power, while the moon continued to gleam and the man and the gorthling watched.

The changes came imperceptibly at first, on an indistinct rumble that barely disturbed the silence of the night. Valorian didn't realize what it was until the second rumble sounded, a little louder and longer. Thunder. He glanced up at the sky to see the first shreds of clouds blowing over the face of the moon. A slight wind stirred the grass.

For a moment, he couldn't believe it. No horse could call a thunderstorm, not even a stallion who had survived a lightning strike. Then a bright flash hid the stars, and three heartbeats later, the thunder boomed through the mountains. Whether he wanted to believe it or not, Valorian realized the storm was coming and he had better be prepared to receive it.

Working only with his intuition and his memories of the realm of the dead, Valorian quickly worked out a spell that he hoped would propel the gorthling through the barrier of mists and back into the mountain of Ealgoden. All he needed was the lightning bolt to blast the opening into the immortal world and the courage to use it. Overhead, the sky was almost overcast, and the night had become as black as burned pitch. There was no light at all except for the blinding explosions of energy that danced across the face of the coming storm. The wind came gusting over the slopes, bringing the damp smell of rain.

Valorian felt every muscle in his body tighten into thrumming wires. To his amazement, he realized the magic around him was increasing, as if something was intensifying its strength. He remembered that same phenomenon had happened before when the Clan crossed the river just before the thunderstorm broke. It had to be the huge forces of the storm and the lightning that produced that effect. It could be a useful thing to remember.

Then he grinned to himself. The strengthening magic could be a useful thing now! He wouldn't have to rely on the gorthling's enhancement when he had magic of his own surging around him in an ever-increasing tide. Quickly he dismounted and carried the gorthling to a flat rock several paces away.

"Don't move. Stay on this rock," he ordered.

The gorthling looked up at him with hatred, its eyes glowing fiercely. "What are you up to, mortal? Are you trying to kill yourself?"

Valorian turned his back on the creature and returned to Hunnul. The storm was close now, its winds blowing flat across the grass. Lightning crackled nearly overhead.

Get ready, master, Hunnul warned him.

Valorian wrapped his legs tightly around Hunnul. The gorthling's influence on his power was gone because of the distance between them, so he drew on the intensifying energy around him to form the beginnings of his spell.

All at once the gorthling understood what the man was trying to do. A blood-chilling shriek rent the night over the sound of the thunder and wind. "You fool! You can't do this! I belong here now! I'll never return to Gormoth." The gorthling jumped up and down on its rock, but because of the gold still around its neck, it could not disobey Valorian's order to stay. It grew even angrier. It shouted maledictions at the top of its lungs at Valorian, Hunnul, the foals, the Clan, and even Lord Sorh, and when no one paid attention to it, it broke into hideous, unending screams.

Valorian shut out its voice. The lightning was close now, and he could feel its power vibrating through his being. His mouth was so dry with fear he could barely whisper a prayer to Amara to protect him. A raindrop spattered on his nose, and a sizzling streak of lightning ripped through the clouds overhead. It was almost time. Slowly he raised his hand toward the sky.

The gorthling saw his movement and its shrieking stopped. "Don't do it, mortal! Don't condemn me to go back to that prison," it shouted in fury. "I will curse you into the tenth generation! The goddess of life has given you and your blood descendants the ability to wield magic, but I will take that away! Some day, in some place, your talent will come to be hated and feared as you hate me. Others will hunt down your descendants and destroy them! Do you hear me, Valorian? Your magic saved your family yesterday, but if you send me away, I will see that it brings everyone who carries your blood to annihilation!"

Valorian hesitated for the space of a breath. He didn't know Amara had allowed his talent to be passed on to his children. Was the gorthling right? Could it possibly place a curse on his descendants?

Then the air began to tingle on his skin and in his lungs from a new charge of lightning that was building in the clouds. It was now or never. The chieftain shut out the gorthling's screaming voice and its imprecations and set his spell in motion. Let the future happen as it will, the gorthling had to return to Gormoth.

A split second later the energies within the turbulent storm instantly fused into a brilliant white streak that was hotter than the sun and faster than the eye could follow. It arced down through the black sky like a spear thrown from the hand of the god Surgart and was caught by the magic of the clansman. In one swift, smooth motion, he pulled the bolt into his right hand. He felt its searing power rage through him to Hunnul and safely into the ground, and only then did he know that Hunnul was right.

Triumphantly he channeled his spell into the furious energy of the lightning and threw the bolt with all his might at the cowering gorthling. There was a tremendous explosion of sparks and light, a howl of rage and despair, and a deafening crack of thunder that shook the hills. Almost simultaneously the backlash slammed into Hunnul and the foals, sending them staggering. Valorian was thrown sideways, and before he could catch himself, he fell from the stallion's back. His head struck a rock, and the night, the horses, and the storm disappeared into black oblivion.

*   *   *   *   *

Gylden found him the next morning lying in the wet grass with blood on the side of his head and Hunnul standing over him. Gently his friend roused him and lifted his head to offer him a sip of Mother Willa's herbal drink from a small waterskin.

Valorian drank gratefully. Groaning, he sat up and put his pounding head in his hands. He knew the gorthling was gone without even asking or looking; he could feel its absence in every fiber of his body. Without the gorthling to feed his power, the effects of his constant use of magic had taken their toll. Every muscle ached, his limbs were sore, and he felt completely and utterly exhausted. His head throbbed with each heartbeat, and he was soaked from head to toe. He wasn't sure he could even walk, he felt so tired.

A soft muzzle touched his arm, and he cocked an eye sideways to see one of the older Hunnul foals peering at him with obvious concern.

Gylden scratched the little fellow fondly. "I don't know what you're doing up here," he said to Valorian, "but the foals were awfully worried about you. They brought me to find you." When Valorian didn't answer, he sat down beside his friend to wait for the medicinal drink to take effect.

It was a glorious morning, fresh and cool, with a light breeze and a sky of perfect blue. Before long the sunshine, the drink, and the realization of his victory brought strength pumping back into the chieftain's mind and body.

It was over. The struggle to unite the Clan, the long journey through Chadar and Sarcithia, the race for survival, the battle against the Tarns, and the summoning of the gorthling. It was all finished. The gorthling was banished. Valorian had lost his armband, too, but he was sure Kierla would understand. The Tarns were defeated. Now the Clan faced a new beginning. Valorian wasn't foolish enough to believe the path would be easy, but from this day forward, anything the Clan did, they did for themselves. The thought was euphoric.

He hauled himself to his feet, clasped Gylden's hand in thanks, and walked slowly down the hill with the black stallion at his side.

*　*　*　*　*

The moon was new and the summer had well begun by the time the Clan left the meadow for the final trek to the top of Wolfeared Pass. They left behind a large mound crowned with spears and flowers, where almost two hundred of their people lay. With them went several wagonloads of wounded still too hurt to ride, a horse herd nearly doubled in size, and almost one hundred black Hunnul foals. Safely hidden in the dark, warm wombs of the brood mares were nearly a hundred more. The black stallion's dynasty was well begun.

A light of joy mingled with sadness glowed on the faces of the clanspeople as they climbed higher into the mountains. The peaks, gleaming with snow, reared above them, and a sharp alpine scent filled their nostrils. They crossed the pass in the late afternoon, and everyone from the youngest to the oldest stared at the hazy, purplish land to the east where they would build a new home.

Valorian deliberately chose to be the last clansman over the pass. He brought Hunnul to a stop on the highest point of the stony trail and watched the last wagon, several riders, and the warriors of the rear guard pass by him and move on down the trail toward a broad, flat plateau where the Clan was setting camp for the night.

He couldn't have described his feelings to anyone at that moment if he had tried. His entire being was a jumble of memories, dreams, and emotions that washed through him in an uncontrollable flood. Foremost, he decided, was gratitude to the Mother Goddess. Without Amara, they would still be scratching out a bare survival in Chadar.

The memory of his discovery of the stone temple on the mountain peak far to the north brightened in his mind, and he suddenly decided that the Clan would begin to leave their own legacy here and now. They would build a monument of their own to Amara, a symbol of their journey and their gratitude that would remain for generations to come. Perhaps down there on the wide plateau would be a good place.

At that moment, a soft wind blew up around him, lifting Hunnul's mane and tugging at Valorian's clothes. It bore a fragrance of incredible delicacy and sweetness that Valorian had only smelled once before in his existence. The flower that shattered the stone. The power of life.

"Amara," he breathed.

The wind wafted past, tickling his face. He felt the same feeling of comfort and familiarity that had nurtured him previously in Amara's presence, and he looked around, trying to see her.

Hunnul tossed his head, neighing a welcome.

You have done well, my son, the wind whispered in his ear.

"Because of you," Valorian replied.

The voice laughed like a breeze dancing through leaves. *I gave you the tools; it was you who put them to use.*

The man felt himself grow warm from the goddess's praise, but there was still something he had to know. "Is it true," he asked, "that you have given this talent to my son?"

To all of them. And to their children after them.

Unfamiliar tears sprang to Valorian's eyes. The goddess had entrusted him with a great gift, and he had ruined it with his weakness and stupidity. "Then the gorthling was right," he murmured.

Yes, my son, and his curse cannot be revoked, for it was spoken by an immortal. But I will give you this promise: Not all of your blood will be destroyed. A few I can save, and when the time is right, they will return your gift to the Clans.

He hung his head and whispered, "Thank you."

In a sudden, gusty twirl, the wind whisked away with its fragrance and its comfort, leaving Valorian and Hunnul alone on the pass.

The chieftain raised his fist in farewell, then he and the black stallion left the Tarnish Empire behind forever and walked the path to join the Clan.

Epilogue

he last word of Gabria's tale fell softly away into silence. Gently she touched the cheek of the golden mask on her lap and looked up at her audience. The tale had taken several hours in telling, but everyone was watching her in rapt attention, the spell of her story still coloring their imaginations. A few people began to stir and stretch. They blinked, and soft voices spoke into the quiet.

Yet one person was staring at her as if he realized a truth he had known but never believed until that moment.

She looked down at him fondly. "What is it, Savaron?" she asked him softly.

The young man sat up, his eyes looking from her to his father and back again. "It's you, isn't it?" he asked with a hint of awe. "That story is also about you."

Gabria glanced at Athlone, and their eyes met in understanding. The same thought had come to them in the past, but they weren't presumptuous enough to completely believe it. The will of the gods was often incomprehensible and obscure to mere mortals.

But Savaron was overwhelmed by the possibility. "It all fits," he cried as he bounced to his feet. "Mother, you and Father are blood descendants of Valorian. That's why you have the talent to wield magic. And it was the two of you who brought sorcery back to the Clans. Amara's promise has been fulfilled!"

Gabria bowed her head to hide the flush that crept up her cheeks. "Perhaps," she said, and her fingers lifted the death mask of Valorian to face Savaron. "If that is so, my son, then it is to you that Valorian's legacy is passed." She looked up at him again, her green eyes as bright as gems. "Treat it with care and respect, for it is a gift of the gods."

Savaron couldn't contain himself any longer. With a whoop of delight, he dashed across the hall and flung open the doors to greet the evening. Fresh air poured in and sent the lamps and torches dancing. Outside, a black Hunnuli horse neighed at the young man as it trotted up to meet him. With a wave to his parents. Savaron sprang to the horse's back.

For just a moment, Gabria fancied he looked just like Valorian as he rode away down the hill. Then she smiled to herself and put away the mask of the revered hero-warrior.